Catinat
Boulevard

Essential Prose Series 211

**Canada Council   Conseil des Arts
for the Arts   du Canada**

**ONTARIO ARTS COUNCIL
CONSEIL DES ARTS DE L'ONTARIO**

an Ontario government agency
un organisme du gouvernement de l'Ontario

Canadä

Guernica Editions Inc. acknowledges the support of the Canada Council
for the Arts and the Ontario Arts Council. The Ontario Arts Council
is an agency of the Government of Ontario.

We acknowledge the financial support of the Government of Canada.

Catinat Boulevard

Caroline Vu

GUERNICA
EDITIONS
TORONTO · CHICAGO · BUFFALO · LANCASTER (U.K.)
2023

Guernica Founder: Antonio D'Alfonso

Michael Mirolla, general editor
Julie Roorda, editor
David Moratto, interior and cover designer
Guernica Editions Inc.
287 Templemead Drive, Hamilton, ON L8W 2W4
2250 Military Road, Tonawanda, N.Y. 14150-6000 U.S.A.
www.guernicaeditions.com

Distributors:
Independent Publishers Group (IPG)
600 North Pulaski Road, Chicago IL 60624
University of Toronto Press Distribution (UTP)
5201 Dufferin Street, Toronto (ON), Canada M3H 5T8

First edition.
Printed in Canada.

Legal Deposit—Third Quarter
Library of Congress Catalog Card Number: 2022952471
Library and Archives Canada Cataloguing in Publication
Title: Catinat Boulevard / Caroline Vu.
Names: Vu, Caroline, 1959- author.
Series: Essential prose series ; 211.
Description: Series statement: Essential prose series ; 211
Identifiers: Canadiana (print) 20230138853 |
Canadiana (ebook) 20230138896 | ISBN 9781771838276 (softcover) |
ISBN 9781771838283 (EPUB)
Classification: LCC PS8643.U2 C38 2023 | DDC C813/.6—dc23

To the children I've met,
thank you for telling me your stories.

Contents

PART 3:
MICHAEL

PART 4:
M & M

PART 5:
APRIL 1975 THE FALL OF SAIGON

PART 6:

THE ORPHANAGE, THE COMRADES, THE RESTAURANT AND THE REDHEAD

PART 7:
The Philippines

PART 8:
AMERICA

PART 1:
IN THE BEGINNING

Stork Heaven

LONG BEFORE MY birth, choices had been made. If I had it my way, there would be laws against illicit sex during times of war. Or at least Stork Intervention preventing the random matching of incompatible people. Unfortunately, it was not so. Fate rarely shows its generous face to us unborn. The determined sperm will always find the egg it fancies.

From my cloud in Stork Heaven, I could see everything. My parents' lives before their chance encounter? I'd witnessed it all. I cried. I wanted no part of that drama. Mama Stork's "Don't worry, everything will be fine ..." couldn't fool me. I shook my head to no avail. Mama Stork's mind was made up. She had chosen a family for me. With one quick stroke of her wings, she wrapped me in a blue bundle. The delivery was about to start. Papa Stork's antsy eyes flickered. He couldn't risk being late. I wiggled so hard during the trip I almost fell out. My left leg dangled in mid-air. My blue blanket turned into a rag wet with tears. "Stop fretting!" Papa Stork grunted through his half-open beak. To my horror, he hung me on a swaying tree branch. I swirled back and forth. Dizzy, I closed tight my eyes. "You want to stay here instead?" he asked. I mouthed "No." He tucked in my leg and resumed his flight down.

OK, maybe things didn't happen that way. Maybe there was no Stork Heaven. No Mama Stork. No Papa Stork. No blue bundle teetering from a tree branch. No observing my parents' lives from above. Maybe I only sensed unease in my genes—was only digesting my parents' sorrowful memories during my stay in Mother's womb. Or maybe I imagined everything. Making up fanciful stories to keep me sane. Whatever, it didn't matter. I knew trouble started years before my birth.

PART 2
MAI

Saigon, Vietnam 1966

IN COMPLICATED SAIGON, my mother led a simple life. The chaos, the war, the corruption. Nothing could sink her floating world. Like a little fairy, she succeeded in maintaining her childhood state of mind—an ignorance made sweet by innocence. Six days a week, she cycled to school in her white satin *ao dai*, its long panels flapping in the breeze. Amazingly, those flowing clothes never once got caught in her bicycle wheels. Never once did she fall on her face to jeopardize her most precious feature: a fine, white person's nose. Starched gloves protected my mother's marbled fingers from the sun. A conical hat kept her shoulder-length hair from eloping with the wind. At thirteen, my mother was not yet a pin-up beauty. Still, her willowy silhouette exuded enough pull to keep a few perverted minds awake at nights. A slender waist, lanky legs, languid bum. My mother's satin *ao dai* left nothing to the imagination. Hawk-eyed shoeshine boys saw right through it.

Even with a trail of admiring whistles following her, my mother never once turned around. She never noticed her hold on those shoeshine boys. She never heard their clucking tongues as she bent down to pick a frangipani blossom. She only paid attention to her flowers. Pink, purple, yellow, white, she collected them all, pressing them inside her textbooks to prevent their withering. Once dried, she'd glue them on sheets of white paper. Alone in her room, she'd contemplate her efforts at making art out of beauty. She'd smile at her works before turning off the light. Images of dancing flowers welcomed my mother to dream-filled nights. Like strings on balloons, they moored her wandering spirits.

Out of the blue one day, Mother decided to tear up her dried flowers. In a fit of rage, she searched her textbooks for petals and threw them all in a waste basket. Somehow one orchid remained intact. Hidden between pages of an old picture book, it would stay there unmarred by time. Years later when she'd stumble on this forgotten fragment of her past, Mother would smile. With her fingertip, she'd caress it tenderly. She'd whisper to it as if addressing an old friend. "Do you remember that day …?" she'd ask. Perhaps she'd even shed a tear for the loss of "those days." Or perhaps she'd only shrug, remembering nothing of "those days." She would not yet know that Time is hungry. Like an ogre, it would devour all unprotected memory.

It was an afternoon of raindrops splashing against her window. Without warning, darkness descended—an eclipse-like darkness that one intuitively knows to last only a few minutes. And during those lightless minutes, all that mattered was a much-awaited downpour with its accompanying cool breeze. In the tropics and in their heat-induced torpor, Mother's family lived for such moments.

My mother twisted and turned on her humid bed. Restless, she spent her afternoon nap cracking knuckles. Two wooden shutters vibrated to the whistle of a monsoon wind outside. A lone dog howled mournfully. Such eerie sounds spooked Mother. She shivered. In the bathroom, she shrieked at the sight of blood in her panties. She doubled over in pain. She hobbled to her mother for an explanation. None was given. She only received four washable pads. "Things happen," she was told. From that day on, Mother stopped picking flowers. She began looking around instead. Overnight my floating little fairy landed with a bang on a concrete sidewalk. Overnight, she became a self-conscious woman.

Surrounded by paintings of voluptuous red-haired beauties—reproductions of French period art her father favoured, Mother eventually learned to compare. Daily she obsessed about her limp black hair, her skin a shade darker than tofu-white, her chest not made for breastfeeding. Rows of fertilized blackheads sprouted from her oily forehead. Her sparse, downward-sloping eyelashes shook with each sneeze. A large mole with its wiggling solitary hair deformed her right earlobe. All these petty worries kept my mother blind to the longings and suffering of the times.

How do I know this? Through gossipy mouths, that's how.

A Childhood Memory

SELECTIVE MEMORY. ATTENTION deficit disorder. My mother enjoyed these typical teenage ailments. At thirteen, she remembered what she wanted to remember. She noticed what she wished to see. Never mind the guerrilla attacks on her city—a pipe bomb here, a sniper there. Never mind weekly anti-government demonstrations in her neighbourhood. Never mind nightly newscasts of her country at war. Once the television turned off, she'd return to her dreams, untouched by grainy black and white images of death.

Only one dark scene lingered in my mother's mind. Flames. Flames in the afternoon. That childhood memory could not be repressed. Self-sacrifice as a protest? Pre-planned tragedy? These concepts were beyond her ten-year-old brain. She'd no choice but to carry that load around for years.

It was a day of unrelenting heat. A wet washcloth around her neck, Mother tried studying. She groaned when drops of sweat dripped down her pages. She tried blowing them dry. Sudden deafening sounds of police sirens puzzled her. She dropped her homework to rush outside. At the intersection, she saw more police cars than she'd ever seen before. She saw neighbours on their front steps whispering to young children. She saw a mass of strangers loitering in her neighbourhood. There were foolhardy boys climbing up precarious mango tree branches. There were men shaking with vertigo atop rusty lampposts. They all wanted the best view. Mother felt a rush of adrenaline pushing her way through curious onlookers. She didn't know what to expect. She just felt energized by hums reverberating down her street. Abruptly she stopped. An old monk sitting in the middle of the road took Mother by surprise. She didn't expect this. Unfazed, the monk bowed to an expectant public. He fixed his saffron robe with a steady hand. He nodded to a skinny boy next to him. In a jerky movement, the boy poured gasoline on his teacher. A strong odour brought fingers to noses. It also brought out hand fans. Waving toxic fumes away from lungs. This was the crowd's spontaneous reaction. The monk smiled at this burst of activity. He took the boy's convulsing hand in his. He whispered some words of comfort. Then he closed his eyes. Transfixed by such an incredible sight, most onlookers refused to disperse. They'd imagined an unimaginable drama and they wanted to see it acted out. From a blue Austin emerged a hunchbacked man with a matchbox. A collective scream broke the afternoon silence. Dancing flames. Mother gasped at the sight of dancing flames. The burning monk, to her amazement, still held his neck erect, his head unbowed, his back straight. Even his legs still maintained the lotus position.

Cameramen ran in all directions, shooting this scene

from different angles. They filmed for half an hour, gave out candies and then left. Give a face to the war, satisfy a public hungry for images. There they've done their job. Of this fiery afternoon, they would only remember a burning saffron robe. They didn't stay to witness flesh turning to ashes. They didn't see a heap of bones with legs eternally crossed in the lotus position.

This vision of death terrified my mother. She couldn't tolerate people's indifference. She couldn't understand their gaping mouths, looking yet doing nothing.

"Why was no one rescuing him?" she wanted to know.

"Well, he's protesting against the president," my maternal grandmother answered.

"The monk burned himself to protest? The president isn't even here to see it! Why? Why?"

"Well, it's a Buddhist versus Catholic problem."

"What?"

"The president is Catholic and repressing us Buddhists. Monk burned himself. To get President's attention."

"What? I don't get it!"

"Yes, yes, there's a Buddhist-Catholic problem on top of a war against those communists. Oh, never mind, it's too complicated. Stop asking questions, Mai!"

Back in her room, Mother prayed for an old monk nobody rescued. She chanted till her mouth ached. "Nam Mo A Di Da Phat, " she repeated over and over. When the musicality of her chanting deteriorated into hoarse whispers, she took a sip of water. Undaunted, she chanted some more. She understood nothing of those Sanskrit verses. Still, she carried on. Melodious foreign words helped calm her distraught spirit that night.

A Fissure on the Street

EVERY DAY MY mother would go looking for traces of the dead monk. What she saw gave her goosebumps. The street's grime did not blur those blackened lines of crossed legs. Cars, motorbikes, stray dogs, runaway chickens, spit, spilled food. Nothing could erase that lotus position etched in charcoal. Mother could still feel flames consuming leathery old flesh. She also felt a strange sense of peace near this place of self-inflicted violence. She returned there often, just to look, to ascertain that the monk was still around.

A flash monsoon rain changed everything. Mother found her street wiped clean that morning. Lines of crossed legs no longer greeted her on her ride to school. Sadness overwhelmed her. For three days, she couldn't sleep. It was impossible to close her eyes. Her lids would automatically pop open the minute she tried lowering them. She fidgeted under her sheets. She thought she heard the old monk calling. She knew she must mark his spot of death. To commemorate it somehow. Only then could she get her sleep back.

For her secret mission, Mother crawled out of her room one early morning. Quietly she gathered her father's pick and spade. The wooden front gate cooperated. It opened without a creak. Outside, she inspected the asphalt diligently. Flashlight in hand, she walked back and forth. She let out a cry when finally, she located a faint black smudge resembling a cross. While her parents slept, while Saigon lay nice and quiet on its back, Mother began to work. On all fours, she started banging. Grating noises echoed in her empty neighbourhood, drowning out the crowing of a rooster. Fifty minutes of banging left Mother exhausted. Her swollen fingers ached. Her scratched knees bled. Her eyes burned from jets of grit shooting up. Her lashes pulled down by the weight of dust. Her brown pupils constricted, the white part of her eyes spiderwebbed by red streaks. Mother's heart sank knowing she could never mark the spot with lines of crossed legs. Only a tiny crack had opened up. It was impossible for her to dig any deeper. She could only honour the monk's death with a small fissure. Tired, she gathered her tools and walked home.

Disappointed at first, Mother eventually came to appreciate her accomplishment. Every afternoon she would check that crack on her way back from school. She beamed thinking of her creation—a portal, a portal through which the monk could pass. So great was her belief, she returned there five sunrises in a row. Like a baby caterpillar, she curled up on the street, her jade green pyjamas damp with morning dew. Pressing her ears to the crack, she listened and listened. In vain she waited for a voice that never came. She only heard rumblings of an earth maimed by too many explosions.

For months, images of burning skin would follow

Mother everywhere. She'd go to sleep with memories of gasoline on saffron robes. Even during her sweetest dreams, she'd breathe irregularly as though choking on some indigestible idea.

Adolescence put an end to those childhood nightmares. Sudden bursts of hormones steered her back to a more normal state of mind. She'd refocus her thoughts on the whiff of sebum emanating from her every pore. As a cure for this teenage scourge, a friend had suggested rubbing lemons and cinnamon on herself. That concoction worked. Satisfied, Mother pranced around, sporting a permanent irritating grin. Her father felt like punishing her for such undeserved happiness. "What's there to smile about in times of war?" he asked, an index ready to point at her face. Somehow common sense took over and his accusing finger stayed still. After all, she didn't break any rules with her lemon-scented hair, he reasoned. Yes, my mother's adolescent resilience allowed her relatively normal dreams while her parents twisted and turned in a state of prolonged insomnia.

1968 A Bloody New Year

MISTAKEN FOR FIREWORKS, the clicking of guns added to everyone's excitement. Ignoring curfews, revellers flowed into streets left dark by non-functioning lampposts. Like fireflies, their flashlights twirled around them. Their laughter cut through humming noises. "1968! Year of the Monkey! Let's make this a good year! Happy, Happy New Year everyone!" They'd toast each other good-heartedly. An hour after midnight, Mother's neighbourhood was alive with fireworks, laughter and indolent talk brought about by too much rice wine. When the first rocket landed, nobody understood their new fate. They stopped laughing for a minute. They looked skyward for cues before returning to their fireworks. A New Year celebration would not be complete without fireworks to chase away evil spirits. A second rocket changed everything. Suddenly lucid, people grabbed their kids to make a dash for home. In their panic, they stumbled over rocks, ripping their New Year finery. A chaotic crowd, a father on his knee, a hand released, a lost child crying. My mother witnessed that scene firsthand. The child's sobs scared her. She too wanted to cry. She coughed instead. Smoke burned her nostrils. Street after street, Mother heard the rattle of glass windows as they shattered then scattered. Concrete walls cracking, failed fuse boxes popping, burned trees crashing on parked cars. She heard it all. Out of breath, she ran home to look for her parents. They were at their front door, frantically waving an old flashlight. Low on battery, the flashlight couldn't pierce the darkness around them. Unable to see clearly, unable to make sense of the raging noises, they screamed. They screamed out Mother's name over and over. "Mai! Mai!" On that moonless night, they only heard Mother's heavy breathing. They couldn't see black soot dripping from her nose.

By pure luck, my mother's section of the street was spared destruction. An island of two dozen pastel-coloured houses stood intact amongst piles of burnt-out bricks. Here hibiscus still bloomed, roosters still crowed, babies still cried. For those unfortunates further down, only smoke radiated from roofless homes. In that damned corner, even cockroaches lay drowned in waves of blood and spilled wine.

My mother's family spent those fearful days locked inside. When they ran out of food, they searched Mother's schoolbag for leftover candies. There were none. They dug into garbage cans and found only ant-covered walnut shells. Driven by hunger, Mother sneaked out her house one early morning. She wanted to check the crack she'd made with her hands. The dead monk would surely give her a sign of some sort. She imagined him offering her sweet lotus cakes and soya milk. She envisioned an orange tree sprouting from that crack. What she saw horrified her. Not far from her crack, a baby tugged sluggishly at a dead woman's exposed breast. It wanted to wake its mother, it wanted to be fed, it wanted to be taken care of. Its hands writhed for a few minutes. Its nose dug into the woman's bosom, smearing blood all over its face. It whimpered. Then it too, fell silent. "Hunger. Makes you hallucinate. None of that scene happened," Grandfather simply said. And Mother hung on to those words. She would believe them. Yes, she was hungry. Yes, she'd hallucinated.

Grandfather dithered a long time before venturing into his garden. A bamboo stick in hand, he tried hitting at mango branches. It was not an easy task. The stick weighed more than he thought. Staggering forward and backward, he almost fell several times. For hours he persevered until three green mangoes finally hit the ground. Trembling with hunger, my grandmother cut herself preparing green mango salad. She saw her blood seeping into the fruit. She only shrugged. There was nothing to be done. Water had been cut off. Wearily my mother and grandparents squatted down to a meal of blood-tinged mangoes. Hunger took away their energy. Fear took away their voice. They ate in utter silence that night. Only their roaring stomachs echoed in the dining room.

The dining room also doubled as a bunker. Under their large mahogany table, Grandfather had installed two mattresses. There they slept, squeezed against each other. There they ate, their backs hunched like shrimps. There they spent hours whispering insults at each other.

"This table will save us," Grandfather murmured.

"From what?" my grandmother said.

"From shrapnel, fallen glass and wood."

"No, Buddha will save us," Grandmother said, shoving her husband away.

Communist rockets eventually stopped raining down on them. Electricity came back after sixteen nights of darkness. Gurgling water announced its much-awaited return. Food markets reopened to an impatient crowd shoving and swearing at each other. My grandfather celebrated that day with a glass of rice wine. Grandmother celebrated by preparing jasmine tea for Buddha. She also lit sixteen incense sticks and kowtowed sixteen times to a porcelain Buddha statue. Yes, Buddha had saved them.

A Sign of Peace to Come

IT IS SAID time can fix all. And it did. Tet '68. Mother managed to repress her memory of that bloody New Year. Midnight rockets, burning houses, dead bodies on sidewalks. She had digested it all. There would be no regurgitation of those scenes. Only images of a burning monk still invaded her dreams. Although she gave up listening for voices from a street fissure, she still glanced at it on her way to school every morning. She still smiled at the crack she had created with her own hands.

A blade of grass emerged from that crevice one day. Mother screamed with excitement. She fell off her bicycle. Ankles twisted, pants stained, hair messed up. It did not matter. She panted. A sign of the dead monk, a sign of peace to come, she mumbled to herself. Proudly she brought friends to witness life growing out of a dark space. Nothing short of a miracle, she told them. They all nodded in agreement. "We should come here to pray. Pray for peace," she suggested.

"I'll pray for my father in the army," one girl said.

"Are we praying for the communist or us?" another girl asked.

"Just pray for the end of war," Mother replied.

"Yes. And for good school marks too," a third girl said.

Cops and Communists

EVEN IN TIMES of war or perhaps because of it, my mother's world centred on a boy. His name was Tuan, a next door neighbour. As children they'd spent whole afternoons playing cops and communists. It was a game Tuan thoroughly enjoyed. Chasing Mother down their alley was his obsession. Rocket craters did not scare him. Monsoon mud could not stop him. Voracious flies hardly deterred him. Tuan felt invincible with a plastic gun in his hand. The tinkling sounds of handcuffs dangling from a belt loop stirred him on. Like the American soldiers he saw on television, he roamed his neighbourhood, two fingers in a permanent V for Victory sign.

When Mother asked to be a cop, Tuan shook his head. He laughed in her face. "Girls can't be policemen!" he said with such seriousness she didn't dare question him. "And girls can't be soldiers either," he added in a teasing voice. Not knowing any better, Mother kept quiet that afternoon. On a gnarled tree trunk sprouting out of crooked sidewalks, she sat. Staring at Tuan, she noticed for the first time his long curly eyelashes. She'd never seen lashes so thick, so dark on anyone else. Her fingers itched. She felt like plucking them. She wondered if

Tuan would holler if she did. The bushes over his eyes kept her entertained for hours.

To make their game more realistic, Tuan suggested Viet Cong outfits. "Ripped black pyjamas are ugly!" Mother protested, her eyes squinting. After much back and forth, she agreed to paste mud on her arms. She winced when Tuan slapped wet soil on her hair. But she managed to keep her red blouse and pink shorts clean. Discreetly she also slipped a frangipani petal inside her pocket. She wanted her communists to be girly.

As Mother grew older, she became less tolerant of Tuan's bullying tactics. One day, fed up with running, she decided to crawl inside an old cardboard box someone had left to rot on a street corner. A glimpse of the words "Made in USA" lifted her mood.

She giggled excitedly. She mistook the musty odour of humid cardboard for the scent of America. Hmmm, what a great fragrance, she convinced herself. Giddy, she breathed deeper and deeper. In the welcoming silence of that carton, her imagination grew. She saw herself flying to America on a Westinghouse box, her flip-flops somersaulting in the air.

She hooted.

Unable to find his communist after a thorough search, Tuan lost patience. "Mai, where are you? Come out you commie Viet Cong girl! Come out now!" To that insistent command, Mother jumped out of her cardboard hiding place. Her eerie "Boo" startled Tuan. Her dishevelled hair glued to a sweaty face scared him. It reminded him of drowned kids seen on television. He yelped. He ran home, dropping his gun in the tumult.

Tuan's plastic gun on the grass mesmerized Mother. For so long she'd dreamt of holding it. To be the hunter instead of the hunted. To live life as a haughty soldier instead of a lowly Viet Cong in black pyjamas. Brandishing Tuan's pistol, she chanted, "I won! I won!" Mother's sudden act of insubordination stunned them both. From that day on, their games changed direction.

Tuan's fixation on the communists eventually ceased. Adolescent, he lost interest in his plastic gun. As a sign of their friendship, he offered it to Mother. Placing jasmine flowers inside its nozzle, he shoved it under her nose. In a hesitant voice, he asked her to smell its sweet scent. The jasmine surprised Mother. She picked at them, till one by one, they fell on her toes. Then she kicked them out of her way. Rolling her eyes, she laughed.

"Oh ... I hate that gun,"Mother said. She accepted it anyway. In her room, she rammed it into her burlap bag of souvenirs. A limbless doll, a badminton birdie and a stuffed rabbit all shifted to make way for a toy gun. And so ended their "Me soldier, you communist" years.

To her embarrassment, Mother's stomach still produced gas hearing Tuan's name. Burping was her way of expressing anxiety. The anxiety of infatuation. Younger, she would burp in Tuan's face and together they would both laugh. Years later, the passing of gas became a solitary game of regrets for the end of childhood obsession. He loves me. He loves me not. Burp. Burp.

Lycée Marie Curie catered to rich kids. No one could overlook its ornate columned façade imitating a French mansion. No one could ignore those miniskirted students loitering in front of its gate. Riding scooters in high-heeled sandals—heads turned for these free-spirited girls. Lycée Marie Curie dished out everything French. French thoughts, French history, French music, French art, French fashion, French snobbishness. Only "La Marseillaise" was missing. Thankfully, Vietnamese students no longer pledged allegiance to La Marseillaise like their parents did a generation before. The end of French colonialism had put a definite lid on that peculiar habit. Students were now asked to read some of France's best contemporary writers. Camus, Sartre, de Beauvoir.

Lectures on the complexity of Nothingness or the meaning of Meaninglessness left Tuan cold. Teachers' pointed Parisian accents got on his nerves. Bored, he spent time looking outside. He daydreamed about rubbing castor oil on his scooter. He imagined zigzagging through Saigon's opium-scented alleys. If life could be cut short by a stray rocket tomorrow, he'd rather be riding his beloved Vespa today. He fiddled in class. He drew images of skulls on his school desk. On the back of his notebook, he listed his favourite foods, not in descending order but according to geographical regions. Under America, he wrote: Chiclets gum.

Trung Vuong, my mother's Vietnamese school, tolerated nothing French. No miniskirts. No high-heeled sandals. No French boot-licking. No French-brainwashing. No Nothingness. No Meaninglessness. No class discussion. Only blind acceptance of an outdated teacher, Confucius. Only rote learning of a grandiose history filled with myths. Monkey Kings and celestial emperors, phoenixes and dragons, a 1000-year-old turtle and its magical sword. They all drove Mother crazy. "Why bother learning dates to fairy tales?" This question earned her a smack on the hand. As a teacher, Grandfather could not indulge that kind of challenge.

Two different schools. Two different education systems. Two different worlds. With time, Tuan's and Mother's thoughts stopped crisscrossing at night. They did a U-turn midway. Only one belief still united them. The belief in the uselessness of their education. What good were French existential angst or Vietnamese mythological history in times of war? They just couldn't tell that to their parents. Daily, death coloured their thoughts a crimson red. A superstitious belief that one of them would not make it floated in their minds. Yet they continued living as if all was a game. A game they had started and must play till the end.

Too Much Pickled Beef

MY MOTHER CAME from a strict traditional Vietnamese family. That meant no mixing of the sexes. It meant sticking to an all-girl school. It meant no alcohol, no cigarettes, no drugs. It meant bowing to one's ancestors' portraits at least twice a year—once at New Year and another time on the anniversary of their death. Forget about celebrating birthdays, no one remembers those dates. With young men pretending to be younger to avoid the draft and older women exaggerating their age to earn instant veneration, birthdays were just random numbers on pieces of paper. Death dates, on the other hand, were real dates engraved on wooden slats kept on family altars. This was information to be remembered by all generations to come. My mother enjoyed celebrating her ancestors' death anniversaries. Far from morbid, she'd look forward to these occasions. She'd count the days on her calendar. She couldn't wait for the food that came after the bowing. Asparagus soup, ginger mushrooms, garlic-fried rice. They all whetted her appetite. They were so much tastier than those overly sweet cakes she had at one of her "modern" friends' birthday parties the year before.

My mother's family was not completely anti-modern. They believed in science, medicine and technology. They swore by their radio and black-and-white television. They popped a multi-vitamin pill every day. If she had more money, Grandmother would sprint toward a scalpel to fix her mono-lid. In the meanwhile, she didn't mind splashing mascara to curl her downward-sloping lashes. And she loved her Revlon lipstick adding red to her meaty brown lips. Grandfather was not completely anti-Western. He enjoyed following French gossip in his *Paris Match* magazines. He admired his imitation Renoirs hanging on the walls. Before his nightly dinner, he'd smack his lips looking at full-bosomed, big-hipped, red-haired women. He'd mutter something about Art and Beauty and Amen. It was a habit he couldn't forgo. It was a prayer he couldn't miss.

No, my grandfather didn't hate all things Western. He just thought it more respectful to commemorate his ancestors' death anniversaries than to have a bunch of giggling girls eating birthday cake. Knowing nothing about the celebration of life didn't bother him. Knowing all about the celebration of death gave him the respectability he so wanted.

Like many of their generations, my grandparents believed in harsh discipline. They couldn't understand this cult of youth they saw on American television. Cult of the dead, yes. Cult of youth, no. Why idolize kids with little accomplishment besides cute looks, they wondered. Why place misbehaving children in a corner when a spank worked so much better? Why pay attention to their whining when it is nonsensical? Can an egg teach wisdom to a duck? Of course not.

If my grandfather was somewhat dimmed by his traditional view, my grandmother was downright myopic. Faithful only to her clan, she dumped all others—Catholics, Northerners, foreigners—into a heap of untrustworthies. Walking with Grandmother, Mother had to keep her eyes on the ground. She wasn't allowed to look at a Catholic or Northern boy, let alone a white or black man. Amazingly, my grandmother could identify people with only a twitch of her aquiline nose. "Hmm, too sour a smell ... must be a Catholic or Northerner. Those people eat too much pickled beef!" Good thing Tuan was of the right stock. He only ate pickled beef once a month.

XX + XY = ?

MY MATERNAL GRANDFATHER earned a living as a schoolteacher. He taught mathematics at a secondary school and made extra money giving private lessons at home. Those private lessons were not always about $X + Y = Z$. My grandfather sometimes got twitching eyes looking at young naive students copying down his every statement, their bosoms heaving up and down underneath their *ao dai*, translucent in the afternoon heat. To see if these girls really understood the mathematics of life, my grandfather teased them with tales of birds and bees. For five bonus points, he'd make them solve his ultimate equation: $XX + XY = ?$

As an educated man, Grandfather was not oblivious to the political conflicts around him. He had read about American bombs being dropped on North Vietnam. He knew about napalm showering down on his own people. Weighed down by a mixture of disgust, guilt, fear and helplessness, Grandfather kept his television off three evenings a week. He preferred to look elsewhere for diversion. That "elsewhere" was not hard to find. Six hours a day, they stared at him in class. Young budding breasts were impossible to avoid. He couldn't pretend not to notice. Sideways glances eventually lead to itchy fingers. Fondling them. He fantasized about fondling those not-quite-ripe peaches. Maybe even put a couple in his mouth.

The Baby Blue Room

OF ALL HIS naive students, Grandfather chose the most innocent for his experiment. She was a petite, wide-eyed girl with skin so pale the blue of her veins stood out like calligraphy on rice paper. Her name was Mai, like my mother's. Unlike my mother, this other Mai came from a family of peddlers. On Saigon's twisted sidewalks, they made their money selling cold beers to American soldiers. Luck was on their side. Not used to Vietnamese heat, American soldiers sweated a lot. Under the shade of an old plane tree, these big thirsty men bought one beer after another. Yes, it was beer that filled Mai's family coffers. It was beer that brought her to my grandfather's private lessons. It was beer that sent her straight into his trap.

"Mai, would you like to see my collection of rare rocks?" Grandfather asked one day. He'd cornered his student on her way out. Seeing her surprised look, he licked his parched lips. Peanut-shaped. Beet-coloured. He slicked back his hair. Coarse. Salt and pepper. Brylcreem shiny.

"Oh, uhmm … yes, Sir," Mai replied. "I didn't know rocks can be rare, Sir."

That remark brought a predator smile to my grandfather's smooth, hairless face. He reached for her hand and held it tightly in his. "Everything can be rare, Mai."

Grandfather led his young charge to a large room behind a courtyard, a room double-locked by keys jiggling in his pocket. This was his private domain—a place to correct homework in peace, a place to store his private collection of knick-knacks, a place for his afternoon siesta away from his noisy family. Secluded, it was also an ideal spot for his perverted fantasies. The room was painted baby blue, his favourite shade. A badly scratched wooden desk, a rattan chair, a roll-away bed and four shelves of collectibles filled the space. On each wall hung paintings of curvy women in various states of nakedness. Grandfather's attempt to brighten his nook with baby blue paint bore no fruit. Marking his territory with youthful colours, he fell flat. He couldn't get rid of that old-man-smell. An unmistakable mixture of cigarettes, stale alcohol, unwashed bed sheets and musty books hung in the air.

Grandfather proceeded to show Mai his collection of 25 rare rocks. The multi-coloured rocks showcased in teacherly order impressed her. Their labels in foreign words intrigued her. She tried ignoring them yet her eyes kept returning to those strange words.

"Those are Latin names," Grandfather explained. When Mai fumbled with her notebook, he slapped her hands. "Put that book and pen away! You don't need to take notes on this." Bewildered, she turned around to stare at him. Her unblinking eyes made him self-conscious. He felt beads of sweat oozing from his palms.

"What, what now? What are you looking at, Mai?"

"Your glasses, Professor. They look so different from close. I never saw such a nice blue colour."

"You mean my frames? It's a speckled baby blue ... Oh, never mind!" Mai's innocent remark gave Grandfather a headache. Ashamed of his dark intentions, he abruptly dismissed her with a wave of the hand. "You can go home now, girl." The eyeglasses slid down his nose. He did not bother bringing them up. On his bed, he pondered his next move. To continue the chase or not? That was the question.

A week later, Grandfather once again stopped Mai on her way out. There are beautiful paintings to see, he told her. They are reproductions of famous French art, he explained.

"I have them everywhere in my house. One day I'll take you on a tour," he said.

The small talk over, he took Mai's hand and led her back to his baby blue room. Her blushing cheeks in front of nude paintings emboldened him.

"Oh, that's a Renoir. Over there is a Monet. Or maybe it is the other way around. I can't remember who's who. Do you like them?"

Mai lowered her eyes. No words came out of her off-centred smile.

After the imitation French paintings, Grandfather showed Mai his collection of old, non-functioning opium pipes. Next came ancient Chinese texts. Then came classic French records that Mai wanted to hear but the turntable had refused to turn long ago. This went on for months. My grandfather patiently explained every detail of his various collections to his student. Afraid to displease him, Mai played along with his game. She pretended to pay attention when in fact she itched to go home. Only paintings of half-naked beautiful women fascinated her. She couldn't care less for the rest. Her feigned interest didn't bother my grandfather. He kept showing her more and more of his collection.

Then one day my grandfather offered to show his student something quite different.

"Mai, would you like to learn about Thai massages?"

"I don't know what that is, Professor Minh," Mai answered, her thin lips twisting every which way in confusion.

"No problem. I will show you. Sit down."

Gently, Grandfather undid the top four buttons of Mai's *ao dai*. He slipped his uninvited hands underneath her dress. Full of confidence, he stroked her shoulders. Caught off guard, Mai froze. She knew it was wrong. Her mind rebelled against such acts of violation yet her shoulders acquiesced to my grandfather's touch. The massage felt good. "It feels nice, doesn't it?" my grandfather, the all-knowing math professor, asked. Mai's nod reassured him. "Good! Enjoy it, just don't tell anyone about this. It is our secret, Mai."

A Slice of Peace in Times of War

SHOULDER MASSAGES EVENTUALLY led to a backrub. For this, Grandfather asked Mai to remove her *ao dai* altogether. Aghast, Mai stood still. She shuddered at the thought of exposing herself. A young girl's consternation, Grandfather had expected this. Her reluctance was a natural reaction. Any other behaviour would've been indecent. He approached Mai with a jovial smile. He wrapped a blue bed sheet around her shoulders.

"Keep your underwear. And cover yourself with this sheet. Then come to bed. I will rub your back."

"This is strange, Sir . . ."

"What is strange, Mai?"

"Being here with you. Where is your family, Professor Minh?"

"Don't worry about my family! They went to the Cercle Sportif club for a swim."

In bed, my grandfather poured coconut oil on Mai's slender shoulders. Patiently he watched it trickle down her back in tiny rivulets. He smiled seeing oil droplets seeping into her bra strap. With the palms of his hands, he massaged her in quick, forceful strokes. To cool the heat generated by his rubbing, he languorously blew air on Mai's sweaty back. The minute he felt her tense muscles relaxing under his hands, he asked her to leave. As a self-proclaimed decent man, he never ogled when, reluctantly, she re-buttoned her *ao dai*.

Grooming Mai didn't take long. She was ready by the tenth massage session. She danced eagerly into his baby blue room that day. Gone was her usual timidity. In its place was an earnestness Grandfather had not seen before. She even winked at him. That daring gesture was met with a laugh. In her haste to take off her clothes, she tripped over his shoes, landing face down on his lap. She turned around, emitting a shrill shriek. She closed her eyes and, in blind anticipation, searched for his thick fingers to guide them up her thighs.

"Not a good idea," my grandfather declared. Before Mai could react, he pulled back his hand. Coyly he said, "Tell me you really want it."

"I really want it. Please, Professor!"

"But I don't want it."

Mai's perplexed look pleased Grandfather. He smiled his wise-man smile. Cool it, he ordered his crawling hands. As a warning, he gave each finger a whack. No toying with thighs today! Not yet. Hair. Hair was safer material, he told himself.

Mai wore her hair in braids. One by one, Grandfather undid those hastily-done braids. He caressed her head. He breathed in her lemongrass smell. He rolled her straight black hair around his thumbs. He twirled and twirled until strand upon strand of it fell on his baby blue bed sheet. Mai's fallen hair brought him out of his fantasy. Swiftly, he picked them up, threw them in the metal trashcan and lit a match. A stranger's hair on his bed. His wife must not see this. The perverse game must end soon. Mai's persistent "Down there please!" was met with a firm "No." "No, Mai. Not today. Maybe later when you're older. How old are you by the way?"

"Sixteen."

"Hmm. I thought so. Still too young. Now just show me your breasts before you go home."

Mai unhooked her bra, exposing her nudity to Grandfather. She cupped his hands around her breasts. The vibration in her erect nipples astonished her. She had never before experienced this form of pleasure.

As my grandfather's lips touched Mai's nipple, another Mai—my mother—came home one hour earlier than expected. Mindlessly skipping through the courtyard ahead of Grandmother, my mother came to a sudden halt in front of Grandfather's baby blue room. Through a slit in his sun-faded curtain, a scene straight out of a trashy book beckoned her. She couldn't look away. Her father's tongue slurping a hardened nipple. His hand squeezing the other breast. The girl's quiet moans.

"Ouch! Ouch! I twisted my ankles! Let's go to hospital!" my mother cried.

"Don't scream, Mai! Your father is taking his nap. Nothing wrong with your ankle. Stop acting like a baby." My mother stamped her feet in frustration. She grumbled as she felt hot urine streaming down her pants. A puddle of yellow liquid at my mother's shoes stunned Grandmother. She shook her head in disbelief. "What?! Mai, you peed in your pants now?"

Mother's cries brought an end to Grandfather's

perversity. The acrid smell of urine wafting through his window cooled all erotic thoughts. Throwing Mai her clothes, he ushered her out his back door, the *ao dai* still only half-buttoned. Mai safely out of view, Grandfather straightened his dishevelled hair. He smoothed his shirt, unlocked the door and went to greet his family. "Urine! Are you alright, Daughter?" He asked in a concerned voice. Dismissing Mother's accusing glare, he turned to his wife. "Nice hairdo," he remarked casually. That got Grandmother cackling.

A phony twisted ankle. This was to save Grandfather's upright image. An imaginary scenario. This was to prevent Grandmother from witnessing the real scene. Bartering for a slice of peace in times of war. This was good business practice. The rule of the game, my mother knew it by heart.

A Vamp with Nowhere to Go

PROFESSOR MINH FELT proud of his daughter's quick wit. Her bogus twisted ankle would save him from months of nagging. Spare him years of mud-slinging. He congratulated himself for passing such versatile genes to her. He felt he owed her one. Yet how would he repay it? Only children pay debts to their parents, not the other way around. His Confucian logic had always taught him this.

My mother seethed in anger in her room. One glimpse of Professor Minh's tongue tickling an erect nipple revealed all. Overnight, Mother's life-goes-on attitude collapsed. She cried seeing her hand-embroidered family portrait unravelling. Stitch by stitch, threads came off in all directions. She wished she could confront her father, make a scene, teach him a lesson. Even slap him. But years of Confucian brainwashing would not allow such impropriety. It would hold her back, tie her down. It would transform her voice of anger into one of fake filial piety.

Resentment for Professor Minh eventually transformed itself into something much uglier—hatred for his hypocritical values. No sex before marriage! Virginity for all young girls! No marriage to a white or black man! Bow to your ancestors' photos twice a year! No, no, no and no! At sixteen and a half, my mother became a vamp with nowhere to go.

A Birthday Invitation

TUAN'S EIGHTEENTH BIRTHDAY invitation landed with precision in the garbage can. Mother gave a snort seeing it stained by the leftover fish sauce. She wondered why he had invited her after so many years of silence. Younger, they had spent hours playing in his garden, at first building sand houses, then as cops and communists. That game had exhausted her. Yet she had continued running back and forth in her flip-flops a size too small. Even if she'd plopped on her back pretending to die, Tuan would coax her into playing Comrade Number Two. Comrade Number One, Number Two, Number Three, Number Four, he'd wanted to round them all up. His incessant desire to catch communists was as insatiable as his thirst for Pepsi. Once he had forced my mother to kneel for a sip of his sweet drink only to withdraw it at the last moment. "No! Pepsi is American and you commies hate Americans." Kicking a pebble his way, she'd licked her parched lips. She'd showed him her clenched fist before scurrying home. Years later, that memory still bothered her. It still left a dry, burning sensation in her throat.

"I won't go to his birthday party! Probably bad cake! Feasts for dead ancestors are better!" Mother said.

"You're right about the bad cake. His mother became 'modern' last year. Ha! Ha! She wants to show off her newly found Western lifestyle. So make peace and go!" My maternal grandmother ordered, deaf to Mother's objections.

"Why? Tuan doesn't like me ..."

"Please, save face ... I promised you to his family years ago. You were two kids playing so well with each other. His mother and I, we made a pact together." Making pacts was my grandmother's specialty. She made them with her neighbours; she made them with Buddha; she made them with her husband. Perhaps she also made them with the Devil.

"Tuan doesn't even talk to me these days," Mother said, looking dourly at an imitation French painting. Already she knew she would lose this argument. There would be no winning against Grandmother's beady eyes and pouting lips. Pressed further, those beady eyes would transform into faucets of endless tears. Her pouting lips would part to let out accusations of "What did I do to deserve such a daughter?"

"Mai, that boy Tuan is stupid. Doesn't know what he wants now. Don't worry. He likes you. Just go to his party."

"But ... but ... how do you know he likes me?"

"I know. I'm your mother."

"I'm your mother"—a signal to stop all arguments—was too well understood in that household. Impossible to have the final word, Mother went to her room, upset yet also thrilled about this party forced upon her. She spent an hour looking through her closet for the most modern outfit she could find. Forget that traditional *ao dai* hiding her slim legs. Those flowing dresses suggestive of female forms under their thin material were reserved for more sophisticated eyes. For stupid young boys, she'd have to show them the real thing. To complement her naturally hairless legs, my mother chose a blue knee-length skirt. Rolled up at her waist, it became a mini. Yes, she was ready!

A Cinderella Ball

IN TUAN'S GARDEN, Mother remembered all their childhood games. She was smitten with him even then. For a seven-year-old girl, Tuan, a year older, represented all that she wished for herself—strength, cleverness, talent, good looks. His fiddlehead eyelashes had mesmerized her in those days. She could stare at them for hours. She loved seeing them flap over his protruding eyes. Typically boyish, Tuan had played with my mother only to show off his superior status. A fawning admirer was what he'd wanted. Otherwise, he'd preferred doing his own thing. To further impress her, he'd once pretended to speak American. "Ya, ya. No! No! OK, ok. Hey, hey. Ya, ya. OK, ok! No, no!" His jumbled GI talk enthralled Mother. She felt transported to another world. America. Inspired, she answered Tuan with her own "OK! OK!" In a flash of quick thinking, she even added a "Hey Mister!", an expression she'd heard on television. Hearing her "Hey Mister," Tuan froze. Incredulous, his jaw dropped while Mother chuckled at her own cleverness.

Mother looked around the room. Five girls chatted in one corner. Sporting the same bouffant hairdo, pink lipstick and green miniskirts, they all looked like half-sisters. Only their barrettes differed. Mother wondered if this wasn't some kind of Cinderella Ball. An excuse to gather and choose the best girl for Tuan? She sneered at such a ridiculous idea. Somehow, she was also glad she'd worn her lime green flower-motif shoes. If she had to run at midnight, she'd leave those shoes behind. Tuan would certainly recognize them. He'd have no trouble tracking her down.

Tuan's living room dazzled that night. Hundreds of yellow and green balloons dangled from the ceiling. Yellow and green confetti turned a plain ceramic floor into fields of chrysanthemums. The sofas had been re-moved. In their place were two rows of chairs facing each other. A long table filled with Pepsi, spring rolls, roast pork, fresh rambutans and lotus cakes stood in a corner. French pop music left Mother feverish. "*Ce soir, je serai la plus belle pour aller danser*," a female voice bel-lowed from a record player. Mother only recognized two words: *belle* and *danser*. That was enough to get her twisting in her seat. She was dizzy with excitement. She wanted to dance too. This was a party to end all parties. Mother had never seen anything like it.

A few off-beat dance steps earned Mother scornful glances. When no one joined her on the makeshift dance floor, she shrugged and continued her arrhythmic move-ment. When her left heel broke, she shielded a nervous laughter behind her shaking hands. To salvage her im-age, she sat down, straightened her back and crossed her legs. On cue, four girls followed suit, even crossing their legs in the same direction. (Oh, how I giggled imagining this scenario!)

"Wow, this is better than my ancestors' death anniversary. Even better than our New Year celebration!" Mother exclaimed to a Cinderella on her left.

"Yes. Tuan should enjoy life while he can. Poor guy. Will soon be up for the draft," the girl remarked.

"Nahhh! I wouldn't worry about it. His father has connections. He'll probably get out of it. Flat feet or something," a second Cinderella said.

Forty minutes after the official invitation time, Tuan showed up with his bunch of friends. Surprise! Surprise! Well, it was not really a surprise party. He just didn't expect to see all these pretty girls waiting demurely for him. To make amends for his lateness, Tuan greeted everyone with a mouthy smile. His white teeth shone while the scents of banana-flavoured gum sprang from his throat. Next, he gave each girl a respectful bow as if addressing his ancestors. For my mother, he posed a delicate French-style kiss on her fingers. Holding them in his hand, he noticed her manicured nails painted a glowing red. He sniffed at the lemon and cinnamon fragrance emanating from her palm. He gave her a wink that seemed to say, "I dare you to burp in front of everyone." It was as if he saw through her womanly artifice, as if he mocked her effort at seduction. No matter what she did, my mother was still a kid in Tuan's eyes. Yet she was taller than him. Even without her shoes, he had to look up to her. Had to tilt his head back and lift up his eyes. This difference in height surprised them both. They didn't expect her gangly limbs to flourish under miniskirts while his knock-kneed legs stagnated inside bell-bottom pants. They could never picture little commie

Mai staring down on a cop named Tuan. Yet there they were, reassessing each other after years of silence.

The bowing and hand-kissing finished, Tuan turned to his friends. He introduced them one by one. There were five short guys in platform shoes. Not used to high heels, they all walked daintily. Rough new leather rubbing against their toes turned their smiles into pouts. Even so, they were happy to have a few centimetres added to their small frames.

Amongst Tuan's newly arrived friends was a girl my mother immediately recognized. Her long hair shielding naked shoulders. Her raisin-like nipples. Her jiggling bite-sized breasts. Her protruding hipbones veiled by cheap panties. Grandfather's baby-blue glasses fogging up. His twirling tongue. His creeping hands. Mother had seen them in action. That memory was impossible to repress. She'd wanted to share it with others. She'd found no willing listener. Dirty laundry in times of war interested no one.

Mai and Mai Ly

WITHOUT HER SENSUAL *ao dai*, Mai looked ordinary. In her drab brown blouse, she stood out from the Cinderellas. One unpolished sentence sufficed to reveal a lower-class background. "I never had Pepsi this cold!" Mai repeated loudly as though promoting a soft drink at Ben Thanh Market. Observing Mai from afar, Mother shook her head in dismay. She wondered what her father saw in this simple girl. Yes, it was easier to judge a foolish girl than to pursue a respected professor.

"Are Tuan and Mai …?" Mother wondered aloud. No, it can't be, she decided. Tuan was looking at neither of them. His whole attention was reserved for a short girl in green across the room. His body language told a tale of infatuation my mother would rather not see. His kiss on Mother's hand was just theatrics. Derailed, my mother turned to Mai.

"My name is Mai, what's yours?" Mother's voice was as dry as sea sand.

"Hey, my name is Mai too!"

"Oh, really? So Mai and Mai!"

"Yes, Big Sister! But you can call me Mai Ly if you want. It's my mother's name. Father likes to call me Mai

Ly when he's in a good mood. My friends also call me Mai Ly and ..."

"OK. You're Mai Ly from now on!" Mother interrupted. She'd only heard, "Call me Mai Ly ..." That was enough. She had no need for explanation. No desire for jumbled talk. She was just glad she didn't share a name with her father's lover. "So, I hear your father deals with Americans. How's his beer business?" Mother asked casually.

"Uh, hmm. Why? How? How did you know, Big Sister?" Mai Ly asked.

"I've eyes and ears everywhere!"

"You're with the Viet Cong, Big Sister?" Cautiously Mai Ly scanned the room for indiscreet ears. Her thin lashes flapped fan-like over her bulging eyes.

"Of course not! What, me a Viet Cong, a commie? Geez, I was just joking! Do I look like a communist?"

Mai Ly's reaction to Viet Cong tickled Mother. She imagined her playing cops and communists with Tuan. Nahhh, Mai Ly wouldn't last a day. Tuan would have her shackled and in prison within an hour.

The girl in green was something else. Clingy low-cut dress. White knee-high Go-Go boots. Red and blue Op Art purse. Short and showy. Impossible to ignore her. Mother wondered which games she'd play with Tuan. A guess-my-bra-size played out on a swinging hammock under a tamarind tree, perhaps. Try as she might, Mother couldn't ignore those large breasts bursting under a tight green dress. "She has more than both of us together," Mother announced in a neutral tone.

"Haha! You're right, Big Sister! And she ..." A loud

giggle from across the room drowned out Mai Ly's words. Bobbing her chest to a captive audience, the green-dressed girl laughed and laughed.

"Mai Ly, can you bring me to your father's beer stand? I want to meet those American customers of his." Stewing, Mother shut her eyes. She tucked in her puckered lips and brought hands over her ears to block out the irritating laughter. She'd come to Tuan's birthday party as a potential Cinderella. She left it as a see-nothing-say-nothing-hear-nothing monkey.

Door to Trouble

THREE WEEKS AFTER Tuan's party, the two Mais—
or rather Mai and Mai Ly—met on *rue* Catinat. Long
renamed Tu Do street, it still stayed Catinat for many
people. The French name gave it a sense of elegance not
found elsewhere. Locals even referred to Catinat Street
as Catinat Boulevard. It added prestige to the place.
Bejewelled ladies loved this part of town. "Who said
freedom from French rule equals freedom from a col-
onized mentality?" they mockingly asked their friends.

Catinat, Saigon's busiest commercial artery, was also
its prettiest. Shaded by large plane trees, it was home to
stately colonial-era buildings. Well-preserved, these imperialist monuments impressed onlookers. Anti-French
nationalists might spit on the buildings' lawns. Still,
their eyes would flutter looking at these memorials to
French culture. Wide sidewalks, regular roundabouts, a
traffic light at every corner, here was urban planning at
its best.

At the corner of Catinat and Le Loi Street stood a
beer stand manned by a hand-waving, black-toothed smiling person. His name was Hung. He was Mai Ly's father.
Nightly he thanked Buddha for his small uncontested

space with a million-*dong* view. The senate's ornate building, the grandiose Continental Hotel, the pots of hibiscus, the graceful women in their *ao dais*. Hung could not ask for more. If outdoor café patrons claimed their share of Catinat Boulevard, so did homeless kids. Rich and poor, young and old. The lopsided sidewalks accommodated them all. Ominous tree roots sprouting from broken cement bothered no one. Like the back of a dragon emerging from water, people took it as a sign of good luck. Superstitious old women would circle those tree roots twice. Younger men would simply squat on them. There they'd spend hours observing Saigon's bustling café life.

Givral Café. It was the trendiest eatery in town. Its bright red exterior was unmistakable. Its extensive French menu ran from *steak tartare* to *croque monsieur*. From raw meat to cheese sandwiches, there was something to please every taste. Day in, day out, ragged street kids fought for a coveted spot in front of this famed place. Once they realized fighting got them nowhere, they decided to take turns. Patient like a blind man's dog, they'd sit outside Givral's rotating door. On the café's marble steps, they'd wait for the scent of fresh coffee and a whiff of its air-conditioned coolness. Sometimes, a here's-for-a-good-deed coin would be thrown into their open palms. On such occasions, smiles would turn a grim face into one of wonder.

From inside Givral Café, Mother watched the street action with disinterest. A throng of colourful people paraded past—elegant ladies in high-heeled sandals, teenaged girls in miniskirts, flip-flopped *cyclo* drivers taking a midday break, barefooted beggars walking aimlessly. The coming and going bored her. To keep busy, she started filing her broken nails.

Out of nowhere appeared six pairs of huge black army boots. Looking up, my mother saw a group of American soldiers buying beers from Mai Ly's father. A couple of glances from one of those soldiers turned Mother into a giggling girl. She grabbed Mai Ly's hand, hoping the human contact would quiet her trembling fingers.

The American eyeing my mother was a husky blond with a scar on his right jaw. His paper-thin lips didn't bother her. Neither did his big nostrils nurturing a web of curly hair. She was too absorbed by his rice-field-green eyes. A large tattoo of an eagle in flight covered his left arm. Mother's bewildered look pleased him. He grinned. Playfully, he held his arm up for a better view. Waving it around, he let his tattooed bird fly. My mother pointed to the soldier's antics and laughed. With that one innocent laugh, she'd opened the door to Trouble.

Western Beauty

MAI LY AND my mother returned often to Catinat Boulevard. Their different backgrounds didn't stop a budding friendship. Mai Ly admired my mother's fashion sense. Her rolled-up miniskirts, glossy hairclips, red nail polish, lemon and cinnamon fragrance—Mai Ly fancied them all. In return, Mother wallowed in Mai Ly's adoration. She loved seeing Mai Ly's eyes widen when shown photos of Occidental actresses. That's Marilyn Monroe and that's Raquel Welch, Mother would point out to bug-eyed Mai Ly. The *Paris Match* magazines stolen from Grandfather's desk would enthral Mai Ly for weeks. She'd never seen breasts so large, legs so long, mouths so full of straight teeth. To copy the actresses, Mai Ly practised sucking on her chopstick. Mother preferred pencils—they were more cigarette-sized than chopsticks. Puckering their lips, the friends would blow imaginary smoke rings into Saigon's smog. Waving their pencils/chopsticks between two fingers, they pretended to be smokers—beautiful women, cigarettes in hand and not a care in the world. To outdo Mai Ly, Mother threw her pencil on the pavement, undid the first three buttons of her shirt and took a deep breath to inflate her chest. Mai Ly shook her head. No, she would not follow my mother in this daring act. She only joined Mother in her giggling fits. Together they marvelled at the boldness of American actresses. "Ah, Western Beauty!" they whispered dreamily leafing through pages on a park bench. It would be years before they'd change their minds. It would take upheaval upon upheaval before Western Beauty became Western Decadence.

Never Losing

AT MOTHER'S INSISTENCE, Mai Ly eventually dropped her Big Sister greetings. Seven months, six inches and hundreds of thousands of *dongs* separated them. That was enough for Mai Ly to look up to my mother. She couldn't wait to show off her fancy new friend. The first meeting with her father was awkward. Mother's manicured toes brought Hung out of his daydream. Briskly he jumped up from his squatting position. With one hand, he tightened the belt around his loose pants, with the other he pulled down his rolled-up undershirt. He didn't want Mother to see grey hairs sprouting around his nipples. Lacking previous contact with proper young girls, Hung stayed silent at first. A mixture of confusion and embarrassment eventually took over. He called Mother "Miss" then switched to "My Child" for no reason. He looked her up and down and wondered what she ate to be so tall. For the first time in his life, he became conscious of his dirty curled toenails stabbing into worn flip-flops.

Hung's blackened toenails never registered on Mother's radar. His loose torn pants were enough. It never crossed her mind to look further down. She only noticed his ease with American soldiers, his laughter, his simple jokes. Hung's wheeling and dealing fascinated her. Like a magician, he'd scam people with a smile. And they'd respond with a bigger smile. One beer for 50 *dongs* somehow became eight beers for 500 *dongs*. American clients didn't care about getting the local currency straight. Curiously, they'd always laugh goodheartedly when given the improper change.

After one month of observing Hung, Mother managed to pick up a few English words. Counting to twenty, days of the week, some simple greetings—they became a part of her new vocabulary. Hung insisted on her remembering: "Yes Sir! Sorry Sir! Thank you Sir!" Good American manners, he wanted Mother to learn them all. "And don't forget that V victory sign. Americans love it. They always want to win. They can never imagine losing," he said with a wink.

The Bird Man

THE **B**IRD **M**AN returned regularly to Catinat Boulevard. He'd go looking for Mother inside Givral Café. He'd ask Hung for her whereabouts. The minute he ran into her, he'd hold out his tattooed arm and float it above her head. Coaxing her to reach up for it, he'd make her bare her midriff. His bird in the air, he'd gallop down crowded Catinat Boulevard. Excited, Mother would bump into sidewalk diners as she chased after him. She would turn bowls of soup upside down. She would make kids fall on their knees. She would separate lovers as she zipped down between them. To catch a tattooed bird, that was no easy feat. Here, Birdie! Birdie!

The tall blond soldier and the dark-haired girl got around their language barrier by chirping like canaries. They tweeted to the sounds of bicycle horns. They hummed to the beat of Pham Duy music. They laughed at their silliness while onlookers watched them with distaste. When monsoon rain flooded Saigon, they'd walk hand-in-hand, nonchalantly sharing an umbrella, oblivious to the brown water seeping up their ankles. When the sun beat down on them, they'd share my mother's hand fan to disperse their beads of sweat. Yet no matter how hard they fanned each other, they couldn't quite cool their bodies in heat.

Besides fanning my mother in public parks, the Bird Man also taught her English. Those lessons occurred in crowded Givral Café. Over iced coffee, the American chatted non-stop. In minute details, he described his hometown, his parents, his former high school friends. My mother's blank stares didn't discourage him. Cool and collected, he pulled out his English-Vietnamese dictionary. Vietnamese equivalents of "Splitting-up," "Suburbia" and "Volkswagen Beetle" were nowhere to be found. It didn't matter. He continued talking. Of all his words, Mother liked best "You're beautiful" and "I like you." To these compliments, she answered, "Yes Sir. Thank you, Sir."

As a soldier, the Bird Man was a man of action. He would put into practice what he preached. "I like you" became a thorough fondling of a jade pendant around Mother's neck. "Beautiful necklace," he complimented her over and over. Her smile encouraged his next move. He lifted a strand of her lemon and cinnamon hair to his nose. "Love your smell," he said as he breathed in my mother's aroma. His index snaked leisurely up Mother's face. Fearless, it entered her mouth. This indecent contact gave colour to her cheeks. Embarrassed, she pulled out the intruding digit. "What is 'splitting-up'?" she wondered out loud.

Challenging Confucius

THE BIRD MAN was a 22-year-old soldier on R&R. He'd recently returned from a jungle reconnaissance mission where he'd killed two Viet Cong. Searching the Viet Cong bodies, he'd found nothing of significance. No name. No address. No letters to families. No photos of loved ones. No cyanide pills. No lucky charms. Not even a cigarette. Ghosts. They were all ghosts. It was true what his captain had said about the Viet Cong. "Have no fear, Boys. These gooks are nobodies. They're just worthless communist shit." Like a drop of vaccine, those words had doubled in strength with each repetition. By the end of their training, Captain Moore had succeeded in building up his troop's immunity. He'd made them immune to fear. And immune to compassion.

Killing two nobodies had tempered the Bird Man's pride. Yet a killing was still a killing. He remembered Captain Moore's smile, his fingers forming a V sign. Ashamed, he also remembered his own wet pants. The Bird Man felt tired all of a sudden. Oh, how he wished to forget everything. To stop questioning his role in this damn country, in this crazy war. To think about nothing except the fact that he was still alive.

"You kill two VC? I mean two Viet Cong?" my mother asked, her mouth wide open.

"Yep, those two communists had fancy Kalashnikovs! Real killing machines shipped straight from Moscow! Haha! But my M-16 was faster. They didn't call me Speedy Gonzales in school for nothing!"

"What Viet Cong look like?" Mai Ly's thin lips quivered. She had no idea what Kalashnikovs, M-16 or Speedy Gonzales meant. She didn't care. She only wanted to see the enemy's face. Even if they weren't her real enemies, she was fooled into hating them.

"Short, skinny guys. Young. I think they were scared shitless. One still had his hands clapped together, like in a prayer. Other guy had his eyes open looking at the sky, praying to God. Dear Buddha, please save me! Haha!"

"Oh, no!" Mai Ly's bulging eyes seemed ready to pop out of their sockets.

"Yep!" the Bird Man said, laughing. Imagine, two Vietnamese girls fretting over two dead commies. What a great exchange, he thought. Why, that's enough motivation to kill more Viet Cong!

The Bird Man was an acquired taste. Once conditioned, my mother craved for more. What she once thought repulsive—his prickly beard, hairy chest, strong armpit odour, cigarette breath—now had her fantasizing at night. He'd introduced her to alcohol on their sixth outing. One reluctant sip had her spitting out the brew. Smartening up, he diluted it with a 7 UP. The sweetened drink pleased Mother. She drank it eagerly. After her tenth sip, she started to whistle. Without warning, she grabbed his index. She noticed dirty crusts under his yellowed nail. Doesn't matter, she mumbled before ramming his finger inside her mouth. Ravenously she savoured it as if sucking on a piece of sugarcane. Yum! It did not take much for the alcohol to unravel my mother's upbringing. Bow to your ancestors! Hahaha! No sex before marriage! Hohoho! Stay away from white or black men! Wowowowow! One diluted beer was all she needed to challenge Confucius.

Her Lemon and Cinnamon Scent

THE FIRST TIME on the Bird Man's bed, Mother had insisted on keeping her fishnet underwear. She'd curled up like a shrimp, refusing to look him in the eye. His vibrating fingers uncurled her a bit. His tongue digging a tunnel through her fishnet uncurled her a bit more. Slowly, ever so slowly, the shrimp transformed itself into a slimy wiggling worm.

Once her ripped veil healed, Mother began to enjoy the Bird Man's zucchini. Twice a week, she'd visit him at his hotel. Twice a week, she'd tell her parents about a fake swimming event at the Cercle Sportif. Instead of treading water, she'd be rocking his bed and screaming Vietnamese holy words. Instead of spitting out chlorine, she'd be drinking his sweat and licking his hairy chest.

One day Mother shook the bed so violently, it stopped a gecko in its track. Surprised, the animal rotated its peppercorn eyes round and round. It had just enough time to stick out its tongue, emit a fearful "gecko" before losing its grip and falling on my mother's naked shoulders. Even with white ceiling plaster narrowly missing his eyes, the Bird Man giggled at this scene. Seeing Mother hysterically jumping up and down amused him.

He wished he'd his camera on him. Geckoes crawling on walls. Mother had lived with them all her life. She just never envisioned their scaly skin touching hers. It was like growing up deafened by echoes of war yet never expecting to be hit by a rocket.

The Bird Man was at first protective of my mother. He wanted her all to himself. Eventually, he realized possessiveness to be pointless in times of war. He just wanted them to have fun. He taught Mother to enjoy each zucchini moment. He told her he could be dead tomorrow. They both knew he would be back in California within a few months. In times of war, there was no time to fall in love. And one zucchini was as good as any other.

Three months after witnessing a gecko in free fall, the Bird Man introduced Mother to his American buddies. Her lemon and cinnamon hair attracted these homesick soldiers craving for a mother's pie. Like hungry dogs sniffling at sidewalks, they followed her trail to the Pink Night Club. There they found her sitting between two men, a beer in one hand, a 7 UP in another. As they surrounded her, she'd smile at each one of them. She'd acknowledge them all and in a fit of laughter, she'd swing her head to better disperse her lemon and cinnamon fragrance.

Mai Ly and the Professor

THE DAY MAI Ly turned seventeen, she became legal prey for her professor. His usual back massages gave way to pelvic rubbings. Mai Ly didn't complain. She'd expected this for months. Professor Minh was gentle with her that afternoon. He talked to her in a soothing voice while putting coconut oil on his fingers. In circular motions, he worked his way up her thighs. Mai Ly closed her eyes. Her uneven breathing signalled anticipation. Perhaps a touch of apprehension? Removing his speckled baby blue glasses, the professor closed his own eyes. The classroom door was locked. His family was swimming at the Cercle Sportif. Only guilt could hold him back. He was beyond guilt by now.

Mai Ly's moans of pleasure, the blood trickling out of her—Professor Minh looked down in dismay. Blood and pleasure, they weren't supposed to go hand in hand. A virgin, she was supposed to be in pain. Not a virgin? Then why blood? Unnerved by stained sheets, he interrupted his love act. "Are you alright, Mai?" he asked.

"Yes, yes, please go on, probably just my period starting … and, and call me Mai Ly …"

Mai. Mai Ly. Blood. Menstruation. Virginity. Pain.

Pleasure. The information spun in his head. Professor Minh decided enough was enough. He gave Mai Ly a towel before running to the bathroom with his soiled sheets. There he scrubbed till his hands turned raw. Swollen fingers or not, he knew he had to clean the evidence before his wife's return.

Back in his room, he found Mai Ly absentmindedly caressing her legs. That innocent gesture unsettled him. He didn't know if he should comfort his lover or deflower her some more. Mai Ly looked up and pouted. "So hot here," she said. Then and there, Professor Minh decided conversation to be his best course of action.

"You changed your name to Mai Ly now?"

"Well, it's still Mai officially. I just like to be called Mai Ly. It's my mother's name. My ... my mother ... she died when I was very young. I don't remember anything about her."

"That's a sad story, Mai. I mean Mai Ly. You have no photo of her? No family heirloom?" Professor Minh enquired with genuine curiosity. He wondered if Mai Ly looked anything like her mother. He wondered if he could ever fall for an older version of Mai Ly. No, he shook his head. No. It was only her youth that fascinated him. It was her innocence that had kept alive his pipe dream of immortality.

"We were poor. Mother had nothing to leave me. No photos either. She only had the clothes on her back, which we buried her in. She left me nothing, nothing except this name ... Mai Ly, do you like it?"

"Of course! Come closer, my dear girl." Mai Ly obeyed. Bending over, he parted her legs with a wet towel. Tenderly, he rubbed the dried blood off her thighs. "Your mother also left you a very nice pair of hairless legs," he whispered in Mai Ly's ear, all the while wondering why sex and death had to be eternally linked.

Love on the Rickshaw

MAI LY'S AFFAIR with my grandfather reeked of perversity. Even now, I find it hard to think of him as my grandfather. That the same blood ran through our veins disturbs my conscience, a conscience under-developed in Professor Minh. Blinded by greedy desires, he saw not the consequences of his actions. Unable to distinguish right from wrong, he felt no guilt. Small, tight Mai Ly—this was all he could think of. Day and night, he lived obsessed by images of her still green peach-sized breasts. Like an oyster around its pearl, he hung on to his grime-inspired fantasy. I could make him more sympathetic, but I won't.

Only Mai Ly's father, the beer seller Hung, lived up to his image as an adult. To his consternation, Hung saw my mother's flirtatious behaviour growing bolder every day. Her giggling fits with a bunch of American soldiers gave him a pounding headache. He wondered if his own daughter Mai Ly was not acting likewise on another street corner. He blamed himself for teaching her English. He regretted not being stricter with the Americans. "You lay off my girls!" he should've told them but he didn't know the English words for "lay off."

Thoughts of his daughter sleeping with American GIs revolted him. It felt like a betrayal to his cause.

◈ As the only boy in a family of three girls, Hung was taken out of school at fifteen. Sent to Saigon to make a living, he learned early to fend for himself. Peddling a *cyclo* in town, he made money riding people around. For every *dong* earned, half would be sent to support his family back home in My Lai. This was a job expected of him. He felt proud of his accomplishments. He never complained.

Every two years, the family would reunite during the New Year festival of *Tet*. Rice wine and evening songs—this was how they celebrated those special moments. His sisters' laughter as they held the gifts he brought them warmed his heart. It was worth a year's hard work. At his last visit, Hung's youngest sister, a skinny cross-eyed girl of seven, had wrapped her arms around his muscular legs. She'd begged for a trip to Saigon. She'd threatened to hug him forever if he didn't agree to her demand. Hung's "maybe next year" had brightened her eyes. She'd let go of her clutch for a minute only to change her mind. The idea of seeing Saigon one day excited her. She hugged her brother's legs even tighter. She covered them with kisses. Fascinated by descriptions of Saigon, she could not contain her joy. Its tall buildings, its cars running around, its strange animals in a place called 'zoo,' its ships floating on water. She wanted to see it all. That night, she fell asleep sitting on a bamboo mat, her head leaning against her brother's lap, her arms still circling his legs. On his wooden chair, Hung also dozed off, his left hand resting on his sister's tangled hair, a hint of a smile making its way across his face.

As the war progressed, long-distance travel became dangerous. Unsafe roads prevented Hung from returning to My Lai. In Saigon, he led a simple existence. To keep company, he befriended a raggedy woman. He'd spotted her selling ginger at Ben Thanh Market one day. Her thread-thin clothes and uncombed hair did not lessen the pull of her smile. Witnessing unscrupulous customers cheating her, he'd spoken up for her. She'd responded with a hearty laugh. Her thick black eyelashes set against her soya milk complexion drove him crazy. He wanted to cover her with kisses. Making love on his rickshaw was no easy matter, and if not there, then where else? The *cyclo*—the rickshaw—had been his only bed in Saigon. At night, he'd park it under a leafy tamarind tree. There, he'd count stars until sleep would relieve him of his backache and transform his uncomfortable resting position into dreams of soft pillows.

Unable to get the woman out of his mind, Hung invited her for a stroll one early evening. She accepted without a fuss. At the first sign of dusk, she snuggled against him. She didn't like being out at night. She was scared of darkness. All her evenings were spent cooking and catching lice inside her friend's shack, she said. Let's sit on this bench, Hung suggested. What's your name, he asked. Mai Ly, she answered. What a beautiful name, what a beautiful face, he whispered. To this, she gave his hand a slight caress. "Mai Ly is also my mother's name. She died stepping on a mine one evening." Her voice broke with those words. All of a sudden Hung felt a worrisome pressure on his heart. It was as if her story had imprisoned him. From that moment on, he no longer wanted to rickshaw her. He wanted to marry her instead.

A combined earning allowed Hung and his wife to rent a space in her friend's bamboo shack. No walls, no doors delineated their spot. Only an invisible line on a mud floor separated their privacy from the friend's. All noises became shared noises. All intimacy became desperate waiting sessions—waiting out the friend's wakefulness, waiting to hear her snoring. It was only then, in the hour before night paled, and to the rhythmic sound of snores, could their action start.

The fruit of those actions didn't take long to germinate. Ecstatic at the news, Hung would don a permanent grin. Every evening he'd rub coconut oil on his wife's expanding stomach. Every evening he'd check for a tiny foot kicking against his oily palm. Sharing a drop of oil with Hung, the friend was also allowed to partake in this ritual.

"What should we name the baby?" Mai Ly asked.

"Well, Hung if it's a boy."

"What if it's a girl?"

"How about Mai? Or Mai Ly, like you."

"No, not Mai Ly. Enough Mai Ly already. I like Mai better."

"Then it will be Mai."

The Hospital

PEDALLING HIS PREGNANT wife to Cho Ray Hospital, Hung almost ran over an elderly woman. At the next intersection, he had near-misses with several cars as he sped through a red light. He became a target for swear words accompanied by clenched fists. On any other day, he would've heard those insults and responded in kind. On this particular day, he only heard Mai Ly's moans.

The hospital was staffed by indolent nurses coming and going as in a dream. Impervious to patients' screams, they went about their business reading charts or writing notes. After a deliberately long wait, Hung was shown a spot on the ceramic floor. On her soiled bed, Hung's wife bowed to everyone. It was her first time on a bed. She wanted to show gratitude. Labour pain caused her to double over. Still, she managed to appreciate her mattress in between contractions. She bowed and bowed.

The hot stuffy room had 21 other moaning women. A horde of mothers, fathers, husbands, sons, daughters ate in utter silence. The smell of fried garlic brought saliva to Hung's mouth. He kicked himself for forgetting his tin can of steamed tofu at home. To take his mind off his empty stomach, he concentrated on two lines of black ants crisscrossing the hospital floor. They were orderly. Unlike Saigon's traffic, these ants moved with a purpose. They didn't ram into each other. They didn't swear at each other.

Mai Ly's screams worried Hung. Her crescendo moans earned a loud "Quiet!" from one nurse. A doctor please, Hung begged. What doctor? No doctor. Just start pushing, came her answer. Before Hung could say more, the nurse walked away. Mai Ly's heavy breathing scared Hung. The smell of her perspiration, urine and stool embarrassed him. He dared not look at her twisting body. Glancing around, he saw 21 copycat scenes. Twenty-one other women were labouring in bed while their family members squatted in silence.

"Take off your pants. You're ready. Push harder!" a nurse ordered one woman.

"You're ready. Take off your pants. Push now!" a second nurse said to another woman.

"Take off your pants. Push more. Your baby is ready to come out," a third nurse told a third woman. As if by miracle, as if they'd heard the command they dared not disobey, three hairy heads slowly emerged from a mysterious space. From a faraway world onto bloody bed sheets, Papa Stork was busy that day.

Hung couldn't accept his wife's naked genitals exposed to strangers. In a moment of quick thinking, he took off his shirt to drape over her legs. A tuff of black hair appeared between her thighs. He gulped. Did it belong to the mother? Or to the baby?

A nurse swiftly threw Hung's shirt on the floor. With one kick, she sent it to the far corner of the room.

Running after his shirt, Hung would miss the most important moment of a delivery—that instant when a mother's body finally let go of her baby, when vaginal resistance finally fell to zero allowing baby to shoot into the world a free being. When Hung next laid eyes on his wife, a baby girl was already in her arms. They would call her Mai. "Mai and Mai Ly," Hung repeated over and over, his eyes misty with happiness.

The Broken Promise

THE WAR BROUGHT misery to many and fortune to others. The arrival of Americans GIs would turn ordinary Vietnamese into gangs of crooked salesmen. There was always something to sell, some services to offer at triple the normal price. Hung's *cyclo* business mushroomed with the boom in war tourists. He doubled his rate for Japanese journalists, tripled it for Western journalists and for those weighty American GIs in their heavy leather boots, he quadrupled it. No one ever made a fuss. Pedalling American soldiers around town broke his back. These new invaders never knew where to go, always had the wrong address or just wanted to go round and round. Stop here! No, stop over there! No, keep going! No, turn right! No, sorry, turn left! They barked at him ride after ride. In return, he replied good-naturedly, "Yes, Sir!" He bowed and bowed, knowing American dollars to be more than just paper. Those green bills smelled of hope, radiated optimism. They'd help him move up his Karma ladder. The day Hung exchanged his old rickshaw for a fancy beer stand, he celebrated with a toast. It was a toast to the power of money. A toast to the heat and the Americans' overactive sweat glands. A toast to the future retirement of all overworked people.

Busy with his new life, Hung eventually ceased fretting about his sisters back home. Instead of regular visits, he sent them annual gifts of dried kumquats, comic books and Chiclets gum. Waiting for his turn at the post office, he felt a tinge of guilt. Those girls deserve so much more, he thought. "Should've bought them those cute dresses," he mumbled. It was too late to turn around. He'd been in line for an hour and had to get back to work soon. A postal clerk shook his head seeing Hung's package. "My Lai, not possible," he said matter-of-factly. To Hung's "Why?" he shrugged. "I sent it last year, no problem!" Hung insisted. The clerk's silence frustrated him. He stamped his feet, banged his hand on the counter and started shouting obscenities. Curious, people turned to scrutinize his unkempt hair and wrinkled clothes. "Will someone get that bum out of here?" a man screamed. "Call the police!" another person suggested. To everyone's surprise, an old woman gently accosted Hung. She took his hand and whispered in his ears. "My Lai no longer exists," she said.

A whole village extinct. Hundreds of innocent civilians killed by American soldiers on a rampage. Hung couldn't believe the woman's tale. In panic, he rushed outside, searching for a newsvendor. He ripped through his newspaper, hoping to see nothing. But he saw it all. Burnt houses, slashed pigs, fields littered with human corpses, a large pit filled with bodies, he could no longer ignore the truth. From somewhere down that pit, Hung thought he recognized his youngest sister's screams.

Memories of her arms hugging his legs brought tears to his eyes. He felt horrible for promising her Saigon's sight and sound when in fact she only heard the clicking of rifles and saw the flow of blood.

At home, Hung sat silent for hours. Dazed, he stared at his daughter Mai Ly asleep on her bamboo mat. Inconsolable, he ran to her, waking her up with his rough kisses.

Safety under the Bed

"**M**AI LY, I** have something to tell you," Mother exclaimed one day. On second thought, she wondered if she shouldn't keep quiet. Keep things as they have always been—under lock and key. Better to pretend she didn't see, didn't know of her father's perversity. Better to salvage his reputation, to save his face, as she'd always been taught to do. Then in a sudden fit of rage, she blabbed, "OK, Mai Ly. Your lover boy, Professor Minh. He's related to me. He's actually my father!"

"Yes, I know," Mai Ly said calmly, looking away from my mother.

"Really? How? Tuan told you? Oh, my God! That damned neighbour's been talking behind my back! What other gossip is he spreading? So is my father good to you?" Mother asked, her cheeks reddened by a late afternoon sun.

"Professor Minh, he's nice. I like his teaching. My marks are all good now. He looks nice, so tall ... and, and ..." Mai Ly paused, struggling to find words that would unlock the vault hoarding her feelings.

"No! Don't say anything else!" my mother warned putting her hands over Mai Ly's lips. She didn't want to hear what would come next. A sense of dread left her head spinning, her ears immune to confidences.

Her friend in love with Professor Minh. Mother could not accept this fact. She drove herself crazy, twisted her own arm. Her father's duplicity, his sordid affair—she must report it to her mother. The thought became an obsession. How would she do it? Send unsigned letters? Make anonymous phone calls? Or tell it straight to her face? In the end her plotting fizzled out. Already fragile, Grandmother's state of mind could not take more hits.

The communist attack of 1968 had transformed my maternal grandmother into a strange night creature. She lived her days like most people do—going to the market, chatting with neighbours, putting up with her husband. In short, she lived a day-to-day existence as if the war would spare them, as if Buddha had spread an invisible holy blanket to shield them from destruction. It was only at night that my grandmother's folly expressed itself. Her matrimonial bed, she'd insisted on sleeping underneath it. There, she kept a pillow, a straw mat and a flashlight. Nightly, she'd wiggle into that closed-in space, her prominent forehead hitting the bedframe. Before turning off her flashlight, she'd check a mousetrap for dead rodents. Despite little critters biting her legs, the place gave her a sense of security she couldn't find elsewhere. Professor Minh tolerated his wife's nocturnal insanity as long as she didn't ask for him under the bed.

Grandmother sharing her mat with mice, sneezing from the dust. This thought tormented Mother. She wanted to scream. She pictured Professor Minh in bed alone while his wife cringed below it. She imagined his eyes riveted on those imitation Renoirs as he pleasured himself with fantasies of young students. Wretched, Mother went looking for her father's collection of rare rocks. One by one, she threw them on the overgrown grass.

Le Cercle Sportif Saigonnais

"**M**AI LY, TAKE my advice, stay away from my father. He's just using you. He's a pervert!" Mother's loud voice echoed down the bus. Used to these kind of accusations, most male passengers remained stone-faced. Six women turned around to check out my mother. It was free entertainment, a diversion from their farm-to-market-to-straw hut lives. Their unabashed laughter stopped Mother from revealing more family secrets.

"Um ..." Mai Ly hummed. Her hand gestures showed her annoyance. "Tone it down," she wanted to say. Leaning into my mother for a whiff of her hair, Mai Ly commented, "Hmm. Smell like lemon and cinnamon ... how do you do it, Big Sister?"

"Don't change the subject, Mai Ly! And stop calling me Big Sister!" She jumped up, grabbed Mai Ly's hands and dragged her out of the bus.

A long walk in mutual silence brought the two girls to a green space in front of a private sports club. Mai Ly's mouth formed an O seeing the letters CSS. Cercle Sportif Saigonnais. That famous playground for the rich, the connected, the foreigners.

"You want to come in? I'll tell the guard you're my

guest. You might see my father! If you like him so much, might as well make it official," Mother suggested in a taunting voice.

"No, I don't want to run into Professor Minh!" Mai Ly's face turned crimson at the idea of seeing his muscular chest outside their secret place. His baby blue room full of collectibles. That was the only spot she'd felt safe.

"Ha! Ha! Just kidding. My father is not here now. Come!" Mai Ly's knitted brows worried Mother. She felt sorry for her friend. Ice cream. Ice cream on a patio will fix all problems, Mother told herself.

At the club's gate, a uniformed employee gave Mai Ly a thorough gaze. He examined her from head to toe, then from toe to head. Even with clean, intact clothes, she didn't fit the typical member's profile. There was something amiss about her. He asked to see her hands and after checking her fingernails, shook his head.

"No maids allowed here," he said in a flat tone.

"What maid?? She's my guest!" Mother insisted.

"Guest or no guest, it doesn't matter. No maids allowed. That's our rule. Miss, there's no need to bring your maid. We have our own waiters and French chef here …"

"But she's not a maid! She's a student! Mai Ly, show him your student ID card," Mother ordered, her hands shaking uncontrollably, her face red with rage.

"Oh, student! OK! Sorry, you can come in then. Welcome to our Cercle Sportif!"

Humiliated, Mai Ly stayed quiet, her eyes fixed on the ground. She still dared not look up once admitted inside the club's lush hibiscus garden. Dragging her feet in silence, she continued staring at her plastic flip-flops. She skirted trees only at the last minute.

For a change of atmosphere, Mother took Mai Ly to the club's restaurant. "*Deux glaces au chocolat,*" she ordered in her shaky French. Hand-in-hand, she led Mai Ly to a terrace overlooking two swimming pools. She asked her friend to breathe in that fresh clean smell of chlorine. "Isn't it wonderful?" she asked. "The scent of cleanliness." Mai Ly did as she was told and agreed. She'd never smelled this in her slum neighbourhood. She'd never seen water so clear, so blue. She even felt like taking a sip of pool water.

From the café, Mother recognized four Americans basking on their lounge chairs. One by one, she pointed them out to Mai Ly. Shrubs of red hair curling around pink nipples. Mai Ly couldn't stop ogling. She grinned when she actually felt like laughing out loud. Directly or indirectly, Mother had known those muscled soldiers. Dancing at the Pink Night Club, twisting in bed or just flirting in Givral Café, the men were a tantalizing series of lips, hands, groins. Thoughts of their muscular bodies brought a craving for their sweet and sour sweat. Nimbly, Mother bent down to lick a line of ice cream dripping on Mai Ly's arm. It was a hot day and ice cream was quick to melt.

A Pig's Tale

"**F**ATHER HATES AMERICANS," Mai Ly told my mother one day. It was her fourth visit to the private sports club. She'd become used to bare-chested GIs sedimenting in the sun. She no longer giggled at their bush of curly underarm hair. She no longer wanted to drink swimming pool water.

"Why?" Mother asked lazily, looking up from her *Elle* fashion magazine.

"Americans killed his family at My Lai. He doesn't talk much about it. Not sure of the exact story. I think American soldiers shot whole village. Everybody's dead. Babies too. 1968. Americans looking for communists. And no, Father's family's not communist ..." Eyes squinted, Mai Ly pointed randomly at a big-bellied white man. "It could be him who killed Father's family." My mother's blank stare reassured Mai Ly. She picked another one. A young man with USA tattooed on his chest. "Maybe it's him. Or the one next to him," she said. Before she could point out more possible culprits, Mai Ly snuggled up to my mother, shivering. "Any one of them could be the killer. Imagine being so near them, looking at them, it scares me!"

Mother took fidgety Mai Ly in her arms. She stroked her hair till all the knots disappeared. "Why such a big fuss?" she whispered. "You've seen Americans before. Your father's beer stand is full of them. It's the same people, so don't worry!" As Mai Ly's breathing slowed down, Mother let go of her embrace. "Is that how your mother died, Mai Ly?" she asked with concern.

"No. My mother died in Saigon. I told you already. Hit by a scooter. Accident. The driver had two pigs in a cage. Little pigs squirmed, cage fell off. Driver lost control. He ran into my mother. She fell down, head hitting the sidewalk. Scooter man picked up his pigs. He just ran off. Everybody saw it. But nobody came to Mother's rescue. She died while Father was busy working. He found her body when he came home. Same spot, body unmoved. I was with neighbours all this time."

Mai Ly with a father from My Lai. The coincidence unnerved my mother. The pig connection also spooked her. Squirming pigs on a scooter. Pigs in military uniforms on a rampage. Both had resulted in death. American soldiers depicted as pigs in uniforms—they were everywhere in Grandfather's French magazines. Since those cartoons seemed nonsensical, Mother had never bothered to ask 'why?' Why were uniformed pigs burning huts? Why were pigs carrying guns? Why were they flying airplanes?

Where Did They Go?

WHEN **MAI LY** failed to show up at their usual meeting place, Mother went looking for Hung. An empty space greeted her at the corner of Le Loi Street and Catinat Boulevard. The beer seller and his daughter were nowhere to be seen. Mother walked up and down the boulevard before checking some side streets. She tapped her feet impatiently, hoping Hung would run to her, excusing himself for being late. He did not. She solicited the help of a street kid napping under a tamarind tree. "Fuck your mother, you fucking whore," was all he said to her enquiries. Inside Givral Café, my mother tried chatting up one waiter. She batted her thin downward slopping eyelashes. She smiled as she asked about Hung. Bowing politely, the black-tied waiter returned my mother's smile. He scratched two mosquito bites on his neck till they bled. He shrugged his stooped shoulders as if to say, "Who knows? And why should you care?" For days, American clients had harassed him for information about their favourite beer seller. Tired of answering all these questions, he'd pointed left to some beer-thirsty GIs and right to some others. "Hung, beer seller? Oh, he went this way. Turn right!" "Yes, he went that way. Turn left ..." My mother scoffed at this bit of information. Polite people, these compatriots of hers. Always smiling, always nodding. Yet completely useless if no money changed hands. Mother gave herself a pinch in the arm for not realizing this sooner.

Conversation with Professor Minh remained out-of-the-question. Extremely testy, he snapped at the least provocation. For days, Mother spied on his private tutorials. Her efforts gave no results. Mai Ly had stopped going to Professor Minh's class. Phoning her friend's home also got her nowhere. She found that number no longer functioning. She went looking for Mai Ly at her school. Stunned, Mother learned she'd dropped out a month ago. Where did they go?

Why Dwell on the War?

PROFESSOR MINH RESUMED his daily routine soon after Mai Ly's disappearance. He continued teaching at the secondary school. His private lessons at home went on as before. He once asked the class for Mai Ly's whereabouts. Without acknowledging him, the girls glanced furtively at each other. Some rolled their eyes. It was as if they could see through his black cotton pants. As if they could picture his grey hair shielding a small limp appendage. Getting no direct answer, he resigned himself to the idea that Mai Ly might be gone forever. Still, he continued calling her name during roll call. He continued preparing her report card, noting 'absent' instead of zero. At home, Professor Minh still shared dinners with his family, still slept alone on the bed while his wife hid underneath it. In his spare time, he'd dust his Chinese pipe collection over and over in an attempt to forget Mai Ly. Distressed at the sight of his baby blue bed sheets, he'd lugged that rolling bed into a musty hangar. On those sheets, he'd braided Mai Ly's hair, had sniffed at her breasts. Now, only her peculiar lemongrass odour remained. He found it ridiculous to be heartbroken at his age over a silly young girl. In times of war on top of it. "Why are you acting like a pathetic teenager? Get over it," he told himself.

Mother naturally noticed Professor Minh's changed behaviour. There was absence in everything he did, inertia to all his actions. He simply was not there for her. Mother too felt the effects of Mai Ly's vanishing act. Rage kept her on the Pink Night Club's barstool. There, she drank one diluted beer after another. Anxiety filled her nights. She'd imagine improbable scenarios to explain her friend's sudden departure. In her most pessimistic state, she'd see Mai Ly disembodied after stepping on a landmine. On other occasions, she'd picture Mai Ly tortured by the Secret Police because one of Hung's competitors had pointed a finger at them. From her American lovers, Mother knew this occurred all the time. For years, innocent people were persecuted simply because someone had pointed them out. "He's a communist sympathizer! She's a Viet Cong! They are all VCs! That one is a commie! Yes, I recognize that communist spy!" To keep their jobs, the Secret Police had a quota to fill. "TWENTY COMMUNISTS CAUGHT THIS MONTH!" helped oil their propaganda machine. "TWENTY COMMUNISTS CAUGHT THIS MONTH!" eased people's anxiety. A monthly catch of ten 'communists' meant a probable promotion. Netting less than two a week spelled trouble.

"Father, can we go to the Secret Police for information on my missing friend?" Mother asked one afternoon. Her request astounded Professor Minh. He adjusted his baby blue glasses to better stare at his daughter. He could hardly believe what he'd just heard. He'd always thought Mother an average-brained teenager more concerned with her lemon and cinnamon hair than with current affairs. How did she even know about the Secret Police, he wondered. Busy checking out difficult French idioms in his French-Vietnamese dictionary, he was in no mood for talk. "Mind your own business," he simply said. "The Secret Police. They question us, we don't question them." Smacking his lips, he returned to his reading. Why dwell on the Secret Police, the war and all its complications when he could escape it all with stories of Brigitte Bardot's love life so deliciously detailed in his *Paris Match* magazines?

The Game of Love and Death

MOTHER LEARNED MORE about the war than she wished to know. Sparing no details, an American lover once described his guilt after dropping napalm on Vietnamese villages. He'd seen photos of his work—of homes on fire, of burned skin peeling off corpses, of swaths of deforested land. Yet those bombs also gave him a sense of power he never had back home. It was a power to decide people's fate, a power to shape destiny. "It's addictive," he said. "Dropping bombs, it's a fetish." His obsession for pushing buttons so horrified Mother she put an end to their afternoon tryst. In the middle of love, she picked up her clothes and walked out the room.

American GIs were a dime a dozen. Replacement zucchinis were not hard to find. Prostitutes on Catinat Boulevard resented Mother for stealing their clients. They hated her spoiled attitude. Having sex for fun, not out of necessity. "You no pay. Just massage me," Mother would say after each session. Her free sex drove those GIs wild. They thought of her as authentic. She was no "Hey Mister, 1000 *dongs*, I love you deep" girl. To these homesick soldiers, she was a true cross-cultural meeting of hearts, a real Vietnam experience worthy of many letters home.

Mother enjoyed her lovers' bedroom gymnastics. Wrestling in air-conditioned rooms after a couple of diluted beers excited her. The alcohol also gave her strange ideas. She once asked a soldier to play dead as she went about preparing his body for burial. The washing, ointment, change of clothes—she wanted to go through that whole ritual. This warped game somehow titillated my mother. Her movements were exactly as she saw them on television. The prostrating bodies of mourners banging their arms and feet on the floor. The hands tearing at dishevelled hair, the open mouth dripping saliva, and the wailing—the incessant wailing. Like those bereaved wives on the daily news, Mother's tears flowed and flowed. Perversely aroused, the American rushed to cover her with kisses. Tenderly he made love to her while she cried for the end of innocence. The games of love and death left my mother aching for a blade of grass to fill the gap in her life. With two fingers, she scooped up warm liquid dripping down her legs. Drop by drop she spread it on her tongue to better savour the fruit of life. It also left a bitter taste of sadness in her mouth.

The Shared Bathroom

MAI AND MAI Ly. One played make-believe communism as a kid, the other grew up knowing only poverty. A shack here, a hut there, a bamboo mat on a mud floor, a plastic stool holding flickering candles. Those had been Mai Ly's childhood homes. Like fish scales, tin roofs in her slum neighbourhood overlapped each other. And like a rotten fish, her home stank.

Mai Ly remembered nights of hunger made worse by the tantalizing smell and singsong voices of ambulant food vendors. Twice weekly they'd come, carrying fragrant pots of noodle soup on their shoulders. Squatting in the middle of her alley, Mai Ly would watch people eat while her stomach howled in protest. Once she begged a vendor for a sip of leftover broth still remaining in a half-eaten bowl. "Go away, kid!" the woman screamed. Hastily she fished out a dead mosquito from that bowl and unperturbed, poured its leftover broth into her steaming pot of soup for the next client. There was no such thing as leftover food in Mai Ly's neighbourhood.

The arrival of Americans changed everything. Clever street peddlers became less poor. After four months selling postcards, they moved out of their cardboard homes.

They exchanged their torn flip-flops for plastic sandals. As their English vocabulary increased, so did the coins in their pockets. Like his colleagues, Hung became the owner of American dollars. For safekeeping, he hid them inside a bag of rice. Eating dollar-scented rice always brought a smile to his face. He didn't mind traces of green on his favourite food.

American GIs wanted to see all. They wanted to experience Saigon from a rickshaw. More authentic that way, they told each other. On a sluggish pedalled ride, everything seemed exotic. The Buddhist temples, the Hindu shrines, the well-hidden opium dens, the bordellos of Cholon. Hung knew where to go. Later, to these young soldiers, he sold beers like the popsicle man at the zoo—luring children to a promise of something sweeter than mere sugared water. Short, skinny, humble, good-natured with a permanent timid smile. No one saw Hung as an expert in wheeling and dealing.

Money enabled Hung to leave the slum. Money landed him in a brick-and-cement rooming house that came with electricity, running water and a shared bathroom. The shared bathroom's nauseating smell bothered Mai Ly. It was still better than floating stool on a rainy day. Defecating into ravines under a monsoon storm. She'd hated the feel of wet, itching clothes clinging to her body.

Unbeknownst to Mai Ly, her shared bathroom was also a place of shared information. Lists of names lay hidden behind loose ceramic tiles. Anonymously placed by one person, to be retrieved by another—this was done by people calling themselves patriots. Hung understood nothing of this patriot business. He did not want to know. When a scrap of paper fell out of a hole in the ceiling, he jumped out of the bathtub. Superstitious, he ran outside, his weekly shower not quite finished. Politics, or the historical context leading to present-day politics, was not for him. He only understood hard work, money and the importance of family.

Family. Hung was once surrounded by them. Now only a daughter shared his surname. Picking up his wife's lifeless body from a bloodied pavement, he'd cursed the motorcyclist who'd run over her. He'd cursed those wiggling piglets Fate had thrown his way. He could not imagine life without a spouse, could not picture raising a daughter alone. Barely four years old, the girl understood nothing of her misfortune. "Where's Mother?" she'd asked. "She went to see her mother up north. Maybe she'll return next week," Hung answered. The wait was long. One week led to another. Mai Ly learned to count to 500, still her mother never showed. To entertain herself, she spent hours tickling a neighbour's dog. She licked its wet nose. She loved hearing its barks. They helped chase silence from her life.

Mission Impossible

THE MASSACRE AT My Lai. A whole village dead and buried in one day. American soldiers on a rampage. Killing because of stress. Was it possible? Yes, it was possible. The memory of his sister's arms hugging his legs flooded Hung with guilt. He developed calf muscle cramps. Coconut oil massages hardly helped. Nightly, he went to sleep haunted by the girl's dreamy eyes. For two weeks, he wept, forgetting to feed his daughter who also wept of hunger by his side.

Hung's tears eventually ceased one day. It was a strange afternoon; he remembered it clearly. A short, balding man had approached his beer stand. The man's bouncy duck walk stood out from all the tired schlepping steps. The Duck Man had observed Hung for months. He'd taken note of Hung's ease with American GIs. He'd seen how the soldiers trusted Hung with their money, how they laughed with him and also at him. The more the Duck Man saw, the more he disliked Hung's servile attitude. He resented the beer seller's fake grin. He shuddered at Hung's fingers in a constant victory sign. He wondered how people could stoop so low

96

for a few *dongs*. Yet as much as he hated Hung's traitorous ways, he knew the beer seller to be his perfect man.

On a rainy day when beer business was at a standstill, the Duck Man came to Hung with an indigestible offer. He invited the beer seller to his *pho* shop across the street. Seated behind jars of snake wine, the Duck Man blended in perfectly. His grey scaly skin was one with the snakes. From this spot, he could see yet not be seen. After two glasses of snake wine, he accompanied Hung home. Squatting on a bamboo mat, he talked the whole night while Mai Ly slept. By morning, without quite understanding it, Hung found himself joining the Communist Party, the party of Eyes and Ears. Spying for the Viet Cong. Hung could never have imagined it, yet there he was, already "comrade this" and "comrade that." Communism, he didn't care much about it. He only wanted revenge for his family's demise at My Lai. He just wished on American soldiers what befell his family. He was promised that would happen if he spied for them.

Hung bowed gratefully after receiving a small television, hand delivered by the Duck Man. Getting a telephone and a book of foreign words a few days later bewildered him. He shook his head in disbelief. No longer just a beer seller, he was now the owner of a dictionary, a telephone and a television set. He understood nothing of the work involved. It didn't matter. He still smiled and nodded. "Watch those crazy American shows and try to follow their accents. That'll be your homework for two months. Start with *Green Acres*. It's about a woman riding a tractor in high-heeled shoes. Not hard to understand, people laugh all the time. Next move up to *Bonanza*, about a bunch of men on horses. A bit harder to grasp. Lastly, finish with *Mission: Impossible.* Wednesday at seven. It's one of their most advanced shows. Full of spies and intrigues. Probably full of hidden messages there. Our comrades are studying *Mission: Impossible* for possible covert material. We'll win this war thanks to their television. But first you must plug it in. Learn to turn it on, change channels, lower the sound. Must also learn to dial a phone. Here's my number. Remember it by heart then destroy the evidence. Now show me how you do all that stuff. Good God! You're a natural with these modern machines!"

Winning wars through television shows? Hung could only nod in confusion. He was just glad no fighting was asked of him. He smiled and nodded some more. He promised the Duck Man he'd do a good job. He'd be Saigon's best television watcher. He'd understand all those American accents in two months.

"I want you to put nice sturdy stools around your beer stand. Catinat Boulevard is too crowded. Not enough space. Move to another location. Near the post office. Lots of space to spread your stools there. You want those Americans to sit and chat with each other. You listen to their conversations. Keep a low profile, pretend you don't understand too much. Just smile and give them their V for victory sign. And you report to me. You leave me notes in your bathroom. Written in invisible ink. I'll show you how later. Don't ever contact me by phone. It's only to be used in life-or-death situations.

Remember that. I see you have a pretty daughter. How old is she?" The question startled Hung. He stiffened. A coughing fit prevented him from answering. He turned away from the Duck Man. Pearls of saliva accumulated at the tip of his tongue. His daughter prostituting for American soldiers? He had to spit that idea out.

The Duck Man saw through Hung's reaction. Calmly he mumbled, "Relax! Who's talking about prostitution? I just want your daughter to hang around the beer stand a bit. Just a few hours after her school. She'd make a good bait for new customers. You'll be watching her. How can she prostitute with you there? Don't worry! Anyway, we're all prostitutes in this war. And there's nothing wrong with prostituting yourself for your country. Remember that!"

PART 3:
MICHAEL

New Haven, USA 1966

IN A LAND far from my own, in a city I had never heard of, with people speaking a language I grasped only partially, a boy named Michael Ross stood stamping his feet on a shaggy rug. Everything about him was foreign to me. Although I was told his story over and over, I didn't always understand his motivation. So I imagined them. I filled the blanks of his childhood with scenes I saw on television and somehow he became complete.

At the rust-stained sink, my father splashed cool water on his face. He threw his schoolbooks on the wet linoleum floor. Barely thirteen, his head already boiled over with independent ideas. Spared of Confucian brainwashing, my father grew up certain his mother owed him more than she could ever repay.

"It's all your fault, Ma!" Father shouted.

"What now, Michael?" my paternal grandmother muttered. Her flexed arms, the shape of giant eggplants, commanded respect in most people. Only her son, my father, showed no fear in her presence.

"Dad ... Uhmmm. David said so."

"Lord, Oh Lord! What does that friend of yours know? What's 68 to the power of 7?" Grandmother looked up from her newspaper. "I bet you can't figure that in your head," she said with a grin. Math quizzes always added lightness to their arguments. They both knew it. My father, the little math genius, would always answer correctly. His calculator mind would invariably earn him a big kiss. "Oh, cut it out, Ma!" he'd always protest good naturedly.

Father's unmoved face told a different story that afternoon. He kept stomping his feet. Her eyes rolling, Grandmother decided to give math a pass. "Eh, I told you a hundred times, child, I ain't got nothing to do with it."

"Ma ... Maybe, hmmm, maybe you should've given Dad more pussy?"

"Oh Lord! Who taught you that word?" Grandmother threw her plastic teacup in the garbage. She ripped the *New Haven Register* in half. Hands on her waist, she stood menacingly in front of my father.

"David. David Kirby," Father answered calmly. Feigning interest, he studied his fingers tapping Morse code messages on his knees. Afraid of his mother's disapproving face, he kept his head down. He didn't want to acknowledge her index ordering him to his room on an empty stomach.

And He Laughed

"**G**O TO YOUR room! No dinner for you tonight."

"But I'm hungry, Ma!"

"I don't care."

Livid, Father slammed his bedroom door twice. Six kiddie posters scotch-taped to cracked walls greeted him. He swore. *Lassie Come Home*. Lassie here. Lassie there. A black felt pen in hand, he went up to each poster. He drew moustaches on all the Lassies. Still not satisfied, he decided to rip out Lassie's ears. He wrote *Star Trek* in their places. Directly on the walls. Upper case letters in un-washable ink. Father could already imagine his mother's "Lord, Oh, Lord!" He'd heard enough of her complaints that night to care. He laughed instead. The desecration of childhood images. It was almost as good as a double scoop of chocolate ice cream.

She Would Be Proven Wrong

LIKE MY MOTHER'S country, my father's native land was also at war with itself. It was a war without bombs but not without police brutality, deep-seated hatred and pent-up rage. While my mother's country-men killed each other over imported ideologies, my father's compatriots fought a conflict that went back centuries. It was a struggle with roots deep in the local soil and deeper in people's memories. It was an unfair duel between bare hands and a revolver. It was a war between the races.

Ideological adherences, like religious belief, can be fluid. Communist one day, capitalist the next. Buddhist one day, Catholic the next. People do change their chameleon minds. The colour of their skin is another matter. It can't be transformed so easily.

How do I know all this? A television told me so. Yes, an old television on a badly scratched table. I watched it day and night. Newscasts and soap operas, both.

Bullets, arson, destroyed properties. New Haven, my father's hometown was spared all that. Here, buildings burned from lighted cigarettes forgotten in bed.

Locals did not lose sleep to simmering racial tensions happening elsewhere. Black men hanging from trees, KKK spray-painted on walls were images seen only on television. The murder of civil rights activists in Mississippi, the violence espoused by Southern white supremacists, the thrashed streets after a protest. They all seemed vague in Father's mind.

"Don't worry," Grandmother would say in her flat tone of voice. Such cruelty came from somewhere far away. No such barbarism occurred in New Haven, home of prestigious Yale University, an Ivy League amongst Ivy Leagues. "No Sundown town, New Haven," she'd repeat over and over. "No, we don't chase coloured people away when the sun goes down," she'd explain with a tinge of pride. In New Haven, Grandmother knew she'd be safe if she behaved properly. Sticking to the right neighbourhood, staying home at night, keeping her mouth shut. These were her survival tactics. For her, life's unfairness came in small doses, not in big events. She would be proven wrong.

The Word

A **SPRINGTIME STROLL** down Chapel Street promised to be pleasant. It wasn't. "Who gave you the right to walk here? Get out of the way, fucking negro!" Father turned to see who uttered such a threat. On a Tuesday afternoon, Chapel Street was almost empty. Two muscular men holding switchblades in their tattooed hands glared at him. For a minute, Father's heart lost its rhythm. It drummed wildly. Panicked, he ran inside the first shop he saw. It was a large toy store full of stuffed animals. Two giant plush Lassies stood proudly in the back. Father ran to the Lassies. He gave each one a pat before sliding down to hide behind them. He tried to be invisible. He sobbed as he hugged Lassie's legs.

"What the hell!" a sales clerk shouted. "What you doing there, kid? Hey, get your dirty black hands off Lassie. Go, get outta here!"

The Photos

MY FATHER WAS only three when his father walked out on him. Father remembered nothing of that event. Only vague memories of big blue eyes framed by orange eyelashes remained. He wished he could remember a caress, a hug, a game of hide-and-seek. All those father-son images on television were unfortunately not a part of his memory. No matter how hard he tried, my father could only dredge up a freckled face looking down at him. For years, he thought he'd dreamt it all since nobody in his family sported such vivid colours.

Rummaging through his mother's bottom drawer for spare coins, Father came upon a stack of old photos. He wondered why his mother had hidden them under her panties. Why were they not in the family albums like those other photos? Curiosity made a stalker of my father. He felt his heart pumping as he slipped the pictures into his shirt pocket. With a pen, he jotted on his palm their exact location. Fourth drawer, left side, under beige polka-dot panties. Whatever he did, he couldn't raise his mother's suspicions. Putting them back in the wrong place would earn him another night without supper. He refolded his mother's underwear and tiptoed out of her bedroom. He felt like Inspector Clouseau on the cusp of something big. Safe inside his closet, Father examined the photos in disbelief. He let escape a sharp cry. Unlike his mom, unlike his grandparents in a curled-up picture withering away on a table, this man kissing his mother, holding her hands, playing with her hair, this estranged father cuddling a baby Michael, was a white man. Such realization dismayed my father. Although he was never taught to hate white men, as a black child, my father could not silence those century-old grumblings in his genes.

The Complexity of Colours

"**M**A, TELL ME again what Dad looks like."
Father finally asked after days of silence. Fear of the truth had kept him muzzled all week.

"I told you a hundred times, child! He's tall and skinny. Long legs. Nice hair. Nice eyes. Now leave me alone. Need to cook. Aren't you hungry?"

"No, Ma. What colour hair? Eyes?"

"Who remembers those things! He left long ago," my grandmother answered without a trace of emotion. To Father's relief, there was neither sadness nor anger in her voice.

"Ma, did he have blue eyes? Red hair?"

"Maybe . . ."

"Then he must be white!" Father exclaimed. Grandmother's shrouded confirmation troubled him. Tense, he pressed two hands against his chest to prevent his wild heart from crushing itself. He leaned on the wall to give respite to his wobbling legs.

"So?" For a minute, my paternal grandmother stopped her frying to look at Father. She felt like throwing another math quiz to divert his attention. No, stop, she told herself. She'd deceived him long enough. It was time to come clean. "Yes, yes. He's white," she said in a quiet voice.

"Ma, why didn't you tell me this before?"

"What for? Black, white, it's all the same," my grandmother replied. She made signs for Father to calm down.

"But if he's white, how come I'm black?" Father asked. The mystery of life, the secrets of families, the complexity of colours. They all left a stale aftertaste on his tongue.

"Who knows? I'll ask them doctors tomorrow. Maybe they'll know."

We, the Dominant People

MY PATERNAL GRANDMOTHER worked as a nursing aide in a subsidized retirement home for coloured people. Day in, day out she changed their bedpans and listened to their melancholic recollections of the bad old days. Torn lives, in retrospect, didn't become rosier. These folks didn't reminisce about a past with better-behaved children, cheaper rent or a healthier lifestyle. They didn't miss their tighter skin, firmer bodies, fuller head of hair. They remembered instead stories of inhumanity told by their relatives. The lynching, the white hoods, the constant dread of fire at night. They remembered those tales of the Old South as if they'd actually lived them. And the fear they carried felt so real, it consumed all hopes of a happy life.

The residence's busy medical staff had no time for tales of sorrows. They encouraged my grandmother to stand in for them. They asked her to play psychiatrist, to lend an ear to these people with nothing left but stories to tell. Unloading second-hand trauma on my grandmother was the old folks' favourite afternoon activity. They would not touch their Jell-O, would not swallow their Tang orange drink unless Grandmother was around.

To their grievances, my grandmother would repeat her usual "Don't you worry, Hon!" No, Grandmother didn't hate her job. She just wished to hear grandchildren stories for a change. Or an ex-wife tale. Even a cat anecdote would've brought smiles to her tired face. At the nursing home, she only heard fearful whispers of a triple K.

"Michael, them doctors said black genes are dominant. That's why you have no white features. So don't forget that. We're the dominant people!" My lip-smacking grandmother announced over supper one day.

Grandmother's words fuelled my father's spirit. It felt good knowing his people excelled at this gene business. He imagined it as a fight with Muhammad Ali knocking all those white boxers out. That feel-good fantasy didn't last long. Remembering his fair-skinned father, he tried hard to repress images of a bloodstained redhead. Ambivalent loyalties, conflicting emotions, incompatible thoughts followed my father night and day.

Moments of Glory

MY FATHER ATTENDED a mostly white private Catholic school run by colour-blind nuns. Black, white, brown or yellow, it didn't matter. The students all got the same strap. They all heard the same weekly lectures about Jesus dying on a cross for them. The similarity ended there. Hard work and a scholarship brought Father to St. Joseph Prep. Money opened doors for most of his classmates.

A strict education kept everyone in line. Spoiled kids from rich families surprisingly spoke with self-restraint. Degrading vocabulary never became a part of their speech. If not welcomed, Father at least felt safe in his school. No racial slurs were ever lobbed his way.

Being different also had its moments of glory. Curious younger kids accosted my father for his opinion on soul music. They wanted to discuss Chubby Checkers, Little Richard, Jimi Hendrix. What about James Brown, they all asked. Busy with his schoolwork, Father had neither time nor interest in music. His Who's Who list only included Nat King Cole, his mother's favourite, and the Jackson Five, his least favourite. He found little Michael annoying. Or rather, embarrassing. Copying adult body movements, the kid looked like a midget performing in a circus. Father wondered if his math skill was not also seen that way. A performance to please his mother's friends. "What's 65.72 divided by 12?" she'd quiz him in front of her church friends every Sunday afternoon. She'd encourage them to do likewise. From her purse, she'd take out a pen and pieces of paper. She'd pass them around so everyone could verify Father's answer. My father needed neither paper nor pen. Like a mechanical clock, random numbers would tick inside his brain's cog and wheels and in no time exited with a "cuckoo!" Grandmother's friends would invariably clap their hands at this flawless performance.

Cool It, Woman

TO HIDE HIS lack of musical knowledge, Father only said, "Cool man, cool ... Nat's still the best." What about the Jackson Five? The kids insisted. "Naah, that's kiddy stuff." Father would dismiss them with a wave of the hand.

The more my father waved his hands, the more young admirers gathered around him. It was as if he'd waved a magic wand in front of them. These students from a lower grade followed my father everywhere, laughing at all his jokes. Girls sidled up to him, asking to feel his kinky hair. "How do you detangle it? Which conditioner do you use?" they inquired with genuine interest. To live up to his image, Father went out of his way with his Blackspeak. Words picked up from television shows became a part of his schoolyard vocabulary. Before trying them out at school, he practised them in front of his bathroom mirror. He rehearsed those words till they sounded natural coming out of his mouth. Fortunately, there weren't that many expressions to memorize. Television shows were mostly about white people, not black ones.

Daring girls giggled upon hearing my father's version

of a Sammy Davis Jr. joke. Tough-looking boys also bobbed their heads in approval. Daily they asked for more. Daily, he gave it to them, mimicking one stand-up comic after another. Bill Cosby, Richard Pryor, Dick Gregory. He knew their lines by heart. With his talent for picking up accents, my father soon became the class clown. Alone in his room at night, he laughed thinking of this bunch of rich kids wanting to play Sanitized Ghetto. He mocked them, unaware that he was also mocking himself. At that age, unease had yet to damper his spirits. It would take decades before truth opened his eyes. Years would pass before he realized he was just an entertainer to his white classmates, a black performer to satisfy their subconscious need to feel superior.

As the only black student in his grade, Father could not goof off. He couldn't hide behind others to snooze during catechism courses. His dark skin always gave him away. He stood sorely out in a sea of blondes, red-heads and brunettes. Among long silky hair, his frizzy head attracted attention. Camouflage was impossible in that setting.

Teachers loved picking on him. Not out of mean-ness, but out of a sense of Christian duty. With preda-tory goodwill, they'd bombard Father with the toughest math problems, the most tortuous spelling words because they knew he could do it. Wanting to instil pride in his accomplishment, teachers went overboard with their challenges. They'd hoped to fill the hole in his heart with extra work. They would've stuffed Yale medical textbooks down his throat had they known the extent of his emptiness. How does a medical textbook replace a missing father, they should've asked themselves. Year after year, they never bothered with this question. To his teachers' extra homework, my father felt like shouting "Cool it, Woman ... cool it." Of course, he didn't.

A Magnum Shooter

MY FATHER'S INSECURITY ceased with the first sign of puberty—stubble on his chin. From a squeaky-voiced kid, he became a man in a matter of months. As his muscles grew, so did his list of bad words. At fourteen and a half, he could've passed for a 20-year-old "motherfucker"—this was his new favourite expression. Two heads taller and 20 pounds heavier than his classmates, Father instilled unease in school. Girls crossed the street when they saw him hunkering down the sidewalk now. They no longer fingered his hairdo, no longer engaged him in phoney ghetto speak. Even real bullies stayed clear of him.

Though he lost friends, Father still kept contact with David Kirby. The two teenagers still loved talking dirty. "Giving pussy" soon led to "eating cunt" and before they knew it, their boyish pickles would turn into huge zucchinis. Awkward at first, they eventually welcomed this opportunity to compare the changes in their bodies. At David's house, they would push his desk against the door to prevent a sudden appearance by blue-eye-shadowed Mrs. Kirby. They would draw the blinds and turn on a radio to mask any telltale noises. David always sat on his bed whereas my father preferred a chair. There, they worked on themselves until a projectile of what seemed like a cupful of cloudy liquid shot out. They compared the consistency, colour, volume, smell of their ejections. Then in a moment of dare, they made a bet one day. The first one to shoot up the ceiling would win a licking from David's still-innocent puppy. Although this idea disgusted them, they didn't show their distaste. "Chicken shit" was the worst insult they could throw at each other. Pumped up, they raced to their spots, both thinking of themselves as Magnum Shooters. They were also glad the bet was made at David's old Victorian house. A 12-foot ceiling was beyond their reach. To their relief, no dog was forced to kiss a zucchini that afternoon.

"Who'd you think of?" David asked. "The new English teacher?"

"Nahhh. She ain't my style, man. I like that girl Suzy in front of me. I like her bum crack always showing under her shirt. And you? Who you thought of?"

"Your mother ... black's cool, man," David replied, making signs of curves with his hands.

"What the fuck! Yeah, fuck you, David!" Father yelled. Or maybe he said something else. I can't really be sure. Maybe none of that scene happened. Maybe I imagined it all.

Electrocuted Hair

BY THE TIME he reached high school, my father's country no longer enjoyed a make-believe peace. The simmering black versus white resentment finally blew up. The Detroit Riot of '67 ended with four dozen death, countless businesses burned and millions of dollars in damage. Martin Luther King Jr.'s assassination gave way to national protests, marches, race riots. Police brutality against innocent black men made the news every week. A foreign policy of international meddling brought wide-eyed Americans to Vietnam. These young soldiers, sent to fight a war they did not understand, often returned in body bags or out of their minds. At home, violence erupted with anti-war demonstrators throwing rocks at masked policemen. That was my father's America.

Father lived those days with a jumping heart. Nightly he'd watch the 6:30 news. Images of a war in a faraway land fascinated and repelled him at the same time. To better locate Vietnam on a map, to better follow Walter Cronkite, Father borrowed an atlas from his school library. He studied all those exotic village names. Recognizing them on television fed his ego. Ten communist guerrillas caught in village A! Bombs dropped on

Village B killed five civilians! Village C neutralized by South Vietnamese troops! With the confidence of a person in the loop, Father nodded whenever Walter Cronkite read from his list. My father wasn't sure what excited him more—watching men in action or seeing the strangeness of the place. He imagined the weight of a gun in his hands, the power of its nozzle. He fantasized about a place where no one would judge him for his skin colour, where, as an American, he'd be superior to the natives. If black lives mattered little to white folks, so would the lives of gooks in his hands. Briefly, he entertained this thought. Ashamed, he shook his head, changed his mind, erased that idea. No, he didn't want to kill all Vietnamese. He only wanted to hunt the communists.

Televised images of dead black soldiers infuriated Father. "Oh, fuck those commies!" he screamed at Walter Cronkite. Violently bobbing his head one day, he fell off his chair. In the tumult, some of his curls—having lost their grips—had decided to straighten themselves out in protest. I chuckled imagining a black man with straight electrocuted-style hair. Ah yes, perhaps I should be less creative in my description of Father.

Guru David

INTEREST IN THE war, yes. Interest in mathematics, no. Interest in girls, of course. As typical seventeen-year-old guys, Father and his friend David obsessed about girls. Rich people's parties satisfied their need for girl-watching. At Westport mansions, they joked around, raided the bar, danced over vomit and smoked. Besides pot, David also experimented with peyote and magic mushrooms. He'd read about them in Carlos Castaneda's books. Their mind-bending qualities intrigued him. "Hey, this stuff would fast-forward my journey of self-discovery," David said with a grin. "Who wants to walk to Haight-Ashbury when we can fly there," he added, seriously this time.

It was easy finding the right supplier. A corner flower shop on Chapel Street. John's Exotic Flowers carried a large assortment of orchids. They also specialized in peyote and magic mushrooms behind closed doors. With these hallucinogens, David imagined himself in Castaneda's footsteps. He saw God in plants. He conversed with birds. In loose cotton tunics, long hair in a ponytail, David attracted misty-eyed followers. Tipsy young women flocked to him like pigeons around trashcans. Pecking at his cheeks, sniffling at his hair, they all hoped to find morsels of subsistence among the garbage.

With no urgent need for self-discovery, Father stayed away from cactus, mushrooms, pot. David's nonsense talk bothered my father. David's empty eyes worried him. David's daily departure from reality gave him goosebumps. A crippling load of guilt shadowed Father's every move. It felt like a clot plugging his arteries. A thousand times he asked himself, "Could I've stopped David messing with drugs?" A thousand times he shrugged, "I don't know . . ."

When Father finally accepted a conclusive "No! Not my responsibility!" he sighed with relief. On that particular afternoon, he'd succeeded in re-packaging his guilt. Perhaps one day, he'd look back on this moment with regret. For now, he enjoyed this deceiving feeling of lightness. Like a hot air balloon floating upward, he felt buoyed by the very flames that could burn him.

Another Blonde Girl

THE **WESTPORT GIRLS** were a group of fair-skinned upper-class ladies. Blessed with teeth straightened by expensive braces, they moved their sinuous bodies with confidence. Peeking through diaphanous Indian blouses, their bra-less breasts jingled alertly. Their shimmering waist-length hair called out to be touched. Father felt like a kid in a petting zoo.

"Well, who do we have here? David, won't you introduce your friend?" a tall blonde asked. Her thick red lips turned skyward. On cue, her eyes changed from blue to a lighter shade of green. Unhindered by a bra, her pointy nipples pushed aggressively against her sheer white T-shirt. Candied cherries. They were candied cherries sticking out of cupcakes to itch Father's eyes. He so wanted to pick them out and swallow them whole.

"Um ... this is Michael, my friend from school," David said.

"Nice to meet you, Michael, I'm Anna. Your first time here? Oh, I love this music, so mellow. I could listen to Leonard Cohen all night. Can you imagine me as Suzanne serving tea and oranges that come all the way from China? Haha! Cohen's from Montreal, did you know? I've friends dodging the draft up there. And oh yeah, remember that John Lennon-Yoko Ono bed-in at some Montreal hotel? Sounds like a real cool place. I should go there one day. Want to join the protest tomorrow? Yeah, anti-war. But also pro-Black Panthers. Ever heard of them? All about black pride. Gosh, you should know, Michael! We'll march to show our support. Downtown New Haven. Starting at Yale's Sterling Memorial Library. 2 p.m. Hope you can join us. Have you tried peyote? It'll blow your mind out! How about a toke, Michael? Here, take it ..."

"Um, naah, no, thank ... thank you, Suzanne ... I mean Ann ... Anna!"

"What you afraid of, Michael? Relax! It's cool! Can I play with your hair?"

Words falling freely like raindrops in a storm. My father had always mistrusted them. His mother preferred weighing her words as if they were gold nuggets. Non-stop chatter gave Father anxiety. He wished he could respond normally. He always ended up stuttering. Father's nervousness doubled in front of fairy-tale Anna. Approaching Father with cat-like movements, she eased herself onto his lap. For a second, this gesture stopped his breathing. Dumbfounded, he stayed silent. Pretending to fix his hair, he took a comb from his shirt pocket. He started fluffing his frizz. Anna laughed at my father's grooming attempt. Playfully she snatched the comb from his hand. Ebullient, she planted a moist kiss on his parched lips. Father closed his eyes. He took deep breaths to calm himself. He ho-hummed for a long minute. He cleared his throat several times. "Yes?" Anna asked expectantly. She'd hoped to hear some Ella Fitzgerald lyrics. Or maybe, a Sammy Davis Jr. joke. There was neither. No words managed to escape Father's choking fear. Anna shrugged at his limp arms and lifeless tongue. Getting off his lap, she returned his comb to its proper place. She gave him a hug then left for greener pastures. She wasn't looking for a softer seat. It was a harder one that she wanted.

Anna was Father's second blonde-girl experience. Instead of rising to the occasion, he plummeted down a dark space. He felt no excitement with Anna on his lap. Only anguish. He remembered earning a slap the first time. It was a school dance with a classmate. Long-legged, rosy-cheeked, deep-voiced Jenny. He'd compared her to Lauren Bacall. Slow dancing, he'd rubbed against her pelvis. Juice leaking through his pants had discoloured her dress. "Dirty pig!" she'd screamed before smacking his cheeks. A black boy sexually abusing a white girl. Such a crime would not be tolerated. Not even in liberal New Haven. Six feet under. That's where he'd be. An electric chair or mob lynching, the result would be the same. Thankfully, Jenny had kept quiet. She'd opted for a cold-shoulder treatment after washing her dress.

"David, let's go! I'm scared. Feel like shit."

"Kiss my ass! You chicken shit or what? Don't tell me you afraid of girls now!" David chuckled. He tried focusing on a group of women. He saw them floating. It was hard to distinguish one person from another. Floating, they were all floating. Yet the details of their garments remained stubbornly fixed in his mind. Their clarity amazed him. The coffee stain on a shirt sleeve. The ripped front pocket of a minidress. The finely embroidered flowers on a pair of faded jeans. Captivated, he stared at those insignificant details for ten long minutes. Then he giggled for no apparent reason.

"You don't understand, do you?" Father's trembling voice brought David back to reality. As the only one stubbornly anchored amongst drifting souls, my father felt lost. He was scared. Black guy, white girl. Could David get it? Could any white guy get it? No, David did not get it. He only gave Father a hiss and a jab in the shoulder.

"Jesus Christ, man! You still hung up about that Jenny girl?" David said. "OK, you want to leave, we'll leave. In an hour, OK? I need to calm down first. And you're not touching my mom's Mercedes! Get me some coffee, will you?"

Unbuckling the Seatbelt

THE 60-MINUTE wait for David to sober up was actually only 25 minutes. In retrospect, my father wished it had lasted two hours. He wished he hadn't pressured David into leaving so soon after his four beers, three tequila shots, a gram of weed, two mouthfuls of peyote and some magic mushrooms shared with languid girls. The drive from Westport to New Haven normally took David 45 minutes. On this particular moonlit summer night, it took him five hours. Barely out of town, David felt his eyes closing. He parked his car, turned off the light and dozed off on the road shoulder. Sleep also overtook my father. A full bladder woke him a few hours later. Hungover and disoriented, he was surprised to find himself in a car. Surprised to see David snoring, his seatbelt maladjusted across his neck, a mosquito flying out of his open mouth. Memory of their Westport party eventually returned and with it, common sense. David strangled by a seatbelt bothered Father. He snorted. "So fucking typical of David, can't do anything right! Can't even buckle himself correctly," he muttered. He wondered if it was that damn peyote's fault. How about those magic mushrooms? Without thinking, he unhooked

David's seatbelt and hopped out of the car. Pine scents welcomed Father to a vast outdoor toilet. He inhaled the aromatic moonlit night before unzipping his pants.

It only takes a minute for fate to change hands. A van speeding down the road took exactly 50 seconds to hit. And run. A deafening metal-hitting-metal noise stopped my father from finishing his business. Turning around, he saw tragedy in action. David's parked Mercedes rammed into a tree. David's body smashed through his front window. David's head hanging from the car hood. Pulled by gravity, David's face slowly slid to the ground while his body hung lifeless above it, his shoelaces still tangled in the Mercedes' hood ornament. Shocked, Father stumbled toward his friend. He turned David over to check for signs of life. Out of David's nostrils oozed so much blood, Father had to turn away. Freaked out, he ran along the road, waving frantically at passing cars. A big agitated black man in the middle of the night, in the middle of the road. Nobody stopped for him. "Get off the fucking road! You want to be killed?" a man shouted as his car wheezed by. "Please, call the police! Ambulance!!" My father screamed desperately. This only earned him fingers gesturing obscenities.

Father sighed loudly as he saw his friend's chest still moving. A highway lamp shone enough light for him to make out a crooked neck, twisted jaws and limbs decked out like a fallen puppet. My father cried. He didn't know what else to do. "I'm sorry man. Sorry! All my fault ... Dragging you from that party ... removing your seat belt ... letting you park in this spot ... not stopping you from taking drugs. David, please don't die!" Father squeezed David's hand, hoping for a reaction beyond the mere thumping of a pulse. He opened his friend's eyes and saw only a pair of doll eyes staring back at him.

Loud sirens brought my father out of his shock. He wiped his eyes. He stopped his mumbling. He got up. "Will he live? Will he live?" he asked repeatedly. He also knew it was a question with no definite answer. Barred from boarding the ambulance, Father found himself facing two policemen too eager to interrogate him.

Yes, Officer

"**Y**OU STOLE THE car?" one policeman shouted while his associate shone a flashlight into my father's face. Father blinked four times before he could focus. Two badly shaven men in uniform burped in his face. Their old garlic breath repulsed Father. He wished to turn away, put a finger to his nostrils, do anything to spare himself the smell of undigested food.

"No! I did not steal it!" That outburst earned Father a slap.

"Don't be insolent, Boy! Call me Sir! We have reports of a black man screaming on the road. So that's you, eh? You with them Black Panthers?"

"No ... no, Sir."

"Causing trouble with all your black protests? I'm sick of all that protest shit. New Haven ain't New Haven anymore these days! Goddamn Black Panther protests ... bringing so many problems to town. So what were you doing screaming in the middle of the night?" The policeman shoved his baton against my father's throat. He liked this move. It was as good as a chokehold. Minus the messy skin-on-skin contact, it was in fact better than a chokehold. Head pressed against a tree, throat blocked by a baton, Father's words could not flow in that position. The policeman knew it yet still insisted on an answer. To Father's " I, I ..." the policeman waved his hand. "What? What you say Boy?" he snickered. "Can't, can't ... ," Father mumbled. Removing his baton from my father's neck, the policeman aimed for his forehead.

"Stand up and stop messing with me, Boy! How'd a kid like you afford this car? Stole it?"

"No!"

"No what? Be polite, Boy!"

"No, Sir. It's ... it's my friend's car."

"Fucking rich kid hanging out with Black Panthers! Probably a Goddamn hippie on drugs. Jesus, send them all to fucking Vietnam! Hey, any drugs in the car, Boy? If I find drugs you'll spend the rest of your fucking life in jail, understand?"

The police released Father after a day of heavy-handed interrogation. During those question periods, they slapped and punched him repeatedly. They threw iced water on his chest to stop the bleeding. Then they handed him a paper cup filled with water. Before he could take his first sip, they hit him again. He dropped to his knees, retching, paper cup still in hand. They laughed as they kicked a rag in his direction. "Clean the mess, Boy," they ordered at the sight of his vomit. They weren't worried about leaving telltale signs of police brutality on his body. The colour of viciousness—the blues, greens and yellows of internal bleeding—were well veiled under black skin.

A policeman's voice on the phone alarmed my grandmother. "Lord, Oh, Lord!" She hung up before they could add more. Out of shame, Grandmother refused to pick up her son. Out of fear she refused to set foot inside a police station full of white officers. After four unanswered calls, the police contacted David's parents. Father could only lower his head seeing Mrs. Kirby at the door. Self-reproach kept him glued to his seat. He turned away to avoid her outstretched arms. "David? David? David?" was all he said. "He's alive," Mrs. Kirby whispered. "They tried draining the blood in his brain."

David's Blinks

ON THE THIRD floor of Yale Teaching Hospital, in a small bare room shaded by salmon-coloured blinds, lay David. Rosy-cheeked David with bandages around his head and both legs in casts. Father noticed with relief the rhythmic in-and-out of David's chest. His heartbeat, like a robot's handwriting, moved mechanically across a monitor screen. David was alive all right. He was also dead. A respirator breathed for him. Liquid medications flowed from a tube into his veins. A second tube bought milkshake food to his nose. A third tube ran between his legs to collect urine. Like an antique pendulum that had ceased swinging years ago, David's left arm hung limply from the bed railing.

"David, you hear me?" Father whispered in his friend's right ear. "Are you there? You hiding in your crazy world, man? No need for magic mushrooms now! You can hallucinate all you want now! Hey, no more term papers! David, blink if you hear me, OK? Or squeeze my fingers. Give me a sign, man! Give me a sign you're still there. I didn't tell your mom 'bout un-hooking your seatbelt. I did it thinking you'd be more comfy. Well, maybe you'd still end up a veggie with the seatbelt on. Who knows? I didn't tell your mom nothing. The drugs, the alcohol … she knows nothing. She hates me enough … I don't need more hate. OK, maybe she doesn't hate me. David! Did you just blink? Did you just blink? I swear I saw it, man! David, blink again! Please!"

Worked up, Father found it harder to whisper. He ended up talking loudly, even screaming into David's right ear. The commotion attracted a nurse's attention. She ordered him to leave the room. Amongst the nursing staff, nobody believed David had blinked purposely. "Your friend couldn't have moved his eyes. Even if he did, it was just an automatic gesture. He didn't hear you," a medical intern said, brought in to calm my father's nerves. The more Father insisted on seeing a neurologist, the more the intern stood his ground. Young and confident, he waved a dismissive hand. "Who do you think you are questioning my knowledge," his gesture said loud and clear. Then he remembered his Hippocratic Oath—Do No Harm. "Sorry, our neurologist is too busy now. You should go home. You look exhausted. Get some sleep."

Father went home that evening angry. He wanted to kick an animal, hit somebody, throw rocks into someone's house. Instead, he spent hours stabbing his pillows with a dull pocketknife.

Only Legit Cactuses

SCHOOL WAS NOT the same without David's jokes. Father even missed David's nonsense talk on Carlos Castaneda. Peace of mind. This was what my father needed most. He so wanted to turn off that constant buzzing in his head. The guilt, the self-reproach wouldn't let him go. It only increased with time. The volume of its voice multiplied day by day till it drove my father deaf to real sounds.

Checking out one of Castaneda's books—Father got a nod from his school librarian. "I don't know what kind of magic it promises, all you students are reading this stuff," she said. Barely fifteen pages into the book, my father threw it down. It was all mumbo-jumbo. Its hocus-pocus exasperated him. He gave up trying to find peace of mind in nonsensical words. He went looking for the real thing. He remembered David mentioning a John Exotic Flower Store near Yale.

"We only sell orchids and legit cactuses in this store!" John said with indignation.

"But my friend bought magic mushrooms here ..."

"Get out before I call the cops! Fucking addict! All a bunch of drug addicts!"

John's scream echoed in Father's head. His empty shop fuelled Father's rage. He imagined beating John to a pulp. Without a witness, he would never be caught. No one would ever know. Abruptly he remembered a police baton on his throat. His grasping for air. His doubling over. His dark skin concealing the colours of violence. Changing his mind, Father gave John the finger. He kicked an empty Pepsi can out of his way and walked home.

If Only

FATHER VISITED DAVID every afternoon. Every afternoon, he'd pinch David's puffy hands to check for a reaction. Next, he'd lift his friend's eyelids to verify for signs of life. Lastly, he'd blow into those opened eyes, hoping for a blink. Then he'd settle on the floor to do his homework. Girls no longer turned him on. Food no longer filled his stomach. Beer no longer satisfied his thirst. During those silent hospital visits, he felt a different type of thirst. It was a thirst for spiritual healing, for calmness, for forgiveness. Only in his textbooks could he find a sliver of that.

Father excelled in school. Early acceptance to Yale, scholarship to Harvard, perfect SAT scores. He collected them all. Yet his 100% marks gave him little satisfaction. The number disheartened him. He wished it could've been 180%. At 180, he would give 100 to David and keep only 80 for himself. He would give Harvard to David and keep Yale to himself. Oh, if only that were possible ...

Chosen valedictorian of his graduating class, Father felt no pride. His mother's resplendent face, her "That's my boy!" in front of church friends no longer comforted him. It only pained him. Memories of his flawless math performances brought tears to his eyes. It was all a sham, he thought. What good were numbers when his friend lay in a coma? What good would lofty words do if they could not turn back the clock?

"We are gathered here on this special day to celebrate our year-long effort. Unfortunately, one of us is missing. No, he's not fighting in Vietnam. He's not hiding in Canada. He's right here in New Haven. As morbid as it is, I wish I could say his spirit is looking down at us, sharing our joy. But I cannot. Like an opened can of Pepsi forgotten for days, his spirit had fizzled out ..."

Reading his text out loud, Father crossed out word after word. No, "fizzled out" is no good. Neither is "can of Pepsi." Dispirited by his literary shortcomings, Father ripped the page to start anew. If only poetry were as easy as calculus. If only he could spew out words like he could solve quadratic equations. If only he'd let me write his speech. If only I could rewrite his life story ...

The Need to Find Meaning

MY FATHER SPENT a summer wandering aimlessly from David's hospital room back to his own place. David's condition might improve with time, he was told. It might improve with talk, the doctors said. So Father talked. He talked for hours on end. Sex jokes, grade school reminiscence, updates on Vietnam. He left nothing out. Vietnam news, no one could escape it now. Two classmates had enlisted, two others were drafted, one hiding in Canada. Father shared all with David. And he waited in vain for David to blink again.

"Ma, I'm enlisting," Father announced over ice cream one summer evening.

"What? Oh, Lord! You crazy, child? You wanna die? Why? Why?" A candied cherry stuck in her throat, Grandmother coughed for a long minute. She dropped her syrupy spoon on the floor. She dirtied her shoes as she kicked it away.

"Like they say, Ma, to fight for freedom. To find meaning." My grandmother's rolled eyes emboldened Father. He repeated with more emphasis, "To fight for freedom. To find meaning, Ma."

"Why can't you do like all them other kids? Go protest the war, not join it!"

"I ain't no sheep, Ma. Gotta find my own way."

"Then do your fighting here first! There's a war here too. Between blacks and whites. Didn't the nuns teach you that in school? Civil War is long over but our people are still discriminated against. Not long ago we had to sit in the back of buses," Grandmother cried, her trembling hands pointing to the back seat of an imaginary bus. "Restaurants, hotels refused to serve us. Your Dad and me, we needed a Green Book to find special accommodations. And he was white!" To my father's "Yeah, I know all that, Ma ..." Grandmother sneered loudly. Fuming, she slammed the table with her tightly clenched fist. "Registration to vote is still hard in the South, Michael! Black churches still being burned. The KKK murdered civil rights workers only a few years ago. Mississippi, yeah. Mississippi, pfff, I'd never set foot in that damned place! Bet them nuns didn't teach you any of that stuff. You too protected in that white school, Michael. Good thing we're in New Haven. You'd be dead in Mississippi!" My grandmother's last words didn't ping-pong in Father's head. They slammed against his skull with the force of a racquet ball. Her son's contorted face put an end to her speech. Immediately Grandmother regretted her talk. She remembered his swollen arms after the police interrogation. She remembered his dazed walk, his absent eyes for months after that episode. Remorseful, she took his hands in hers. She placed them on her heart. She kept them there for a long time.

"You haven't been the same since that day at the police station. That's what bothering you? That's why you want to leave here?"

"Don't want to talk about that, Ma. Don't remind me, Ma!"

"So stay home, Michael. Fight this war first. No need to fight some Chinamen."

"It's Vietnam, Ma, Not China."

"Same to me. I don't care. I want you alive, Michael. What did I do to deserve this? And what about college next year?"

"I asked for deferment. College can wait, Ma. The war can't."

"Jesus Christ!" my grandmother screamed in disbelief. All her life she'd dreamt of her son in college. She'd pictured her genius kid in engineering school. She'd saved, skimmed, worked hard for this goal. Two metres from the finishing line, she suddenly found herself tripping on someone's foot, the gold medal slipping from her grasp. The disappointment reminded Grandmother of her failed relationship. A lanky Jimmy Stewart lookalike—he had promised her so much. Elopement, New York City, money, freedom, eternal love. His whispered words on their lovers' bed had lulled her into a trance-like state. Gladly, she surrendered to his spell. She thought she'd found a pine tree—forever green, strong, dependable. He turned out to be a December snowman—freshly white and lasting only one season. Her act of defiance was met with a changed lock on the front door. As pastor and wife, her parents could not accept their only daughter running off with a white man. New

York City turned out to be Hoboken, New Jersey. Freedom turned out to be freedom to have mistresses. Money meant money for gambling halls. Eternal love lasted only hours. Outside their bedroom, eternal love was in fact a mixture of self-love and self-loathing. Returning home with a child in arm, Grandmother was greeted with indifference. Nobody bothered to tickle her baby's chin. Nor pinch his cheeks. They didn't even ask his name. Ashamed of harbouring a single mother under their roof, they begged her to leave. They gave her enough money to cover a year's rent before closing the door to that unfortunate part of their lives. A pastor's family must lead by living exemplary lives, they'd preached to their flock. No, no kid out of wedlock in their home.

Grandmother spent her years of abandonment devoted to her son. She lulled him to sleep with multiplication tables sung to a Nat King Cole's melody. Forbidden to have pets in their apartment, she threw her hard-earned money on Lassie toys. She sent him to a coveted school to open doors that would normally be closed. Though he talked back to her, she knew their love to be genuine. She wept now at the thought of losing him too. Bitterness made my grandmother repeat words she knew to be blasphemous. "Jesus Christ!" she hollered again and again.

Me Measure You

SAIGON'S LAWLESSNESS CAUGHT Father off guard. Honking cars, speeding mopeds, flat-tired bicycles, hawkers screaming their wares. They all ignored optional red lights. Traffic ran in all directions, at all times of the day. Blowing on their whistles, white-uniformed policemen slapped fines haphazardly. With children to feed, these men of the law didn't refuse little gifts. A 5000 *dong* bill discreetly placed under a driver's licence worked wonders. Driver's licences—like school diplomas, normal chest X-rays and negative syphilis results—could so easily be faked, they sold for next to nothing on the black market. Only passports and exit visas stayed out of reach for most people. For that, one would need connections in the Ministry of Foreign Affairs.

"I see you have a diploma in English literature, a normal chest X-ray and a negative syphilis test. It's not enough to get an exit visa to America. Sorry, Big Sister! Oh, and I see your 500,000 *dongs* in an envelope. It won't work either. So beat it!" Unfulfilled dreams of foreign escape. That would make for great lyrics and memorable songs. Wouldn't it?

Saigon's diverse residents intrigued Father. The city

buzzed with people from all over. As a remnant of the last war, French ladies still graced gritty streets with their chalk-white skin under flowery sundresses. On outdoor terraces, American, British, Australian and Canadian journalists formed one group while Yankee GIs formed another. Japanese NGO workers, South Korean soldiers, Indian salesmen and adventurous backpackers of the world were also everywhere. Fervent, these sweaty foreigners rushed around with a sense of purpose, always with a camera in hand. After all, they were there to witness history. They were there to experience a country seen nightly on television. A God-forsaken backwater not letting American politicians sleep in peace? Yes! Self-satisfied, these amateur historians sent home photos of ambulant ear cleaners and street dentists. Removing earwax on the sidewalks, pulling rotten teeth in public parks. The photos depicted an exoticism alluring even to other Asians. "Watch out for your camera! There's a thief lurking behind you!" Father would shout to unsuspecting tourists. And there were many of them.

My father hated the smell of diesel in the morning. The omnipresent swarms of flies and mosquitoes drove him crazy. He cursed most Saigon's unrelenting heat. Nightly, he questioned his decision. Life meaning, there was none to be found in this country. The Vietnamese were no less racist than those he'd left behind. If anything, they were even more racist. Their stares, their snickers vexed Father. Even with American Dollars stamped on his forehead, no Vietnamese hawkers bothered to hassle him. It was as if they feared catching his blackness.

Father suffered occasional bouts of melancholia. He missed home. He missed the golden colours of autumn, the cool breeze of winter. Did David ever come out of his coma, he wondered. He thought about his own mother changing diapers at the senior residence. News from home, he so longed for it. Only a Hallmark birthday card reached him after months of silence. It was a typical card with ten generic lines about a son who'd grown up to be a man the nation could count on. "Happy Birthday, Michael! Be safe! Love from Your Mom" These were Grandmother's only hand-written words. Still, her card touched Father. He knew she must've spent a whole Saturday searching for the right image. Of course, there were no right images. Those Hallmark boys all had white skin.

Saigon's oppressive atmosphere felt like lead on Father's shoulders. He became restless. To lighten his sombre mood, he hung around bars. He drank and talked nonsense with prostitutes. These girls didn't mind his skin colour. They actually sought him out. Tales of huge black zucchinis tickled their imagination. They all wanted to see it in live action. One day, a stocky prostitute pointed to his groin before whisking out a plastic ruler from her purse. "Me measure you!" she yelled to her friends' cheers. My father chuckled at this bit of cross-cultural conversation. He wondered if all Vietnamese girls carried rulers in their handbags.

A Bullet in the Jungle

THE JUNGLE TAUGHT my father one thing: black or white, it didn't matter, when you die, you die. The communists weren't racist. They rejoiced as much over a dead Black as over a dead White. Men Father imagined with KKKs tattooed on their arms became his buddies under the monsoon rain. Their worlds would never meet again back home, that much they knew. But in Vietnam, they looked out for each other. They helped carry each other's burden.

Alabama Ben, a medic fresh out of medical school, wasted no time spotting my father. He saw in Father's idealistic "to fight for freedom" his own "to heal the wounded." Enthusiasm for the war was so lacking, it didn't take much to recognize a soul mate. "What movie you like?" Ben had asked Father the first time they met. From his cot below Father's, Ben could spend hours giving his opinions on actresses. Excited by images of a particular actress, he'd hop on Father's bed. Brushing against Father's feet, he'd smoke one cigarette after another. He'd describe in detail his dream actress. He'd whistle while caressing his groin. Top on his list was Raquel Welch. Next came Marilyn Monroe. Then Vivien

Leigh. Ben loved Vivian Leigh tightly corseted. He thought *Gone with the Wind* a great period film with technological feats way ahead of its time. It didn't take much to shred Ben's white man fantasy. "Freed black slaves moping over the good old days of slavery? Give me a break," Father simply said.

Ben's talk with my father kept them busy at night. It helped take their minds off the fear of dying. It reminded them of their humanity. Freedom fighter and wound healer, they were. Not some evil Americans to be killed. Idealistic young men discussing their country's cultural merits. They deserved to come out of there alive.

A hike through the humid jungle in fatigues and leather boots was nobody's idea of fun. The soldiers all dreamed of an R&R on windswept China Beach. Or even better: a week in Pattaya, Thailand. The absence of direct sunlight, the oppressive smell of mould, the flies constantly in their faces, the leeches penetrating their boots through loose lace holes, the dread of serpents snaking down tree branches and of course the terror of being ambushed by a vicious enemy—all these threats kept everyone on edge.

The soldiers feared booby traps more than a fatal shot. Inadvertently falling into well-camouflaged foot-long poisonous spikes was their worst nightmare. They had been warned about these Viet Cong instruments of torture. Maiming, paralyzing, spreading infection. These silent bamboo spikes were King of the Jungle.

My father was hit by enemy fire on the fourth day of his mission. A solitary clicking of a distant rifle. A lone bullet piercing his left arm from behind. Father heard nothing, felt nothing. Fear had paralyzed his faculties, dulled his perception of pain. A tree branch, a tree branch entangling me, he'd thought. Unaware, he drudged on. Blood seeping through his sleeve finally stopped him. "Fuck, I've been hit!" he cried. With that one complaint, his platoon turned around to discharge a hundred rounds of vengeful bullets. As usual, the enemies had disappeared. Ben rushed to my father, and in an automatic gesture, tried stopping the trickle of blood with his bare hands.

"Bullet exited in front. No major artery hit! It barely grazed the biceps! Bandages are in place. Michael's arm will be as good as new in a few weeks," Ben announced to everyone's relief. "Fuck, there's the bullet," he mumbled, seeing a glittering object half embedded in a nearby tree. Taking out his knife, he carved around it. The bullet that had hit Father, the bullet that Ben had found. This would be their new bond. It was better than Hollywood films.

PART 4:
M & M

Beyond Cultures

OF ALL THE Bird Man's American colleagues, one stood out from the rest. This man talked much less than the others. His skin was also dark, very dark. He studied my mother with intense eyes as she flirted with two GIs. He liked her straight nose, her small waist. He admired her mixture of spunk and timidity. He found her low voice rather sexy. Her broken English in a foreign accent charmed him. After a week observing Mother, he approached her with a ruler. "You measure me," he said.

"Your arm OK?" my mother asked. The afternoon was hot, the air conditioner was broken and my father had rolled up his T-shirt sleeve.

"Viet Cong shot me last month. My arm still painful." Out of his pant pocket appeared a shiny bullet. Mother gasped. "How and when?" she asked, clamouring for more details. Gory stuff, she wants to hear gory stuff, Father told himself. No measuring tonight. He sighed and then smiled.

My father's melancholic smile troubled Mother. She could not undo its grip on her. His humility, his keeping quiet about American greatness intrigued her. She was not used to such behaviour. All the other soldiers bragged

about America. Father's scarred arm moved her. She'd
seen photos of maimed GIs before. She'd even met some
of them at Hung's beer stand. Faces misshapen, they
didn't smile. They only gave her dirty looks. "Why is
your father not fighting your own dirty war? Stop ogling
me, girl!" Unable to answer, she'd walk away in silence.
Father was different. His benign wound expressed no
rancour. It spoke to her in whispers instead. A bizarre
desire to smother it with kisses took roots. His broken
spirit, she wanted to fix that too. Mother had noticed
him eating alone while others traded barbs. She saw him
bent over his beers, morosely studying his fingernails.
The black soldier might share none of her culture. Still,
she recognized signs that were beyond culture.

Sadness and Infatuation

WHITE DEVILS AND Black Devils. My mother had been warned about them. Grandmother loved singling out Black Devils, especially Black Christian Devils. They pray to that man on the cross, Grandmother said with pouting lips. They forget their own ancestors. They eat reincarnated meat. What if their steak were their great grandfathers in another life?? And they even drink wine in churches! My mother actually liked the idea of drinking wine in churches. She also liked the singing, the dressing up, the celebratory mood found there. She could be a good Buddhist if only Buddha allowed her some fun. But no, she must meditate. She must renounce all earthly desires. She must eat chemically modified food. Tofu mock chicken, tofu mock pork, tofu mock fish. As true vegetarians, why couldn't they simply eat carrots and oranges? Why the hypocrisy of tofu-this and tofu-that?

Unlike Mother, my Black Devil father was a virgin in the game of sex. He'd imagined himself a robust seducer, nothing short of a Magnum Shooter. In fact, he was hand-led to bed by a slim innocent-looking young woman. Her lemon and cinnamon hair brought back memories of aromatic songs. "Are you going to Scarborough Fair? Parsley, sage, rosemary and thyme …," Father sang under his breath. The catchy tune caught my mother's attention. She grinned. Playfully she thrust his right index in her mouth. Her little nibbles surprised Father. He froze. His finger stayed as rigid as a dead branch.

Father's left arm glued to his side perplexed my mother. The other GIs would be all over her by now. Puzzled by Father's reluctance, she tried tickling him. He laughed. "Help," she said as she glided his hands over her chest. She needed help to undo her two dozen buttons.

Small erotic breasts. Father could never picture them. Chesty *Playboy* pin-up girls had always been his point of reference. Now he marvelled at my mother's little lithe body doing tricks on him. The feeling was unimaginable. It was nothing like those adolescent zucchini games in David's room. "Oh Man, if only you knew what it's really like," Father mumbled in between kisses. He imagined crazy, earnest David wagging his virgin zucchini, and laughed. Sudden memories of David plugged to a respirator and cardiac monitor turned his laugh into funereal whimpers. "Are you still a man, David or did you become a machine?" he murmured.

Father's anguish, Mother mistook it for the anguish of the uninitiated. The nervousness of first-timers. She had seen it before. To calm him, she caressed his face, chewed on his earlobe and whispered sweet Vietnamese words in his ear. Next, she worked on his chest, wetting his nipples with the tip of her tongue while scratching his groin with her uncut fingernails. His zucchini responded to her teasing. He closed his eyes and took a deep breath. Still, images of David on a hospital bed persisted. Sadness overwhelmed Father. Sadness also deepened his infatuation. Melancholic, he fell madly in love with Mother the night she rode him home.

Hitting Herself

IN HER TYPICAL careless ways, Mother ignored the early signs of pregnancy. Four missed periods didn't ring any bell. Thanks to Grandmother's overuse of ginger in her cooking, the nausea of pregnancy never showed its face. Without this telltale sign, with deceiving non-messages, my mother didn't know any better. She continued her nonchalant afternoons in bars—drinking diluted beers and smoking without inhaling. Only after her sixth missed period did Mother panic. She heard the cursed news at the doctor's office. "Don't try that hanger trick at home. You'll kill yourself," he said. Mother had no idea what the hanger trick entailed. She was just afraid, very afraid. Out of fear, my mother kept the news from her parents for another month. Dread cut off her appetite. She lost weight when she should've been gaining. Her cheeks caved in, her hair fell off in chunks, dark circles popped up under her eyes. What she saw in her mirror, I also saw. When her belly ballooned beyond hiding, she decided to tell Grandfather. And I heard it all.

"Whose child is it?" Professor Minh yelled, hitting his desk so hard Grandmother could hear its creaking noise from the kitchen below. Wiping sweat off her face, she ran upstairs to check on her husband.

"I ... I don't know ... Father. An American ..."

"You fucking whore!" Professor Minh hurled one obscenity after another. His heinousness hung like smog around Mother. Blinded, she couldn't see, couldn't understand. "But ...," she protested. "No but!" he screamed. In an uncontrollable rage, he slapped her. A kick in the stomach sent her to the ground. My grandmother's attempt at intervention only got her husband more worked up. He gave Mother's curled-up body another kick before tossing her down the staircase. It was my first exposure to physical violence. Surprisingly I didn't feel any pain. I only felt a loss of grip as my world tumbled downstairs. I wished my mother had held out her hands to protect me. Instead, she used her own fists to repeatedly hit herself. Then she howled.

Losing Her Scent

THE NIGHT MY mother rolled down a staircase, Father sat alone at the Pink Night Club. A ceiling fan cut through the humidity. It moved the sluggish heat with its noisy rat-tat-tat. Pink bulbs shone light on the usual crowd—two prostitutes for each GI. In one corner the Bird Man shared beers with his group of drunken friends. In another corner, young women in miniskirts gossiped as they prepared themselves. Passing a hand mirror around, they double-checked their teeth for lipstick stains. Next, they fixed each other's limp hair using a can of hairspray. As soon as the music switched to a slow song, they marched out in gangs. They approached male customers with teeth-revealing smiles. It was a sight familiar to my father by now. Only my mother was missing. She'd been missing for weeks. Her absence worried Father. He hoped she wasn't flirting with other guys in another bar. He missed her lemon and cinnamon hair. He feared he'd never come across that scent again. It didn't take long before a thick-lipped prostitute closed in on Father. She wanted to dance. He shook his head wearily. He gave her a ten-dollar bill. "Go buy some cinnamon and lemons," he said. With a smile of collusion, she pocketed his money. "Markets all closed at this hour," she whispered in his ear.

Tearing out the Bible

"YOU WANT A kid at your age? A kid with no father? You want to stop school? You want to ruin your life?" It was an interrogation with too obvious an answer. No, no, no, no. "I should hit you but I won't. It won't solve any problem!" Grandmother snapped. On a night without electricity, without the whirl of a ceiling fan, without the television's hum, she felt the void of unspoken words. Back and forth she paced till her feet wore out. She so wanted to return to her hiding place under the bed. "You go to the convent. Have your kid there. Then your kid goes to an orphanage. Orphanage and convent run by same people. Nuns. Nuns will take care of it," Grandmother finally said after a long silence.

"You know nuns, Mother? We're not even Catholics."

Before my mother could say more, she felt a sting on her face. Her mother's swift hands were faster than she'd thought. The force of her fingernails more painful than expected. Dumbstruck, Mother sat paralyzed on her seat. She dared not wipe her bloodied cheeks.

Professor Minh on his bed and his wife underneath it shared few words in their room. His sighs echoed her sniffling. A pregnant unmarried teenaged daughter, what could be worse? Having lost face to their friends, they locked themselves in the house. How to avoid crossing paths with Tuan's parents became their shared obsession. Their daughter's anxiety wasn't worth addressing. She was as good as dead in their eyes.

They checked their lunar calendar for a good-luck-day. Getting rid of me was no ordinary matter. It must be done properly or bad luck would descend on them. To their consternation, the next auspicious date came only in a fortnight. The two-week wait tortured them. They blocked their ears when my mother cried. They closed their eyes seeing her shameful expanding body. They counted the hours before they could safely ship her off to a convent. On the appointed good-luck-day, Mother was given a piece of candy after her normal meal of fried rice. At the last minute, Grandmother added two lemons and three sticks of cinnamon to Mother's suitcase. She had nothing else to give, nothing to say. A pat on the shoulders, a brief caress of hands and Grandmother returned to her kitchen. Outside, Professor Minh honked the horn four times. He glanced repeatedly at his watch. To avoid neighbours' gossip, he threw Mother his vest and cap. He wanted to turn her into her a boy, to hide her bulging stomach. Perhaps he also wanted to turn back the clock, to deny me my existence.

Professor Minh dumped Mother's suitcase in the car's trunk. He ordered her to lie low. "Don't show your face and put on my jacket and cap!" Without another word, he whisked across town. Driving my mother to the convent, he thought he was safe from prying eyes. At 90 minutes before curfew, Saigon was already quiet.

Only merchants, waiting for a last bus home, still roamed. In his haste, the professor passed a red light, narrowly missing a street vendor. While the woman escaped unharmed, her merchandise had splashed against his windshield. Blinded by noodles, beef strips and green onions, he came to a halt. A crowd instantly formed around him. To the woman's gutter words, people in pyjamas and ready for bed, appeared out of nowhere to add their own Fuck-Your-Mothers. Professor Minh scowled. He threw her some coins, paid someone else to clean his car, then took off without looking back. He couldn't afford to be late. The nuns were waiting. Five minutes late and Mother's spot would be given to another unfortunate girl. There were so many of them.

As an amateur, Professor Minh could not compete with the professionals. His secret plan full of holes fooled no one. Mother's disappearing act did not go unnoticed. Beady eyes registered her family's every move. From their vantage point, they saw everything while Professor Minh understood nothing. Anxious to leave the accident scene, he hadn't noticed a short duck-like man watching him from a second-floor balcony. His arrogance, his attempt to buy peace of mind with money, his daughter's trembling hands, her unbecoming clothes. The Duck Man saw it all. He laughed at her attempt at disguise. An oversized vest couldn't conceal her pregnant stomach. A man cap couldn't hide her long hair. He knew no amount of money could still her disquiet heart. He felt sorry for her even if she'd slept with the enemy.

"Your daughter's friend, the tall one fucking Americans, is pregnant. She's at the convent." A note written in invisible ink fell from a crack in the wall. It rolled about on the bathroom floor before landing on torn flip-flops. Bending over, Hung picked it up. He gave the room a quick glance then resumed washing his hands. Yes, there were eyes and ears everywhere.

Arrived on time, Professor Minh sighed with relief. He handed his pregnant daughter to two old nuns. He reclaimed his jacket before hurrying away. "Father!" Mother called to a disappearing silhouette. Desolate, my mother went to the nuns for comfort. They only shrugged. They gave her two towels and a Vietnamese Bible. "Read it, my child," they said in unison.

The Bible made no sense to Mother. In a waste-basket it went after the fifth paragraph. Changing her mind, she retrieved it and began tearing out its pages. She crumpled those torn pages into balls. One by one, she threw them against her whitewashed walls. This mindless gesture kept her busy. After an hour of throwing paper balls, she decided to gather them for her bed. As if planting trees, she laid them row by row under her bed sheet. She also stuffed her pillowcase with crumpled paper. Transforming her bed into a field of paper land-mines, turning it into a place of comfortless, sleepless nights—this was how she punished herself. This was her way of getting back at me.

Some Would Live and Others Would Die . . .

MY FATHER MISSED my mother. He wanted to see her again before his flight home. He looked for her at all their usual spots. Sniffing here, sniffing there, he found no traces of her lemon and cinnamon scent. Givral Café, Catinat Boulevard, The Pink Night Club, Ben Thanh Market, Le Cercle Sportif—all these places, once so familiar, became foreign territory in my mother's absence. Without her know-how guiding him through convoluted local mentalities, my father became utterly lost. He sought the help of The Bird Man and his GI friends. Tethered on The Pink Night Club's vinyl-covered stools, they all shook their heads. Mother had also vanished from their lives.

It took my father four days rickshawing around town to trace Hung. No longer at his usual spot on Catinat Boulevard, he now waved his V sign in front of the post office. His fake grin, his V sign were special treatments reserved for Americans. To his fellow Vietnamese, Hung only nodded coldly. "Hello Mister! Beer, Mister? I serve, you drink. Yes? How many?" Hours of watching American TV had turned Hung into an expert. An expert on America. He could sing "The Star-Spangled Banner." He could impersonate Dean Martin. He could identify all the Boston Red Sox players. Yet he must act dumb. That was the deal. He'd often fantasize about yelling: "You shithead Yankees, why don't you go home?!" And this in a mock Texas drawl on top of it. At home, he'd even practised those sentences using a New York accent. He gave up when he couldn't get it right. The Texan rhythm was easier on his tongue.

"Hello Hung. Hung, that's your name, isn't it?"

"Yes. And?" A ten-dollar bill changed Hung's tune. "America Number One!" he said with a grin.

"No, Saigon Number One!" Father replied. He patted Hung's shoulders. At this gesture of familiarity, Hung shuddered. Slowly he removed himself from my father's black hands.

The shoulders slipping away from Father's touch didn't go unnoticed. Insulted, he grabbed Hung's tattered T-shirt. "Where is your daughter Mai Ly? Where is her friend Mai? Tell me!" he shouted. Hung's misty eyes stopped Father in mid-sentence. He regretted his sudden move. The beer seller's flustering lashes reminded Father of his mother's on their last evening together. Besides her usual 'Lord, oh Lord!' she'd not said much that night. Finding her still asleep next morning, Father had decided to leave quietly. A no-goodbye was better than a melodramatic wail. Their kitchen on that last morning looked no different from previous days. His box of Kellogg's cereal and plate of banana were at their usual place. Only one thing stood out: a note on a saucer with three words, "Be safe, Son!"

Shaken up, Hung blurted out, "Pregnant! My Mai

Ly good girl. But your Mai pregnant! Baby coming, no father!"

"Oh My God!" Father exclaimed.

"Not God! Just nuns. Mai with nuns. Convent. Cholon."

"Hmmm, where?"

"Cholon. Chinatown. Take *cyclo* over there. 30 minutes!"

"Thanks Hung! Here is another ten dollars for you."

The rickshaw ride took an hour. Opium's vinegary scent greeted Father at Cholon's entrance. Chinese characters on windowpanes told him he had arrived. Two swirling dragons on top of Quan Am Pagoda caught his attention. Noodle-making men plying their trade on sidewalks fascinated him. He made a note to return with a camera. He wanted to capture it all. Unhurried limbs of emaciated girls. Headless chickens dangling from a street vendor's arm. Fish carcasses strewn on the pavement. This was Cholon, Saigon's Chinatown.

A black iron cross atop a slender spire crowned the convent. Fresh coats of white paint gave its brick facade a clean, imposing look while shrubs of hibiscus added a touch of colour. Proudly it stood out from surrounding moss-covered houses.

"*Oui?*" a voice said through a crack in the door. Father racked his mind for a half-decent French sentence to flatter the tiny blue-eyed woman in front of him. St. Joseph Prep had taught him nuns were like the rest of us. They too, succumb to flattery. Yes, flatter and you'll enter. Sister Tremblay. His French-Canadian teacher. What was it she always said? Ah yes: "*Mon Dieu! Mon Dieu, sauvez ces enfants de leur ignorance!*" The students had never understood this expression. They just liked its cadence coming out of Sister Tremblay's mouth.

"*Mon Dieu, mon Dieu, sauvez ces enfants de leur ignorance*," my father said in a heavy accent.

"*Quoi?*" The nun raised her eyebrow in puzzlement.

When Father tried repeating his sentence using a different intonation, she laughed in his face. "Save which kids from ignorance?" she asked in English. Her words flowed. They followed the current down a river while my father's imbedded themselves in a tangle of vines. She shrugged off his grateful smile and asked coldly what he wanted.

"Please Sister, I'd like to see a girl here. She's pregnant. Her name is Tran Cuc Mai. I'm going back to the States soon. I need to see her before I go."

"Sorry, we let no men inside."

"Please Sister, I think I love her."

"That's what they all say." She rolled her eyes.

Realizing there would be no bypassing this unflinching gatekeeper, Father searched his duffel bag for pen and paper. Love letters on the fly were not his specialty. Still, he managed to scribble down a few words of longing. The French nun took his note, with distaste read it, then slammed the door in his face. She felt no need to tell him Mother was in labour that very instant. That a premature baby was about to be born gave her no worry. She'd seen enough of those wretched creatures coming out of wretched orifices to care. Some would live while other would die. That's the nature of things, she'd tell herself. She could hear my mother's screams as she walked down the hall. Hands on her ears, she marched straight to her room for an afternoon nap.

Her Poison

BEFORE A MIDWIFE severed my umbilical cord, before I survived on my own blood and oxygen, before I formed my memories, I saw the world through my mother's eyes. I shared her thoughts, emotions, nostalgia. Her fear, I felt it in my palpating heart. Her cravings, I felt them in my growling stomach. Her contentment, I felt it in the warm liquid with which she bathed me. We were one.

That all changed lying on my mother's stomach. One look at me was enough. Shrieking, she pushed me away. "Oh God, no! A dark baby! Father will kill me! Please get it out of here!" In those few short minutes, my mother's regret filled every space in my body. Carried in my blood, her melancholia fed each one of my cells. Her bitterness overwhelmed my mind. It left me with a deep sorrow no amount of milk can soothe. My mother preferred me dead ... I promised myself to stop growing. Premature, I was small. I wanted to be smaller.

The cord finally cut, I began to forget my mother's thoughts. I let out a cry, allowing my tears to wash away her poison.

PART 5:
APRIL 1975
THE FALL OF SAIGON

A White Christmas in April

THE DAY SAIGON fell into communist hands, Professor Minh lost his mind. Visual hallucinations haunted him. Images of his young lover taunted him on every street corner. "Where are you going? Why do you wish to leave?" Her mocking voice echoed in his head. Memories of Mai Ly's silky hair on his sweaty back caught him off guard. Like a tentacle, they wanted to hold him back. "No! Let me go!" he shouted. He knew he must leave. The new Saigon had no sympathy for people of his kind. Dragging his body around town, frantically he searched for a last-minute exit out of his nightmare.

For months Professor Minh had followed newscasts on television. The capture of one South Vietnamese town after another had disheartened him. Stubbornly, he'd refused to imagine Saigon's last days. Armed with American rifles, South Vietnamese soldiers would surely defeat their northern brothers in rubber sandals. So why were rusty Soviet tanks rolling down Saigon's boulevards? Why was the communist golden star already flapping in front of the Senate?

Noise filled the packed sidewalks. Women ran to catch a glimpse of these young victors squatting on their tanks. The self-acclaimed liberators looked commanding in their green uniforms. They smoked one cigarette after another. They littered the street with their butts. They smiled and waved at throngs of girls screaming in ecstasy. People putting on a spectacle for their former enemies turned Professor Minh's stomach. The fake welcome was nothing more than a last-ditch effort to save their skin. Like him, these girls would rather be on one of those American helicopters that had flown out of Saigon a week before. Now it was too late.

Professor Minh blamed himself for his stupid sense of pride getting him nowhere. He should've left with his family two days ago. Mai's American boyfriend, he should've ignored his crude words. Bursting uninvited into his house after kicking his fence down—the professor should've forgiven that guy. He just couldn't. The American's dishevelled look, vulgar bird tattoo and beer breath had left a bad impression on him. Neither man was in a mood for introductions. "Mai, you come with me. We'll take a helicopter out of Saigon tonight. Go pack your bags now," the American ordered. Taken by surprise, Mai pointed to her parents. "They can come to the embassy. I don't guarantee a place for them on the helicopter. I'm only here for you. Be quick. The communists are very close. Can't you hear their rockets? They are more and more frequent!" The American's shaking hands were all Mai needed to see. She ran to her room to pack her bags. Her mother did likewise. She too understood all that was needed to understand.

"He'd impregnated my daughter! Son of a bitch!"

Professor Minh thought, furious. "Why couldn't he dispose of his sperm in a Kleenex like I did with my Mai Ly?" He soon worked himself into a rage thinking of his self-imposed sacrifice while this American boor went all the way with his daughter. Ruining her reputation, leaving her with a child out of wedlock. How could he ever forgive him? No, he would not add to this American's sense of self-importance. He would obey no orders. He would not run to pack his bags. Thoughts of Mai's baby—a grandchild he could never accept because of its mixed blood—depressed him. Bitterness weighed him down. It turned him into a chipped block of limestone. Heavy and heavy-hearted.

Mai made a show of pleading with her father. For a moment, his wife joined in, even shouting obscenities at him. "Don't be so damn stupid! Go prepare your damn bag, you stubborn pig!" Such crude words from his wife shocked him. He wanted to slap her but his hands stayed limp by his sides. Sudden realization of his unimportance, of his inability to control his family, of the futility of his life, frightened him. His head ached. He felt dizzy. His vision blurred and a strange numbness slowly crept up his left limbs. Slumped on a sofa, he tried removing his speckled baby blue glasses. If only he could clean them with his shirtsleeve, his normal vision would surely return. This simple gesture was harder than he'd thought. The glasses only slid down his nose. Professor Minh's catatonic state worried no one. His wife only sneered. "You don't want to move? Then you can stay! There's enough rice in the pantry to last you two weeks.

We're going now," she said without the tenderness of a goodbye. He looked at her, unable to utter a word. Only wheezes came out of his open mouth.

An hour later, he was still slumped on the sofa, head still dizzy, vision still blurred, left limbs still numb. As he pondered his new fate, a neighbour's radio pulled him out of his rumination. A loud 'White Christmas' played over and over from across the street. That song baffled him. What does April 28 have to do with a white Christmas? He wondered if he wasn't also losing his mind.

Enough, You Son of a Bitch

"**B**OTTLE-NECKED SAIGON. Shit, that's worse than the jungle!" The Bird Man swore loudly. Repeatedly he banged his horn. The honking echoed down the street and glided across town. Yet no one moved. Saigon was at a standstill. Evening traffic. This was a never seen. For years, curfews had forced cars to snooze, had allowed exhaust fumes to dissipate. No one bothered with curfews today. Frenzied policemen were first in line to get out of town.

"We're catching that 7 p.m. helicopter tonight. Must get to the embassy before it closes. Damn! Listen, Mai … Hey, hey look, look at me, Baby! Take only what's most important from your suitcase. Tell your mother to do the same. Here, put your stuff in my knapsack. We'll walk to the embassy. Look at all these idling cars. Crazy traffic! We'll get nowhere sitting here. Hurry!"

Before Mai could reply, someone answered for her. "Tell your American lover to get his mother fucking car out of my way! Goddamned whore!" Mai saw two pumped up fists knocking at her window. She felt hands rocking their car back and forth. Menacing limbs didn't bother Mai's mother. 'Whore' did. She flinched. She thought about replying, then decided to keep her mouth shut. 'You-son-of-a-bitch' were already exchanged left and right. She didn't need to add her own.

Running for the Helicopter

THE TREK TO the American embassy took exactly forty-two minutes. A crowd of distraught Vietnamese banged on its closed gate. Others tried escalading its high walls. Humility no longer mattered. Young women let expose raw flesh as they wormed through barbed wires. Blood dripped from their open wounds. Mai's mother shivered. She wondered if she'd have to go through the same humiliation, the same pain. Without warning, she collapsed from anxiety and exhaustion.

A sweaty Vietnamese woman dragging a large steel suitcase accosted the Bird Man. "Full of gold. For you, Mr. American. Tell them I'm your wife!" Her hands tightly clasped, she bowed. "Sorry, Lady!" he shouted, pushing her away. "Open the goddamn gate! Open the goddamn gate! I'm an American! There is a sick older woman here! Josh, where the fuck are you? Josh! Josh! You hear me? Open the gate! It's Ron! I'm an American!" The gate stayed closed even with those magic words. A minute later, a voice announced from above: "Climb up, Ron. We can't open. If we did, those Viets would flood us!" The Bird Man groaned seeing Mai's mother still collapsed on the gravel. "Look away," he told Mai. He bent over and slapped the old woman's cheeks. Then he spat into her nostrils. At once she came back to life in a coughing fit. Disoriented, she looked around. She asked one question after another. Mai only shook her head. She too was shell-shocked. The Bird Man took two long-sleeved shirts out of his knapsack. He checked them for tears. In one swift movement, he hauled Mai's mother on his back, then secured her using his shirtsleeves as rope. "We're coming up!" he shouted to four Marines manning the wall. Three warning shots in the air interrupted the pushing and shoving below. A moment of shocked silence, then angry screaming. Immediately, two Marines brought their guns down. Aiming at people's chests. It was crowd control at its best. Still, some young men persisted in their climb. Unafraid, they hoisted each other up. Reckless, they encouraged each other on.

To these insistent Vietnamese intruders, a more forceful method was used: gun butts to smash fingers, soldiers' boots to stamp on hands. This tactic succeeded. The men released their grip and howled as they hit rocky ground. Pushing back a panicked crowd took nerves of steel. Many young Marines came here to shoot point-blank, not to look desperation in the eye and do nothing.

The Bird Man felt no unease piggybacking Mai's mother. Combat training had prepared him. He climbed the iron door with a sure foot. Once inside, he promptly handed Mai's mother to a Marine. "Give her some water, she'll be OK. I gotta go get her daughter now." Outside the compound, Mai was nowhere in sight. Her spot had been taken over by a dozen Vietnamese women jostling for his attention. They pulled on his shirttail, hung onto his arms, hooked their fingers around his belt loops and refused to let go. To free himself, he resorted to his Swiss Army knife. He used it to slash the thick air around him, not caring if he slashed a few fingers in the tumult. He finally found teary-eyed Mai squatting under a star fruit tree. In her hands was a frangipani flower with half its petals gone. She threw the flower away and hopped on his back. Mai's sweat running down his neck bothered him. He was so hot already. Yet her heartbeats against his back somehow calmed him. It reminded him of their Saigon siestas—napping after heated sex. This was what he remembered most about their embassy escape.

Screams on the embassy's rooftop scared Mai. A shaky ladder leading to a helicopter pad terrified her. She'd always been afraid of heights. A gale blew her long hair in every direction, making knots in the air. The helicopter's chopping noise disoriented her. She felt vertigo coming on and wasn't sure if she was above ground or below it. For a moment she thought she was doing the 100-metre breaststroke. The sensation was the same. Fatigue and dizziness. The Bird Man had to hold her in his arms for her last five steps up the ladder. Mai briefly blanked out. She remembered nothing of being pulled into a taxiing helicopter. She never heard the back-and-forth between her lover and an impatient pilot.

"No space for that old lady!"

"I got Ambassador Martin's permission. Call and check!"

"Fuck you and your whore! OK, fucking get in. What you waiting for? Hurry! This isn't some funeral procession!"

Mai? Or Mai Ly?

PROFESSOR MINH FOLLOWED the evacuation of the lucky few on television, He watched from beginning to end. He sat glued to his TV set. He wanted to see it all. He wanted to witness history live on his screen. He saw one helicopter after another taking off from the American embassy's rooftop. He heard the panic of those left behind. Anarchic scenes of locals climbing embassy walls gave him palpitations. Images of hands smashed by gun butts dismayed him. He stamped his feet. He wanted to scream. Only a little whimper came out. He tried looking for his wife and daughter on television. He wondered if they got through. Of course, they got through, he reassured himself. They went with a blonde, green-eyed American GI after all. He knew connections would open doors and at that moment he had run out of connections.

After a day of deceiving calm, the sounds of war returned. Roaring tanks, whistling rifles, crackling fires. Professor Minh heard them all on his street. He realized then he'd have to escape fast. The communists were at Saigon's door. And he could neither run nor drive. Weaker limbs, less steady gait, vision doubled. He could only limp now. Dragging his body through town, he couldn't believe what he saw. While fighting continued in some neighbourhoods, others had already crowned the new winners. Red communist flags popped up everywhere. There was nowhere to go, no place to hide.

The procession of communist tanks gave Professor Minh a headache. He thought he was going crazy. He blinked over and over for a clearer look. He couldn't believe what he saw. On top of a Soviet tank sat his young lover Mai, or rather Mai Ly as she liked to be called. Waving at a crowd beneath her feet, she exuded a self-confidence he'd never seen before. There she was in her Viet Cong uniform, a rifle hung on her back, her hair cut short, her skin darkened. Although older, she still sported that innocent wide-eyed look. Radiant, she shared one joke after another with her comrades. Out of nowhere, someone's hand stroked her back. Professor Minh closed his eyes to let pass this moment of jealousy. "Mai! Mai! Mai Ly! Mai Ly!" he whimpered from his spot on the sidewalk. He waved nervously at her.

With a trembling elbow, Professor Minh managed to inch his way through a screaming crowd. His double vision worsened as he approached a row of tanks. Someone jostled him. He fell on a piece of steel rod sticking out of wet grass. His hands bled. Excruciating pain prevented him from thinking properly. He saw a tank coming yet did not move. Perhaps he couldn't move. In a crushing sweep, the armored car came down on his torso. Before dying, he managed to whisper, "Mai, I'm sorry." Trampled by dirty shoes, those last words stayed buried under dust. Even if someone had witnessed his final uttering, they wouldn't know which Mai he was referring to. Mai, the daughter? Or Mai Ly, the lover?

Out of the Ceramic Tiles

FROM ATOP HER Soviet tank, Mai Ly noticed a familiar face waving at her. He reminded her of somebody. She just couldn't put a name to him. Everyone else also waved but only half-heartedly. She could tell it was all for show. They would rather throw tomatoes at her if they could. In the old days, these people would've hurled insults at her after reporting her to the Secret Police. She would've been tossed in jail and tortured for information she didn't know. April 30, 1975, changed all of that.

April 30, 1975 marked the beginning of a new era. Mai Ly smiled jubilantly looking at the crowd beneath her feet. For years she had dreamt of this day. Victory had arrived sooner than expected and with so little fighting. Who would've expected the capitalist army to give up so easily? Deserting their uniforms, running half-naked into villages to hide amongst civilians. Their cowardice surprised everyone. Surreal images of abandoned army boots plugging up highways angered Mai Ly. She wanted to see flowers lining roads, not dirty, stinking boots left by those retreating soldiers. Mai Ly was proud she worked for the other side.

The exact date of Mai Ly's conversion was not noted

anywhere. She only remembered an exceptionally cool day. In her shared bathroom, a ceramic tile had fallen off that afternoon. Out rolled a crumpled piece of paper. Curious, Mai Ly had picked it up. She recognized with surprise her father's childlike handwriting. His strange words making no sense puzzled her. When asked about his cryptic message, Hung denied ever writing it. He cursed. "Stupid invisible ink not working," he mumbled. A second obscure note gave Mai Ly palpitations. She couldn't hold back her question: "Father, are you with the Secret Police?" Hung reacted by slapping his daughter across the face.

"Don't ever mention those shitty words again! Why should I work for those fucking sons of bitches?" Pushing Mai Ly's forehead backward with his pointed index, Hung looked at her with contempt. He couldn't believe his daughter's ignorance, an ignorance further sullied by arrogance. How dared she imply his collaboration with the Secret Police? A Secret Police that was neither secret nor policing, that was only good at hauling poor-looking young men into jail. In their simplistic paranoid minds, these well-fed males only saw the enemy in poverty-stricken boys. No one else would be susceptible to communist ideology, they'd reassure themselves. Thoughts of the Secret Police turned Hung into a rabid dog ready to bite. His convulsing hands were set to strike again. "What does that mean? Think! I didn't pay for those private lessons so you can stay stupid! What did your damn Professor Minh teach you?"

"The professor, he, he taught mathematics, Father," Mai Ly replied in a halting voice, her arms by her side.

Even in pain, she dared not minister to her burning cheeks. "You, you hate the Secret Police. So ... so you must like the Viet Cong, the VC, the communists," Mai Ly said.

"Shhh! Never say those words out loud, understand? Look at me! Never reveal your true nature to anyone. Get it? Now, I need you around my beer stand. Pay attention to what those Americans say. I'll teach you more English. *Mission: Impossible* is good for learning. Just remember: keep your mouth shut. You look, listen and smile. No talking. Don't ever ask 'Why?' Just obey me and report to me."

"Yes, Father," Mai Ly said, nodding, sweaty hands still by her side, still not able to caress the hurt on her face, her mind still bewildered by her father's revelation, still rebelling against the idea of spying on her friend's lovers. The black soldier, the Bird Man—she had genuinely liked them.

Mai Ly's Journey:
The Lesson in Hatred

MAI LY HAD never imagined her father a communist sympathizer. So well hidden was that part of his life, she could only react with shock the moment truth showed its real face. Shock also shut off Mai Ly's brain. Shock would transform filial respect into blind obedience. "Yes, Father," was all she said to Hung's orders.

Mai Ly never pictured joining the Party herself. Yet her conversion was inevitable after Hung's talk. Trading the carelessness of youth for a cause still nebulous in her mind. This was not easy. She did so with much hesitation. Her sexual awakening, her formal education, her social-climbing lessons. All must be sacrificed. In their place, a different type of learning was introduced. A small shack in the back of a candy store, five people squatting on a mud floor, complete darkness and a hushed voice. This was her new classroom. Mai Ly's initial mistrust eventually melted after a few mind-bending classes. She'd let her guard down by the fourth meeting. She'd no longer cup her hands to block her ears. In that space lit by moonlight, she listened attentively to a melodious voice telling her the other history of her country. The voice instilled in her a sense of love for the nation, a feeling of pride for her people. This was a pleasant sensation she'd never experienced before. Instead of phoenix and dragon tales, instead of boring texts on emperors dead centuries ago, Mai Ly learned of the injustice of French colonialism. She learned of the battle at Dien Bien Phu where idealistic Vietnamese soldiers had put an end to French rule in Indochina. She learned of a humble man named Ho Chi Minh and of his life-long effort to reunite Vietnam. She learned of American duplicity—mouthing the virtues of independence on television yet crushing nations fighting for self-rule with bullets. She learned and she learned.

Introduced steadily, these lessons inspired. Mai Ly longed to know more. She raised her hand and asked questions. She listened intently. Every Tuesday, she'd come home with a febrile heart. Febrile heartbeats eventually led to rage. She learned to hate and to wallow in resentment. American imperialism. American hypocrisy. American decadence. American this. American that. She learned to hate it all.

Codename: The Student

AS AN INFORMANT working at her father's beer stand, Mai Ly performed well. Her slim adolescent body attracted a horde of American soldiers. They didn't care about her age. They didn't want to know. All Asian women look young anyway, they reassured themselves. Heeding her father's order, Mai Ly kept a permanent smile. "Hello, Mister, one hundred *dongs,* one beer, thank you." Those were the only words Hung allowed her to say. She'd put on her calculated spaced-out look if American GIs attempted more talk. Frustrated, they'd eventually brush her off. They'd turn to each other to complain about the danger of bedding young Vietnamese girls. The weather was another popular topic. Everyone hated Saigon's unbearably humid heat. Occasionally, amongst typical chatter on ex-girlfriends, diarrhoea or tropical leeches, an important exchange of information would arise. "Did you know General Westmoreland is coming to town next week?", "Hey, we got a new shipment of jeeps yesterday. Look like fucking good armour to me. Impossible for those damn VCs to ambush us now!", "My Dad wrote that Jane Fonda sides with the commies! I'm gonna boycott all those Fondas films! Jesus!"

The bits of information American GIs threw carelessly around, Mai Ly would pick up with care. Like frangipani petals strewn on sidewalks, she'd gather them all. Diligently she'd note everything in her schoolbook, using the code she was taught. Deleting every second and fourth letter, it was an easy-to-crack code. As a low-level foot soldier, she didn't need more. Unfamiliarity with more complicated codes was in fact a blessing. If caught, she'd be spared high-level torture.

Mai Ly was never caught. Never tortured. Her coded notes passed from one hand to another. Their final destination: the Duck Man's wrinkled fingers. Her beautiful penmanship mesmerized him. He admired her cursive more than the actual content of her messages. Like a homesick lover, he'd ask for more notes. Obediently, she'd provide him with more information. The American said this. The American said that. The American looked worried. The American laughed today. Gladly, she reported it all.

Then one day there was nothing left to report. Overnight, American GIs stopped coming to Hung's beer stand. Magically, they disappeared from Saigon's streets. Mai Ly could not understand this sudden departure of so many soldiers. The boulevards less crowded. The hustling calmed. The bars half empty. The prostitutes out-of-work. It all seemed strange to Mai Ly. This was information her Eyes and Ears had failed to pick up.

Things were less hazy for the GIs. Their newspapers had predicted an American withdrawal long ago. Their political analysts had seen it coming in their crystal balls.

Global Anti-War Protests + Mounting Casualty + Large Federal Debt + Rumours of Political Scandals = Electoral Promises of Peace.

It was an easy equation to solve. Mai Ly should've figured it out. She didn't. The Duck Man was less naive. He knew about the political scandal. He'd read about Watergate in the newspapers. He chuckled at Nixon's misfortunes. He despised the man's dishonesty. It only confirmed his view of Americans as crooked business brokers. "You vote for me. I give you peace. And we forget Watergate. Ha! Ha!" The Duck Man laughed at his impersonation of Nixon. His friends loved this performance. They hooted.

The Duck Man was right. Once re-elected, president Nixon kept his electoral promise of peace. He ordered the withdrawal of American troops by 1973. But 1973 saw no peace for Vietnamese families. The war between brothers still raged on. Russian lackeys and American puppets still shot at each other in the jungle that was Vietnam. The Cold War was still very hot.

With American GIs gone, Mai Ly found herself out of a job. No more information to gather. No more coded messages to fill her notebook. Hung's beer stand lost clients, yet he carried on. There were still enough American military advisors and embassy staff to support his business. Mai Ly went out of her way to smile at these pasty-faced men in sport shirts and loafers. She even put her hands on their shoulders. She tried swatting away their dandruff. She spiced her dialogue with "What's up, Sir?"

Nothing worked. Impossible to milk information from these discreet types. They never talked outside of their concrete bunker. They'd come for their afternoon break, drink a few beers, then leave. Their robot lips hardly moved during this whole time. Perversely, Mai Ly missed the rowdy GIs. She missed their screams, their swearing, their insults. "Fucking country! All these Viets are crooks out to cheat you!" She had hated them so much. Now, there was no one to hate. No one to blame for the deaths around her. Their sudden departure left her with a strange emptiness. Years would pass before she'd learn the truth. Time would fly before she'd see the hated GIs as victims too.

Frustrated at having nothing to do, Mai Ly decided to join the real army of fighting soldiers. She wanted to fight those South Vietnamese puppets licking their American bosses' boots. She wanted to contribute to a socialist paradise promised by Uncle Ho. To Mai Ly's dismay, her father forbade her to take up arms. "Too dangerous," he simply said. She was told to take up the pen instead. In neat cursive letters, she wrote simple tracts dictated by her father. "Comrades, don't be discouraged!" "We'll win this war against the capitalists!" "Thieu is an American puppet!" "Vietnam will be reunited!" "Long live Uncle Ho!" 'Long live socialism!" "The Future belongs to the masses!" "Down with the rich!" "No more Exploiters!" The writing was straightforward. Mai Ly even enjoyed practising her cursives. Daily she wrote 25 copies of each slogan, resting only when her fingers ached. If the production of propaganda seemed easy, its distribution wasn't. To avoid suspicion,

Mai Ly hid her tracts inside her schoolbooks, which she placed inside her school bag. A few months earlier, when she fell off her bicycle, the school bag had dropped to the ground, its latch had opened and some tracts had managed to escape her grasp. A gust of monsoon wind had dispersed those papers beyond her reach. It was impossible to gather them all up. Quietly Mai Ly had retrieved her school bag. Head bent, she pedalled as if late for class. She knew keeping a low profile to be important. Running after pieces of flying papers would only attract attention. Had these papers landed in the wrong hands, her two-faced comrades would all be shot. "Please Buddha, please let some illiterate vendors find those tracts and use them for their oven fires," she prayed that night. Fear of being caught with communist propaganda gave Mai Ly twitching limbs. She was forever bumping into trees or zigzagging down boulevards. Her heart thumped so hard she could feel it fissuring against her rib cage. Palpitations or not, she knew she had to soldier on. She had to deliver those tracts. A flower stand at Ben Thanh Market. A candy shop on Hong Bang Street. A bookstore in Cholon. Mai Ly did the same route every Wednesday afternoon. Her contacts were all elderly women—shopkeepers during the day, grandmothers at night and communist middlemen in late afternoon. For her delivery trips, Mai Ly always wore her white schoolgirl *ao dai,* always carried her schoolbag full of schoolbooks stuffed with anti-government messages. Her codename was "The Student." Nobody wanted to know which school she attended.

No More Legs to Grow

A **FEW YARDS** down the boulevard, Mai Ly suddenly remembered the bespectacled man waving at her. His speckled baby blue glasses, oh yes, how could she forget? How many times did they slip down his nose as they kissed? He'd have to push them up every ten seconds, regularly interrupting his tongue's walkabout in her mouth. Images of Professor Minh's muscular torso now flooded Mai Ly. Her years underground had been a time of idealistic self-sacrifice. She had no time for selfish love then, no energy for useless dreams, no desire for caresses by enemy hands. She had forgotten Professor Minh. Now she remembered him. The speckled baby blue glasses brought back memories of a doting lover, always eager to please. Mai Ly assumed him to be balding now. Or with white hair. He would be older, yet still virile. His arms would still be bulging with muscles. The man she saw on the street looked frail. His distorted face hardly resembled her old lover. Mai Ly searched the crowd for a familiar pair of glasses. He was no longer there. She shrugged seeing nothing worthy of nostalgia. She convinced herself an imagination finally let loose had played tricks on her. Had she noticed a pair of baby blue glasses crushed under her comrade's tank, she might've let out a mournful howl. Fortunately, she could not picture such a scenario. Muzzled for so long, her fantasy no longer grew legs.

Curiosity or Love?

SQUATTING ON THE helicopter floor, Mai felt tiny feet crawling on her back. A centipede perhaps. Maybe a caterpillar. Or a bedbug? Such a bothersome itch. She wished she could scratch it. If only she could push other people's arms, chests and legs away. If only she could carve out a space for herself. Then she'd know if that itch belonged to her. Squished against half a dozen people, it was impossible to differentiate her unease from that of others.

The overcrowded helicopter smelled of sweat. The odour reminded Mai of her father. She hated his perverted, hypocritical and domineering ways. Even so, he was still her father. She should've forgiven him his weakness on their last day together. Should've shown him some form of warmth, held his hands, talked gently to him. Instead, she'd left their house without a goodbye, without a care for his drooling face, for his immobilized legs. Now it was too late to change destiny.

Whimpers from a nearby child troubled Mai. It brought back memories of a bloodstained mattress. A dark baby on her abdomen. Its tearless cries. Her palms pushing it away. Its freefall off the bed. Its legs caught in mid-air by the midwife. Its convulsing body once again placed on her stomach. No, get it out of here, she'd repeated. Head in hands, Mai sobbed remembering those words of rejection.

Mai had never visited her baby. Had never mentioned its existence to friends. Had never reminded her parents of those shameful days. Still, she could not forget it. Alone at night, her thoughts often turned to the kid. How much does it weigh now? Can it walk? Can it talk? What was its first word? What does it like to eat? Curiosity kept her awake till early morning. Curiosity was a form of love, wasn't it?

Somewhere inside the helicopter, a baby screamed. Its ear-piercing cry overpowered all other noises. Then it went quiet. That sudden silence spooked Mai. The lamentation of a young child, its abrupt descent into muteness reminded her of something she'd seen on live television recently. Operation Babylift? Yes.

Operation Babylift. Mai liked those fancy words. So American. What a perfect name for a large-scale evacuation of kids. An honourable effort at parachuting Vietnamese orphans into American homes. An admirable attempt to repatriate unwanted children of American GIs. Mai had watched those babies being brought onboard airplanes. Seeing neatly dressed stewardesses with their blonde hair in a bun excited her. She swore she could smell America. A mixture of pine fragrance and air conditioning, it must be it. Yes, the smell of coolness. That was America to Mai. The more she watched, the more she wanted to hop on those big planes. To go to

America too. She tried looking for her brown baby on television. Then she shook her head. She'd forgotten what it looked like.

Operation Babylift. It was also a tragic plane crash that had killed half those onboard. Images of silent infants scattered on burned grass so distressed Mai, she cried. She pictured them screaming a minute before. A scream of protest against Destiny. Only to be followed by a quiet surrender to bad luck. Those tiny lifeless bodies also horrified Mai's mother. She ran to the kitchen. There she lit two incense sticks. Eyeing a hazy sky, she mumbled a prayer before bowing three times. Mai too, looked upward. She too prayed for a dark child that came out of her. Without exchanging a single word, the women had understood each other's skyward glances. They were two mothers imploring God to spare an unwanted kid.

A Spook for a Spook

FROM HER WINDOW, Mai saw rows of cars still in gridlock. She saw abandoned vehicles with headlights still on, still plugging streets, still blocking other people's hope. These roadblocks to freedom. She had contributed to them. Saigon's fear and panic. Her American lovers had a hand in shaping them. Which torture method did they use on the communists to foment so much hate? Which propaganda message did they drum into their South Vietnamese ally to create such mass hysteria? Mai sighed.

"You came back for me?" Mai shouted over other people's talk. She still could not digest her life's drastic changes. Less than 72 hours ago, she was still watching television with her parents. The news was bad. One town after another had fallen into communist hands. Professor Minh had smashed his glass full of rice wine against a wall. "Cowardly soldiers! Corrupted generals! That's us!" he'd raged before sinking into his armchair, feet stomping. Three days later she was on a helicopter fleeing her tyrannical father, fleeing a war that was so much a part of her life, fleeing a country that had shaped her first thoughts and moulded her earliest beliefs.

"No. I didn't come back for you, Mai. Sorry!" The

Bird Man laughed, his loud voice distorted by the heli-copter engines. "California in '73 was a huge disappoint-ment. Couldn't talk to my parents. They thought I'd be happy being back with no limbs missing. They don't understand the war may be over for us, it wasn't over for you guys. Six months home was enough. I wanted to be back here. Got a job and bought myself a ticket for Saigon. Yeah. For a while, I hung around our embassy and took Vietnamese lessons."

"Oh! You speak Viet now? *Anh nói tiếng Việt với em nào!*" Mai said teasingly. The Bird Man's badly pro-nounced Vietnamese surprised her. She raised her eye-brows. In all their time together, he'd never bothered to learn a few expressions of love and here he was, speaking to her in her language. With his atonal voice flattening out every word, it wasn't easy following his conversation. Mai thought she heard: "working at American embassy, spying on communist spies …" Then again, she couldn't be sure of the exact meaning of his sentence. Full of curiosity, Mai exclaimed, "What? You CIA?"

The American grimaced at Mai's outburst. He man-aged to quiet her down with a thick index in front of his mouth. "Shhh! Did I say those words? No. So don't start rumours, Mai! Anyway, I was a just small fish in a big pond …" This veiled admission got Mai panting. Like a dog waiting for a treat, her tongue stumbled out of her open mouth. She was desperate for diversions. Anything to take her mind off her father still at home, her mother still refusing to look at them, her future as unsure as next week's weather prediction. She wanted those fish stories—he would tell her fishy tales. He pondered a long moment before deciding on the White Christmas story. It was a recent story. It was a simple story. It was a true story. "You remember hearing 'White Christmas' playing all afternoon on the radio a few days ago? Why 'White Christmas' in April? Well, that was a code for us to get out. It was to tell us the communists are very near. I thought of you. I wanted to save you. Yes, there are many other secret codes. And no, I can't tell you any more. Sorry, Mai!" To put an end to their conversation, the Bird Man stretched his neck. He moved someone's shoulder out of his way. He licked his sandpaper lips before planting a light kiss on Mai's cheeks. Appeased, he inhaled her lemon and cinnamon fragrance.

PART 6:
THE ORPHANAGE, THE COMRADES, THE RESTAURANT AND THE REDHEAD

A Plastic Bag on the Doorknob

THEY THOUGHT I had forgotten. No, I remember everything. What should I tell them? That for years, you bound my body in a blanket? That you placed me in two plastic bags and hung me on a doorknob while you were gone? That I was fed diluted snake wine to keep me happily drowsy? Nobody would believe me. Even doubled, those plastic bags would surely rip, sending me to the floor, they'd tell themselves. My cries would then alert the other nuns, they'd convince each other. How wrong they were! I wasn't always a big fidgety kid. My branch limbs and twig fingers weighed less than those cushions on your bed. Like a hand towel on your bathroom rack, my useless legs never moved, never caused trouble. You thought I was a mindless infant. In fact, I was already wiser than my years on earth.

Waking me each morning with a nudge of your left elbow. Rolling me onto the cold floor to change my cloth diaper. Washing my face with a wet towel. You performed all those tasks wordlessly. To my whimpering, you'd mutter, "Stop fretting! I'm reheating your rice porridge and snake wine now. Be thankful! Kids like you would be dead out there ..." You always said the same thing. Those were your favourite words day and night. With a small spoon, you'd feed me the only meal I knew. Then you'd hang me on your bathroom doorknob. Before leaving, you'd pull the curtain, allowing for a bit of light. You'd caress my head and tell me not to cry.

Our evening rituals never changed. You switched on your television the minute you returned to our room. At low volume, it kept me company while disturbing no one. Spoon-feeding me my rice porridge, you sometimes lost patience. "Open your mouth, eat!" you said whenever I took too long to swallow. My meal finished, you washed your hands, fixed your tunic and waited for the usual knock on the door. "Prayer time, Mother Superior." This was a signal for you to leave me once more.

Television voices kept me company in your absence. Television lights turned our dark room into shades of grey. I followed those talking images every day. They spoke to me in ways you never did. Eager, I watched and learned. Yes, I learned so much.

Back in our room, you wasted no time taking me down from your doorknob. My clothes off, you brought me to the sink for a quick wash. "Look at your horrible curly hair all tangled again," you grumbled. You didn't bother brushing my curls. You only wanted to point out their ugliness. I turned away from the bathroom mirror. I hated seeing my reflection there. I hated looking so different from you.

Your rough scrubbing of my chest hurt me. I let out a cry that you never bothered acknowledging. The washing done, you placed me on a table, propped up by two pillows. I loved these moments. I loved seeing our room from this height. I loved watching you brush your hair and meeting your eyes as you turned to check on me from time to time. I loved those television programs we watched together while others slept. "God, please forgive me for watching American shows!" you always said before turning to that black and white image box. It did not take long before you fell asleep, your head lurching forward, your shoulders leaning against mine.

I remember you rushing into our room one day. In your panic, you didn't bother closing the door. Loud footsteps and snapping voices came clear to me. "Unannounced District evaluation! Hide all the American kids!" someone shouted. "Oh, let the communists take them all away! I'm tired of these foreign devils!" someone else screamed. I heard running feet, slamming doors, cries of babies suddenly woken up. Beyond those sounds of alarm, I also heard children's laughter and singing voices. I knew then that I was not alone in this place, that others played while I hung on a doorknob.

Sweat drenched, you pushed our mattress against a wall. Hands quivering, you removed a loose ceramic tile from the floor. There, in a dark hole, you placed me. "Be quiet!" you said. Before I could react, you replaced the tile and pulled our mattress back to its place. I must have fainted or fallen asleep for when I awoke, I found myself back in my usual place, snuggled in two grocery bags, hung on your bathroom doorknob.

I'd never heard the word "half-breed" till I saw it discussed on television. Do you remember us watching it together? You watched intently that evening. I couldn't decide what shocked me more—seeing light-haired kids with slanted eyes or witnessing tears streaming down your cheeks. "Oh, should've let the Americans take him away that day. Don't know why I kept him! Giving myself so much trouble!" you mumbled to yourself. My sneeze put an end to your complaint. You turned to look at me with pouted lips. Your right hand reached out to touch my hair. Right away it retreated as if it had changed its mind. You were full of mysteries. Our evening was interrupted by an unexpected knock on the door. "What is it?" you muttered with irritation. "Excuse me, Mother Superior. Sister Tam is sick! Please check on her," a faint voice said.

The rest of that night alone, I so missed your breath on my back, your arms around me.

Black Devil

I **TOOK ON** weight despite my meagre diet. Slowly, ever so slowly I outgrew my plastic bags. Too heavy for the doorknob, I was allowed to wiggle on your bamboo mat. A cockroach on its back, that was me. Kicking my legs in the air felt good. Bringing my hands to my mouth was harder. I kept missing my mark. I kept hitting my nose instead. Rolling over was the most difficult task. I succeeded only after many trials. Not used to carrying weight, my arms and legs collapsed under my body. My forehead hit the ground on my first attempts at movement. Determined, I continued. By the second day, I managed to take a few steps before knocking over your lamp. The broken floor lamp angered you. "What now? What did you do?" you snapped. If I'd been able to talk, I'd have explained my fear of being left alone. And wondered if you'd care.

Weeks of falling taught me what I needed to know. Accumulated bruises finally made me smarter. Moving my arms, one at a time, before dragging my knees— those were the proper steps to take. As I crawled on all fours, I sniffed at every scent in our room. Obsessively I searched for your familiar odour. When the camphor of your shoes billowed out from a closet, I let out a cry. I had finally found you.

One day you brought me outside. I gaped at colourful flower beds shaded by blooming trees. Everything looked so much brighter than what I saw on television. Sunrays bothered my eyes. I had to blink repeatedly before I could see properly. A group of big kids in torn clothes pushed each other in one corner. In another corner, a nun sat reading her book on a bench. Smaller kids played around her. You never sensed my hesitation. You only egged me on. "Go play with them," you ordered. I crawled back behind a rose bush. "Don't worry. Go! Go play! I'm going for my nap now. Will check on you later." Did you know I never played? Hidden behind a rose bush, I watched kids jump rope and throw balls. My loud sneeze put an end to their games. They stared at me for a long time before someone cried, "Let's get him!" In groups of two or three, they circled me, pebbles in hand. As hard as I tried, I could never outdo them. They stood upright while I stooped on all fours. While I crawled turtle-like, they skipped ahead of me, blocking my way in every direction. "Black Devil! Black Devil! Come and get us!" they shouted tauntingly. Hands circling above their heads, eyes squinting, they aimed for me. The sounds of stones banging against gravel terrified me. Even if most had missed their target, some rocks did land on my arms. I screamed in pain and frustration seeing my shirtsleeves full of dirt marks. I dragged my bloodied knees across pebbles, hoping to find refuge under the nun's bench.

"Help me!" thundered in my head yet no words came out of my mouth. You hadn't taught me to speak.

"You kids be quiet and leave the Black One alone!" the nun scolded. She finally looked up from her book.

"But he's a black devil, Sister!"

"Shhh, I said! No more nonsense! Mother Superior is napping. Continue screaming and she'll whack you all when she gets up!" Seeing my scraped knees, she grunted. "Put some grass on it. It'll stop the bleeding." I did exactly what I was told. I applied grass to my knees that whole afternoon. I understood then your reason for hiding me in your room. You wanted to protect me.

"Learn to stand up and walk normally! I'm tired of carrying you around like a baby. You're four years old now!" you shouted at me that evening. Your sharp tone of voice scared me. Your words alarmed me. If you wouldn't carry me, who would? If you were tired of me, how would I get my porridge and snake wine? I could only answer you with my downcast eyes.

A week later, you brought me to a chubby-cheeked nun reading her newspaper in a small stuffy room. "Sister Tam, here's your new challenge. Teach this boy to walk and talk. He's already four. Still can't run, still can't utter a word. May God be with you!" Your loud voice surprised Sister Tam. "Of course, Mother Superior," she replied. She turned to check on my wild un-brushed hair. Cautiously, she examined the rest of my body. It was as if she couldn't decide on her emotions. Disgust or fear? Perhaps both. Perhaps she saw in my useless, flailing limbs the tentacles of a half-octopus. Perhaps she saw in my dark skin, the unwanted son of the Devil himself. She hesitated a long moment before taking my hand. Then she held me up and wrapped me under her white shawl. I liked the smell coming from her breath. It reminded me of the bananas you used to eat for lunch.

Comrade Mai Ly

MAI LY HATED the weekly neighbourhood meetings. She hated seeing people cowering in her presence. Even if nobody forced them, older men kowtowed before her. She found the reversal of fortune unsettling. Their new socialist society was supposed to be one of equality. Not one where young communists could elicit so much fear in the population. This was not the utopia she'd hoped for. It was not what she'd imagined when she wrote all those socialist tracts years ago. Time and again she tried repeating the same message, "I'm not here to send you to re-education camps!" Only downcast eyes greeted her outburst. Nobody believed her words.

Mai Ly took her usual seat behind a rickety wooden desk next to a blackboard. She looked anxiously at the old ceiling fan circling unsteadily above her head. One of these days, it would fall, she was sure of that. It was dusk, yet the heat had not abated one bit. Mosquitoes still buzzed, competing with flies for air space. A wrinkled kerchief in hand, Mai Ly dabbed at her sweaty forehead. She made signs for people to enter. Like shackled prisoners being led to the courtroom, tired-looking men and women slowly filed in, their feet shuffling as if held back by an insurmountable languor. No one dared to look Mai Ly in the eyes. Silently they went to their seat.

"Come in and sit down!" Mai Ly shouted to those still standing outside.

"Hey, Big Brother over there, can't you give your chair to Old Aunty next to you? Can't you see she's limping? There are not enough chairs for everybody!" Mai Ly pointed to a tall, bearded man. She opened her notebook filled with blurry numbers and blinked for a few seconds before focusing on her task.

"24?" Mai Ly called.

"Yes," someone answered.

"30?"

"Yes."

"36?"

"Yes."

"43?"

"Yes."

"51?"

"Yes."

"54?"

"54?"

"54 Tu Xuong Street is not here today? Can someone drop by 54 Tu Xuong Street and tell them to come next week? 54 already missed a meeting last week. I don't want them to miss more meetings." A dozen numbers later, Mai Ly looked wearily up from her notebook. On the blackboard, she scribbled three numbers on the right column and one number on the left.

"24, 30 and 36, your street cleaning is very good

this week! Congratulations. Keep up the good work. Please stand up so everyone can see you."

A round of applause was heard as three women stood up.

"All right, that's enough applause. Now stand up 51. 51, I have reports that you were wasting water to clean your bicycle. Water is precious! Do not waste it. Capitalist ideas need to be cleaned out of your mind. Bicycles do not need to be cleaned. The rain will take care of it!" As 51 bowed her head, loud sneering sounds rose from the back.

"Be quiet in the back! There is no need to sneer at 51. She has learned her lesson tonight. Now any questions? Yes, over there, What's your number, Comrade?"

"66. I'm at 66 Tu Xuong Street."

"How many people at 66?" Mai Ly asked without real interest. She was still thinking about the old ceiling fan falling one day.

"We are 15 people, Comrade Mai Ly. Me and my four children plus two other families. Thanks to the Party, we all have a roof over our heads."

"Gratitude to the Party is a good sign. Where are the other two families?"

"They can't come to the meeting tonight, Comrade. Their children are sick. I am representing them, Comrade."

"So what do you want to know, Comrade 66?" Mai Ly asked impatiently.

"There are fewer vegetables at Ben Thanh Market this week. I waited hours in line yesterday. When my turn came, there were only onions left to buy. How can I cook with only onions?"

"The weather was bad this season. Crops are not as good. The Party cannot control Nature! We must all learn to sacrifice for the nation. Is anyone starving? No? Then stop complaining! Before the revolution, you were probably living on the streets or in the slum. Now you are in a fancy area of town. The Party provided you that house. You should not ask for more."

"I hear we're sending soldiers to Cambodia. Is that why there's less food in the market? I thought the war was over, why are we still fighting?" Comrade 66 said, undaunted by Mai Ly's forceful tone.

"What does war with Cambodia have to do with food in the market? There's no relation! Don't get counter-revolutionary ideas, Comrade. The American War is over, yes. And yes, we are sending soldiers to Cambodia. That crazy Pol Pot is murdering his own people. Did you know millions of Cambodians are dead because of him? He'll kill anyone wearing glasses. Are we crazy like that here? No! Does the Vietnamese Communist Party treat you like that? No! That Cambodian Pol Pot is no longer a true socialist. He has become an enemy of the people. We must liberate our Cambodian brothers and sisters. Get those counter-revolutionary ideas out of your head. Any other comments, Comrade? No? Good! Now sit down."

Accusations of counter-revolutionary ideas automatically shut people up. Counter- Revolutionary—there was something sinister about that term. People always shuddered hearing it. Mai Ly knew the exact moment in a meeting to bring up those dreadful words. She was good at psychological crowd control. Half-heartedly, she put a little X next to number 66. Checking her notebook, Mai Ly was relieved to see only three other Xs. Four families will lose their food ration cards next month. It wasn't socialism at its best ... but she had a job to do.

Before Mai Ly could end the meeting, another woman raised her hand. She stood up and glared at a man next to her. When she complained about a neighbour sexually touching her young daughter, three nursing mothers screamed "Child Molester!" This outburst turned the class upside down. A frenzied shouting match followed. Fingers pointed here and there. Tears flowed. Heads shook in denial. "Where did he touch the child?" an older man asked. "His hands should be cut off!" someone said. "His penis too! Cut it off!" a third woman suggested. Red-faced, Mai Ly slammed her fist. "We're here to talk street cleaning, not sex! Quiet now!" Even with that order, the back and forth persisted. "Child molester" continued its bounce around the room. From rage to shame, from confusion to guilt—it left no one indifferent.

"Discourse on sex is counter-revolutionary!" Mai Ly finally cried. With that, the class quieted down.

Reclaiming her Lost Youth

THE DREADFUL WEEKLY meeting exhausted Mai Ly. "Child Molester" unsettled her. She'd never heard those words before. Never considered their implications. Never saw herself a victim of one. Now she wondered. No, impossible, she whispered. Hastily, she banished Child Molester from her thoughts. A mimosa branch fell on her flip-flop. She kicked it away before crossing the crowded avenue.

Meandering along tree-lined Tu Xuong Street helped clear her mind. Its graceful French colonial villas soothed her. Their wrought iron gates, circular driveways, grand staircases leading to huge wooden doors impressed her. Mai Ly tried imagining previous owners in their pastel-coloured houses. She felt neither jealousy nor contempt. Only curiosity pushed her to peek into their open bay windows. She wanted to check the colour of their sofa, the size of their dining table.

At a busy intersection, Mai Ly stopped to wait for her light. There she noticed a newly boarded-up house. Empty houses meant one of two things: their occupants had been sent to re-education camps or had escaped by boat. Mai Ly hated both possibilities. She marched up to the house. She gasped when she saw number 54. 54! The 54 that didn't show up at her meeting this evening. She wondered if they'd ended up in re-education camps. Under a streetlamp, she checked her notebook for negative reports against number 54. There were none. Always good street cleaning these past two years. Relieved, Mai Ly put her notebook away. No, she hadn't sent number 54 to whatever fate they'd met.

Dark, silent houses. Homes boarded up. There seemed to be more and more of them every month. Families escaping Vietnam by boats, mothers risking the open sea with their babies in arms. It was a half-veiled secret nobody dared to address. These empty houses were an insult to Mai Ly's beliefs. Free of American and French aggressors, Vietnam was finally independent. People should not be leaving. They should not dream of a different freedom. There should not be Boat People lining up in front of America's doors. Images of emaciated hands pleading for bottles of water and parched lips mouthing words of self-pity disturbed Mai Ly. She did not fight a war to see her own people escaping through a back door.

The abandoned homes reminded Mai Ly of her empty life—a void left by departed friends. So many comrades had died during the war. So many others had boarded boats in search of a paradise called America. They had left her behind. Fifteen or twenty, she had lost track of their number.

Of all her former friends, Mai Ly remembered Mai most clearly. Colourful, she stood out from the nameless comrades. Yes, Professor Minh's daughter was full of life. Her miniskirts, French pastries in Givral Café, fancy ice cream at a private sports club, cool "Hey there" expressions picked up from American GIs—Mai Ly had once revelled in them. Nostalgic, she yearned to hear again stories of a blond man with a tattooed bird and a black man with a ruler. She smiled thinking of that ruler.

On a whim, Mai Ly changed her bus route. Instead of going home, she headed for Professor Minh's house. Obeying her father, she'd cut ties with him years ago. She'd stopped going to his classes. She'd avoided his neighbourhood. She'd repressed all memories of a baby blue room full of knick-knacks. She'd found passion in that place. Or was it damnation? Losing her innocence to a child molester was a curse she had to carry.

Mai Ly expected her lover's house to be empty. Professor Minh and his family would surely be in America by now. From afar the house looked unchanged. Same blue and tangerine-coloured walls. Same mango trees. Same hibiscus shrub. No traces of abandonment. Fried garlic wafting through a window startled her. A flickering light upstairs gave her palpitations. Through a half-open door, she could see moving shadows. Thoughts of seeing her lover again emboldened Mai Ly's steps. Would she embrace him or arrest him? It wasn't an easy decision.

Sixteen was such a confusing age. Mai Ly had craved both lollipops and manly hands. Professor Minh should've guided her out of that labyrinth. Instead, he'd dragged her deeper into a maze. Her un-ripeness had been his comfort food, her tightness inspirations for his vulgar poetry. Fooled by a man thrice her age, she wished she could go back and change destiny. Yes, perhaps she'd arrest him. Taking a deep breath, Mai Ly rang the doorbell.

"Who is it?" an older female asked, a toothpick hanging from her mouth.

"Excuse me, Aunty. My name is Mai Ly. It used to be Mai." Mai Ly imagined the woman facing her to be Professor Minh's wife. Despite numerous afternoons spent in his blue room, she'd never caught glimpses of a spying shadow, never heard cries of a jealous voice, never found hidden photos of a betrayed spouse.

"I don't know any Mai. Or Mai Ly. What do you want?" Not bothering to look at Mai Ly, the woman continued picking her teeth. Successfully dislodging a piece of green onion, she placed the used toothpick in her pocket. She let out a long "Ahhh."

"I am sorry to bother you, Aunty. I am looking for my friend Tran Cuc Mai."

"I told you I don't know any Mai!"

"Then why are you living in their house, Comrade?"

'Whose house?"

"Professor Minh's. Tran Van Minh to be precise. This is his house."

"Are you checking up on me? Where is your badge? Oh my God! This is going too far!" In a rage, she broke her toothpick in half.

"Here it is, Comrade," Mai Ly said in her official voice. "Now show me your papers! Since when are you here? This house belonged to Professor Tran Van Minh."

"Bao! Bao! Come down! There's someone here asking for our papers! These young kids are too much!"

Ashen-faced, the woman went inside to pour herself a glass of water.

"What is it?" a short, duck-like man descending the staircase asked. His peculiar walk reminded Mai Ly of someone. Vague memories of a foul-smelling bathroom came to her mind. She brushed that image off since it made no sense.

The Duck Man immediately recognized Mai Ly. He understood perfectly her presence in his house. Mai Ly, the beer seller's daughter, the professor's lover, the student turned communist spy. Her beautiful penmanship on all those secret reports. Here she was, a disillusioned idealist looking for her old lover, reclaiming her lost youth. She wanted to hear stories. He would tell her stories.

Writing Is Not Enough

THE DUCK MAN'S stories shook Mai Ly. She cringed. They were more horror tales than recollections of a lingering past. There was no nostalgia, no memory of sweetness to neutralize the bitterness of his words. Smoke from his hand-rolled cigarette further added to Mai Ly's discomfort. Her eyes stung, turned red. Still, she couldn't cry.

Her father's death, Mai Ly had never known how or when. He'd just left one early morning as she lay in bed. "I'm going on a mission today, see you later" was all he'd whispered in her still-sleepy ears that day. The first few weeks after Hung's departure, she'd wait patiently for his return. She'd spend her nights writing socialist slogans while praying for his safety. She'd drag Hung's beer stand to its usual place in front of the post office. She'd lower her price for regular clients. She'd shout "Beer, Mister?" from across the street, her fingers wagging the V sign. She'd wink at young men, hoping to make a sale. She'd manage to keep herself alive while waiting for her father's return.

Hung's prolonged absence confirmed Mai Ly's fear. By the second month, she understood her new fate as an orphan. For help, she turned to those women dealing in anti-government slogans. Grandmothers at night and communist sympathizers in the afternoon. They all shrugged their shoulders. "Who are you? Go away," they said to Mai Ly's pleading. Distressed by such blatant rejection, she lost sleep. Her insomnia made her listless. Her socialist tracts became unreadable. Full of spelling mistakes and sloppily written, they were only good for wrapping fish at the markets.

Unbeknown to Mai Ly, word did get around. To her surprise, she found a basket of bananas and oranges in her room one day. Another basket magically appeared a few weeks later. This time, there was money hidden underneath. The food baskets lifted Mai Ly's spirits. They gave her hope of seeing her father again. After all, only her father had a key to their place. Only her father knew of her favourite fruits: orange and banana. Perhaps Hung was not dead. Perhaps he was only hiding.

Mai Ly screamed when the tenth basket came with a handgun hidden under eight oranges. Her piercing cry woke a neighbour from his nap. "Sorry, sorry to disturb you, no problems here," she said in a cracking voice. That dark, silent object of death scared her. It could only mean one thing: Hung was indeed deceased. It was now her turn to join the guerrilla fighters. Writing socialist propaganda was all that Hung had wanted from his daughter. He'd forbidden her from taking up arms. "Too dangerous," he'd warned that day. But writing slo-gans was not enough for the Cause. They wanted her to kill and to shed blood too. Tenth basket and eight oran-ges. They wanted her in by the tenth of August.

Never Steal from the Dead

THE FIRST THING the Duck Man said caught Mai Ly off guard. "Stop calling me Comrade. I'm old enough to be your father! Call me Uncle." A cigarette in his mouth, he made a show of inhaling. Slowly, deeply, he took his time breathing in the bitter smoke. Between puffs of cigarette, he turned his attention to two lines of mosquito bites along his legs. One by one he scratched them while Mai Ly waited in silence.

To test Mai Ly's patience further, he ambled to his fridge for two bottles of beer. His duck feet made plopping sounds against the ceramic floor. He gave Mai Ly an indifferent nod when she shook her head. "Thank you, Uncle, no beer for me." Leisurely, he checked for a can of soda. "No soda. You want mineral water?" he asked. He threw her a bottle of water and sat down. Across a table from Mai Ly, he started his tale by blowing smoke into her eyes. He wanted her to close them. To hide those bulging orbits that so bothered him. Opened eyes. He'd seen too many during the war. Glassy and unreactive. He was forced to close dozens of them before piling on the earth. He coughed at this memory. Mai Ly reacted by pressing cold bottled water against her temples. She needed it to cool her nerves, to prepare herself for the story she was about to hear.

You want to know how your father died? Simple. He died in the jungle. So many of us died fighting there. But his story is different ... I don't have an exact date. Unfortunately, there wasn't time for an official burial in the jungle. There's no need for it. The leaves, tree roots, snakes, ants, they took care of it. I think he died on his second week out there. He was scavenging for food. Searching an American corpse for something to eat. You know how those Americans always carried lots of food with them. Enough for a picnic! Candies, chocolates, nuts, crackers and so much more. Yes, they were well-fed while we starved. Our ration of rice and salt left us obsessing about food day and night. In his frenzied search for something to eat, your father accidentally detonated a dead GI's grenade. We found him lying on top of a disintegrating GI. He'd killed himself with the enemy's weapon. Or maybe someone else threw a grenade that killed him. I don't remember those details. Anyway, your father was almost unrecognizable ... his bloodied nose-less face, his hands blown off. It wasn't a nice sight. We found the hands four metres away. Left hand hanging from a tree branch with a watch still ticking, the other in a ditch. The one in the ditch was clutching a package of gum. That was all he could find to eat. A package of sugarless American gum!

Learn from your father's mistake: don't steal from the dead. They will never forgive you, will never let you sleep in peace. Your father didn't die a hero in battle. Trying to take a dead enemy's food. What a shameful, cowardly death! But we have forgiven him. By the way, we found a partially burned-out photo of you in his pant pocket. I've meant to give it to you years ago. Sorry, I never found time to do it. We sold his watch on the black market to buy food for our comrades. So yes, he was useful to our revolution after all. I've always wondered where that watch came from. Was it another robbery? Stealing from another American corpse? Or was it a gift from one of his American clients at his beer stand? I'll never know. Anyway, it doesn't matter now. My Other Half, can you please bring me that capitalist photo. It's on my desk. Thank you.

Catinat Boulevard. Hung's old beer stand. The photo showed everything. Mai Ly could even see her father's hand making a V sign in the background. It was the hand that had spoon-fed her after her mother's death. The hand that had picked lice out of her tangled hair at night. The hand that had opened beer bottles all day on the scorching sidewalks of a Saigon still under the illusion of a future victory. All his life, her father had tried to be handy. With his bare hands, he had survived poverty, widowhood, war. The hand that lay in a ditch, clutching a piece of gum, had finally betrayed him. Yes, don't steal from the dead.

Seeing her younger self brought a hesitant smile to Mai Ly's thin lips. It was the first and only time she'd posed for a camera. To her friend Mai's order, she'd fixed her hair and straightened her shoulders. She'd giggled the whole time. "Don't move, Girls! No, stop moving, you two!" The Bird Man had scolded them before clicking on his special machine. A Polaroid, Mai Ly suddenly remembered its name. A Polaroid with instant pictures to snap shots of Saigon life. Perhaps it was also to spy on its people.

Mai Ly knew she couldn't hold back much longer. She didn't need much prodding for her tears to start rolling. Unabashedly, in front of a top communist spy, she cried for her innocence, now lost. And she cried for the loss of a father she had never understood.

Mai Ly's distress left no mark on the Duck Man. He looked at her with disinterest. Out of his mouth came no words of sympathy. Might as well go all out, tell the girl everything and get it over with, he reasoned to himself. He coughed for a few seconds before clearing his throat.

One More Dead. So What?

*B*Y THE WAY, *I know all about you and Professor Minh. Yes, yes! No need to blush. We all knew your stinky secret. Your professor died on the first day of liberation. It was an accident. The street was full of people out to welcome us. Your professor tripped. Or someone accidentally pushed him. He landed in the path of a moving tank. He couldn't get up, couldn't save himself. In the tumult, nobody noticed his crushed body. I saw everything from another tank. Before dying, he tried to get close to you. He wasn't sure it was you sitting up there. He squinted his eyes to see better. One side of his body was not working well. I think it was his left arm. It looked paralyzed. He tried wiping his glasses with his right shirtsleeve. It was a very clumsy move. They almost fell off. I immediately recognized those peculiar baby blue frames of his. He waved to you. Too bad you didn't notice. One more dead. So what? Hundred of thousands of others have died during this war ... What's one more? Anyway, there is no place for someone like him in the new Vietnam. You know that. That worm did nothing to earn respect. His daughter—your old friend Mai, the tall one—remember her? Your father and I, we'd been watching her for years. Indiscriminately, that traitor slept with*

American GIs. She wasn't some poor peasant girl doing it to feed her family. No. It was all for fun. She survived the war when she should have died.

Spying on American soldiers and writing all those secret notes. You did your part for the nation. Your handwriting was beautiful. I still remember it. What did Mai do during those times? Cavorted with our enemy for some cheap thrill. She was scum. Mai and Mai Ly. So different! I wonder how you two stayed friends. That whore had a kid out of wedlock. Did you know? No? Well, guess what? The kid is half-black. Abandoned in an orphanage. Cholon orphanage. Mai left for America with a GI. The Bird Man, we used to call him. That guy was an American devil. A spy. CIA. He stalked all of us. So I had to keep an eye on him. Um ... what else can I tell you? I know you still have lots of questions boiling in your mind. You're dying to know why am I staying at Professor Minh's house. You are wondering what right have I to take over his home. I'll tell you this much: I'm the eyes and ears of the Party. The Party needs me. That should answer all your questions. I hear you're doing a decent job with your weekly meetings. Keep it up! And by the way, number 54 Tu Xuong Street, the whole bunch of them, are in jail. We caught them trying to board a boat last week. Their house is empty now but will be taken over by the Party soon. We need more space for our committee reunions. Now good evening, Girl. My supper is waiting for me.

The American Dream

THE BIRD MAN'S beer breath gave Mai's mother stomach gas. He got Mai pregnant, he should've married her, she daily fumed. His vulgar tattoo, his unpolished talk, his badly pronounced Vietnamese bothered her. He represented everything she wished to leave behind: the war, Mai's illicit affair, her illegitimate kid.

The helicopter flight out of Saigon was a confused blur in the older woman's mind. Of her first month in California, she remembered only the tears. They'd burned her eyes and itched her cheeks. Trickling down her blouse, they'd left goosebumps on her chest, wrinkles in her heart. These days, her eyes were as dry as a burned pot of tea. No more water. No more crying. She'd cried enough to last a couple of reincarnated lives.

Memories of her first welcome-to-America meal still gave Mai's mother cold sweat. In a noisy church basement smelling of garlic and onions, she'd shuddered at the sight of roasted chickens. Killing an animal amounted to annihilating a soul, she'd been taught. How to explain this belief to others? It was not possible. Hugged by strangers, she'd felt awkward. Unable to reciprocate their gestures, her hands had stayed in her pant pockets the whole time. In front of well-dressed, nice-smelling ladies, she felt dirty in her brown trousers and spotted beige blouse. Listening to their talk, she could only smile. She nodded humbly, pretending to understand all. Her rudimentary English allowed her to grasp only simple words. "Vietnam …", "Vietnam …", "Vietnam …" That American matrons knew more about her country than she did made her blush with shame.

Through church connections, a rent-free room with hand-me-down furniture welcomed Mai and her mother to California. Father McMillen, The Bird Man's uncle, had arranged everything. Well connected in his community, well respected at church, he could easily turn water into wine. In her American kitchen, Mai's mother bowed gratefully as she admired an electric can opener. She'd never had this contraption in Saigon. The first can she tried opening splashed all over her counter. Then it rolled on the floor, spreading its contents of noodle and chicken bits on her feet. She screamed when she realized those small beige squares actually came from a chicken.

When Mai landed a job in a Chinese restaurant, her mother bowed even lower. As a favour to Father McMillen, the restaurant owner had hired Mai even if she spoke no Cantonese. He understood he gotta give some to get some. Catholics or Buddhists, it all amounted to the same thing.

Mai hated her job. She knew nothing about taking multiple orders, serving hot soup without spilling or giving back the right change. After two weeks of training, she was left to manage by herself. Mai tried her best to serve each client. She only received frowns in return.

"Miss, we ordered one hour ago!" "Waitress! You got our order mixed up!" "There's a dead ant in my hot and sour soup!" "Speak no Chinese? No English? What you speak?!" Tongue-tied, Mai would respond with a "Sorry!" and the V-for-victory sign. She did not forget what Hung had said about that V sign: Americans love winning.

To clients' irritation, Mai would hop from one table to another, her right hand in a permanent V sign. "Victory for you! You win, I lose," she'd wanted to say. Sadly, some twisted minds would interpret things differently. If one erect finger means "fuck you," two such fingers must mean "fuck you twice over," they'd conclude with indignation. They'd respond by writing, "Fuck you too!" on paper napkins before walking out, their food untouched, their bills unpaid.

Continuously mixing up her orders got Mai fired one spring afternoon. Not understanding the word fired, she shook her head. "I caused no fire," she said. The owner's bland look perplexed her. "I no smoke," she insisted. Confused, she sat hunched on a toilet seat, the washroom door wide open. She picked absent-mindedly at a ripe pimple on her chin. Only when pus and blood oozed on her fingers did she stop squishing. Moping around, she annoyed the cook, who nevertheless offered her a glass of soya milk out of pity. Mai stayed at the restaurant past her shift. She stayed till the owner kicked her out at night. "Go, go home!" he said as he handed her a Styrofoam container full of leftover chow mein. Flicking out his cigarette, he muttered: "Good riddance!"

Mai's empty bank account worried Father McMillen. Her downcast eyes pierced his conscience. He wasted no time digging around. Stella and Joe. Italians. Devout Catholics. Regulars at his church. Restaurant owners. Washing dishes. Surely Mai could do this, Father McMillen told himself. He genuinely wanted to see a success story.

"Don't worry about breaking these dishes, they're all plastic," Mai's co-workers had said on her first day. Plastic or not, she'd wash them all with reverence. She never threw them in the sink. She never banged them against each other. Her respectful handling of their dishes pleased the owners. Stella called her "Our Chinese dish-washer and her Ming porcelain." Joe gave her two all-dressed pizzas each evening.

Less stressed, Mai came home with shoulders less slouched. She'd even smile occasionally. Instead of an-swering her mother's enquiries with groans, she offered to teach her new English words. She'd add a few Italian expressions just to see her mother's frowns. When the older woman insisted on a translation for fettuccini Alfredo, Mai simply shook her head. "No Vietnamese equivalent, Mother. Don't ask questions. Just learn it by heart. Isn't this what you always told me in Vietnam?" These words of challenge burned Mai's mother. She wanted to put Mai in her rightful spot. She wanted to slap respect into her. Somehow the scolding could not find its way out of her mouth. Her hands couldn't move.

Stella & Joe Pizzeria gave Mai the independence she needed. The money earned boosted her self-confidence. Every other Thursday she'd go for a gelato after cashing her paycheque. In that 25-minute walk down her street, ice cream in hand, she felt a fleeting burst of happiness.

A Simon and Garfunkel tune in mind, she rock 'n' rolled her way home. She exaggerated her twists and turns in front of neighbouring kids. They pointed at her and giggled. She waved back.

Saving for the future, undoing her mother's grip, finding her way. These were good things. *Mademoiselle* Magazine said so. One day, the American dream would be hers too. One day she'd be her own Stella & Joe.

Four years of washing plastic dishes gave Mai ideas. Observing tricks of the trade fed her dreams. Bank loans were easy with help from the Bird Man. Demand for exotic food was high. And her mother knew how to cook.

A Vietnamese Restaurant in Los Angeles.

MAI LOOKED WITH disdain at a group of American students adding soy sauce to her mother's *pho* soup. She'd tried teaching them about fish sauce. They'd instantly grimaced hearing "fish sauce." Their puckered lips, twitched noses and raised eyebrows surprised Mai. It was as if she'd said 'shit sauce.' "Oh, well, these kids would never know authentic Vietnamese cuisine," Mai muttered. She shrugged and returned to an old *Cosmopolitan* magazine. She chuckled as she read about ancient Oriental sexual positions. The *Kama Sutra.* She didn't know her Saigon sexual games had a name. Ah yes, she'd tried this position with the Bird Man. And that one with Michael. And this one with ... Her mother's sneezing fit put an end to her fantasy. Annoyed, she hoped the older woman had used a Kleenex instead of her blouse.

Coaxing her mother to cook meat took time and effort. Mai had to resort to lie after lie. "American animals have no soul," she had said. When that did not convince her mother, Mai tried another angle. "Alright, all animals have souls; they were once humans in another life. But these are American animals. There is no chance any of them were once your Vietnamese ancestors! These reincarnated chickens are safe to cook! And Americans do not care about eating their ancestors! So please relax, Mother!"

To Mai's menace of "Cook meat or face bankruptcy!" the older woman trembled. She felt cold sweat rolling down her back. She acquiesced to Mai's blackmail with reluctance. Cooking meat, OK. But only frozen meat, she insisted. Blood, she couldn't bear seeing blood on her hands. She couldn't stomach the stench of dead souls lurking in her kitchen.

It was an unusually quiet Friday evening. Mai was grateful for the lull in business. This last week had been crazy. She was tired of running around serving non-Vietnamese clients on the lookout for cheap ethnic food. These crowds of students exhausted her with all kinds of questions. "Do you put MSG in your broth?" No, never. "Is your green onion organic?" Umm, no. "Do you have vegetarian *pho*?" No, but we can take out the meat if you want. "No, I mean do you have *pho* made with bean sprout broth?" No, it wouldn't be *pho* then. Our traditional dish is cooked with beef stock. "Oh, is your beef antibiotic-free?" Umm, not sure. At times Mai felt like shaking those privileged students a bit. UCLA T-shirts here, UCLA backpacks there. UCLA everywhere. Wouldn't it be fun to tell them about her minced-cat imperial rolls? Mai imagined their look of horror as they fluttered their UCLA lashes. Ah, the challenges of serving safe exotic food.

"Mother, why can't you use a Kleenex for your nose?!" Two translucent blobs on the old woman's blouse confirmed Mai's suspicion. Her mother had wiped herself with her sleeve. Getting no answer, Mai sighed loudly. Her mood ruined, she returned to her *Cosmopolitan*. She flipped its pages without interest.

The front door locked, Mai opened her cash register. Counting their day's earnings was her job. She'd always count twice, noting the amount on a piece of paper. Placing bills inside a black plastic bag, stuffing it in her purse, filling her jeans pocket with loose coins. It was a ritual she enjoyed.

Money in her hands. Mai needed this reassurance. It made her 11-hour workday worthwhile. The chopping, boiling, frying, serving, washing, mopping was not for nothing. Money meant she had survived. Survived the war. Survived the evacuation. Survived weeks with a sobbing mother and a ten-dollar bill in her pocket. Survived despite the lack of paternal care. Survived even in the absence of love.

Professor Minh. Mai pictured him in a re-education camp, being tortured for wearing glasses. In her more pessimistic state, Mai imagined her father killed by tidal waves. His corpse floating in the South China Sea. His speckled baby blue glasses washing up on some Southeast Asian beach. Then she snorted as she remembered his tongue tickling a young girl's nipple. Nahhh, her father didn't die ... couldn't die.

Mai had never revealed Professor Minh's indiscretion to her mother. The more the older woman aged without grace, the more Mai felt a need to protect her. Her mother's stooped shoulders, sprouting grey hair and garlic smell worried Mai. To lift her spirits, Mai would offer her beauty cream every month. To entertain her, she would recap some soap operas she'd seen on TV. Mai's overreaction to American soap operas elicited a laugh from her mother. "Stop dramatizing Mai. In Vietnam, lots of men have two or three concubines. The older they get, the younger they want their women. Nothing new." In a flat tone, the mother reassured the daughter.

Prolonged exposure to American soap operas calmed Mai. Somehow her feeling for her father took a turn for the better. What he did was no worse than what played on television day in, day out. Certainly not worse than those scandals she saw on grocery store tabloids. Roman Polanski. Impossible to avoid photos of this Hollywood director. His face stared at her from most checkout lines. Despicable acts were not restricted to her father alone. Even rich, famous people indulged in this kind of stuff. The realization somehow freed Mai from a long-standing sense of shame. The shame of being a child molester's daughter. It must be a male thing. A horny, insecure, ugly, older male thing. Mai snickered at this thought.

The Letter

MAI SPENT MUCH time waiting at Saigon Noodle Restaurant. She waited for clients to take their seats, waited for them to decide on their orders, waited for *pho* soups to be reheated, waited for the verbal authorization of their credit cards. On certain nights the waiting seemed to stretch forever. During those dead minutes, Mai's mind would wander. It would hop outside her restaurant. It would jump on a helicopter for a return trip back to Vietnam. It would revisit a smoky Pink Night Club in search of a black soldier. Finding him, she'd hug him tightly. She'd tell him how happy she is to have finally found her youth. She'd relive a time that had too easily escaped her clutch.

It was not easy tracking Michael down. Letters to the US Army produced no results. Mai was simply told confidential information could not be given out. Phone books proved equally useless. She found four dozen Michael Rosses in Los Angeles alone. There must be thousands of Michael Rosses across the country.

Michael's old letter was Mai's sole source of consolation. She could not sleep without first going over a few simple words. A toothbrush in her mouth, a crumpled letter in her hand. It became a nightly habit.

On her bed, Mai would rehash her last day at the convent. A package and a letter. A package and a letter. That image stuck in her mind. "Here's a Bible for you, my child," a nun had said that afternoon. "We know you tore the first Bible. Please keep this one safe. There is also a letter from your male friend. May God bless you." A male friend? Which male friend? Mai shook with curiosity. Her convent stay had been a time of loneliness. No friend had contacted her. Even her mother had written her off. Cramming the letter in her bag, Mai had rushed out. She didn't dare waste another minute. Her father was already honking his horn impatiently. On her ride home, Mai only answered "Yes, Father, no, Father" to Professor Minh's numerous enquiries. She couldn't think properly. She didn't hear well her father's words. Her mind was on a letter delivered six weeks too late. Mai smiled reading Michael's message that night. Then she cried.

Mai Baby!

Where have you been? I've been looking for you all these weeks! Somehow you just disappeared from my life. Then I found out you're pregnant! Sorry about that! A nun at your convent refused to let me in. What a bitch. I'll be going back to the States soon. Might not see you before you get out of that place. This is not much of a love letter ... but

I want you to know you're very special to me. I'll always remember you. A young Vietnamese girl in a flowing ao dai *walking languorously down Saigon's boulevards ... Geez, am I poetic or what? Perhaps, we'll meet again one day, when the war is over. I really hope so. Remember that blade of grass sprouting from a crack on your street? I do. Sign of peace to come, you'd said. Yes, I hope that peace will soon come. Mai, I miss your shy laugh and caresses so much.*

Love XXX,

Michael—alone on the street without you— Saigon 1972

Los Angeles Bingo Nights

MAI KEPT BUSY writing notes to herself. She had a list of groceries to buy, a list of bills to pay, a list of broken things to fix and a list of other Asian restaurants to visit. Checking out her competitors upset her. These new eateries offered a mishmash of Asian food for trendy people expecting the unexpected. *Pad Thai* and *pho* soup. Spring rolls and sushi. Fried rice and samosas. *Gado gado* and *kimchi*. Mai knew she couldn't compete with their eclectic menus. Her mother could only prepare traditional Vietnamese fare. She was a professor's wife, not a cook without borders.

On her sofa bed at night, Mai pondered her life's acute twists and turns. From a spoiled teenager flirting on Saigon's streets to a businesswoman weighed down by responsibilities. From bedding indiscriminately to an empty bed. The change had been drastic. The Bird Man had been her suitor at first, handing out pity-sex and lending her money. Eventually, he'd lost his interest in Mai. In sun-splashed Saigon, her exotic charm had worked wonders. In California, she became another immigrant with bad English.

The Bird Man's muscular body. Mai would routinely

evoke it. Under her bed sheets, she'd touch herself, imagining her hands to be her former lover's. She'd rub her nipples till they turned hard. Stealthily she'd work her way down her groin. To muffle her uncontrollable "Bingo!" cry, she'd chew on a pillow. No, she couldn't afford to wake her mother sleeping in the next room. Stingy, she wouldn't let anyone partake in her solitary pleasures. Playing with the Bird Man in her fantasy, Mai was guaranteed a win. "Bingo! Bingo!" she'd hum under her breath as her fingers glided round and round.

Bingo with Michael was another matter. It was on another scale. His generous, red lips reining in an impatient, forceful tongue. She could still taste its mint flavour. His sharp incisors on her earlobes. She could still feel their playful bites. She twitched remembering his passionate thrusts inside her. Oh, yes, it was Super Bingo with an imaginary Michael.

How often did Mai play Bingo in the solitude of her sofa bed? Every night? Three times a week? Twice a month? She stopped counting. It didn't matter. What mattered was her escape from drudgery, her sweet flight from self-pity.

No Birthday Parties

HER MEETING WITH the Duck Man left Mai Ly so unsatisfied, so itching for a resolution to something, she knew she couldn't go home. She felt the need to linger on, to hang on to memories of this neighbourhood. Its massive tamarind trees, hibiscus shrubs and pastel-coloured villas beckoned exploration. Turning left, Mai Ly noticed a large house shamelessly taking the space of three other homes. Its simple rectangular lines stood out from neighbouring imitation Greek columns. Even with paint badly peeled, Mai Ly could still make out patches of yellow, purple and green. Its modern shape and grand scale tickled Mai Ly's memory. A gigantic eyesore. A birthday party. A Pepsi shared with another Mai. Talking nonsense while waiting for a first dance that never came. A skinny youth in platform shoes. Tuan. It all came back.

A heaviness tugged at Mai Ly's heart. Her father's sacrifices, she only realized them now. His fake victory signs, forced smiles, long hours toiling at his beer stand. It was all for her. He'd sold his soul so she could attend a decent school, so she could mingle with children of the more fortunate. And for what? To spy on them later?

Mai Ly ran toward the house and rang its doorbell.

Getting no answer after a third ring, she kicked it. Door kicks. This was to squash those 'bell not working, didn't hear you' excuses. It was the first thing Mai Ly learned during her neighbourhood round-ups.

A thin young man in tattered jeans peered out. Mai Ly's official badge dangling from her hand exerted an immediate effect. He hesitated, taking a step back. A mixture of fear and contempt flashed across his eyes. Still, he managed to greet Mai Ly with a smile. Since the communist takeover, Tuan had learned to conceal his true feelings.

"Good evening, Comrade. Can I help you?"

"Good evening, Big Brother. I am looking for an old friend. His name is Tuan."

"Err ... may I have your name, Comrade?"

"Don't worry, Big Brother. I am not here to arrest anyone." Mai Ly changed her tone. Tuan's effeminate voice was unmistakable. His torn clothes surprised her. She'd expected to see nobody. Or a spoiled young man in platform shoes. Not this pitiful person shaking with apprehension in front of her. She suddenly felt sorry for him.

Mai Ly introduced herself, reminding Tuan of their mutual friend Mai. Their class difference couldn't break a common bond of time and space. They'd both experienced the war. They'd both walked the same crooked sidewalks in town, listened to the same Pham Duy songs, swallowed the same American propaganda on television. Mai Ly laughed, reminiscing about Tuan's birthday party. "A sexy girl in green and a bunch of short guys in platform shoes. Do you remember, Big Brother?"

Tuan trembled, hearing "birthday party." Vehemently

he denied ever hosting a party. "No, no. I don't remember any such thing! We never had any birthday parties here! That's counter-revolutionary, Comrade!" Tuan's white lies bothered Mai Ly. She wondered if he had been tortured. Why such blatant falsehood over an insignificant event? She stroked his right hand gently. She peered into his eyes. "Tuan, you don't need to call me Comrade. Am not here to arrest you. Tell me, were you sent to re-education camps?"

'Re-education Camp' elicited in Tuan the usual responses: sweaty palms, light-headedness, irregular heartbeats. He stiffened. Memories came back. He saw again a grey field lined with weary-looking men. Green-uniformed soldiers shouting commands. He remembered digging for worms to supplement his diet of rice water. He remembered cold monsoon nights spent shivering under a leaky straw roof and the dizzying pull of mud sucking him out of his hut. The sensation returned, strong enough to throw him off balance. Tuan lurched forward, almost hitting Mai Ly. "Excuse me." He coughed reflexively before sitting down to steady his spinning head.

Tuan's Journey

*I*T WAS THREE *years ago. I hadn't noticed anything unusual when I showed up at my prearranged meeting point. It was early evening, the sun had begun to set, clouds had turned pink. A dark-skinned cyclo driver greeted me with a silent nod. He recognized my striped yellow shirt and motioned for me to get in. For an hour, we went around town, stopping here and there for a pack of cigarettes, a bottle of water and some tasteless candies. The bottled water went into my shoulder bag, the cigarettes into my pant pockets, half the candy into my mouth. I gave the other half to the driver. We talked about the weather. "Weather's good, calm sea tonight," he said. We went into dark alleyways. One small street after another. I turned to check for fishy movements. There were none. No one was tailing us that evening. We headed for the pier. It was deserted and badly lit. Only one street lamp worked. My driver pointed to a bobbing object on the horizon. I recognized my fishing boat docked nearby. I counted my last dongs then paid him his fare. He turned his cyclo around and wished me good luck.*

The boat trip had already been paid for. In gold bars. My parents had taken care of everything. They were good parents. You know, I was supposed to leave with them a month earlier. I still remember that chaotic scene. One minute I was fighting for my spot on the boat, next minute I was pushed out with a gun on my chest. I can still feel that gun. "Do not shoot!" my mother had yelled. My place was given to the captain's extended family at the last minute. No amount of negotiation could change his mind. "No more space! The kid takes next boat out with my cousin!" he'd insisted. Mother cried seeing me left behind that night. She screamed my name over and over till someone knocked her out with a slap. Alone on the beach, I followed that boat's light until it disappeared. My mind was empty. I could only hear the captain's words, "The kid takes next boat out . . ."

The empty pier spooked me. Returning to the same spot that saw my mother being slapped around bothered me. I could not forget her cries. I tried calculating the chances of us reuniting one day. That chance was low, very low. Where would I find her? In the middle of the ocean? My cries scared a big rat nibbling on garbage. I looked at Vung Tau for the last time. I loved swimming here. I loved returning to its beaches every summer. Somehow it was more home than Saigon. "This way . . ." someone whispered, holding out his hand to guide me. The minute I set foot onboard, an alarm went off. A policeman appeared with a headlight projected straight into my face. It was only then that I realized I had been tricked.

Young, male, healthy. I got the worst punishment. The others—children, women, elderly people—I heard they were released after two months in prison. For me, it was two years. Two years in a re-education camp. What can I *say about that? The dry season was bad. Tilling fields under a hot sun with only three glasses of tea a day made me sick. I was very weak from exhaustion. Monsoon season was even harder. Heavy rain drowned my vegetables. It soaked my straw bed. I survived on rainwater and floating earthworms. That was when I realized how much our farmers suffered while we lived off their sweat. I can only thank the Party for opening my mind! Long live Uncle Ho! Long live socialism! Down with the rich!*

Tuan could not finish his story. His last rehearsed words riled Mai Ly. She cut him off with a sharp hiss. She'd had enough of this kind of phony talk at her weekly meetings. She didn't want to hear more. Stop the exaggeration, she told him. She only wanted to know why he'd wished to leave? For what? What's missing here?

Unconnected Dots

MAI LY'S WORDS appalled Tuan. He shook his head in disbelief. He found the labels "out-of-wedlock birth" and "half-breed kid" especially hard to swallow. He could not imagine his former neighbour mixed up in such scandals. He racked his mind trying to visualize teen-aged Mai in a long *ao dai*. The image eluded him. He'd never noticed Mai growing up in front of him. In his memory, she remained the little neighbour kid he'd chased around with his plastic gun. Cracked heels overhanging flip-flops a size too small. This was how he remembered Mai. Oh, how he'd tortured her with his "Bang! Bang! I got you, commie girl!"

Tuan squirmed in his chair. He licked his lips and cracked his knuckles. He tried getting up for a glass of water only to be pushed back. Mai Ly hadn't finished her speech. She continued with tales of a Mai he didn't know. Hearing "half-black kid," Tuan shook his head. He looked blankly at Mai Ly. He hadn't understood, didn't connect the points. Had he been more quick-witted, he would've recognized a sad storyline instead of seeing only random dots. Tales of less fortunate people might've touched him. They might've opened his eyes.

On that cloudless afternoon, Tuan only saw uncon-nected dots.

"Black? I don't understand ..." Tuan stammered.

"What is it you don't understand? The kid's father is a black American soldier. Yes, Mai's abandoned child is black!" Mai Ly snapped. Once again, she pushed Tuan back into his seat when he tried getting up.

The Polka Dot Girl

SISTER **T**AM **SCARED** me. She talked a lot. One minute she'd tell me stories from a picture book, next minute she'd shout at me. She'd get upset whenever I forgot words for certain objects. "It's a *helicopter*! Can't you remember it? How stupid are you?" My "Helicapta" earned me a knock on the head. "No! No helicapta! It's a *helicopter*! *Un hélicoptère* in French and *Vertolet* in Russian! Go to the corner and repeat it 45 times in English, 35 times in French and 25 times in Russian."

My mumblings finished, she ordered me to do 30 sit-ups. I did not mind these physical chores. The more my shoulders ached at the end of the exercises, the prouder I felt. Excitedly my arms and legs wagged doggy style. At last, they could function like everyone else's. They'd know what to do when faced with a bully. "Black Devil, we're going to kill you!" no longer paralyzed them. Obedient, they'd run. They'd save me from pebbles, rocks and grit. When younger kids missed their aim, they'd show me their clenched fists. They'd stick out their tongue and make fart noises with their armpits. Or they'd point to my frizzy hair and laugh.

Older kids never laughed. Pushing me down the

stairs, tripping me with their foot. They'd always keep a straight face. In our common bathroom, they'd pull down my pants to check on my eel. "What colour is your penis, Black Boy?" they'd taunt me over and over. Sneaking an older girl into our dormitory, they'd made bets. Will she laugh or scream, they'd asked each other. It was neither. She simply eyed me with a pout. "How disgusting," was her only comment.

Not everyone made fun of my dark skin. A pale, skinny girl actually sought me out. It was a windy morning. We were on our way to the yard for our daily break. Her name was Thu. She asked for mine. She didn't react when I answered, "Black Devil." Her hand in mine, she dragged me to an empty corner of the yard. Her gesture so surprised me, I could only stay silent. No other children had touched me in such a manner. Her damp hand reminded me of Mother Superior's. From her hoarse whispers, I learned she was sick. Many doctors had seen her, yet no one could cure her. Could my blackness do magic healing, she wondered. "The sickness, please get rid of it," she begged. Hidden behind a big plane tree, she lifted her shirt. She put my hand on her stomach. She asked me to touch it, to feel her pain. I did and gave a start when I felt a big hot bump under her belly button. Curious, I squeezed it. That simple gesture got me into trouble. Thu howled before fainting in my arms.

Sister Tam marched to our spot behind the plane tree. My left hand on Thu's stomach shocked her. Her first reaction was to slap me. "What did you do to Thu?" she demanded. I could only reply, "I don't know.

I, I touched her." Sister Tam slapped me again. Then she bent down to lift Thu's body. Through tears, I saw her skinny legs dangling from Sister Tam's arms. Covered with blue and violet spots, they looked more like ink blotters than legs. That image terrified me.

Thu returned to the courtyard a few weeks later. Alone on a bench, she seemed lost in her own world. Her eyes were closed. Her mouth whispered words no one could hear. Her face looked paler than on our first encounter. The strange colours on her limbs glowed brighter in the sunlight. They looked like polka dots.

Thu didn't react when I approached her. Her eyes opened for a minute to glance at things beyond my vision. She let her gaze wander around. I kept quiet sitting next to her. A mixture of Tiger Balm and banana scent emanated from her hair. I breathed in the concoction, held my breath for a long time before letting it out. If I could, I would hold it in forever. Thu searched for my hand and whispered, "It hurts . . ."

"I am sorry Thu. I didn't mean to hurt you the other day!" I protested.

"It's not you. It hurts all the time. It's my sickness. I wish Mother were still here. She always held my hand when I get sick. Made me feel better."

"Where is your mother?" I asked.

"Don't know. She disappeared one day. Sister Tam said she probably died stepping on a mine. Someone found me walking alone and brought me here. Don't remember any of that. Just remember Mother's hands. They smelled nice . . . like lemons."

"Don't know where my mother is either. Mother

Superior said she was bad person. 'Sleeping around with American soldiers!' That's what Mother Superior said."

"Shhh. Can you hold my hand a bit tighter?" Thu ordered.

Her squinted eyes and twitching lips worried me. I knew she was hurting. Silently I said a prayer for her, exactly the way Sister Tam had taught me. Both my hands holding Thu's, I could not make the sign of the cross. It was an incomplete prayer. Still, I hoped it would take away some of her suffering.

In a gesture of dismissal, Thu released my hands. "I'm tired, want to sleep now." She got up and with much effort headed for her dormitory. Halfway over, she stumbled on a rock. Slowly, she managed to straighten up. She turned to look at me before continuing her jittery walk. A minute later she disappeared from sight. I never knew what longing was until that day in the yard.

Going to the Moon

I SAW THU regularly that summer. She looked thinner with each advancing week. Her voice croaked, her hands trembled, her breath laboured. Yet she insisted on being with me. If I were in the latrine, she'd wait for me outside, squatting patiently on wet grass. If I were hiding from bullies, she'd wander around till she ran into me. "Black One, where are you?" her hoarse voice so echoed in my ears, I knew I could not escape her clutch. Our meetings were always behind the big plane tree. In our private corner, she'd place my hand on her stomach. Out of people's view, she'd ask me to blow cool air on a hot lump below her belly button.

We'd often talk about our mothers. Her mother's lemony hands. That lemon scent obsessed her. She'd smell it in her dreams. She'd smell it sitting under the plane tree. It was a memory she could not let go. Thu asked about my mother. "Her hair, it smells nice?" she wondered. "Don't know. Never met her," I replied. "Then just imagine," she said. "Imagine her pretty. Nice hair. Lemon scent. Lemon and cinnamon too." Right away, I said "yes" to this image of a pretty mother with lemon-and-cinnamon hair.

After many weeks imagining lemon and cinnamon

hair, I asked Thu for permission to touch hers. She had long black hair, sparse on top, tangled at the bottom. She agreed if she could also touch my frizzy curls. We made a bet to see who would catch the first head lice. I always did. She was full of them and searching for them through her thin straight hair was easy. Hidden inside my thick curls, my lice were harder to find. Her smile. I'd sometimes pretend to come up empty-handed just to see her smile. For a brief upturn of her lips, I did not mind the occasional loss. Playing with each other's hair, counting each other's lice—this was how we spent our days.

"Where's your father?" Thus asked one day.

"In America. You know, that place with beautiful houses, big cars and lots of snow."

This allusion to snow impressed Thu. She opened wide her eyes. "Well, my father is in heaven. Killed in battle and went straight to heaven. Mother said so. There are flying angels in heaven. Better than big cars."

Not to be outdone, I said, "There is a flying nun in America. I saw that on television. Mother Superior loves watching her fly every Friday at six. There's even a talking horse. Mr. Ed, his name. I saw that on television too."

"Yes but heaven has Jesus. He can walk on water. Jesus is number one!" To this remark, I nodded. I took her hands and we both laughed at the idea of a talking horse.

"Horse language or our language?" Thu wondered.

"He speaks English but I don't understand much."

Thu coughed then yawned. Her eyes closed for a moment. I knew she was tired. It was time for her afternoon rest. Not wanting to see her go, I asked, "Can you see the moon from your bed at night?"

"Yes," she replied drowsily.

"Well, there are Americans up there. They walked on the moon. I saw that on television."

"Did they run into Jesus on the moon?"

"No. I don't think so . . .'

"Why go to the moon if you can't find Jesus?" she asked. I could only shrug at this question. Going to the moon to find Jesus. Going to America in search of a talking horse. Looking for impossible things in unreachable places. Perhaps we'd only wanted to find our parents.

Holding Her Hands

INEVER KNEW when I'd see Thu again. Her sickness forced her to spend more and more time in bed. Some evenings she'd miss dinner altogether. I tried saving my food for her once. Out of Sister Tam's view, I rolled my uneaten rice into a ball. I shaped that ball into a hand with five distinct fingers. I placed it in my shorts' pocket, taking care not to squish my work.

The entrance to the girls' dorm was well guarded. Sister Tam's shout startled me. "NO boys in there! You know the rule!" Showing her my rice creation made things worse. She shouted even louder. "Rice is to eat, not to play with! Stop wasting food when there are hungry people out there!" Her lecture ended with a slap on my face and my rice hand in the garbage.

Thu's prolonged absence worried me. I decided to follow Sister Tam. I spied and listened behind doors. Long periods of eavesdropping revealed what I had feared. "That poor kid has cancer," Mother Superior said. "Leukemia, doctors said so. Serious sickness. She can die. Has nothing to do with the Black One. No witchcraft. No black magic, Sister Tam! Now stop spreading rumours!"

Sister Tam's swift exit took me by surprise. I tried to step backward. Wet ceramic tiles transformed my simple movement into a strange dance. I slipped, my knees skidded down the hall. Falling, my elbows hit the ground, my flip-flops flew in the air. My bloodied shirt did not alarm Sister Tam. She only scowled. "Pushed by a big kid again?" she asked. When I nodded yes, she muttered, "Learn to defend yourself!" She shook her head and went on her way.

Thu's sickness scared me. Perhaps Sister Tam was right. Perhaps she'd understood my blackness's true nature. Perhaps she'd seen my skin's morbid side. Perhaps I'd really caused Thu's illness. Weeks after Thu left for the hospital, I still dreamed of her at night. Her thinning hair, her polka-dot legs, her hands clutching mine, I saw it all. "Holding hands was something my mother always did," she'd whisper. "Holding hands was something my mother never did," I'd respond. Then I'd wake up in sweat, words of longing thumping in my head.

Back to the Plastic Bag

ALONE, I SAT under the plane tree, waiting for Thu's return. Week after week, I prayed for her health. When she didn't show up by Christmas time, I went looking for her at the gate. My fingers grabbing an iron grill, I stood for hours, searching for a car that would bring her back to me. I only saw drenched cyclists pedalling against tides of brown water. I only saw dead rats floating belly-up down a flooded street. My own soaking clothes didn't bother me. My shivering limbs couldn't discourage me. I stood and waited, my wrinkled fingers refusing to budge.

I so wished to hold Thu's hand again. I so missed playing with her hair, breathing in her Tiger Balm, listening to her stories of a caring mother. A shared melon soup, a nightly embrace, a voice whispering lullabies. Thu's tales of her mother had me dreaming about a normal childhood.

Sister Tam's voice woke me from my trance. "You crazy boy! What are you doing there in the rain? You want to be sick?" She ran to me with an umbrella, clasped my hand and pulled me back inside. To my attempt at an explanation, Sister Tam shook her head. Her scolding sounded less severe that afternoon. "Stop wasting time waiting for that poor girl. Time is precious. Use it to do better things. Go review your French verbs." With a dry towel, she patted my face. The wetness, that's from the rain, I tried saying. I didn't cry, I wanted to add.

News of Thu finally reached me. "Nothing more to be done ..." Her doctors had already predicted a death date. Thu had asked for me. "The strange dark boy, I want that strange dark boy." So desperate was her voice, the nurses could only acquiesce. A dying last wish should always be accorded. That was Sister Tam's teaching.

My ride to Nhu Dong Hospital excited me. I had never been outside our building, never been on a crowded bus, never seen so many cars, *cyclos*, bicycles, pedestrians.

Saigon's streets looked nothing like what I'd seen on television. Crumbling houses, people sleeping on sidewalks, dirty kids urinating on lampposts. It was all new to me. Television shows were full of good-looking people in nice cars. Sometimes they'd kiss in their back seat. More often they'd shoot at each other. Laughter spilled from the screen. So did a lot of Bang! Bang! Bang! You're dead! Blood leaking from dead bodies, yes. Dirt and poverty, no.

The hospital smelled strange. A bitter odour tickled my nose. I sneezed repeatedly. A short, old woman met me inside. She took my hand to lead me down a long white corridor. Through wooden slats, I heard children crying everywhere. I turned to the old woman for an explanation. She only shrugged with indifference. At the end of the corridor, we descended two flights of stairs. A cold draft and complete silence greeted us on this floor. It was the silence of the almost-dead.

I could barely recognize Thu on her bed. Her bald head shocked me. She looked so skinny I feared her bones would break with the slightest touch. The purple blotches covering her limbs had spread everywhere. There seemed to be no pale skin left. Her eyes closed, she already looked ghostly. Her Tiger Balm smell no longer floated like pollen in the wind.

Thu opened her eyes. Recognizing me, she managed a weak smile. "Hold my hand," she said hoarsely. "Hold my hand like my mother did." Those words flooded me with memories of our friendship. She was my only friend, the only one wanting to touch me. Now she was dying in front of me. My eyes stung. I tried to turn away from her.

"No, hold my hand," Thu said again. I touched her hands, feeling her dry, cold skin. I caressed them with my fingertips before bending to blow warm breaths onto them. She suddenly grabbed my wrist with surprising force. She held me in her clutch for a few minutes. In that brief time, we shared smiles. We assured each other of our mutual longing. Then the minute passed. She closed her eyes and I felt her grasp loosening. "No! Thu, don't leave me!" I cried. The words rang in my head. Yet no sound came out of my mouth. Without hope of seeing Thu alive, I'd reverted to a defenceless, mute kid hung from a doorknob.

To Have in the Present Tense

THE HOSPITAL VISIT ruined my appetite. I picked at my rice bowl, eating only dried sesame seeds. I also stopped talking. Nobody noticed my silence. Only Sister Tam reacted to my speechlessness. Snapping her fingers, she eyed me with suspicion when I failed to answer her math question. "Math too hard for you? Recite the days of the week in English then," she ordered. I shook my head, pointing to my throat. To her "Bad cold? Sore throat?" I nodded.

"Alright, go write those English days in your note-book. While you're at it, conjugate the French verb "avoir" and its English equivalent in the present tense. I want to see your work tomorrow. And try to write neatly!" From her pocket, she pulled out a mint candy, placed it on my open palm then left.

> Avoir—To have
> J'ai—I have
> Tu as—You have
> Il a—He has
> Elle a—She has
> Nous avons—We h

I stopped in mid-sentence. I couldn't continue with this exercise. "Je n'ai pas," I wrote instead. "I do not have." Don't have. Didn't have. Never had. Never had a mother to hold my hands. No longer had a friend to share longings. "Je n'ai rien" I scribbled on my notebook, my fingers tremulous. "I have nothing" I noted its English equivalent at the bottom of my page. On the margin, I added in Vietnamese: I've nothing left.

A Small Wooden Box

THU WAS BURIED on a hot sunny day. As her only
friend, I was allowed to accompany Sister Tam to the
cemetery. Lost, we walked round and round till a small
group of people waved us over. I recognized the old
woman from the hospital. Next to her stood Mother
Superior, furiously wiping her forehead. Two bare-
chested men kept busy tying knots around a wooden
box. A small wooden box. I tried imagining Thu inside.
Her skinny legs. Her violet spots. Her colourless face.
Her Tiger Balm smell. Her hoarse voice telling me the
stories of her mother. Her hands holding mine. But I
couldn't imagine her anymore. I only saw a wooden box
being lowered into the ground. I only smelled freshly
dug earth. I only heard her casket creaking as it hit a
rocky bottom. On a hot sunny day, I shivered. My teeth
clacked. My lips turned blue.

Back at the orphanage, Sister Tam handed me another mint candy. "Your throat better? Got your voice
back?" she asked. I shook my head vehemently.

Thu was gone yet nobody cried.

Mr. Oreo

MICHAEL'S AFRO HAD grown back since getting out of the army. Big and wild, the way he liked it. However, on this day, he was having it trimmed.

"Cut it shorter," Michael told the barber.

"Yeah, Afro look is over, Bro."

At home, Michael checked himself in the mirror. He liked his pectorals still bulging underneath a tight T-shirt. He pinched his flexed arm for hardness and nodded with satisfaction. It was still very hard despite his lax exercise routine. His grin gave way to a groan as he looked down. Shrunken and out of shape, that other muscle hung limply between his legs. He wondered when it would fall off.

Susan. A blind date. Michael got talked into a blind date once. She was a petite dark-skinned woman with pleasantly curly eyelashes, full red lips and straight brown hair. He liked her hearty laugh. He liked the tone of her voice. It reminded him of Natalie Cole. Her fashion style intrigued him. An oversized rumpled jacket over open white shirt over men's jeans over red high-heeled sandals. He had never seen such a cool combination before. To impress her, Michael took her to a wood-oven pizzeria. In the intimacy of their booth, he pulled out stories of Yale University, Carlos Castaneda, Vietnamese jungle. In that order. Her bored smile worried Michael. His first round of stories barely finished, she was already on her way to the washroom. She returned a few minutes later a different person. Shiny pink lipstick, skin less oily, a whiff of perfume around her neck. They were signs for Michael to stop the talk. Stop the talk and start the action. Her wink got Michael sweating. He stuttered as he tried to whisper in her ears. "I bet you like Natalie Cole ..." This lame attempt at seduction exasperated her. She shook her head. She snorted. Michael attempted another tactic. He put his hands on her head. Sweat from his palm trickled down her neck. He took her shudder as a sign of pleasure. Emboldened, he started playing with her long silky hair. He remembered Mai liking this gesture. Blind Date Susan obviously didn't. She frowned. Before he could grasp the subtlety of the situation, he felt her hair shifting under his hands. It was only after it moved another inch that Michael reckoned his mistake. A wig. He'd been toying with a wig all along. He blamed himself for being so stupid. Witless, he'd forgotten those random laws of nature: black girls don't have straight silky hair. Discreetly he tried readjusting her dislodged wig. Too late. His cluelessness would not be forgiven. Pushing Michael's hands away, she said bluntly, "Don't bother!" She got up, murmured "Goodbye, Mr. Oreo!" and with gliding strides, strutted out.

The Oreo label perplexed Michael. It stung. It brought back memories of his high school days—of a thirteen-year-old boy miming Black Speak to entertain his white classmates. Black outside, white inside. Was that how people saw him? A race traitor?

Michael brushed his teeth twice. He wanted them to outshine his new silver watch. Over and over, he combed his just-cut hair to give it the right shape. He practised his smiles till his lips ached. Thoughts of his upcoming media interview gave him the jitters. He sweated so much, the comb fell from his hand. As New Haven's only black Purple Heart soldier, he was in demand. Local television, local newspapers all wanted to hear his version of the war. Michael knew he must look good on screen. His lines, he must rehearse them. He must sound authentic. Whatever he said, he must not come off as Mr. Oreo.

The Monk Again

VIETNAMESE BOAT PEOPLE. The world could not take its eyes off these dehydrated bodies packed into rickety boats. A mixture of curiosity, horror and true concern pushed readers to read on. Nightly television viewers followed newscasts in silence. High Nielsen ratings brought Vietnam back into people's living room. National news outlets interviewed important people. New Haven media went after purple-hearted Michael. Yale University radio station, The *New Haven Register*, WTNH-TV, Michael did them all. His mother wallowed in his celebrity.

Before each interview, Michael would read as much as he could on the subject. Diligently he'd watch televised newscasts of Vietnamese boat people. Images of tired eyes, torn clothes, crying babies distressed him. Photos of jammed boats slanting dangerously troubled him. He felt guilty, seeing again these passive Oriental faces. He'd enlisted to fight for their freedom once. That was pure illusion. No longer could he delude himself. He'd left. The American army had left these people behind. Overnight and with little warning, they'd all forsaken their South Vietnamese allies.

Recognizing familiar faces was Michael's secret mission. Again and again, he searched for Mai in all those boat people images. When he couldn't find her, he tried sniffing the photos. After all these years, lemon and cinnamon still obsessed him.

The possibility of miracles. Vietnam had shown Michael this. Mai's tale of a monk on fire had fascinated him. Her description of charred bones in the lotus position made him twitch. Realizing they'd been talking about the same person, Michael screamed. "Wow! The monk on fire—I saw that photo in the States! It was everywhere! TV, newspapers, magazines!" To this outburst, Mai simply said, "I saw it in front of my house."

"Come, I show you," Mai announced one eerily cool evening. She took him to her neighbourhood. Two blocks from her house, they got out of a taxi. Even in the greyness of dusk, she preferred keeping her sunglasses and straw hat on. A black man by her side, she wanted to be incognito. She couldn't risk being slapped in public by her father. Asked to see her house, Mai shouted, "No!" She preferred describing it to him. Two levels. Painted blue and white. Some light orange too. Wood and iron front gate. Interior courtyard for car and trees. Two mango trees. One lime tree. Hibiscus shrubs. One big room in back for Father. Baby blue colour with faded curtains. Slit in one curtain. Father with his speckled baby blue glasses fogging up and ... and ... and ... All of a sudden Mai stopped describing her house. "And what?" Michael asked. "And nothing," she answered. To change the subject, she whispered, "Come.

I show you miracle ..." In between green lights, she pulled him into the street. She lit a match to show him blades of grass sprawling out of a fissure. "Old monk died there. I did that crack in road," she proclaimed proudly. "Grass growing out of crack? That's sign of peace. Peace to come." And Michael would totally believe her.

The Interview

MICHAEL PERFORMED SURPRISINGLY well on radio. His dreaded stuttering never manifested itself. His initial apprehension soon gave way to self-confidence. Yale student journalists understood nothing of the war. Its causes, its origin remained a blur in their minds. They only remembered what they could explain to themselves: massive street protests. flowers in rifle butts, anti-war songs, John Lennon, Give Peace a Chance, Kent State. four white students killed by soldiers. They remembered all that. What about the Orangeburg Massacre of three black students by patrol officers? Hmm, never heard of it. When it came to facts, they'd keep mixing the Battle of An Loc with the Battle of Khe Sang. They'd get their dates all twisted. They didn't know the names of any generals. Their ignorance grated yet also pleased Michael. "No, no, that's not it at all," he would say in his professorial-like voice.

Of all the student journalists, Michael remembered only one. Amanda Knock from the *Yale Daily News*. Amanda's flaming red hair falling over turquoise eyes had Michael wondering about the hue of her other body parts. There was a certain charm to her fluttering lashes, arched brows and lips the shade of week-old cherries. In her diaphanous Indian blouse, Amanda reminded Michael of those '60s Westport girls. Only one thing differentiated them: the bra. Amanda hung on to hers while the Westport girls burned theirs.

"Thank you for agreeing to this interview, Mr. Ross."

"It's my pleasure to be here, Amanda. And please call me Michael."

"OK, Michael. I understand you were a soldier in Vietnam in the early '70s. You were injured in combat and were awarded the Purple Heart. I understand you enlisted. You chose to go to war at a time when people were protesting against it. Why?"

That's an easy one, Michael thought. He'd been asked this question too many times. It became boring. He wanted to go off-script this time.

"Idealism had nothing to do with it. I was under no illusion about saving the world against communism! Like every other boy, I played with toy guns as a kid. I thought it would be fun to hold a real one. You know, like on TV ... put a gun to someone's head. Bang! Bang! Let's kill some commies!" For emphasis, Michael pushed two fingers against Amanda's temple.

"Oh!" exclaimed Amanda, wide-eyed. She swiftly moved her chair away from him.

"Hey, I was just kidding! Haha! Holding a gun wasn't fun at all in real life. Believe me! It was scary as hell. The thought that I could kill someone freaked me out. I didn't want to kill anyone. Nor be killed! I guess I enlisted 'cause I didn't know what else to do with my life in those days. I was a confused kid. My best friend was in a coma. I felt weird, you know? I also needed money. Not easy to find a job as a black kid in New Haven. Army helped me maintain my cigarette and beer habit. Actually, no. No, that's not all. I did have naïve ideas about saving the world. I did fantasize about fighting for freedom and all that crap. In reality, I was only fighting for my dignity, my self-worth. That police baton against my throat, I had wanted to push it away. OK, never mind …"

Amanda's next question exasperated Michael. He'd heard it so many times. "Why are Vietnamese refugees still coming here five years after the end of the war?" Amanda asked. "Are these people true political refugees or merely economic migrants? Should our government still accept them?" No longer afraid of Michael, she moved her seat back to its original position. She wished to see his amber eyes from close. Michael took a deep breath. What he was about to say, he'd already repeated over and over. Yet boredom had never shown its face. Indifference had never hijacked his indignation.

"Amanda, I can't tell you if these people are true political refugees or just economic migrants. They may be both. What difference does it make? During the war, our American Air Force had dropped tons and tons— sorry I don't have the exact number—of napalm and Agent Orange on Vietnam. Years later, there are still people suffering from sickness and malformations because of our chemicals. There are still deforested lands where nothing can grow. There are still unexploded landmines all over the country. It is understandable people want to get out of this hellhole we helped create. These Vietnamese boat people are risking their lives on the high seas. Many have drowned. Others have succumbed to robbery and rape by pirates. Do we turn our back on them? Do we build walls to keep them out? I hope not." The passion in Michael's voice so surprised Amanda, she stopped her note-taking in mid-sentence. Seeing him choking on his emotions, she passed him her handkerchief. For a second their hands touched. Did she know about a Mai in Michael's past? No. Could she understand this emotional attachment to a country not one's own, to a people so different from oneself? Maybe not.

Michael's strong reaction to her comment did not stop Amanda. She was intent on moving on. She had a piece to file that evening. She hesitated a moment before bombarding Michael with questions of a more personal nature. She wished to hear his experience as a black soldier. She wanted to know about racism in Vietnam. Instead of answering her directly, Michael decided to quote an excerpt from a 1967 Martin Luther King Jr.'s speech. Out of his pocket appeared a folded piece of paper. He cleared his throat before reading. This act, he'd also done many times on television.

"We were taking the black young men who had been crippled by our society and sending them 8,000 miles away to guarantee liberties in Southeast Asia which they have not found in South West Georgia or East Harlem. We have been repeatedly faced with the cruel irony of watching Negro and white boys on TV screens as they kill and die together for a nation that has been unable to seat them together in the same schools. So, we watch them in brutal solidarity burning the huts of a poor village, but we realize that they would never live on the same block in Detroit."

"Wow, strong! Could I have a photocopy of it?" Amanda asked. Before Michael could answer, she launched into her next question. Like every other interviewer, she wanted to know about Post Traumatic Stress Disorder.

"Woah! Slow down, Amanda! Yes, racial tension existed in Vietnam. The '60s were times of racial tension in the States. George Wallace, Martin Luther King Jr., Malcolm X, the Black Panthers, the murders of civil rights workers, etc. The early '70s were no better. We didn't leave that heritage behind when we landed in Vietnam. Black soldiers were over-represented over there. Most of the time, we had to do the dirty work. So yes, racial tension existed in the barracks and on Saigon's streets. But deep in the jungle, we were united against the Viet Cong."

When Amanda insisted on returning to her Post Traumatic Stress question, Michael tapped his feet impatiently. It was such a typical run-of-the-mill question. He'd rather discuss Hollywood war movies. Unfortunately, he must answer what was asked of him. He must give people what they want to hear. Like a math genius entertaining his mother's friends, he must now perform for Amanda.

To add spice to his ho-hum interview, Michael decided to bring back the machine gun image. Going off-script might hurt his reputation. He didn't care anymore.

"Yes, seeing your buddies die can fuck you up for life. Same thing with losing your leg. And losing your sanity will fuck your family forever. The movies, the media, the books, they all talk about these problems. Yet the trauma of Vietnam is more complicated than that, you know … The loss of a friend, of a limb, of a normal mind—yes. What about the loss of self-importance? Self-importance. Is that a word? Most of us were nobodies, just young kids straight out of school. Vietnam changed that. We felt important over there. It was a false assumption, of course. Our lives meant nothing to those who sent us there. Yet we felt important. You know, some of us liked that feeling of a machine gun in our hands. It gave us a sensation of power we never got at home. The Vietnamese are short people. They are humble. Or they pretend to be humble. Being so short, they had to look up when they talk to us. They were always bowing and nodding in agreement even if they didn't understand a damn thing. Some of us felt uncomfortable with that kind of relationship. No, I won't kid myself. Deep down, many of us enjoyed that feeling of superiority. Who wouldn't? So going back to ordinary life, to being a nobody—that can be tough. No movies will talk about this. It is too awful to admit." Before ending the interview, Michael decided to add another atypical comment. "While many of us died in that war, so many more Vietnamese died: the civilians, the North Vietnamese soldiers, the South Vietnamese soldiers. Bombs had destroyed a large part of their country. Do we ever talk about their Post Traumatic Stress? No. Perhaps we should."

"Good point," Amanda said. Putting her notepad

away, she got up to leave. "Thank you, Michael for your time."

"You are welcome, Amanda. By the way, can I ask you a private question?"

"Sure."

"Do you like Leonard Cohen?"

"Is that a trick question? Am I supposed to like him 'cause he's Canadian like me? Nahhh. I prefer Joni Mitchell. Why you want to know?"

"Just asking. You from Canada?"

"Pembroke, Ontario. Friendly, small town. Nice people. We got some draft dodgers holing up there during the war."

"So, why, why are you here?"

"My cousin studied at Yale. I came for her graduation and fell in love with New Haven. So pretty! And so near the Big Apple too!"

"That is great, Amanda! Hhmmm, glad you like New Haven."

Michael felt his right eye twitching nonstop. Hastily, he lowered his gaze. From contact with Vietnamese people, he'd picked up enough of their superstition to know a right-eye twitch equalled good luck. He gave Amanda a salesman smile then pranced outside. He was afraid his twitching right eye—convinced of its good fortune—would try sneaking its way into Amanda's translucent bra if he stayed any longer.

Sitting on humid grass, Michael smiled. He couldn't stop smiling. It was a smile so wide it exposed his wisdom teeth to the wind.

No Phony Story

TODAY IS THE day. Time to make my big move, Michael convinced himself. Amanda wouldn't wait forever. First, he must clean up. Yellow walls, green wall-to-wall carpet, blue Salvation Army sofa. Nothing matched. On the second floor facing busy Chapel Street, his studio stank of street grime. Daily, Michael woke to diesel fumes and dozed to motorbikes screeches. Even so, he liked it there. He liked its proximity to coffee shops, cheap restaurants, bars. He liked eyeing girls from his balcony. He liked, even more, sending them catcalls and seeing their confused looks, necks twisted every which way in an attempt to locate the culprit.

Into a closet went stacks of *Penthouse* magazines. Out the door went an overflowing garbage bag. On hangers went scattered clothes. In their places appeared a patchouli kit, rock crystals, lavender candles. Michael rearranged them four times before finding the correct yin and yang combination. Not quite satisfied with his still life, he went looking for his knapsack. From assorted textbooks, he fished out two: Hegel's *Philosophy of Rights* and Kant's *Political Discourses*. Yes, while some printed material should be put away, others deserved to be shown.

Michael dialled Amanda's number using a red pen. Red for good luck. Another Vietnamese superstition. Amanda's busy signal untwisted his stomach. He slammed the receiver and laughed with relief. It was only after four beers that he dared try again. A melodious voice answered on the second ring. Michael wished it had rung a bit longer. He wished he had more time to prepare his opening line.

"Umm ... Hi Amanda, it's Michael Ross. Remember me?" Michael slapped his head. He couldn't believe he'd just uttered such a boring greeting.

"Michael! I was just thinking of you," Amanda said.

"Really? Then it must be telepathy ... I, I, err ... really enjoyed reading all your articles in the *Yale Daily News*."

"Thanks, Michael. What I wrote about you got a lot of good feedback. Hey you're famous!"

"Hmm ... OK. That's great ... Amanda, Hmm ... Are you, are you busy this weekend?" Michael decided to blurt it all out. There was no point torturing himself with useless pleasantries. No point in dragging out the moment of rejection. In a suddenly determined voice, he asked her for a coffee date. Amanda giggled and agreed. Using an eyeliner pen, she scribbled Michael's address on her thigh.

"I'd love to discuss journalism with you. I'm, hmm, you know, I'm doing an Honours in Poli Science now. I, hmmm, I hope to get into the Master's program one day. Politicians and journalists, we need each other. Ha! Ha!"

Political Science. Michael's mother had never understood his choice of study. She'd never condone it. Trading the certainty of mathematics for a shadowy subject like political science? Why?? For months she'd complained to deaf ears. Political Science instead of Math. That decision was made long ago. Movies of families in gas chambers, photos of black corpses hanging from trees, newscasts of napalm dropped on civilians. Those images had haunted Michael for years. If numbers no longer held any secrets for him, the oppression of one people by another still kept him wondering at night. Why, why and why?

"Hey, Honours in Poli Sci, that's fantastic Michael! Congratulations!"

"Hmm, yeah ... that's thanks to affirmative action. You know—quotas for minorities. Like, it helps to be black sometimes."

"Come on! Don't fib the facts, Michael! Affirmative action had nothing to do with it. You got accepted on merit. Your scholarship was based on marks. You were valedictorian at St. Joseph's."

"Oh ... how, how you know all this, Amanda?"

"You were one of the best in your grade. I looked you up. I asked around ... I have my sources."

"You looked me up! Boy, you're a real journalist, Amanda! No phony story!" Michael chuckled. As he twisted on his seat, the phone slid from his sweaty palm and landed with a little bounce on the carpeted floor.

Michael Forever

MICHAEL ROSS IN the *Yale Daily News*. The Bird Man couldn't believe his eyes. Stumbling on this newspaper piece brought back memories of the war years. Catinat Boulevard. The Pink Night Club. Givral Café. Hot crowded sidewalks. Street urchins peddling Chiclets gum. Knock-kneed prostitutes selling cheap love. Mai curled up on his bed. It all came back.

Michael Ross. A solitary black man at Saigon's Pink Night Club. The Bird Man could still picture him. They'd mumbled greetings whenever their paths crossed. They'd had a short conversation on *Mission: Impossible* once. Other than that, they'd stayed strangers. Only Mai's constant pestering for information had kept this name buzzing on his radar. She seemed desperate to find Michael. What for? A long-lost lover? He wondered then brushed it off as none of his business.

It was the month before Christmas. November 24th. Fuck the holiday shopping, the Bird Man muttered. He hopped in his car for the 100-mile drive to Mai's restaurant. The *Yale Daily News* would be her Christmas gift.

Mai had made a name for herself. Her hard work had paid off. Saigon Noodle Restaurant was always full.

Instead of serving trendy fusion food her mother couldn't possibly prepare, she gave out customer loyalty cards. These cards didn't offer a free spring roll after five meals. They offered a free spring roll cooking class after ten meals. This, her mother could very well do. Instead of all-you-can-eat buffets, Mai organized poetry-reading nights. Located in Westwood Village, within walking distance of UCLA's English Department, her restaurant attracted creative writing students. They would come for its authentic ethnic atmosphere. Vinyl tablecloth, plastic flowers, fat Buddhas, Vietnamese singers wailing from a boombox. The students noted all those details. Plastic flowers mutated into *blooming orchids* in poems. Fat Buddha became *his face of contentment*. Sucky songs got renamed *notes of longings*. Mai loved such transformation. She gaped at the talent around her. She wished she could write like those UCLA students. Dishing out free beers, she considered herself a true patron of the arts. "Drink up! Will calm your nerves before the reading!" she'd tell each aspiring poet. Mai knew very well one free beer would lead to multiple paid ones and an order of food at some point. A subversive patron of the arts and a fine homeschooled MBAer she was. No need for fancy diplomas. No need to go to business school for this.

Mai's back to him, the Bird Man approached quietly from behind. He pinched her waist. He puckered his lips. He blew puffs of nicotine breath on her neck. The unexpected gestures so startled Mai she let loose a series of swear words. "Shit! What the fuck!" Swinging around, she dropped her notepad on the floor. In an old teasing move, the man let his bird tattoo circle above

Mai's head. She automatically reached up for it, giggling like a schoolgirl on her first date. This scene earned a few raised eyebrows. Some regular customers snickered. In their mind, she was a quiet owner-cum-waitress. Not an excited woman, flushing in front of her ex-lover. Had they known Mai's ex-lover to be a former CIA spy, they wouldn't snicker so much. Or perhaps they would snicker more. Such an absurd scenario would keep them busy writing for weeks. Sex and spies in the hands of the talented would make for one unending erotic poem.

His arm around her waist, the Bird Man led Mai to the kitchen. Away from clients' eyes and in full view of her mother, he gave Mai a long kiss. She resisted at first, only to acquiesce a few seconds later. She so missed this human touch.

"Well, hello! Hello!" Mai's mother smacked her tongue.

"Hello, Mrs. Tran! How are you?"

"Fine. Long time no see!" she answered in a sarcastic tone. She'd meant to ask, "When will you marry my daughter?" but refused to cheapen Mai's value with such a question.

Michael's story in print surprised Mai. She grabbed the newspaper from the Bird Man. Out of her mother's view, she scanned it. A young Michael in uniform. A Purple Heart medal in his hand. An older Michael in jeans and sweatshirt. His smile revealing sharp incisors. Yes, she'd been searching for those teeth, been anticipating those lips. His snug fit inside her. His in-out to the tempo of jazz music. Ah, her forever indulgence! He was now in New Haven, Connecticut. "That's near New

York City," the Bird Man said. "Yale University, my Alma Mater! I still have friends there. No problem finding Michael's address."

Michael's photos left Mai with a painful heart. She felt pressure on her chest. Perhaps it was just her stomach complaining of hunger. A squeezed heart or a stomach devoid of food? It was hard differentiating them. It was delicate facing an old boyfriend while holding pictures of a lost lover. What she had done with one, she could never tell the other. Her secret black child would forever stay that way.

Mai opened the fridge to pour herself a beer. Her mother's gaze bothered her. It followed her every movement. She could imagine her barrage of questions. "What's going on? Why is he here? What's in that newspaper? Since when do you drink beer?" Mai made a show of throwing the Yale article away. She gulped her beer in one shot and pulled a confused Bird Man outside. "Please hurry up with your spring rolls, Mother. Customers are waiting," she said through grinding teeth.

Overwhelmed by curiosity, Mai's mother bolted for her garbage bin. A pair of chopsticks in hand, she fished out the soiled article. A black man under the heading "Vietnam Vet Speaks Out" stared at her. She understood nothing. That didn't stop her from pouting. She turned to her ancestor altar. In a whiny voice, she began her praying, moaning and complaining.

Looking for the Orphan

MAI LY RANG the doorbell four times without success. On her fifth try, a young nun in a white outfit marched noisily out. She suppressed a "Hey, stop ringing!" Her eyes did a quick up-down. Wordlessly, she turned around. This is a matter for Mother Superior, I have nothing to do with these communist types, she thought. Even without her starchy green uniform, Mai Ly couldn't hide her Party look. There was something about her walk—back straight, head lifted—that sent ominous vibes to a people raised on the Confucian virtue of humbleness. In vain, Mai Ly called after the nun.

A minute later, a bespectacled middle-aged nun came out. She walked with deliberate slowness as if needing those extra seconds to plan her next move. Her dragging feet scratched a cement walkway. At the rusted gate, she fumbled for a key around her waist. She sighed when her keychain fell from her grasp. Picking it up, she sighed some more. She unlocked the gate door and cursed when she couldn't re-lock it. She waved Mai Ly's official badge away with her dismissive hand. Awakened from her nap, Mother Superior was in no mood for Comrade Talk.

"Yes? How can we help you, my child?"

Surprised at being called "my child," Mai Ly could only stutter, "Eh ... um. I hear there is a half-black kid here, Comrade."

"Call me Mother Superior."

"Yes, Mother Superior. Is there a half-black child here? I ... I was a friend of the kid's mother. She left for America in '75. And ... um. Well, I wonder if I could see the kid?"

"Name? Age? Sex?" Mother Superior yawned. Mai Ly shook her head in embarrassment. She shrugged. Scanning the clouds for an answer, she found nothing. No hint of a doll. No suggestion of a car. Nothing to help her guess the child's sex. Clouds only looked like clouds that day.

Mai Ly's awkwardness brought a grin to Mother Superior's face. She bent down to gather frangipani petals still wet from the previous night's downpour. Catlike, she sneaked up to Mai Ly. One by one she applied petals to the girl's red burning cheeks. Sucked in by the heat, they managed to cling for a second before making their spiralling dance downward. "Frangipani, good antidote for blushing cheeks," Mother Superior said.

"There are many half-breeds here. Half-breed babies meant sleeping with foreigners, it meant loose and easy girls. You know how it was during the war with all those foreign soldiers. They were homesick lonely men. It was not hard to meet poor peasant girls eager to please them for a few *dongs*. That's how we ended up inheriting all those unwanted babies. Half-black, half-white, half-Korean, half-Japanese, half-Filipino, we have them all.

Can't keep track of who's who. Sorry, I can't help you. Come back when you have a birth date, a name or a gender. It would be easier to find then. Good day now, I have things to do."

Back inside and safe from Mai Ly's curious gaze, Mother Superior crossed herself. She ran toward a large marble statue of Mary standing prominently in the interior courtyard. On her tippy toes, she kissed Mary's marble feet. "Please forgive me for my lies," she whispered.

Mother Superior understood the communists' obsession with bi-racial kids. These children were their enemy's offspring after all. Did they carry that dreaded gene of capitalism in them? Or even worse, inherited traits of American imperialism? Did they pose a menace to socialism? A whole generation of sleeper cells, perhaps? Mother Superior giggled as this image crossed her mind. She remembered that old TV show *Mission: Impossible* and shook her head.

The orphanage did not house a bunch of half-black kids. There was only one and until two years ago, he shared Mother Superior's bed. She couldn't explain her fondness for this tiny, frail child. His helplessness had stirred something in her. Dark and minuscule, this rat-like premature baby had annoyed all the other nuns with his constant yelps. His skin colour had frightened younger children who would instantly cry in his presence. He was a tailless rodent nobody could love.

Only pity emanated from Mother Superior when she noticed him for the first time. Pity eventually transformed itself into something more generous. After a third look, she picked him up from his bug-infested bed, stuffed him into a plastic bag and carried him to her room. There she hung him on the bathroom doorknob. She swung him pendulum-like till the crying stopped. When his crying restarted at midnight, Mother Superior gave a loud curse. Impatient, she unlocked a cabinet next to her bathroom sink. A bottle of snake wine in hand, she poured half a teaspoon into a glass. She took a small sip for herself. She flushed the rest down the baby's throat. It gagged. It coughed. It cried for five long minutes. It hiccupped for a few seconds. Then it went silent. Sleep. Blissful sleep in her arms.

Mother Superior eventually got used to the strange creature sharing her mattress. She found his regular breathing sounds reassuring at night. She enjoyed his warm back rubbing against her stomach. She took comfort in his eyes. Like two guardian angels looking out for her, those big brown eyes shaded by curly lashes followed her everywhere. They'd blink when sneezing fits descended on her. They'd stare intently when prayers transformed her rough voice into soft music. Yes, that half-black orphan was her favourite.

Brandishing Their Americanness

BESIDES A HALF-BLACK kid, the orphanage also housed two half-white pre-teen boys. Their large eyes, fair skin, big frames gave them the self-confidence lacking in others. Thinking of themselves as superior beings, they stayed away from everyone. They never bothered with bullying games, never wasted time ganging up on the half-black kid. All that petty stuff was beneath them.

Climbing over a fence one evening, they laughed at their act of defiance. They dared each other to spend the night outside. To their surprise, they succeeded. No harm, no fear, no tears. No one disturbed their sleep on overgrown grass. No policemen dragged them back to the orphanage. They'd imagined life on Saigon's streets to be full of freedom. They found instead a hand-to-mouth existence, which thrilled them nevertheless. Barely two weeks after their escape, they became street-smart, picking up enough Russian to hassle this new breed of tourists. They learned to steal after consorting with petty criminals. As a last resort, they preyed on people's charity by begging in front of temples.

Mother Superior had read about all the vagrant kids wandering aimlessly. She laughed at the new name given them: *bui doi* or 'dust of life'. Such poetry! And a slap on the Party's face! Propaganda about a classless society didn't fool her. There were still beggars lining the streets of socialist Vietnam.

The boys' escape incensed Mother Superior. It gave her orphanage a bad reputation. She was still glad to see them go. Two fewer mouths to feed. She didn't like these boys. She hated their self-righteous attitudes no amount of whipping could fix. They'd go around brandishing their white Americanness as if it was something priceless. They'd pretend to speak "American" to each other—keeping everyone else out of their game. "Hello, papu ti mo ti ti ti ra fa fito America!" one of them would say. "Hello fi fu fi fi fo fo me ro na ti America!" the other would answer in a haughty tone. They'd talk louder when Vietnamese kids laughed at their gibberish. They didn't care about sounding ridiculous. Their tall frames gave them an indisputable advantage. They could look down on everybody and bat their big long-lashed eyes. Yes, Mother Superior could certainly do without these two half-white kids corrupting her younger orphans. Two days after their escape, Mother Superior ordered Sister Tam to set barbed wire on the fence. She didn't want them climbing back.

The Writing Exercises

NOW THAT I could walk and talk, you banished me from your bed. My portion of snake wine also dried up. Only glasses of warm water welcomed me to the night. Spitting it out on the first day earned me a slap. You didn't say much that evening. You were too busy stuffing my plastic bag with torn old clothes. You'd turned it into a bumpy pillow that you threw in my direction. A thin bamboo mat by your bathroom door. This was my new bed away from you. So far away from you. Deprived of snake wine, I couldn't sleep. Images of Thu in her wooden box haunted my nights. I wondered if her purple spots had changed colour. Did her belly become less hot, less painful?

Sister Tam's class started at seven each morning. We always began with leg exercises. She read her Bible as I ran around the room. Next came rope jumping. She threw me a rope and motioned for me to jump. That task looked so easy on others. It fooled me into thinking I could do it too. Of course, I couldn't. Terror kept me grounded to the floor. I just couldn't move. "Jump!" Sister

Tam ordered. "I can't," I replied, looking shamefully at my bumbling legs. Fear of falling in front of her added sweat to my already dripping clothes. I didn't want to disappoint her with my graceless limbs after so many months of her coaching.

"Try harder," Sister Tam said, eyes still fixed on her Bible. I could not jump. I could only step over the rope. "That's not how you're supposed to jump!" After many failed trials, Sister Tam lost her patience. She snapped the rope from my hands and flung it to the floor. I ducked, afraid she would hit me. She didn't. "Take out your exercise book. Recite the table of seven and read me what you wrote yesterday." The multiplication table was unchallenging. I had learned it by heart days ago. Effortless, I recited tables of seven, eight and nine. Sister Tam frowned at my earnestness. "Stop showing off! Now read me your writing," she said. My voice cracked during this part. Revealing myself on paper, making sense of my world through words. It was more painful than I had thought. My sentences often left me tight chested.

"I miss Thu, the little skinny girl," I said, reading out loud. "She was my only friend here. I still dream of her hands. Her Tiger Balm still floats in my head."

"I like that last line. 'Her Tiger Balm still floats in my head.' Pretty good! Now, how did you spell 'skinny'? Show it to me. And pronounce the word better. Repeat after me: skinny."

"Skinny . . ."

"Good, no spelling error. I want you to stop writing about Thu. I'm tired hearing about that girl. Let her die in peace. Can't you write 'bout something else?" Sister Tam's inverted V eyebrows were enough to keep me quiet. "Well, what do you have to say?"

"Hmm … Hmm … what should I write about, Sister Tam?"

"Use your imagination! How about your mother? Write about her."

"But I do not know my mother," I said. This earned me a rant.

"Didn't I tell you to use your imagination? God didn't give us brains to stay dull. Imagine your parents' lives before your birth. All those television shows you watched from your plastic bags should give you ideas."

Imagining my mother before my birth was not simple. I wanted her to be both beautiful and nasty. I pictured her to be like you, Mother Superior. Yet no matter how hard I tried, I knew she could never be like you. Her hair would not smell of your eucalyptus. It would be lemony instead. Lemony with a hint of cinnamon.

Imagining My Mother

BACK IN OUR room, I found your note addressed to me. Dust the table, water the plants, mop the floor. These were my twice-weekly chores. My first try was a mess. I'd left watermarks all over. You'd slipped and fallen on the wet ceramic tiles that day. Pushing me away, you'd used a table leg to propel yourself up. You'd muttered, "Go! Go!" You didn't have to say much for me to know I'd failed you. Your few words of annoyance stung more than your scolding.

Practice made me better. I no longer left water on the floor. Your furniture didn't just shine after my polishing. It actually reflected my white teeth and your silver fillings. I wanted you to notice the improvements. I wanted you to comment on my hard work. Alas, you never paid them any attention. You only asked Sister Tam to re-mop after I've done my job.

I wasted no time carrying out my tasks. I wanted to be done with them before lunch. I started with the easiest job: watering the plants. I finished with what I hated most: mopping the floor. Lugging buckets of water hurt my back, wringing excess water hurt my hands, scrubbing gritty ceramic tiles hurt my shoulders. It was such a useless chore. You knew you'd dirty them again the minute you walked in. You'd point to black marks left by your shoes and you'd gripe.

My housework finished, I sat down to ponder my schoolwork. I knew my mother was young when she had me. My father was a black man, I was also told. From these two bits of information, I had to imagine a tale. I had to build myself a life story. I sat for a long time trying to picture my mother. Only images of an ailing Thu came to mind. "My mother was a very sick girl," I scribbled. Changing my mind, I crossed that sentence out. In its place I wrote: "My mother collected frangipani petals." My hands trembled as I added: "Like a fairy, my mother soared. Nothing could moor her floating spirit." How those words ever found me, I'd never know. Yet there they were, on paper for Sister Tam. They made me dream. They also made me sad.

"What's this 'Nothing could moor her floating spirits' nonsense? Don't get so fancy! Stick to things you understand. Are you Victor Hugo??" Sister Tam demanded. I shook my head No. "No, Sister. I'm no Vuctor Yougo." But I did stick to things I understood. My mother's spirit did float. It did drift beyond my reach. Unmoored, it did wander away from me. So far away. Nothing could bring it back. I understood that too well.

The Squatters

MAI LY RETURNED often to Tuan's house. Her frequent visits mystified him. He couldn't fathom her motives. Was she eyeing his parents' big villa for herself? As a well-connected Party official, she must've known it now housed six other families. They had taken over the best space, leaving him only a small room—the former maid's room. These families that came out of nowhere regularly spilled soup on his parents' damask covered sofas, thought nothing of scratching their rosewood dining table and bred carps in their marble bathtub. The disrespect toward his parents' possessions bothered Tuan. Yet he smiled knowing how these state-sanctioned squatters sweated in his frilly house. Non-functioning glass windows refusing to slide open, air conditioners gone, fans no longer available. This could only mean one thing: unbearable heat.

Tuan was scrubbing his kitchen floor when the first wave of squatters came banging on his iron gate. Looking up, he saw with surprise a bunch of sniffling kids. Behind them stood four head-scratching adults in clothes so tattered he could make out their private parts. He had to look away. He didn't want to see sagging nipples sticking out of holes in a blouse. Yet his eyes kept wandering back to those two wrinkled raisins moving in and out with each deep breath. "Let us in, damn it!" a woman shouted. Getting up, Tuan almost fell on the wet ceramic tiles. He unlocked his gate with reluctance. A hunchbacked man shoved a piece of paper into his face. "Look! We've permission to live here now!" he said to his friends' cheers. The man spat in Tuan's direction, kicked a pebble out of his way and marched in. Two kids followed, imitating his every move. Once inside, he picked up Tuan's old newspaper to fan himself. "What it says?" one kid asked. Holding the newspaper upside down, he made a show of reading. "Nice weather tomorrow!" he announced ceremoniously. With the confidence of a television broadcaster, he winked at each kid. An upside-down newspaper in hand, he continued pontificating. He read and on yet couldn't tell a M from a W.

Pre-Revolutionary Bourgeois Excess

TUAN'S BANKER FATHER might've left, he didn't leave his son penniless. Nor witless. An ardent collector of Western know-how, the father had filled every corner of his house with brand name equipment. Those old appliances now danced in Tuan's mind. They did a few cha-cha-cha steps before turning to the tango. Westinghouse air conditioners, Singer sewing machines, RCA radios, General Electric televisions, Sunbeam hair dryers—they all sang in unison. "Sell me!" they hummed in Tuan's ears one evening. Inspired by this vision, Tuan jumped out of bed. Pen and paper in hand, he quickly sat down to make a price list. Like the American PX store, there'd be no bargaining at Tuan & Father Shop. "Fixed price, Comrade! Only fixed price!" Tuan repeated those lines with a smirk.

Oiled and polished, the old gadgets took on a new life. Overnight these authentic Made-in-the-West pieces became collectibles. Fed up with malfunctioning Soviet goods, communist cadres from Hanoi fought over Tuan's offerings. For a peek at pre-revolutionary bourgeois excess, high-ranking Party cadres lined up in front of Tuan's house. These glum-looking men all pretended not to know each other. They all gave the same excuse for visiting Tuan: to confiscate his parents' collection of American sex magazines. Everyone knew such printed materials no longer existed. Panicky collectors had burnt them years ago when a communist victory became evident. No readers would risk going to re-education camps for some photos of naked blondes. Everyone knew that. Even so, the old excuse still worked. "Ah ... I'm just checking them for decadent American books. Oh, you too, Comrade?"

It didn't take long to sell all the appliances. Comrades hid radios under their raincoats. Bicycles carted away sewing machines camouflaged by old bedsheets. Midnight rickshaws discreetly transported air conditioners. This thirst for American goods shamed the comrades. It was a vice they must keep secret.

If old toasters satisfied some fantasies, exotic vintage jewellery tickled others. Russian tourists preferred hunting for small collectibles. "Real antiques but I give you fake certificates saying they just imitations. So you can take out of country. Understand?" Such universal language of con men—the Russians didn't need to understand. They shrugged. They didn't care much for certificates. Certificate or no certificate, it made no difference to them. They knew no Vietnamese custom officials would dare open their suitcases at airports. They knew what everyone else knew: it was Russian guns that had defeated American tanks during the war. Certain of their untouchable status, Soviet tourists felt no qualms hoarding Tuan's exotic antiques. They loved his mother's lacquered jewellery boxes, her ebony nail filer, her mother-of-pearl combs, and all other useless things she'd left behind when she'd boarded a boat for freedom years ago.

The Road Home

MAI LY WAITED patiently for Tuan to open the door. She liked his newly cut hair, ironed shirt and mended pants. He looked so much better than on their last meeting. Clean clothes. Mai Ly knew he could afford them. His mother's knick-knacks sold well on the black market. There was no shortage of money.

Tuan's muscles twitched upon spotting Mai Ly's Party badge. Everything about her—her brisk walk, loud voice, green uniform—reminded him of his re-education days. Two years spent tilling a barren field from dawn to dusk, his half-empty stomach could never forget that time. In the evening, two hours of political lectures followed the physical labour. He remembered those mind-numbing sessions too. Nightly, he'd listened to an age-ravaged face shouting into a microphone. Mechanically he'd nodded in agreement. Heartily he'd clapped his hands after each speech. He'd understood little of that revolutionary discourse. Only his bowl of porridge made any sense to him.

Tuan's last day at the re-education camp came as a complete surprise. A white-haired man had interrupted his morning routine in the latrine. Hobbling with an arthritic limp, he had waved to Tuan. Without a word, he gave Tuan his old possessions: a silver watch, a pair of platform shoes, some clothes, a crumpled wallet containing 2000 *dongs* and a house key. Tuan kowtowed at the sight of his watch. Then he stopped in mid-act. The first words grilled into his head came back to him: "There will be no feudal gesture in a classless society!" How about a simple handshake then? Would that be seen as too American? Fearful, Tuan stood motionless against a tree. His eyes darted back and forth. He wondered if this was a trick, a mid-term exam to test his incorrigible attachment to material possessions. He thought about throwing the Timex watch against a tree trunk. That show of disgust for American goods would prove his complete repentance, his successful re-education. No. He changed his mind. A functioning American watch would make a better bribe than a broken one. Gifts had opened doors in the good old capitalist years. Doors might stay shut these days. But who says rusty windowpanes can't be oiled?

"Thank you, Comrade Uncle. However, I can't take these. They aren't mine anymore. The Party should keep them. The watch is still good."

"No. They're yours. Take them. You're to leave today."

"Why?" Tuan asked, astonished by this sudden dismissal.

"You've done your time. We need space for others. Lots more like you from the city."

"Uncle, where do I go?"

"Back to where you're from."

"Uncle, how do I get home?"

"Go to the entrance. Turn right on the road. Walk till you see a bus stop. You have money for a ticket."

The old man's word sounded genuine. Tuan still feared reprisal. On his walk down the camp's entrance, he dared not look back. If he were to be shot, he'd rather not know it. "I'm just some rich man's kid. A nobody in the larger scheme of things. No true revolutionary would waste a bullet on people like me," he said, trying to reassure himself.

Four guards milled around. They seemed to expect Tuan's departure. "Name? Date of birth? Home address?" A few correct answers and two iron gates opened wide. "Send us some dried longans when you get home," one guard ordered. "And some coffee too," a second guard said. "Yes, I will, Comrades. Long live Uncle Ho!" Tuan replied haltingly.

Tuan felt strange walking down the road in his platform shoes. He wanted to jump up and down. He wanted to run a marathon. He wanted to do the rhumba. Only rough leather rubbing against his heels stopped him from dancing. His long, uncut toenails felt squished in that closed space. The three-centimetre heels made him unsteady on a pebble-covered road. For an instant, he missed the old plastic flip-flops left behind.

Loud thunder brought Tuan back to reality. Running for cover from the rain, he nearly twisted his ankle. On a rock, curled up under yellowed banana leaves, he sat. Carefully, he took off his shoes. He tucked them under his armpits and let out an "ah!" Protecting a pair of shoes was his main concern that afternoon. Monsoon rain poured for a long time. Gushes of water washed off all the grime under his dirty toenails. Delirious with joy, Tuan whistled a Pham Duy tune.

The first bus didn't bother stopping. Six hours later, a second bus came to a screeching halt when Tuan jumped in front of it. "Fuck your mother! You want to die? Get in!" the driver shouted, his cheeks red with anger. The standing-room-only bus smelled of chickens. They were everywhere—in cages, on laps, tied to hands. They clucked noisily while their owners catnapped. Tuan tried his best to ignore two hens pecking at his feet. Hunger turned him into a depraved person obsessed with chicken slaying. Twisting and turning a sharp pebble in his pocket, he imagined gouging them. If he could get away with it, he'd drink chicken blood straight from their squirming necks.

Two days on a hot, crowded bus brought Tuan home. He cried seeing his house still intact. He thought it had burnt down. Or been taken over by the Party. It was only boarded up. A piece of flat rock and a large tree branch worked wonders. Tuan succeeded in prying off ten badly nailed-in wood boards. From his pant pocket, he took out a key. One click and the deserted house came back to life.

Dark, humid, hot. Very hot. The house smelled of rotten garbage. It smelled of abandonment. Yet electric light bulbs still worked. Tuan stepped inside cautiously. He did not want to see a dead body. A dozen scared cockroaches scurried around. In another corner, a colony of black ants moved calmly about, each soldier transporting a grain of blackened rice on its back. Disciplined, they went about their business, impervious to Tuan's sudden appearance. In his absence, they had claimed this dark, silent space. They had taken over the garbage he had forgotten to burn years ago.

Dragging two full garbage bins outside exhausted Tuan. He sighed seeing overgrown grass and frenzied rats. Pigeons encircled him. Their flapping wings blinded him. He felt dizzy with hunger. Back inside, he ran for the kitchen cupboards. Nothing. He checked the fridge. Nothing. There was nothing to eat. What about that lacquered chest? Ah yes, the lacquered chest. His mother's beloved piece of furniture. Ceramic statues of Buddha, photos of dead ancestors, pots of incense, vases of plastic flowers. They were still there, still untouched. That chest also served as a spare pantry. Its bottom drawer often held extra food for unexpected guests. Tuan's eyes moistened seeing its content intact. A bag of rice, four bottles of Pepsi and five cans of Spam welcomed him home.

On wobbly legs, Tuan poured warm Pepsi into his parched mouth. It still bubbled. Yes, Buddha had blessed Pepsi, had looked after it in anticipation of his return. Halfway through his drink, he stopped to say a prayer. He turned and bowed four times to a statue of Buddha. Two years in a communist re-education camp could not wipe out his religious beliefs. If religion is the opium of the masses, so be it. Let me smoke some more, he muttered sarcastically.

A tour of his house reassured Tuan. No burglary. No petty theft. Even his mother's rings—small enough to be swiped without attracting attention, still lay in their original lacquer boxes. This was unheard of before the communist takeover. Directly or indirectly, almost everybody stole in the former Saigon of his youth. From petty street thieves to high government officials. No one was spared this vice. "A national addiction with little chance of re-habilitation," was his father's favourite expression. Communist re-education camps had fortunately put an end to that nasty habit of corruption. Then again, why steal from the rich when you could literally move into their house, scratch their dining tables and spill tea on their damask sofa? Sharing is such a lofty concept.

Rings Will Open the Door

"**G**OOD MORNING, COMRADE Mai. How are you?" With a forced grin, Tuan opened the door to his unwelcome visitor.

"Stop calling me, Comrade. I told you my name is Mai Ly now. Don't forget that. I'll make this short. I need to find wedding rings. They can be fake gold, doesn't matter. I know your mother left lots of jewellery behind. Can you find me something?"

"I'll try, Mai Ly. What's it for?"

"For you and me. We need to show them we're married."

"I don't understand." Tuan shook his head hesitantly. Two years in a re-education camp had not prepared him for this choosing-a-mate communist style. He stared at Mai Ly for a long moment. Then with a shy smile, he put his arm around her shoulders. Immediately she pushed him away.

"Don't be ridiculous! Nobody's getting married. I just need to fool those nuns. Can't adopt the kid if I'm not married. My Party badge can't open doors at that damn orphanage." Tuan's silence annoyed Mai Ly. She could see through his cluelessness as he tried figuring out which kid she meant. If he'd dared to ask "why?" she would've said, "why not?" Because the kid, my old friend and professor were once all linked, she would've explained. Because that kid is all I got left now, she would've added. Because your former neighbour was once my lover, she would've whispered in a faltering voice. Tuan asked no questions. "Revolutionary glory to you Comrade," was all he said.

Hola Mi Amigo!

THE *YALE DAILY NEWS*. Michael Ross on its cover. An old lover finally located. A letter written, edited, re-edited and ready to be mailed. Yet it still remained in Mai's purse. Re-establishing old ties was harder than she'd thought. Michael scratching his head in bafflement, that image unsettled her. "Who's this Mai? What baby is she talking about?" She feared hearing those words.

The child that nobody wanted, Mai knew neither his name nor his whereabouts. Was it even a he? Maybe it was a she. Mai couldn't be sure. In her haste to push her baby away that day, she didn't pay attention to its sexual organs. She'd only noticed its skin colour. No one had cried out, "It's a boy!" The delivery room had only been filled with her heavy panting and a midwife's nervous steps. The infant had taken a long time before releasing its first mournful cry. During those minutes of silence, so worrisome to the midwife, Mai had only felt remorse. Remorse for letting her parents down. Remorse for giving birth to a kid when she herself was still a child. Short of maternal instinct, her breasts had remained dry. Not a drop of milk trickled out of them. In its place flowed regret for all the tenderness she couldn't give her baby. Guilt for all the absences that would follow it throughout its childhood.

A letter addressed to Michael fell out of Mai's purse one day. Her mother didn't hesitate to pick it up. The male name intrigued her. Like pigs searching for truffles, she sniffed the envelope from left to right then top to bottom. She placed it against a light bulb and tried guessing its content. She imagined it to be full of forbidden words, words she'd never known. To her frustration, she saw nothing. The whistle of a tea kettle gave her ideas. Ah yes, steam. Steam would do the trick. Opening the steamed letter, she found only smudged wet ink. Mai's liquified words dribbled down the kitchen sink. Drop by drop, they meshed with the leftover soy sauce.

Mai screamed seeing her ruined letter. Then she laughed bitterly. Why are you snooping in my stuff, she wanted to ask. She made a cynical joke instead. "Are you a communist spy now, Mother? Haha!" Embarrassed, the older woman pretended to laugh.

There was so much information Mai couldn't share with her mother. The older woman only knew of the Bird Man. All the other nameless shadows had stayed quiet. Like a good child, Mai had always returned home before sunset. Supper with her parents followed by a solitary sleep in her small bed. That was her routine. She'd never fancied an overnight embrace. Her Saigon afternoons had filled her with more semen than she could hold. "Yeah, I was a daylight lover." Mai had wanted to tell her mother this for years.

Mai approached her mother with outstretched arms begging for a physical touch. A simple "Are you OK?"

would have been nice. The older woman reacted by backing away. She preferred attending to her broken nails. All her years in California couldn't change her ways. Physical discipline, yes. Hugs and kisses like they do on television, no. She was not ready for that. Aloofness was her defence mechanism against a daughter fitting too well into a society that still excluded her.

Mai let out a long sigh before settling at her desk. She must recover her melted words flowing down a drain. Fortunately, she remembered most of her twisted sentences by heart. She only needed to change the date and greetings. No more "Dear Michael." In its place, she would write *"Hola mi Amigo!"* This new expression, picked up from her clients, would throw sand in Michael's eyes. He would think her cool when in fact she was hurting.

Wit in a Cookie Jar

FROM HER CLIENTS, Mai learned more than Spanish expressions. She learned to write a sort of English her mother could never comprehend. Run-on-sentences, stream of consciousness paragraphs lacking punctuation, new nonsense words. UCLA poets were all reciting this stuff. Hearing them read at her restaurant, Mai shook with giddiness. She knew she could write like that too. "Brrr … beautiful solace full of holes scary scary nights ahhrrr me alone … again—why?" This, Mai's first attempt at poetic prose was met with such applause from clients, she had to give everyone free beers. Encouraged, Mai continued writing texts her mother never bothered to read, revelling in the fact that finally, she had found her own words in her own world.

In between clients, Maid would jot fragments of poetry on paper napkins. On discarded receipts, she wrote one-liners while waiting for imperial rolls to be cooked. She kept all those bits and pieces of wit in a large cookie jar behind her cash register. As an alternative to fortune cookies, clients would be shown Mai's poetry jar. They'd make a show of picking a piece of paper. The personal hand-written message always brought a grin to their faces. "So cool!" they'd exclaim. They'd sometimes return to her restaurant just to read a few lines of heartache. Exotic food served with words of sadness. Who would've thought? Mai did. An unlicensed yet talented MBAer, she was.

The Writing Group

MAI'S STOMACH ACTED up the minute she walked into the room. Bubbling gas was ready to pop. There was no way to suppress her burp. A hand in front of a mouth proved to be useless, Mai realized too late. She wondered if she shouldn't call it quits and go home. Luckily no one had noticed her belch. The crowd was noisy that night.

Mai took a seat next to a gum-chewing guy. She almost knocked over his bottle of Dr Pepper. "Hey!" he cried. "Sorry," she replied. She looked around with apprehension. All earnest UCLA types. Their eager, young faces reassured her somewhat. Mai could already imagine their I-love-him-he-loves-me-not tales. She was so fed up with those weepy scenes on television. She knew she had better stories to tell. If only she could find the right words.

It seemed everyone had met before. Mai was the only newcomer. A baby-faced, dark-haired young man walked up to her with a wooden box. He asked her to pick an image from it. "Why me?" she wondered. "'Cause you're new," he answered. Amused, Mai picked an image of a boat. She immediately tried exchanging it for another picture. "No exchange! A boat it will be," he said. Holding up that picture, he told the group to give a narrative to boats.

Her eyes wide, Mai studied people writing furiously, page after page. Ten minutes later, her pages were still blank. She couldn't understand how so much could be said about a boat. She wished she'd picked the image of a family. There would be stories to tell there.

The scent of fountain pens gliding effortlessly across pages worried Mai. It gave her a headache. Everyone was writing. She must write too. She must scribble a few words of her own. "So this is a writing group? Maybe I won't come back," she wrote in big letters. She drew some flowers and smiley faces to further fill her notebook. Mai had thought she'd learn proper grammar. That was what she'd signed up for. She never expected writing groups to be about inventing stories from kiddie images.

A shrill bell marked the end of the hour. "Please stop now," the young man ordered. Obediently, people put their pens down. Some nodded while re-reading their story. Others massaged their sore hands after such a writing frenzy. It was not long before Mai heard words that made her want to burp again. "OK, now we all read our stories. We'll start with Bea and go clockwise."

Mai felt nauseous. She couldn't go through with this. She couldn't read her nonsense story to the group. She was ashamed of her fresh-off-boat accent. Two Asian women sporting bandanas had ignored her when she tried smiling at them. Chinese-Americans born in L.A. They both had that made-in-America pronunciation allowing them to blend perfectly in while Mai still stood sorely out.

Mai emitted a few fake coughs. "Sore throat, bad cold, can't read …", she said in an agonizing voice. The baby-faced guy looked at her with a poor-you look. "Do you mind if Peter, sitting next to you, reads for you? We all share our writing here. It would be nice if you did too." Mai shrugged and gave Peter her notebook. She blushed as she snatched it back. She crossed out the part about not coming back. She underlined a few sentences to be read and handled it back to Peter.

> *The beach behind the old man's house stretches far. A full moon sheds light on a bobbing boat full of people. Already it looks unsafe. Yet how can I turn around? The trip has been paid in full. And I don't even know how to swim. I search the beach for a familiar silhouette. But she is already gone.*
>
> *"What happened on the boat?" they always ask. It is late. We are tired yet they clamour for more. I would like to tell them fanciful stories but my mouth aches from dryness. "We were lost. We floated for days and days on the South China Sea," I say. "That's it? That can't be all!" they insist. And perhaps that's not all.*

"Thank you. I like it. Foreboding. Next time try to limit your use of 'but' and 'yet'," commented the baby-faced guy. He gave Mai a thumbs-up while others stared at her in awe. They wondered if she was writing from personal experience. A flesh-and-blood Vietnamese boat person in their writing group? How cool! "Tell us more! Tell us more," they begged. Mai shook her head. There was nothing more to say. She'd never stepped foot on a boat. Never floated for days on the South China Sea. She'd only run for a helicopter out of Saigon. Her fear of falling off the embassy's roof had made her scream obscenities at her mother. Floating for days just sounded more book worthy than screaming at one's mother.

Mai headed for the bathroom during coffee break. On a toilet seat, she closed her eyes. Her hands on her ears, she tried blocking out the ventilator noise. She imagined her father lost in the South China Sea. She saw him floating on a boat to nowhere, his skin burned by a tropical sun, his limbs emaciated from lack of food. She heard his plea, "Mai! Wait for me!" Words of regret. Words of desperation. Addressed to Mai Ly, the lover? Or Mai, the daughter? It didn't matter. Tears for her father—tears she'd refused him for so long, finally started their course down her cheeks.

Too Much Purple Prose

A MONTH LATER, Mai still felt nervous sharing her texts with the writing group. Her accent didn't improve. Her imagination did. "No big deal to stray from an image. No reason for public humiliation. A boat didn't have to be a boat," Peter said in between sips of Dr Pepper. Mai nodded at this revelation. She could've written about a single leftover Cheerio floating in a half-empty bowl of stale milk. That would be fine too.

Someone picked an image of the sun. He held it up for all to see. Mai felt energized. She would write creatively this time. It would be so creative, nobody would recognize that bright hot planet. In fact, she would write about a cold rainy night.

> 'It was a dark and stormy night,' she writes. A loud knock on the door suddenly interrupts her. The girl closes her diary and looks up from her spot at the cash register. She recognizes her next-door neighbour, a handsome black man. They had talked a few times in the elevator, he smiling, she pretending not to feel the thumping of her heart. She opens the door and sees him soaking wet. He

322

shivers in the rain. It is a dark and windy evening.
She takes his hands and leads him inside. She gives
him a napkin to dry his hair. Quickly he pulls her
toward him. Her fantasy is finally coming true. As
his lips touch her neck, she feels a shiver down her
spine. She gives the black man a radiant smile
and rubs her stomach against his. She wants him
to feel the heart beating below her heart.

"Hmm ... lots of purple prose there." The baby-faced guy couldn't help himself.

"Oh, really? Thank you!" Mai pressed the written page against her chest. She grinned.

Do the Right Thing

MICHAEL FOLDED MAI'S letter in half. He slid it under his stack of books. There was a whole lot of mumbo-jumbo in it. Only four words stood out: 'The child is dark.' So what? Michael asked himself. Doesn't mean I'm responsible, he concluded. He remembered Mai being quite flirty around other GIs. He also re-membered being the only black soldier at the Pink Night Club that summer. The only one pestered by prostitutes' rulers. "Me measure you! Me measure you!" came back to haunt him.

A sharp pain squeezed Michael's chest. He felt his breathing becoming difficult. Alarmed, he reached for his phone. He dialled 9-1 but hung up before he could do the last 1. No, I'm too young for a heart attack, he mumbled. Taking a deep breath, he ripped Mai's letter to pieces. His pain doubled seeing her torn letter. He'd longed for Mai once. He'd dreamt of her long hair sweeping his chest. Now he only wished to hide from her accusing words.

Michael roamed around his neighbourhood in a daze. Sleepwalking to classes, he learned nothing. A permanent hum in his ears blocked out all other noises.

No one could pull him out of his stupor. Amanda's "Are you OK, Michael?" was met with half-hearted shrugs. At home alone, he mixed vodka with beer to drink in one shot. He wanted so much to forget it all. To be spared those long hours waiting out the night. To sleep soundly again. Sleep never came. Only hyperventilation and palpitations greeted him in bed.

"Oh, it's just panic attacks," the family doctor said in a calm voice.

"Really? How come my heart beats so fast? And I can't breathe sometimes!"

"Don't worry about it, Mr. Ross. All part of the symptoms."

"You sure my heart is OK, Doc?"

"Yes, both EKG and Holter came back normal. Here's a prescription for Lorazepam. Put a tablet under your tongue whenever you feel anxiety or palpitations coming."

"That's it, Doc? That should do the trick?"

And yes, Lorazepam did its trick.

Another finger-pointing letter landed on Michael's desk a week later. It stayed unopened. It stared at him for days. Michael could imagine words of reproach and recrimination stewing inside that envelope. Oriental women were good at this kind of thing. Sweet and docile at first, expert in mind games later. Hmmm, Michael wondered where he had picked up that idea. Probably from some Hollywood movies. James Bond. Must be James Bond.

Michael decided to pay his mother a visit. He ironed his shirt, polished his Adidas sneakers and went to a corner store for two bouquets of red carnations, her favourite flowers. He also dropped by Mister Donuts. A half dozen custard-filled chocolate doughnuts would do her good. "Lord, oh Lord!" was his mother's first reaction upon hearing the news. One doughnut after another, she ate till there were none left. A long silence passed. Patting Michael's shoulders, she voiced her second opinion that evening. "Do what is right." Lovingly she reached up and kissed his forehead. Such an unexpected move humiliated Michael. Stepping back, he detached himself from her embrace. He didn't want to be a little kid again.

Do what is right. Do the right thing. Back and forth, those words flew with the grace of a badminton birdie in Michael's heart.

Pig in a Blanket

THOUGHTS OF **A**MANDA eased some of the tight lines on Michael's forehead. He remembered his efforts to woo her on their first date. Cleaning his apartment, buying patchouli, checking out tofu recipes, even purchasing new records to serenade her. "Forget Rock & Roll on the first date. You want to impress her? You want hugging and petting? Romantic 19th-century music will do the trick!" And so it was "Best of Classical Music" from beginning to end.

Amanda lilted her body to Chopin's "Tristesse." She savoured Michael's homemade vegetarian pizza. She listened intently to his Vietnam stories. She guffawed at his jokes until she felt something biting her ankles. A scream ended their evening's possibilities. Jumping on her chair, Amanda pointed nervously to some swaying dark spots on the floor. "A mouse, a mouse!" she shouted. Upon closer inspection, she sighed with relief. No mouse, no ants, no spiders, no centipedes. There was only a maze of pizza crust whirling to a ceiling fan. "Probably just a fly," Michael said with embarrassment. Amanda too, blushed at her overreaction. Sorry, sorry, they both murmured. It was impossible to salvage their evening after that.

A fly was all it took to send Amanda home.

In bed that evening, Amanda fell into a deep sleep, her plastic slippers still hanging on unvarnished toes. A wet bed sheet and two twirling index fingers woke her up hours later. Running a relay race, her fingers had worked in synchrony. Passing a torch back and forth, they made sure she reached the finish line. As if they had minds of their own, they did not stop until she won. The last lap left her exhilarated. Wet and warm, she waved to a full moon.

It was a wet dream with Michael. Amanda had gasped at his muscular chest as he strutted around. He'd lifted her nightgown for a peek at her breasts. Like a guilty priest discovering *Playboy*, he'd closed his eyes. "Come here, Michael," she'd whispered over and over. He'd turned away and exited her dream, leaving her with unsurmountable yearnings.

One nocturnal wandering and Amanda's insect phobia fixed itself. Overnight, her white-girls-don't-bed-black-guys education got sent back to Mom and Dad for a much-needed fine-tuning. Pembroke, Ontario. It was time she got out of there.

Except for a whisky-flavoured goodbye kiss, their second date was as chaste as the first. Kissing under the influence, Amanda's mouth had found its way to Michael's tongue. He had blushed at these lost lips driving without a map and thanked God for his dark skin emitting no external colours of emotion.

The day they finally did make love, Michael felt like

a Magnum Shooter. So much liquid came out of him, he wondered if he didn't also urinate in Amanda. Tipsy, he couldn't think properly, couldn't tell which was which. Too embarrassed to ask, he fake-kissed his way down Amanda's body. Twitching his dog-like nostrils, he sniffed at her sticky thighs. When he detected no urine odour, he mumbled, "Oh, Thank God!" He gave Amanda a dog lick in all the right spots before falling asleep in her arms.

Amanda or Mai? Amanda's voluptuous breasts were the stuff of Michael's adolescent dreams. He loved burying his face in that generous, welcoming flesh. To turn Amanda on, he'd wrap her breasts around his penis. Her dirty talk about "pig in a blanket" excited him. Mai, on the other hand, never talked dirty. She'd only grunt as her small light body twisted in different complex positions. And her tightness was a thing he so missed. Gold medals. They both deserved gold medals.

A redhead and a black man. It was a difference Michael could handle. The gap between him and Mai was harder to bridge. It only widened with each passing year. A different culture, a different language, a different geography. It was impossible to realign their paths. Only a miracle would bring them back together. And an unwanted child was more a tragedy than a miracle.

Mai's letters arrived on a weekly basis. Sometimes it was only a postcard. Once she even sent a telegram. Her message was always the same: "A dark baby. Do something about it." Do something about it. The words whirled in Michael's brain. He hobbled to his desk searching for her last letter. Still unopened, it laid buried under his stack of notebooks. Crushing anxiety overtook him. He didn't want to know the truth. Didn't want to accept responsibility. Didn't want to be a father. Without thinking, he lit a match to set ablaze Mai's letter. He immediately regretted his cowardly move. "Can't run away forever!" he said loudly. Taking out pen and paper, he sat down to answer Mai. He hoped he was doing the right thing.

"Morning Baby! Why you up so early?" Amanda asked in a sleepy voice. She wrapped her arms around Michael. Her unexpected presence in his study unnerved him. He reacted by ripping his half-written letter. He turned it into a jigsaw puzzle no one could solve.

"What's up? Why are you tearing up your letter?"

"Oh, nothing, just writing some stupid stuff … no, no, don't bother picking up those pieces of paper, Amanda!"

"You've been acting really strange these past few months! Are you having an affair, Michael?"

"No! Swear to God!"

"So you're with the CIA or something?"

"Haha! You got some wild imagination!" Michael laughed all the while knowing he'd have to deliver more than that. One pinkie after another, he scratched his head. Checking them for dandruff, he lamented lazily, "Psoriasis, so itchy and …" Her hands on Michael's groin, Amanda interrupted him in mid-sentence. Snuggling up to him, she said coyly, "Pig in a blanket now?"

WTH

SEVEN UNANSWERED LETTERS. Mai could not take it any more. She began snapping at her mother. She stopped giving free beers to aspiring UCLA poets. Sullenly she sat through those poetry readings, her eyes checking the clock every five minutes. Her witty poems on the back of receipts got shortened to three words. What The Heck. Sometimes she even pared them down to the bare necessity. WTH.

As months passed without an acknowledgement from Michael, Mai started questioning his character. She'd thought him a good honest man. Drinking alone at the Pink Night Club, she'd thought him naive and lonely. A quiet black soldier. So different from those boastful white GIs. How could she not like him? And the scar on his shoulder—left or right, she couldn't remember. It didn't matter. What mattered was the blood he'd shed for that crazy, meaningless war. Other GIs only bragged about girls they've bedded or communists they've killed. They'd even compare statistics and make bets like at horse races. Crunching numbers was not Michael's thing. He'd preferred humming Nat King Cole songs. He'd preferred watching Mai lick her ice cream. He'd preferred sniffing her lemon and cinnamon hair. He'd preferred rubbing her knees. These wordless dialogues had comforted a messed-up Mai. They'd re-assured her on Saigon's chaotic streets. They'd made her feel worthy of love.

In America, those wordless conversations continued. Only they were now one-way chit-chats. Unacknowledged mail with no response. WTHs screaming at nobody.

That's How It Started

MAI STUDIED HER reflection in a hand mirror. Her nose was still plastic surgery straight. Her body still holding up on its own—slim waist, perky breasts, a young boy's bum. The oily skin had given way to a few lines on her forehead. All in all, she was still a looker. "How much for all the work?" an older client had once asked. "Oh, lots of money! Carpenters, painters, plumbers. They make more money than doctors in Vietnam!" Mai had answered.

What had changed? Time. Time had changed all. Maternal instinct. Guilt. Both kept under lock and chains during adolescence. Both growing like summer vine in adulthood. Mai lived obsessed with thoughts of finding her rejected child. She'd spend hours writing postcards to the kid only to tear them up later. Mickey Mouse, Disneyland, Hollywood sign, Universal Studio— they'd all finish in her trash can. There was no point sending anything. Previous letters to the orphanage had gone unanswered. Perhaps they'd been confiscated. Or simply lost. Lost like a kite after a tornado. Like a memory after a head trauma. Or like a sense of inner peace after war. They would not be found again.

Love letters. Imagine a love letter, her writing group moderator said. The assignment proved difficult. Penning a love letter to Michael was impossible. Four times Mai tried. Four times she found only sarcasm on her pages. The reverse was possible. The reverse was even therapeutic. An imaginary love letter from Michael. She would make him caring. His words would be warm. He would call her Sweetheart. He would remind her of their Saigon days. He would apologize for his lack of interest in their child. He would promise to be more proactive. He would end with four baffling words: Love, Yours Always, Michael. Neutral, non-committal, run-of-the-mill ending to a letter. Yet they managed to stir something in Mai's heart. Satisfied with her writing assignment, Mai decided to make a copy for herself. Unzipping a tattered leather purse in her bottom drawer, she slipped the copied letter in. From that same purse, Mai retrieved Michael's old love note. She read it out loud, then sighed. Her only love letter, she intended to save it for happier times. Running into her kid one day, she would show it this piece of prose. "Your father and I, that's how it started," she would say.

The Devil's Hand

STUBS OF HAIR on her young ward's face gave Mother Superior a headache. She shivered. She knew trouble to be around the corner. She took his squeaking voice as a message from God: Get that kid out of your room! Married to Jesus, Mother Superior could not afford rumours of infidelity at 57.

Undressing in front of the toddler had never bothered Mother Superior. From his bathroom doorknob, he'd look at her intently. Inside his plastic bag, he'd wiggle every time she took off her smock. His unblinking stares made her laugh. She once shone a lamp in his eyes. "Blink!" She'd wanted to see him blink. "Babies, no different from lizards," Mother Superior concluded after a week of observation. Lizards too would eye her without a blink whenever she cracked open a jackfruit.

As the boy grew in height, so did Mother Superior's modesty. At first, she'd turn her back to him. Eventually, she'd stop undressing in front of him altogether. In his presence, she'd only brush her hair. One day he'd asked permission to feel her silky hair. She'd shuddered when his hands wandered on her head. She hadn't felt this good in a long time. Go on, she'd said when she felt him hesitate.

The kid's new tufts of hair distracted Mother Superior. His head massage no longer gave her pleasure. The Devil's Hand. His coarse dark hair reminded her of the Devil's Hands. Before he could finish his usual 30-minute massage, Mother Superior pushed him away. She felt sullied by such hairy hands. "Go!" she ordered. He obediently retreated to his mat near the bathroom door. There he sniffed his fingers. Eucalyptus fragrance drifting from his nails kept him awake that night.

Clueless Tadpoles

MOTHER SUPERIOR DIDN'T recognize Mai Ly. She'd come asking about a black baby years before. She'd been insufferable then. She was friendlier now. Without her communist badge and official attitude, Mai Ly actually looked pleasant. A sorry-looking young man in old platform shoes accompanied her. Nodding at her every utterance, he was introduced as Tuan, the slow-spermed husband.

"Thank you for this meeting, Mother Superior," Mai Ly said, bowing respectfully.

"What can I do for you?"

"If possible, we would like to adopt a child."

"'Cause we can't have kids," Tuan said meekly, looking down at spots of mud on his shoes. He proceeded to scrub them with his saliva and long fingernails.

"We have many children here. Any preferences? What age? Boy or girl?" Tuan's shoe cleaning act amused Mother Superior. She snickered. She felt sorry for this bourgeois guy missing his boat. To this capitalist left behind with nowhere to go, she said, "Bless you, my child."

"A dark child if possible, Mother Superior. Boy or girl, doesn't matter. Around thirteen, fourteen or fifteen."

Mai Ly's preference for a dark-skinned adolescent jolted Mother Superior. She stiffened. Hmm … another message from Heaven. Mother Superior could no longer ignore them. Yes, God had decided and God would provide.

Mai Ly's performance as the main actress wasn't too bad. It was Tuan's role as her useless husband that convinced Mother Superior. She could picture his clueless sperm running around in circles. She cracked up thinking of those lost little tadpoles. Immediately she crossed herself. "Forgive me, Father," she whispered.

Illegal adoption gangs posing as childless couples. Orphans sold for profit on the world's market. Mother Superior wasn't stupid. She'd read her newspapers. Cute Oriental girls, yes. A clumsy dark-skinned boy? He would be almost worthless on the black market. Mai Ly's request for a dark kid must be for an honest reason. It wouldn't be for monetary gains. This thought reassured Mother Superior. It also nagged at her heart. Used to her ward's puppy eyes and yelping, she was loath to give him away.

A Bigger Longer Eel

MY VOICE NO longer belonged to me. It croaked. It emitted eerie sounds. Younger kids laughed so much, Sister Tam had to brandish her whip. "Hey, hey Monkey, show us some tricks!" They tortured me incessantly with their tongues sticking out of foul-smelling mouths. Even you, who used to defend me, looked at me with distaste. "The Devil got your voice. It'll soon get the rest of you. You'll become a beast." Your comment terrified me. I felt shame witnessing my changing body. Dark, coarse hair sprouting everywhere, my eel becoming bigger, longer, my chest bulging out like a stuffed beast, my voice, so strange, so inhuman. What else will the Devil do to me? Will I turn into an animal to entertain those other kids?

Sleeping by your bathroom door was not enough. You had to banish me to the dining hall. Locked me up all night. My monstrous body must've disgusted you. The Devil in me must've frightened you. Did you know nothing changed in that vast, silent room? My chest hair didn't fall off. My broken voice didn't revert to its normal tone. I could only howl.

The dining hall's emptiness scared me so. Oblique rays from a banana moon allowed me to see things I didn't want to see. On her usual chair, Thu sat moaning in pain. Her polka-dotted fingers pointed to me. Her bloodshot eyes fixed mine. Her head lice hopped toward me. She screamed out my name. Then she was gone. Her ghost terrified me. I cried out for you. Lost, my estranged voice could no longer find its way to your room. Our room.

The door handle moved up and down. For a few seconds, I breathed with relief. Perhaps my scream had wakened you. Perhaps you'd come for me. Stepping closer, I heard only silence on the other side. There was no "Stop fretting!" There was no habitual clanking of keys as you searched for the right one from a chain around your waist. That moving door handle spooked me. I imagined the Devil coming to punish me for all my forbidden dreams. Dreams of touching again your eucalyptus hair. Dreams of sleeping again next to you. Dreams of seeing again your naked shoulders from a plastic bag. You thought I remembered nothing but I remembered all.

Sudden laughter from outside the door calmed my fear. I recognized those laughs. I recognized their "Black Devil, show us some tricks!" No, no Devil lurked outside. The Devil was only me. Reassured, I went back to my mat. The dining hall was cold that night. Its floor so littered with old food crumbs, I could hear scurrying rats. I could feel their coarse tails flapping on my toes. I rolled my mat in disgust and jumped on the head table. Soiling Sister Tam's place with my big eel, I didn't care anymore.

She Wants a Starring Role

HER EVENING MEAL finished, Mother Superior wasted no time waving to Sister Tam. "Meet me in the chapel," she said. Inside the small chapel she kissed Jesus's nailed-in feet. She closed the heavy wooden door and motioned Sister Tam to a chair.

"What do you think of that adoption request, Sister Tam? Would it be good for the brown kid to go? I don't know what to think anymore." For the first time in years, Mother Superior felt disoriented. If the sign from God was clear—Let That Kid Go! —the murmur from her heart was less obvious. It was full of static.

Mother Superior's question caught Sister Tam by surprise. The old nun, always giving orders, had never asked for opinions. Mother Superior's tapping feet rattled Sister Tam. She knew she must talk. She must paint an accurate portrait. She decided to start with some annoying details. "That kid is causing a lot of disruption here, Mother Superior. Well, he doesn't do anything bad. He's just different from the others. So he gets picked on. He's scared to fight back. He comes crying to me with a list of his torturers. He probably comes crying to you too. Every day I have to whip those other kids.

My hands are sore from too much whipping. Do you think they are afraid, Mother Superior? No! They just become rowdier and rowdier." Wiping sweat from her hands, Sister Tam pointed to three red marks left by a forceful handling of the whip. "This kid has few things going for him. Still has problems with fractions and square roots. Can't do any sport. Gets his French and English words all mixed up. Only his writing homework is decent. Actually, it's quite good for a kid his age. I'd even say he has some talent."

"Oh? I didn't know that. What does he write about, Sister Tam?"

"He writes about his mother. He's obsessed with his mother and that girl Thu who died a few years ago. He also writes about you, Mother Superior. He has a wild imagination."

"Oh, really? Show me his writing homework next time." Mother Superior could not imagine the kid writing stories. Still, she hoped to get a starring role. She didn't want to be a shadow to an imaginary mother or a dead kid. "Alright, I'll take your advice, Sister Tam. We'll give him away. But first I must give him a name. 'Black Devil' is no good!"

No More Generic Nguyen

MOTHER SUPERIOR WAS an ardent follower of Jesus. She was also an ardent television watcher. Night after night, she'd watch American shows with the kid sitting next to her. She remembered a black American singer with so melodious a voice, she'd thought it was God himself singing. Squirming on her seat, she spent half an hour trying to remember his name. On the verge of giving up, a word popped up: Nat. Yes, Nat, but Nat what? The forgotten name drove Mother Superior crazy. She knew she wouldn't sleep trying to figure that one out.

All worked up, Mother Superior brushed past Sister Tam. Back in her room, she pushed her mattress away, removed a ceramic tile and went looking for entombed treasure. From a deep, dark space, she brought out an old *Time Life* magazine. Her hands shaking, she leafed through dirt-encrusted pages, stopping only once to admire images of a pope on his Vatican throne. The shaking hands went into a spasm when photos of a black singer finally appeared. Nat King Cole was his name. Her Black Devil would be called Nat King Cole from now on. Repeating that name out loud, Mother Superior changed her mind. No, no Nat King Cole Nguyen. Too long. Nobody would want a simple kid with such a complicated name. Nat Nguyen was enough.

In bed that night, a suddenly remembered Nat King Cole song filled Mother Superior's head. "When a lovely flame dies, smoke gets in your eyes …" Such a catchy tune. Nothing could silence it. Oh, how she wished to pluck that earworm out with her tweezers! If she could, she'd roll the bugger around her chopstick four times before going for the kill.

Wide awake, Mother Superior's brain started tinkling. She wondered if Nat's surname was actually Nguyen. She'd always shipped her orphans off with that generic name Nguyen. Nguyen A, Nguyen B, Nguyen C, Nguyen D . . . Nobody had ever complained. This kid was different. She wanted him to be reunited with his real family one day. To do that, she must find his true surname.

Impossible to sleep with Nat King Cole crooning on and on, Mother Superior bolted from her bed. It was 3 a.m. A flashlight in hands, she dashed for her office. There she unlocked a filing cabinet containing all the orphans' information. It was chaotic. Bits of information were filed haphazardly. Nothing was in alphabetical order. Nothing in chronological order. Mother Superior grunted at Sister Tam's lazy layman work. She kicked a newspaper out of her way and returned to bed.

The sun barely out, Mother Superior was back in her office. She tried putting order into Sister Tam's mess. "If he's around fifteen or fourteen, he must've been born in '71 or '72," she said out loud. Checking all those births, she noticed only five girls. The rest were boys. Of these boys, seven were underweight. "Aha!" she exclaimed, pleased at her discovery. Word by word, she scrutinized seven pieces of paper attesting to seven sorry lives. Nothing. She found nothing about an American father.

Mother Superior was ready for a temper tantrum. Four times she banged on her wooden desk. At the fifth pounding, a fearful Sister Tam crept in. "The kid's birth certificate. Where is it?" Sister Tam's shrug infuriated Mother Superior. She threw everything on the floor. On its flight downward, a red hand-drawn star flapped its wings It beamed its light. It caught Mother Superior's attention. She had not noticed it before. In a jumble of black and white, its red ink stood out. It glared at her from the dirty ceramic tiles. Mother Superior bent to pick it up. This star symbol was not seen on any other papers. Could this be a subtle indication of the kid's difference? Ten minutes of reflection was all it took to convince Mother Superior. Yes, the red star was to mark Nat's otherness. There was no other reason for it. Mother Superior crossed herself. Mary. It must've been the Virgin Mary who'd helped her in this search. And why not? She was after all a Mother. She'd know how it felt to lose a son. She'd want her Son to be found.

In flowery calligraphic handwriting, Mother Superior wrote in her notebook:

> Name: Tran Nat
> Date of Birth: January 14, 1972
> Mother's name: Tran Cuc Mai
> Father: unknown.

From Black Devil to Nat Tran—the change only took one day. No, no more generic Nguyen.

Last Day at the Orphanage

NAT'S LAST DAYS at the orphanage were like any other. Under Sister Tam's watchful eyes, he did 15 sit-ups. Next, he sat down to geometry and writing exercises. As a goodbye gift, Sister Tam added a square root-solving problem written in French. For lunch, he ate his usual meal of rice, fried tofu, eggplant. His task of cleaning toilets remained unchanged. Younger children still mocked him while older ones still shoved him around. Only the television viewing changed. It didn't last long on this night—the eve of his departure. One minute of Soviet peasant dances was more than enough. "Turn off that television," Mother Superior said. There was only so much she could take of stomping Cossack boots. She gestured for Nat to come closer.

"Do you know how lucky you are?" Mother Superior asked. "No other kid can come into my room. No other kid can watch television. However, that will end soon. Do you know what awaits you tomorrow?"

"I think so, Mother Superior." While Nat's voice throbbed with excitement, his drooping eyelids told a story of sadness. "That will end soon" felt like dent marks on his stomach's interior lining. Longing filled his eyes with tears. Only he had no idea what it was he longed for.

"Here, take this and dry your eyes. No need to cry! So, what do you remember most about this place?"

"The plastic bag, Mother Superior. A plastic bag by the doorknob."

"Good memory! But forget that plastic bag!" Mother Superior clicked her tongue. A craving for something bitter overwhelmed her all of a sudden. She got up to search for her bottle of rice wine hidden in the cupboard. She found only a flask of snake wine. Shrugging, Mother Superior poured herself half a cup. In one shot, she gulped it down. To Nat she offered the few remaining drops still clinging on its side. "Like I said, forget that plastic bag. Try to remember better things!" His tongue twisted, Nat managed to lick the cup dry. Mother Superior laughed. His movement reminded her of a kitten she once had as a child. In fact, everything about little Nat had reminded her of that black kitten—his warm body against hers, his yelping sounds, his big brown eyes, his thick fuzzy hair. For old times' sake, Mother Superior poured Nat some more snake wine.

"Sister Tam did a good job with you. You speak like a normal kid now. And you write better than a normal kid. What will you miss most about our place?"

"I'll miss watching television with you, Mother Superior."

"Alright, that will be our secret, understand? Don't go telling everybody that," Mother Superior said, an index finger pressed against her lips. "And don't look so gloomy! You'll have a new mother tomorrow!"

"What if she's mean to me, Mother Superior? "
"Don't worry! I've vetted her."
"What if she'll leave me like my mother did?"
"You're being dramatic! Now go to sleep."

Coming for Nat next morning, Mai Ly found him sitting morosely next to Sister Tam. His teeth showed chunks of bananas wolfed down in a hurry. The space under his fingernails was filled with old rice. Traces of oil parenthesized his mouth. He obviously didn't want to look his best for this occasion. By looking dirty as usual, he hoped his world would stay the same. On the wooden bench, Nat's downcast eyes never moved.

Mai Ly took her time reading the adoption papers. She wanted to go over every word of every sentence. Her "Hello Nat!" went unanswered. Not used to his new name, Nat showed no reaction. He kept busy chewing his fingernails. A sharp nudge from Sister Tam put a stop to this bad habit. "Hello, Aunty Mai Ly," he said without looking up. Automatically he went back to fidgeting with the plastic bags on his knee. In one bag, Sister Tam had packed his notebook, three shirts, two pairs of pants and four pairs of briefs. In another, she had placed gifts wrapped in old newspapers. They were coloured pens. "Use red pens when writing about your mother, green ones to describe your father and blue ones for square roots," Sister Tam said over and over. Send me those stories of yours, she was about to say when Mai Ly approached Nat. "Time to go, my boy!"

A pat on the shoulder. This was Mother Superior's goodbye gesture. Sister Tam did likewise. "Be good, listen to your new mother!" they both said. "And don't forget your new name. You're named after a famous black American singer! Be proud," Mother Superior added with a wink. At the orphanage's gate, Nat managed a limp wave that nobody saw. Both nuns had already turned around.

Nat kept his head lowered throughout the bus ride. The plastic bags twisted and turned in his hands. He punched holes in them with his uncut fingernails. Glancing at his clenched jaws, Mai Ly feared she would never see a smile. She imagined pulling his wisdom tooth with a string. Yes, it'd be easier to extract his teeth than to get a smile out of him.

Mothering. What did Mai Ly know about mothering? Nothing. Her own mother, she wished she could remember more than a name whispered at night. "Oh, Mai Ly, Mai Ly, Mai Ly," her father had sobbed for months after his wife's death. That had been her only childhood lullaby.

The Smell of Tiger Balm

MAI LY KEPT her eyes fixed on the conductor. She looked at me only once during our long ride. "Bus making you nauseous?" she asked, her voice shaking. My "no" calmed her anxiety. Turning away from me, she sighed. She kept her legs crossed to avoid touching mine. She kept her hands in her pockets so they wouldn't have to hold mine. I leaned over for a sniff of her hair. Tiger Balm. The Tiger Balm Thu had spread on her diseased stomach. It had promised her relief from pain. It had given her fake hopes. It would not fool me.

He Did THE RIGHT THING

THE DAY MICHAEL revealed his secret, all hell broke loose. It started as a quiet evening watching television. Flipping through channels, Michael stopped at a PBS documentary. Live images of Saigon flashed on screen. Animated, he jumped up from his seat. He babbled, pointing to familiar street scenes. Catinat Boulevard and Le Loi Street —yes, he'd hung around that corner. Yes, he'd drunk beer and talked nonsense with prostitutes there. He recognized the Continental Hotel, Givral Café and Pink Night Club façades. Eagerly he pointed them out to Amanda. "Hey! Hey! I know those places!" he yelled. Saigon's streets hadn't changed. Its mob, its clamour, its exhaust fumes from motorbikes had him grinning nostalgically. He could even feel its tropical sun burning his skin.

"What a blast from the past!" Michael exclaimed. He laughed. Sudden images of tall, fair-skinned kids changed his mood. Their shifty gazes, their emaciated bodies, their torn clothes made him gag for air. On street corners, they begged in gangs of three or four. They hassled tourists for free pens. "Cigarettes, Mister? Postcards, Mister? Me American, take me home!" they shouted to the film crew. Michael panicked seeing dark-skinned, curly-haired boys asleep on overgrown grass, their gangly legs intertwining. This documentary on bi-racial children abandoned on Saigon's streets distressed him. He zapped it off. He placed the remote control in his shirt pocket.

"No, leave it on. Seems interesting, I want to watch it," Amanda said.

"Um, no."

"What is it, Michael?"

"Nothing, nothing."

"Give me that remote control, will you?" Turning to Michael, she tried fishing it out of his pocket. He resisted. She tried again. Distracted, he threw it above her head. He'd aimed for a cushion. Unfortunately, it hit a vase. Pieces of broken glass put an end to their tug-of-war. "What a stupid move! I'll clean up. Sorry," he said. "How silly of us," Amanda said. They hugged each other and laughed.

"I feel bad for those kids," Michael finally said.

"Yeah, me too. All those horny GIs leaving their sperm behind! That's your great American army alright! Good thing we Canadians are not in this mess."

"Eh, um, um ... Amanda ... I was one of those horny GIs."

"I know you're horny, Baby! That's why we're together."

"I mean I was a horny GI in Vietnam."

"No! What?? Don't tell me! You have a kid somewhere in Vietnam??"

"Maybe."

"Why didn't you tell me this before??" Like wasp bites, Amanda's accusing words stung. Michael felt darts all over his chest. Buzzing in the air, her reproach would not let him be. He reacted by bending to kiss her neck. He didn't know what else to do. She gave him a hard push. "I'm going out for a walk now," she said.

Peace with Amanda didn't come easily. Chocolates, pink geraniums, dim light, Beethoven sonatas. Nothing worked.

"So what's the girl like?" Amanda shouted upon her return.

"Oh, a young Vietnamese girl. Nothing much to say. Well, she has long black hair. She is tall for a Vietnamese. Her English not that good. Probably not very smart ..." Michael rambled on. Desecrating his memory of Mai with a ready-made answer tormented him. He stopped in mid-sentence. No, he had lots of things to say about Mai. And yes, she was smart in her own way.

"She's still in Vietnam?"

"No. She's here. In California."

"Oh, Jesus Christ, Michael! You've been writing her all these years??" In a rage, Amanda smashed the flower-pot and one by one threw chocolates against the white wall. For a long minute, she looked at Michael with narrowed eyes. She wasn't sure if she hated him or pitied him.

Amanda's foul mood troubled Michael. He regretted withholding the truth from her. He regretted hiding from Mai. He regretted not playing level with his kid. Bent on changing his ways, Michael took out pen and paper from his knapsack. He sat down to write Mai the words she longed to hear. To quiet his shaky hands, he fed himself a Lorazepam.

The short letter took a circuitous route to express a few simple thoughts. It took hours to reach that final *Love, Michael* line. It was four in the morning when he put his pen down. Too late to join Amanda in bed. Bleary-eyed, he settled on his sofa. Hours later, he woke to the tick tock of a leaky faucet. Like a wailing, it echoed in his bare bathroom. It cried out in protest. Already it found the emptiness unbearable. Amanda's things were gone. Only a handwritten note on their un-made bed greeted him: "I'm off to my parents' for a while. Don't call."

For weeks, Michael waited. When Amanda didn't return, he went shopping for binoculars. He looked for her everywhere. On his balcony, binoculars glued to his eyes, he spied on all red-haired women. No, that's not Amanda. Not Amanda either. No. No. No. Discouraged, he slumped on his knees. "I'm sorry," he moaned. An apology to no one and to everyone.

"Ma, I listened to you. I did the right thing," Michael whispered. Then he hung up. He didn't want to share his pain.

No Wicked Stepmother!

AMANDA PUT HER suitcase down. One look around sufficed. She was tempted to walk out. The place was messier than usual. Old cheese slices drying on a sticky cutting board, dirty socks blocking doors, empty beer bottles lined up like pins in a bowling alley, ready to be knocked over. Michael at his worst. Amanda stormed into their bedroom. She checked the closet, looked under their bed, lifted her favourite quilted cover. There were no forgotten bras, no panties. She found only islands of wine spots on white bed sheets. Doggedly, she sniffed for a scent of female perfume or nail polish. There were none. She inspected garbage pails for used condoms or bloodied tampons. She stopped when she found only old Kleenex strangled by dental floss.

Amanda's unexpected presence so surprised Michael, he stood motionless in the corridor. For a long moment, he looked at her in silence, his hands in his pockets as if stuck there by glue. He opened his mouth to say something only to stop in time. He didn't want to stutter in front of her. Sliding up to him, Amanda pulled him to bed. Michael had often dreamt of this moment of togetherness. Yet now with Amanda by his side, he was at a loss for words. He began to perspire. A gust of wind from the open window threw beads of sweat into his eyes. He became momentarily blind. He shivered.

Amanda too found herself struggling for words. Her months away from Michael had been a time of self-reckoning. She'd done so much research, learned so much. The Amerasian Homecoming Act of '87, proposed and adopted by Congress, troubled Amanda. This bill which would facilitate the repatriation of Amerasian kids tortured her conscience. It revealed her two-faced nature. Opening doors to offspring of American GIs, yes. Bringing Michael's kid into her life, maybe not. Giving abandoned bi-racial children a future, yes. Becoming a stepmother, no. Amanda trembled as tears of guilt streamed down her cheeks. Without a word, she curled up against Michael, feeling his warm breath on her naked back. It was easy sharing her body. Not so easy sharing her odious thoughts.

As photos of Le Van Minh flooded local newspapers, Amanda's brooding changed direction. Her heart constricted at the sight of the small Amerasian boy crawling ant-like on Saigon's streets. Dragging his hunched back and emaciated limbs around, he spent his days selling flowers. Flowers made from discarded cigarette foil paper. Those *Newsweek* photos shocked Amanda. She couldn't take her eyes off them. Like a voyeur, she inspected every detail of the boy's handicap. His wobbly body on all fours. His bony hips shifting upward. His inward pointing feet. His unsmiling face. His curly hair and hazel eyes screaming "Me, American. Take me home!" She studied the crowded streets of his environment. Dirty pavement. Garbage-filled sidewalks. Blind beggars on street corners. Indifference everywhere. She imagined Michael's kid living that kind of life. Agonized, she phoned her mother and all her high school friends. They talked for hours during dinners. Sometimes even past midnight. "His kid and me, we could get along. I think we could be friends," she muttered. To this, they all repeated words she longed to hear: "Yes, of course and you'd make a good stepmother."

Flexing her journalistic muscles, Amanda went searching for information. For months she dug and dug. This new challenge buoyed her spirits. When at last she found a contact address for Michael's child, she hopped excitedly. With her right hand, she waved that important piece of paper. With her left hand, she flung her guilt onto the scorching sidewalk. There it frittered away, desiccated.

Plov Is Russian for Rice

HOW SHOULD I address her? Aunty Mai Ly? Or Mama Mai Ly? Comrade Mai Ly? Perhaps just Miss Mai Ly? I preferred that last choice. Miss Mai Ly. I preferred keeping our relationship formal and distant. She was not mean to me. She never hit me, never scolded me, never mocked my bumbling limbs. Not a bad person, yet I couldn't allow her an entrance into my world. She could never replace Sister Tam whose whipping taught me all that I knew. Sister Tam, whose white skin, chubby cheeks and large brown eyes I could not get out of my mind. It was her horned-angel face that rocked me to sleep every night. Naturally, nobody could replace you, Mother Superior. Our shared mattress. Our midnight spoonful of snake wine. Our forbidden television shows. Yes, I remembered. I remembered too well.

Squinted eyes greeted me at Mai Ly's place. None of her roommates took Mai Ly's words seriously. "He's my long-lost nephew ..." was met with snickers. Some even hissed at the suggestion of a family tie. One by one, five women approached me for a better look at my wiry hair.

"What's the matter? Never seen a brown kid?" Mai Ly asked so aggressively, no one dared to answer. She pushed me into her bedroom and closed the door. Small and stocked full of old carton boxes, the room left little space for walking around. A bamboo mat in a corner beckoned me. I knew it was for me. I went there without being told. The rest—a stained cot, a badly scratched desk, a plastic blue chair—that was for Mai Ly. I knew that too. I could smell her Tiger Balm all over that furniture.

Besides a large poster of Uncle Ho staring down at me, Mai Ly's room reminded me of yours, Mother Superior. Same beige walls marred by cracks. Same loose ceramic tiles on the floor. Same non-functioning ceiling fan. Same black curtains repelling curious eyes. I wondered if I hadn't also brought with me the same geckoes and cockroaches.

Except for one woman, Mai Ly's four roommates looked eerily like her. Their stiff green uniforms, their caps punctuated by a red star, their curt talk, their stomping around—I couldn't tell them apart. They all scared me with shiny handcuffs hooked to their belt loops. They all mystified me with their coded Uncle Ho talk. *He needs to be Uncle Hoed. Did you Uncle Ho her? I hear Comrade X started Uncle Hoing her own family!*

"What did the nuns teach you?" one of Mai Ly's roommates asked. Her crossed eyes intrigued me so much, I couldn't stop staring at her.

"Big Sister, I learned mathematics, writing, some foreign languages and physical education,"

"Call me Aunty. I'm old enough to be your mother! Which foreign language? The colonialist language? Or capitalist language?" Not knowing which was which, I blurted out, "*Plov. Plov* is Russian for rice. I learned

Russian, Aunty." Her nod of approval prompted me to continue. "I also learned some French and English. Sister Tam is very good at languages. Mother Superior too." For some unknown reasons, turning those nuns into saints became my mission. I wanted to forget their whips, their criticism, their screams. I wanted to let bloom only generous memories of the two women who'd mothered me when my own mother had pushed me away.

"Hmm, I thought so. French and English. Colonialist and capitalist languages! Did you learn any history? Political lessons? Did you even know there was a war??"

"Yes, Aunty. I saw that on television …" Immediately I regretted my remark. I'd promised Mother Superior to keep quiet about her television. And there I was admitting to it at the first interrogation. Yes, it felt like an interrogation. It felt like *Mission: Impossible.*

"Television! Those nuns are too spoiled. I bet it's an American brand too! Do you even know what communism is?"

"Hmm, Hmm, yes Aunty … Hmm. Long Live Uncle Ho!" I said after a minute hesitation. *Long Live Uncle Ho*, this was Mother Superior's automatic uttering whenever electricity went out during her favourite television shows. Frowning at my ignorance, Cross-Eyed Aunty tapped her foot. She played with a pair of handcuffs on her belt loop. Petrified, I screamed, "I Uncle Hoed those nuns every Monday!"

"Nonsense! I see you know nothing about socialism! You'll be taking lessons with me from now on. Every day at five. Now get those foreign language ideas out of your head. *Plov* is Russian for rice! Yaya! Haha!" Cross-Eyed

Aunty's mocking laugh would've echoed down the hall were it not for Mai Ly's sudden interruption. "He is right. *Plov* is Russian for a rice and vegetable dish." Looking up from her newspaper, Mai Ly gave me a smile. It was a smile that swayed across the room. Like a twitting canary, it was a smile that said nothing while saying all.

Counter-Revolutionary

MY HISTORY AND political lessons left me whirling. The French, Americans, Soviets, Chinese, Cambodians, communists, socialists, capitalists, imperialists, colonialists, enemies of the people, Buddhists, Catholics, atheists, Marxists, Leninists, Nixon, Uncle Sam, Uncle Ho, Mao, Pol Pot, Viet Cong, CIA ... How was I to digest all of this in one week? I couldn't keep track of who was fighting whom, who was right and who was wrong. Oh, I shouldn't even ask that question. Uncle Ho and his Vietnamese Communist Party were good and blameless. The bad ones? Those imperialist Americans, of course. At least that was clear. Cross-Eyed Aunty made sure I got that part correct.

My hands itched for a pen. I missed filling my notebook with stories. Oh, how my tales had kept Sister Tam twisting on her seat! She'd laughed at my parents' absurd flirting scenes. Description of Father's index snaking up Mother's necklace pleased her. She'd given me a 9/10 for that. At times, she could also turn violent. Once she'd screamed "pig!" while reading about Father's black eel. She'd slapped my fingers and forced me to erase that paragraph. I knew that scene to be improper. I just couldn't help putting it in. I was carried away in my fantasy. Perhaps I'd wanted Sister Tam to read it.

Each political lesson would start with a quiz. A quiz about my origins. Cross-Eyed Aunty would not let me forget my father. Day in day out, she'd pound into my head his status as an enemy of our people. As an American, as a capitalist, he was an oppressor to trillions of labourers worldwide. Not a writer, Cross-Eyed Aunty didn't care about description. My father's looks, his clothes, his walk, his speech. None of that mattered to her. A faceless monster was how she painted him. This was what she wanted me to remember.

One day Cross-Eyed Aunty astounded me with a speech so different, I didn't know how to react. "Listen, Boy. Your father was our enemy. Yet he was also an enemy of those rich white people where he's from. American politicians sent black men here to die during the war. Did you know that? It was a way to get rid of them. Did they send rich white boys from influential families here? No! We never saw sons of millionaires or politicians in those days. They all had fake medical notes to exempt them from the draft! They bought their way out with stuff like flat feet, bone spurs or some such nonsense. That country is one of the most racist places on earth!"

"Well, we're pretty racist ourselves," Mai Ly said from her chair. Her voice was surprisingly calm. Or maybe it was a voice of disappointment. It was hard to read her. Mai Ly's shifting ideas often left me confused. I wondered if she was only half-communist like I was semi-Catholic. Waving her hands, Cross-Eyed Aunty managed to shut Mai Ly up. Tired of interruptions, she turned her anger on me. She muttered incomprehensible words as she glared at me. I felt like Judas the traitor. Sister Tam had always reserved for Judas a most bizarre put down. "Scum of the earth," she'd always say. Scum of the earth. I wondered if it meant milking one's eel in a field.

"Your father was our enemy, Boy. He fought on the wrong side. However, he earned points for being black. We don't resent him. He's part of the global repressed people we wish to liberate. We don't have anything against your skin colour. You should count yourself lucky. Now go do your self-criticism homework." Unsmiling, her face stayed as rigid as a statue of Jesus on his cross.

"Yes, Aunty," I replied, trying hard to remember the fancy word I've just learned. Ah, yes: Counter-revolutionary. I jotted it down on my hand before it could escape my memory once more. Yes, 'counter-revolutionary' will be indispensable for my self-criticism homework. Those counter-revolutionary nuns had brainwashed me with their counter-revolutionary Garden of Eden fairy tales. My mother, who had consorted with an American soldier, was nothing other than counter-revolutionary. On a scale of counter-revolutionaries, she'd be high up there. Perhaps the equivalent of Uncle Sam, whoever he was.

Oh, how I missed writing about Mother's flirtatious moments. How she milked my father's eel. How she measured it with a ruler. Do a simple math calculation. What's the length before and the length after her milking? Oh, but that will have to wait. At Mai Ly's place, I could only write about counter-revolution.

Filling a Book with Stories

MAI LY SOMETIMES took pity on me. My struggling with the self-criticism homework amused her. My half-empty page didn't bother her. She understood my situation. Born an unwanted baby, left in an orphanage, mocked day and night. I was a star victim. I did nothing wrong, nothing worthy of self-recrimination. Hours staring at my pencil, still I could not fill those pages of self-criticism expected of me. There was only so much I could say about watching American television with Mother Superior. Yes, that was very counter-revolutionary. So was praying to "that bearded guy on a cross"—Mai Ly's nickname for Him. But what else? What else did I do to offend Uncle Ho?

My non-stop pencil nibbling bugged Mai Ly. Its noise disrupted her reading. Putting her newspaper down, she scanned my empty notebook. "What do you know about your mother?" she asked as if expecting to hear a story. What could I say other than Mother had left me? I could add that Mother had a black American boyfriend during the war, that she'd left for America later. That would be counter-revolutionary enough to fill my pages. Alas, I had already mentioned that two weeks before. I must find new material with which to whip myself.

Mai Ly snatched my pencil to scribble "speckled baby blue glasses" on my blank page. Next, she added "very pretty and popular girl ..." at the bottom. I responded to her intervention by drawing two question marks on the paper's margin. She smiled at my scrawl. I wasn't sure if it was a wicked smile or just a watered-down smile.

"Your grandfather," she started to say, then shook her head. "No. My father ..." Mai Ly took a long time telling me her story. Captivated, I listened without so much as a twitch of the eye. From bits and pieces of her tale, I was able to link her to my family. She had known my grandfather, a math professor famous in school for his speckled baby-blue glasses. She had befriended my mother, a pretty and popular girl at Saigon's Pink Night Club.

Was it counter-revolutionary to wear glasses? I asked Mai Ly. No, she replied. "People need glasses to read. The speckled baby-blue colour is another matter. That's a sign of vanity." A minute passed before she added words that made me smile. "The Regime doesn't tolerate expression of selfish pride. Our goal is to act for the common good. Not to look good in order to chase young girls." Ah yes, my grandfather's speckled baby-blue glasses. His vanity. I thanked Mai Ly for my new counter-revolutionary material. Denouncing my grandfather, I could fill two pages of my self-criticism notebook if I wrote in big block letters.

I dreamt of my mother that night. She came to me dressed in a pink *ao dai*. Her long thin hair, white skin and bony hands reminded me of Thu. Only there were no purple dots. Unlike Thu, my mother laughed a lot. She laughed as she let a black boyfriend caress her neck. She laughed even louder as his fingers crawled into her mouth. The dream left me so uncomfortable, I woke with chest pains. It was the pain of ambiguous longing. I knew I had to write it all down. I went looking for a pen and pieces of paper. On my way out, I tripped over Mai Ly asleep on her cot. Her snoring stopped for only a few seconds. It soon resumed as if my disoriented hands hadn't accidentally flattened her chest.

I wondered if Mother looked anything like Mai Ly. Mai Ly with her scarecrow hair repulsing birds. Mai Ly with her smacking thin lips and bullfrog eyes. Still, there was something pretty about her. Maybe it was her smooth skin, enhancing a straight nose. Maybe it was her tangerine-sized breasts under loose pyjamas.

Mai and Mai Ly. Two young friends during the war. One flirted with Americans, the other with ...? My imagination ran in all directions. I could fill three notebooks with forbidden tales.

Yves St. Laurent

BEAUTIFUL NUMBERS. NOTHING in red. No minus signs. Only money pouring in. On a wood and chrome stool, Mai tapped her feet to Chick Corea's notes. Her restaurant was beyond trendy by now. Turning-clients-away, her Catinat Boulevard Teahouse had reached this coveted stage. A new name, an updated menu, a complete re-decoration had transformed her *pho* shack into L.A.'s newest go-to. Mai loved her new staff. Three Vietnamese women laboriously chopped and fried under her mother's command in the kitchen. Three young Americans sporting ankle bracelets took orders in front. It was so hip.

Freed from her waitressing job, Mai spent her time writing. Behind the cash register, she'd look dreamily outside. A dented red Ferrari parked illegally. A just-trimmed French poodle tearing away from its owner. An empty beer can rolling down a deserted street. Any image would do. Once inspired, she'd jot down one stream-of-consciousness sentence after another. Leafing through her journal, Mai scoffed at her early works. She couldn't believe the improvement in her prose. She could barely speak English fifteen years ago. Hand gestures had been her main mode of communication with the Bird Man. He'd misinterpreted her gesture of "Deeper! Deeper!" for "Harder! Harder!" Mai didn't want it harder. She'd wanted it gently, slowly and deep. She'd also wanted to play hard-to-get. Play-hard-to-get-with-me-Baby. This was a fantasy no hands could convey. It was an idea beyond digital manipulation.

Thoughts of the Bird Man invariably brought up memories of Michael. Like fraternal twins, they were somehow linked in Mai's mind. Two homesick American GIs medicating their anxiety with beer. Two horny men sharing their beds with her. Two lost souls navigating the minefield that was Vietnam. The similarity ended there. Even twins grew apart with time. She appreciated the Bird Man's irregular contact. She resented Michael's silence.

When a letter finally made its way into Mai's mailbox, she grunted. She felt only rage reading it. Michael's nine-sentence note expressed neither concern nor love. 'Dearest Mai, You must know I'm in no position to look for the baby now. Still very dangerous for me to return to Vietnam. But things might change. Congress just passed the Amerasian Act. The kid could come here one day. Will let you know when I have more info. Promise. Very sorry I didn't write earlier. Sending you much positive energy. Yours Sincerely, Love, Michael.' Scissors in hands, Mai decided to strip the letter of its meaning. She spent an hour cutting out each word. Gluing them on a blank page, she composed herself a different message. *Dearest Mai, I Promise I Will return to Vietnam to look for the baby. You know, things change But I'm Still Yours.*

Love You Very much, Michael. A text decomposed and recomposed. She would tell her writing group about this new technique. The baby-faced guy would appreciate it. Surely, he would stop mocking her "purple prose."

A male customer in his 40s approached Mai. He gave a nice impression with his tousled auburn hair, blue eyes and straight teeth tinted by nicotine. He winked at Mai's usual question. "Would you like an original poem?" His head cocked, he answered with a smile. "Since words are free, I'll take three poems." Mai came back with her own quick wit. "Yes but paper isn't free. So please take only one!" The man made a show of dipping his right hand into her poetry jar. His eyes closed, he picked a piece of paper at random. Mai's abbreviated poem confused him. "What the fuck! It says WTH, WTH, WTH." Red-cheeked, she grabbed the paper from his hands. She wrote the first words that came to her: Watch Those Hens, Work The Hole, Will They Hatch? She nodded at her instant baloney poem. She marvelled at her new ability to churn out absurd words under stress. "Words Under Stress," that would make a good title, she thought. Better yet: "Words Under Duress." Yes, her writing had improved. No more purple prose.

The man shrugged at the new poem. He understood nothing. Still, he gave Mai a thumbs-up. At the door, he turned around to send her a second wink. That was enough to leave an excited Mai twisting on her chair. She noted his name on a credit card receipt: Yves St. Laurent. It reminded her of the French designer Yves Saint Laurent everyone talked about after Oscar night.

Oh, Jane Fonda wore Yves Saint Laurent! So did Meg Tilly! Who wore it better??

Mai's thoughts turned to Yves St. Laurent that night. She wondered if French lovers were as amazing as everyone claimed them to be. To answer her question, she played solitary Bingo till 1 a.m. Naturally, she won. "Bingo! Bingo!" she murmured under her breath as her fingers twirled round and round. *Oui, Oui*, Frenchmen are hot.

Sixteen Again

LANKY YVES ST. LAURENT came regularly to Mai's restaurant. Each time he'd eye her intently, following her every move. If she turned to meet his gaze, he would smile timidly. Then he would look down at his *Newsweek*. He pretended to read but it was obvious nothing caught his attention. He stayed on the first page all evening. Spring rolls with iced coffee were his usual order. Mai didn't mind him nursing a coffee for hours. From the corner of her eyes, she saw him ogling her. That knowledge pleased her. It added lightness to her feet as she greeted new clients. Yves St. Laurent's thumbs-up at her bit of poetry delighted her. She felt sixteen again.

Forgetful, Yves often left without his *Newsweek*. In neat stacks, those abandoned magazines waited to be reclaimed. They waited and waited. Yves never asked for them. Mai's "Mr. St. Laurent! Mr. St. Laurent! You forgot something!" never got an acknowledgement. He'd walk straight out as if the name belonged to someone else. She once asked him in her well-rehearsed accent *"Parlez-vous français?"* He reacted by blinking. Then he replied, "Thank you. Very good! Very good!" Mai beamed thinking of his absentmindedness. It was cute. A grown man forgetting his name, getting his languages mixed up. Behind her cash register, she tried recalling flowery French expressions she'd seen in her father's *Paris Match* magazines. Those words of seduction so nicely strung together had impressed a young Mai. If only she could remember them now. If only she could lure passion back into her world.

The Fall

AN INSISTENT KNOCK prevented Mai from counting the day's proceeds. She looked up to see Yves St. Laurent's face, wet from the December rain. Perhaps it was just his sweat glistening down his neck. Mai couldn't be sure. He looked distraught. His hands gestured frantically, his face mouthed words Mai couldn't hear. A gut feeling told her he was in trouble. Although she never unlocked her door after closing hour, she found herself walking toward him. His smile reassured her. She grinned back. Maybe he wasn't in trouble.

"Sorry to bother you at this hour! I think I forgot my credit card here!" Yves exclaimed, his face rosy from the cool air. Embarrassed to admit his forgetfulness, he looked away to avoid Mai's gaze.

"Hmm, I don't know. Didn't see any credit cards lying around."

"Please could you check for me? I'd be in so much trouble without my card!"

"Maybe Caroline put it in the cash register. I'll check. Here, take this napkin to dry your face. You're all wet!" Handing Yves a newly folded napkin, her hand grazed his. Mai smiled seeing his shaking fingers. He was nervous, that was obvious. Mai unfolded another napkin discreetly. Out of Yves St. Laurent's view, she blotted excess oil from her nose. She wanted to look good too. French. Tonight would be a different game of love, using a different language of love.

A strange out-of-body experience consumed Mai. She saw herself lying face down on the floor. She saw her arms stretched out, as if in trying to salvage her money, she'd failed to protect her body, had forgotten that automatic reflex to cushion her fall. Her ribs, her shoulders, her knees. She could hear the crackling of their displacement. She could feel heat searing through her disjointed body. She could sense her heart pumping disillusionment. His shove, his punch, her fall. It was all too fast for Mai to digest. Fractured spirits, broken bones. It was all too painful for her to remember.

A piercing cry followed by a loud thump startled Mai's mother. She wasn't sure which came first, the cry or the alarming sound of a body hitting the wood floor. Maybe they came together, hand-in-hand in perfect sync. Rushing out of her kitchen, she saw a scene beyond her understanding. A slumped body on the ground. Brought about by what? A stroke? A heart attack? A fall? It was something she expected Mai to find, not vice versa. She could never imagine this scenario-in-reverse.

Like a blue-lipped child emerging from cold water on a late fall day, Mai's mother shivered. Her teeth clacked. Goosebumps popped up all over her body. Saliva dripped from her open mouth. Her state of shock lasted five minutes. Only afterwards did she notice the open cash register. A rapid glance reassured her. Money was still there. Coming to her sense, she ran to her daughter. Lines of blood trickling out of Mai's nose scared her. She managed to stop it with a Kleenex from her pant pocket. Mai's regular breathing calmed her fear. She trembled as she tried to check her daughter's pulse. She'd seen this done enough time on television. She knew she could do it. On her first trial, she succeeded in tracking it down. Yes, the pulsating sign of life was there. Mai's heart still functioned. It still squirted melancholy.

"Give us details," a brown-skinned medic asked. Haltingly, Mai's mother answered his string of questions. No, she didn't hear any arguments. Only talk and one scream. No gunshots. No banging of furniture. No breaking of glass. Cash register opened. Money still there. 75 dollars. Only credit card receipts missing. Strange. No, Mai had no enemies. No health problems. No drugs. No alcohol. No medication. No family history. "So why the fall? Why the fall," she wondered out loud. In an inconsolable voice, she repeated her question over and over.

Mai saw her mother sweating in the ambulance. She heard the siren overhead. She wanted to reach out. She wanted to hold her mother's hands, to both reassure and be reassured. She yearned to shake her immobilized body, to wag her frozen tongue. She could only watch helplessly as she fell into a deeper state of sleep. Maybe she needed this sleep after running around all day. Maybe she needed to forget Yves St. Laurent. Maybe she needed to repress all thoughts of her dark child left in Vietnam. Yes, sleep would do her good. She would wake up refreshed tomorrow. Ready for another day at her restaurant.

An Official Change in Policy

MOTHER SUPERIOR RAISED her eyebrow as she spotted a short duck-like man wobbling toward the front gate. She recognized his peculiar walk. He was her plumber during the war. And now? Now a high-ranking cadre judging by his impeccable uniform. From her window, Mother Superior watched the man's wormy little finger wiggling up his left nostril. She cringed as he flung his snot on her fence. Nose cleaned, he rang the doorbell.

Mother Superior rushed toward her adoption cabinet. Her hands shaking, she verified all the papers. They were in order. Even so, she must expect the worse. An Important Party Person didn't visit for nothing. Did one of her orphans end up a murderer on the street? Did that brown kid spread gossip about her American brand television set? Or what? What could bring the Duck Man to her orphanage? A quick once-over reassured her. No guns. No handcuffs either. Perhaps he hadn't come to cause trouble.

A "Hello Sister," rubbed Mother Superior the wrong way. Her nose twitched. Like a bulldog flaring its nostrils before a fight, she sniffed. She wasted no time putting him in his place.

"It is 'Mother Superior' and what can I do for you? Please be fast because I'm busy." Niceties with communists were not her forte. After all, their goals ran diametrically opposite to hers. While she directed her prayers straight up, heavenward to Jesus, they preferred looking down—searching the ground for unexploded landmines, testing water for traces of Agent Orange, digging up mass graves for proof of American evil. Finding that evidence forced them to dig deeper. And the deeper they dug, the more their messages of hate spread on television. Images of kids born with no limbs had tortured Mother Superior. Dizzy, she'd turned off her television. Dragging her shocked body, she'd fumbled toward the dark-skinned kid in his plastic bag. There she'd held him against her until she felt his heart beating in sync with hers.

"I'll make this short, Sister. We have new orders from Hanoi. All half-breed kids can now go to America to find their fathers. We are to make the paperwork easy for them to get out of Vietnam. It's our new policy. Also new American policy. I must obey it. Where's your half-black kid?" The Duck Man's words gave Mother Superior's sluggish heart a shot of adrenaline. It was like pouring snake wine straight into her veins. She told him about Mai Ly, wished him Revolutionary Glory and ushered him out.

The visit was too much to be brushed off as coincidental. She'd just received a letter from America. It was a short, typewritten note on thick white paper. In a simplified English with a French *merci*, a man called Michael had asked for Nat's whereabouts. Now a local bigwig wanted the same thing. Add to it an official change in policy from Hanoi. And a new policy from America too. Everything was lining up. Heaven must be interfering somewhere. Mother Superior wondered if it was Jesus. Perhaps it was Mary. She couldn't tell. She knelt to say a Hail Mary. She shut her eyes, crossed herself, mumbled her prayers of thanks. Tears of relief rolled down her wrinkled cheeks. Perhaps they were also tears of sadness. Leaving her prayer half-finished, Mother Superior marched to her room. She had a sudden desire to re-read Nat's letters. Hidden under her sink, in a safe spot away from Sister Tam's prying eyes lay dozens of Nat's neatly scripted pages. She devoured them now with a smile on her face. She liked that bit about having to dig up counter-revolutionary examples to fill his self-criticism notebook. Mother Superior laughed, imagining herself a covert counter-revolutionary amongst a sea of revolutionaries.

Comrade Sister Number Two

I GOT USED to Mai Ly. I appreciated her slow hands not so ready for a slap. Her Tiger Balm hair, I appreciated less. Its medicinal smell made me nauseous after a while. I wished she would rub lemongrass on it. How about lemon and cinnamon, I once suggested. "No! Plain water is enough," she replied. Living an austere life, Mai Ly never allowed herself the pleasure of fresh fruits. Dinner never varied: white rice, tofu, sesame seeds everyday. Willingly she'd give all her meat ration cards away. The recipient of those coveted cards wasn't me. It was Comrade Sister Number Two.

Comrade Sister Number Two gave me headaches. Although young, she could outtalk Cross-Eyed Aunty. She could scream louder than everyone else. Her shrill voice woke us before cocks crowed every morning. Two chicken-wing arms flapped from her short body. Her hands' sole two fingers intrigued me. Like crab claws attached to chicken wings, they were a strange sight. "Stop staring!" she'd said. I couldn't stop. So, I spied on her all day. How she managed to finish her chores without complaint put me to shame for whining about my awkward limbs. With a spatula in her mouth, she'd fry tofu. With a hammer in the crease of her elbow, she'd pound lice out of our clothes. With a pen lodged between her third and fourth stubby fingers, she'd write letters. She wrote an incredible number of letters. They were all addressed to some person in Hanoi. Perhaps she had relatives in that city, I asked one day. It was a mistake I thoroughly regretted.

"No, no relatives in Hanoi and mind your own business!" Cross-Eyed Aunty said. Mai Ly added through gritted teeth, "She is asking for extra help. More food cards. More medicine. Her body hurts all the time."

"I see," I replied. I didn't see. I didn't understand. Mai Ly saw through my blank look. She wasted no time scolding me. "Ignorance of the war is also counter-revolutionary. Write that down in your self-criticism notebook. Didn't you notice how her hands, arms and fingers are strange?"

"Yes, of course, Aunty Mai Ly."

"Do you know why?"

"No." I shook my clueless head.

"Agent Orange. It's a chemical sprayed by American soldiers. Its purpose? To kill trees. To expose our comrades hiding in the jungle. The result? Poisoned lakes. Sick people. Deformed limbs."

"I'm sorry Aunty Mai Ly!" I cried. 'Sorry,' was now my automatic response every time 'American soldiers' came up. For everything they did, for all the mess my father left behind, I was made to feel responsible.

"Be quiet and listen! Agent Orange. Years later babies are still born disfigured because of it. Or born with disease like cancer. Ever heard of cancer? It's a deadly sickness. It makes you suffer before it kills you." My mind wandered hearing the word cancer. Images of Thu's purple splotches returned to spook me. Like a prayer wheel, her words "the pain, the pain," swirled round and round in my head. Mai Ly brought me back to reality with a smack on my right hand. It didn't hurt. It only caught me off guard. "Pay attention when I speak," she said.

Mai Ly finished her lecture by asking who sprayed Agent Orange. This was one lesson she wanted me to remember. I wasted no time answering: American soldiers. She then asked if I felt guilty. My "Yes, of course, very guilty," earned me a nod of approval. "That's all part of self-criticism. Now go write it down."

I wondered if my father had sprayed Agent Orange on our forest. Did Thu drink water poisoned with this stuff? A black man, an orange chemical, a body covered with purple spots. My head spun.

Agent Orange. I wished I hadn't learned about it. There was still so much to know about this war. So many more facts to weigh on my conscience. Those Communist Aunties would not let me be. I knew there would be additional lessons, further feelings of guilt. I could no longer hide from the truth.

I dreamt of Thu that night. She had grown to be my height. Breasts had developed where a flat chest had been. A closer look revealed the same skinny legs covered with purple dots. Her face was still sickly white. "Hold my hands," she said, pleading. Reaching out for her, I felt two claw-like fingers snapping furiously at my wrist. I screamed out in pain. "I'm sorry! I'm sorry!" I said. Then I woke up to a groaning Mai Ly. "Be quiet and let me sleep!" she muttered.

A Two-Legged Headless Giraffe

THEY'D FOUND ME. Someone far away, in another country, over so many oceans, had found me. That someone was my father. Michael Ross from New Haven, America. Mai Ly announced this news with a smile so wide, I could see two black teeth in the back of her mouth. My own throat throbbed as if strangled by a large hand. I coughed and fought for air. To calm my heavy laborious breathing, Mai Ly handed me a glass of cool tea. She sat down next to me and hesitated a few seconds before taking my hand.

Going to America thanks to some new American law scared me. I looked around to make sure we were alone. I feared the other Aunties hearing this. I was counter-revolutionary enough. I didn't want more guilt heaped on me. My frowning face puzzled Mai Ly. She reassured me this was good news. I was not a traitor for going to America. Hanoi had agreed to this deal. To cheer me up some more, she whispered in my ear, "Most Americans are bad but some can be very good. Just don't go repeating this to Comrade Sister Number Two!"

Comrade Sister Number Two eventually learned of my good luck. She didn't say much to me at first. On the third day, she came to me with a piece of paper and a pencil. She sat down in front of me, her face sweating from the afternoon heat. She held her pencil between two agitated fingers. Exhaling loudly, she drew a few crooked lines. "Guess what it is," she said. Her disproportionate image reminded me of kids' drawings at the orphanage. Four lines resembling a couple of long sausages converged into two lines on top. It looked like a strange two-legged headless giraffe. At the bottom of the page, Comrade Sister Two wrote "2." It was her autograph. She was proud of its distinct curve and unwavering line. I offered to slide her drawing into an old, yellowed envelope. She pushed me away. Using her lips and two fingers, she succeeded with her task. "Take that drawing to America, show it to your father," she said. "It's my deformed hand, I drew. Show him my two fingers. Let him see the results of his work."

Even if my estranged father meant little to me, I still had an automatic reaction to defend this elusive Michael Ross. "But," I blurted out. "No, but!" Comrade Sister Two snapped back. OK, no 'but', how about 'what if?' What if my father had nothing to do with her short arms and missing fingers, a fleeting thought ran through me. Could I tell her this? No. I could not dash her hope that one day someone would listen, that someone would take responsibility for her misfortune. "Yes, of course. I'll take your drawing," I said.

America. What would I do there? How would I find my way around? Where would I stay? What would I say to my father? Sister Tam's English lessons were basic stuff for eight-year-olds. I had passed that stage long ago.

And my mother. Where in America could she be? Would I ever find her? Could we forgive each other?

So many questions without answers trotted in my mind. Two questions stood out: 'Did he?' and 'Could I?' Did my father spray Agent Orange to slowly kill my friend Thu? If so, could I ever love him?

Official Papers, Her Specialty

TUAN COULDN'T BELIEVE his good luck. Just as he was running out of his mother's old brooches, just as Russian tourists' interest in Vietnamese knick-knacks began to wane, Mai Ly came to him with some incredible news.

It was a sunny monsoon afternoon. A bright interlude between two downpours. Squatting on his mattress, Tuan counted the remaining jewellery. Only three brooches and four hairpins left. Everything else had been sold to survive. Three broken gold brooches, four dull silver hairpins. They weren't worth much. Money would soon run out. He'd have to join the mass of labourers one day, breaking his back for a weekly ration card of two dried fish. Memories of sun-stroked farmers bent over rice paddies gave him vertigo. He didn't want to go back there.

"Big Brother Tuan! Come out! Comrade Mai Ly here to see you!" someone screamed.

The cry jolted Tuan. He quickly jammed the jewellery into a straw-covered pit under his mattress. He straightened his shirt, combed his hair and checked his mouth for bad breath. Before greeting Mai Ly, he ran to the backyard for a sprig of mint. He wanted to be presentable.

A visit from Mai Ly always brought unease to Tuan's lungs. He'd often cough, wheeze or sneeze in her face. Two lines of clear discharge would also flow from his nostrils while tears of allergy swelled in his eyes. Mai Ly had become less threatening since posing as his barren wife. Their trip to the orphanage was even funny in Tuan's mind. No longer a foe, Mai Ly was still far from being a friend.

"Comrade Mai Ly! How are you? Please come in. Let me get you a glass of water." Tired of hearing platitudes, Mai Ly dragged Tuan to his room. Locking the door, she motioned for him to come closer. Without a prelude, without an introduction, she mentioned Nat's twist of fate. Nat's upcoming departure for America overwhelmed Tuan. He could only react with big bulging eyes. For an instant, he seemed more fish-eyed than Mai Ly. His long silence finally gave way to a shaky "It can't be true!"

Ignoring Tuan's outburst, Mai Ly went straight to the point. "I need to ask you a favour. Nat's still a minor. He doesn't speak much English. He's not street-smart. He doesn't know his way around our town. How can he go to America unescorted?"

"Err, you're asking me to teach him more English? No problem! *Ohh say can you see? by the dawn early light!*" Eager to show off his Americanness, Tuan sang loudly, oblivious to the eyes and ears lurking next door.

"Not just that. Nat also needs an adult to accompany him. You're to go with him." Mai Ly's words so shocked Tuan, his feet buckled. He stumbled on a chair. His heart palpitated. His restless legs twitched. He got up and hopped around the room. He felt like a galloping horse after weeks tied to a post.

"Huh, I don't get it. Why me?" Tuan stammered, still bewildered by Mai Ly's order. He was afraid of being tricked.

"You speak English. You understand American thinking. Will be good for the kid."

"But, but how will I get to America, Comrade?"

"New American law. Half-American kids can go there now. Minors must be accompanied by an adult family member. America let them in. Hanoi just goes along. So you're to go with Nat."

"But, but ... I'm blacklisted. Re-education camp, remember? Why would Hanoi let me out?"

"Don't worry! Nobody keeps track of people like you. There's too many of you ... no one cares." Mai Ly's impassive voice perplexed Tuan. Going to America. How could she act so detached? It was like ordering him to buy a dozen bananas at Ben Thanh market.

"I'm not even related to Nat!" Tuan's protest was met with a slap on his back. To shut him up, Mai Ly placed her index on his lips. She could get him fake papers, she murmured. He would be Nat's half-brother. She could make him younger. Dates and names, she took care of those things. "'Official' paper—that's my specialty," she said with a straight face. Before leaving, she told him to avoid the sun. She handed him a pot of coconut oil from her bag. "Apply this oil to your face. Every day. It would give younger-looking skin."

"You, you don't want to go to America, Comrade Mai Ly? You could be Nat's sister. Or his mother," Tuan suggested hesitantly. Offering his spot to Mai Ly was pure show. They both knew it.

"Why should I go to America? My home is here. Only people like you want to leave!" Mai Ly's sea-salt tone stung. Belittled, Tuan lowered his head. He tried picking at the dirt under his fingernails.

America, America, Tuan whispered in his half-dream that night. Perhaps he'd find his parents in America. His neighbour Mai. Perhaps he'd run into her too. The years of silence, the chronically empty mailbox, did not dampen his hope. "Confiscated mail, that's all it is," he'd tell himself. He laughed imagining a nameless comrade in some dark room checking his mother's letters for counter-revolutionary messages. Of course, they would be full of counter-revolutionary gossip. His mother's chitchat had always been about new American appliances, fancy jewellery or the latest French restaurants opening in town. She would not change in America. If anything, she would be doubly counter-revolutionary there. "Confiscated letters, that's all it is," Tuan would repeat this every night as he pondered his room's empty walls. "No, they didn't drown. Couldn't drown," he'd say before falling asleep.

Repulsion and Fascination

TWO MONTHS BEFORE my departure for America, Mai Ly busied herself with cutting and sewing. She measured my arm's length over and over until she got it right. On newspapers, she drew shapes I didn't quite recognize. Pinning the paper on an old blanket, she cursed her malfunctioning rusty scissors. Her creation took shape only after four days of cutting and swearing. A coat. Her old blanket became my new coat. "It is cold in America," she said matter-of-factly.

All four Communist Aunties chipped in to help. Comrade Sister Number Two showed the most enthusiasm. With her ration cards, she ran to Ben Thanh market for two spools of thread. At home, she insisted on recuperating buttons from old ripped shirts. Unable to cut with her deformed hands, she resorted to using her teeth. Chewing thread with her sharp incisors, she managed to yank off old buttons. The final result looked odd. The hem was short in front, long in the back. Buttons didn't match. Despite multiple washings, black stains persisted. Yet it didn't matter. The Communist Aunties all grinned. They clapped till their hands turned red. They hooted at their finished product. Comrade

Sister Number Two hooted louder than everyone else. She insisted on a show. Turn right, then turn left. Take the coat off, then put it on. Lift an arm here, lift an arm there. "Stop slouching," she screamed, as I cringed in front of her. Then she gave my back a tap to prod me on. Maybe she wanted more than just a spectacle. Maybe she wanted to go to America with me. Maybe she wanted to find the pilot who'd poisoned her village with Agent Orange. Or maybe she just wanted to see snow.

Mai Ly made an effort to spend more time with me. She no longer turned off her light at eight o'clock sharp. Her legs swinging from a cot, she'd tell me stories of my mother. She wanted to see my reactions to those tales. I listened without blinking, without twitching a muscle, without betraying any emotions. Yet I was completely torn inside.

"Your mother was pretty enough to attract hordes of American soldiers," Mai Ly said. "The more they pursued her, the more she made herself available to them. Despite her facility for arithmetic, despite her father being a math teacher, she couldn't keep track of all her lovers. One, two, three or ten, it was all the same number. She took them all in yet loved none of them. On the last day of the war, she ran off to America with one of those men. Did she think about her father left behind? Did she spare a thought for her abandoned kid in an orphanage? I don't know." Mai Ly turned away from me and coughed. After a long silence, she continued, "Younger, your mother cared only about fashion, even during times of tragedy. Hers was not the innocence of youth. It was the ignorance of privileged, ideal-less kids. But I looked up to her. I envied her carelessness. Foolishly, I idolized her." Mai Ly's description of my mother repulsed and enchanted me equally.

"Your mother knew my secret," Mai Ly confided offhandedly. "Your grandfather and I ..." She started a sentence that she could never finish. Those four words stuck to my burning chest. One by one, I removed them. Wiping my sweat off them, I changed their direction. "Your grandfather and I," became "My grandfather and Mai Ly ..." Carefully, I glued them in my notebook.

When it comes to my father, Mai Ly's words dried up. She remembered little besides his shoulder wound. Shot in the jungle, he'd kept that bullet as a lucky charm. "He'd seduced your mother with songs by a certain Leonard Cohen. Or maybe it was a Nat King Cole—those American names are so confusing, sorry! Ah, yes, he also carried a ruler." She giggled. "He wanted girls to measure him!"

For weeks after, I imagined my father walking down Saigon's boulevards, a bullet in his right pocket, a ruler in his left. Or perhaps it was the other way around.

All the Straight and Crooked Information

MY CONVERSATION WITH Mai Ly wasn't always about a past that was. Often it was about a past that wasn't. An imagined past concocted in Mai Ly's head. It was a fake story I had to memorize. Nightly, we rehearsed my lines till I got them right. High-heeled Tuan was to be my half-brother in this new scenario. My origins, already muddled, must be made murkier before I could go to America.

"What's your brother's name?" Mai Ly loved these late night tests. I yawned. My eyelids tightly shut, I let my mind wander. I let it uncoil the snake in Mother Superior's snake wine jar. "What's your brother's name again?" Mai Ly repeated impatiently as I rubbed my eyes.

"Nguyen Tuan," I replied, not bothering to look at the notes pushed in my face. I already knew everything by heart.

"And your name?"

"Tran Nat."

"If Tuan is your brother, why do you have different family names?"

"Because we have different fathers."

"Explain."

"My mother's late husband was a Nguyen. He died stepping on a landmine one day. To support her family, my mother had to do dirty work. She had to work in bars for Americans. Served them beers and did other things with them. Soon she got pregnant with me. My father is an American. He went back to America before I was born. My mother can't remember his name. So she gave me her maiden name Tran. She feared her dead husband's ghost. 'That kid is not mine! Do not give him my name! No Nguyen for him!' She heard his haunting words every night. It was a warning she couldn't ignore. That's how I was born a Tran ..." Mai Ly's rolled eyes at this bit of spontaneous information made me blush. I felt my cheeks burning with pride.

"My God! You got imagination. But slow down when you talk. Don't just recite. Put some emotion into it. So, where is your mother now?"

"My mother died too. Five years ago. Tuberculosis." I lowered my voice for effect.

"What does your half-brother Tuan do for a living?"

"He sells things at Ben Thanh Market."

"What kind of things?" Mai Ly asked, eager for the details that'd make our story real.

"Old watches and men shoes with high heels," slipped out of my mouth before I could realize my mistake.

"No! He sells bananas and mangoes! Remember that! Stop improvising. Just learn your lines by heart. This is serious!" Mai Ly yelled, her right fist aiming for my cheeks. She changed her mind, uncurled her fingers and brought them back into her pant pocket. To atone for my mistake, I ran to the bathroom. Furiously I mopped her floor, scrubbed her toilet, washed her sink. I didn't know what else to do. Mai Ly's straight yet crooked information. Yes, I would learn it by heart. I would regurgitate it to her liking. I would fly to America on its wings.

A Convincing Love-Hate Act

MAI LY BROUGHT me to Tuan's house the minute I mastered my lines. "Note all the details of his room," she said. The smell, the look, the heat, I had to commit them to memory. A lumpy bloodstained mattress caught my attention. Full of fat, freshly squashed mosquitoes, the bed was as welcoming as a dirty toilet seat. Brushing two dead mosquitoes away, I spread their blood further. Unwittingly, I turned Tuan's mattress into a battlefield aftermath. Looking around, I noticed moss on every wall. There were enough green smudges to block my breathing, to raise a few allergic wheals. I sneezed. I wheezed. I tried walking out. Mai Ly pulled me back. In that mildewy room, we practiced Tuan's lines. Mai Ly was as tough with him as she was with me. For hours she quizzed him, stopping only to gulp some water.

Tuan was no actor. The simplest lines eluded him. "My mother died stepping on a landmine ..." earned him a dirty look. Mai Ly shook her head. "No, it is tuberculosis!" She clenched her teeth so hard, I could hear their grinding sound. When twice Tuan forgot my American father's name, Mai Ly lost all patience. She snapped at both of us. She turned to Tuan with her bulging eyes and steaming cheeks. "It's goodbye America if you can't get your lines straight! Lots of people would love to take your place." She got up, slammed her notebook and marched outside.

Even with such a threat, Tuan dragged his feet. The right answers came only two weeks later. I clapped on and on after that successful interrogation. Tuan shot me a sheepish glance. He knew I'd gotten my act together only after three days of practice.

Getting our acts together meant visas to America. It meant adventure. It meant freedom. We were excited. We were also scared. Our pulse quickened upon hearing the words New Haven. Our limbs trembled whenever we saw the name Michael Ross. Only Mai Ly stayed calm. She paid our hearts no attention. She was only interested in directing our make-believe story. She didn't care about visas. She didn't care about America. She only wanted to mould us into perfect actors. To turn us into mirror images of herself: a high-functioning performer. "Start talking to each other as if you were real blood relatives. Make your dialogues authentic," she said at the end of each day.

Mai Ly's coaching paid off. Our hours rehearsing for a convincing narrative worked. After five weeks, I managed to think of Tuan as my brother. My love-hate act seemed so genuine, I fooled both American and Hanoi officials. Four interviews. Four simple interviews and our exit visas were granted. Ecstatic, Tuan jumped up and down, his hands pumping in the air. Melancholic, I was not sure if I should laugh or cry.

Remembering the Plastic Bag

A WEEK BEFORE my departure, Mai Ly took me to the orphanage. She understood my strange longing for that place. No words could explain my nostalgia for a time of humiliation. We remained silent on our bus ride. The sight of Sister Tam's hands waving from her window tightened my heart. It started thumping in my ears the minute Mother Superior approached the gate. As usual, she had trouble finding the right key. Her fingers fumbled awkwardly. They were perhaps more awkward than before. I could not return her smile. I could only stare at my feet. Mother Superior, how could I say goodbye with a simple smile?

Sister Tam rushed out, two whips in hand. Her wide grin revealed a row of crooked teeth I hadn't noticed before. I almost laughed at her stooped body, bowed legs and whips twice the length of her limbs. Her face, still smooth, her skin still spotlessly white no longer stirred my imagination. It was perhaps for the best.

Her hands holding mine, Sister Tam gave me a tour. Nothing had changed. The dining hall where I'd seen Thu's ghost still smelled of stale fish sauce. Dried grains of rice still littered its floor. Oil still coated its dining tables. A marble Mary still dominated the yard where kids still played ball. Accompanied by Mai Ly, I felt safe. Hopping around, I winced at the younger kids. No one dared to utter the words that had so tortured me: Black Devil. They only pointed their dirty fingers my way.

The only room I wanted to re-visit remained off-limits. A plastic bag on a bathroom doorknob. An old television set next to a snake wine bottle. I yearned to see them again. Only by re-visiting that room, could I confirm my childhood memory. "No!" Mother Superior said firmly. Her refusal surprised me. It pained me but I dared not insist.

With two fingers, she waved me over. She cleared her throat twice before talking. "You have a future now. So, forget that plastic bag! Soon you'll meet your real father. Maybe you'll find your real mother too. Talk to them. Get to know them. See if they're really what you've imagined them to be. Look ahead. Don't look back. Try to forget us. I enjoyed your letters but don't write anymore!"

Mother Superior's words left me in tatters. I responded with mumbling lips. Could I stop writing? Could I forget her? Could I erase images of a plastic bag? No. Impossible. If only she knew how it felt to leave home forever. If only she understood the mixed emotions of a soon-to-be-foreigner. Perhaps then she'd grant me my last wish. The nostalgia of that room, I'd have no choice but to carry it with me to America.

Don't Do It

FOUR CYCLOS OR three *cyclos*. That was the question. That was the back-and-forth between Mai Ly and four rickshaw drivers. They suggested four rickshaws for our ride to Tan Son Nhat airport. Mai Ly insisted on three. Two for us humans and a third for our suitcases. Mai Ly eventually won. Sullen, the fourth driver returned to his spot under a mango tree. He spat on a rock. He scratched his young, muscle-less chest. My last morning in Saigon. His first day on the job.

I followed Tuan to his rickshaw. My decision piqued Mai Ly. Grabbing my hand, she pointed to the one with her green cap already claiming its spot. A gesture of affection or a show of ownership? I'd never know. The hunchbacked driver squinted his eyes as I approached. He rolled up his pyjama pants to scratch his legs. "Two people, too heavy!" he said. "Me and the kid, we weigh next to nothing," Mai Ly muttered. Out of her purse, came her Party badge. That dangling official paper exerted an immediate hypnotic effect. "Oh! Going to Moscow, Comrade? Or Havana? Lucky you! Long live Castro! Long live Lenin! Long live Uncle Ho!"

"Quiet with your nonsense. Uncle Ho is already dead!"

"Yes, of course, I know it, Comrade! He's still in my heart!"

"Good. Can you pedal faster now?"

The trip to Tan Son Nhat airport took over one hour. It was a painfully slow ride with the rickshaw driver coughing and spreading phlegm on our heads. Trails of diesel turned my stomach. Clouds of exhaust fumes choked my lungs. The incessant honking of mopeds kept me on my toes. So, this was my city. This was Saigon. No, this was Ho Chi Minh City. Better get used to its new name. I made a note to remember all its sights and sounds, to remember this fleeting moment before it'd turn into a distant memory.

A blonde woman stood frozen at a roundabout. Her fearful eyes darted back and forth as motorcycles whizzed by. Nobody bothered stopping for her. One hesitant step forward, two quick steps back. She reminded me of ducklings at their first swim. Our driver snickered. "Hmmppphhh, I make more money with people like her," he said. Once again, Mai Ly took out her badge to shut him up.

Passing a tall, pink structure, our driver shouted, "There, Cathedral!" The church's twin crenelated towers impressed me. Inspired, I mumbled a prayer. My murmuring lips got Mai Ly twisting on her seat. Mockingly she asked, "Yeah, talking to your old man on his cross, Nat?"

A broad tree-lined street full of large brick buildings came into view. Mai Ly gave my arm a sharp nudge. "Look! The old Catinat Boulevard! Renamed Tu Do, then Dong Khoi. My father had a beer stand there. Your mother met all her American friends at that corner." I turned around to observe that famed spot. The sidewalks were crammed with people. Street hustlers in torn clothes. Local women in *ao dais*. Comrades huffing with self-importance. A tall black youth carrying a harmonica stood out from the crowd. A slim Vietnamese girl ran after him. He turned around, his hand making the V for victory sign. She bowed. They both laughed. Their playfulness told me their worlds intersected on many planes. I longed to call their names, to see their reactions, to spook them out. Let them know their future is observing their every careless move. I had to cover my mouth to stop from screaming, "Mai! Michael! Don't! Don't do it!"

Chicken over Beef

A<small>RUSTY BLUE</small> car cut in front of us. Its driver turned around to stare at me. "Fuck your mother! Never seen a brown kid?" our *cyclo* driver screamed. Mai Ly's face turned so red I thought she'd pop. She searched her purse for her Party badge. By the time she found it, it was already too late. The car ran off, leaving us with a whiff of its black fumes. We all coughed. Mai Ly's left hand sought out mine. She held it for the rest of the ride. It was a gesture I hadn't expected.

Mai Ly's Party badge worked wonders at Tan Son Nhat airport. Zigzagging through foot traffic, we skipped lines. We cut shamelessly in front of sweaty tourists. I actually preferred waiting for my turn, biding my time, delaying this moment of departure. Why, I wondered. What's there to miss about this place? Was there anything more than memories of a plastic bag, a bullied kid and strands of eucalyptus hair? I didn't know then. I still don't know now.

We finally exchanged goodbyes. Mai Ly placed her arm on my shoulders. I also received a caress on both cheeks. "If you find your mother, send her my regards. Tell her I still think of her." Next, she added words that would weigh on me for years. "Don't forget Sister Number Two's drawing. Her deformed hands. Don't forget to show it to your father."

Fear of never landing overshadowed the excitement of my first flight. Television images of the war—of planes disintegrating in mid-air and bodies charcoaled by flames—blocked my view of fields and clouds. Looking out my cabin window, I only saw a frail girl covered in purple spots. "Hold my hand," she said. "I'll guide you back to Mama Stork's abode. You can start anew with another family. Come, come with me." No! I didn't want that scenario. Panic-stricken, I buried my face in a travel magazine. Page after page I flipped through its colourful photos, searching for promises of a better life. I found it on page 79: Palawan, the Philippines. White sand, clear blue water, palm trees, no one in sight to dirty its beaches. Tuan sneered at that Palawan article. "Read the fine lines! There's a Vietnamese refugee camp there! Full of boat people. Look closely and you'll see shit everywhere! We're no boat people. We're going to be American immigrants! We're going to big city Manila, not some hick beach town!" Patting my head, he managed to mess the curls I'd spent so much time taming.

"Stir-fried lemongrass chicken with straw mushrooms! Look at it, smell it, taste it!" Tuan exclaimed when our food came to us. He'd chosen it for me. It's better than beef stew, he'd said. One bite of that tender, fragrant chicken made me realize all that I'd missed growing up in an orphanage. The mixture of crispy and soft, of salty and sweet, of spices and vegetables I'd never heard of, overwhelmed my tongue. Although hungry, I could only eat slowly, taking little bites in between sips of water. The meal's colourful presentation pleased my eyes. Its aromatic scent satisfied my nostrils. Go ahead eat, wolf it down, my senses cried out. Yet my mouth hesitated. In its nostalgia, it longed for that burning sensation of snake wine. In its distorted memory, only snake wine equalled fulfillment.

PART 7

The Philippines

A Welcome

MANILA AIRPORT WAS bigger than we'd imagined. We were lost. Tuan's knowledge of English was great for choosing chicken over beef. It was useless when exposed to words like Customs, Transit, Immigration. He could only cough mousily every time I asked: "Where do we go now?"

"Follow the other passengers?" I finally suggested. This earned me a smile. "Good idea, Nat! Smart kid!"

A sallow-skinned Oriental man with our names on a cardboard sign stood at the exit door. Seeing our names, Tuan jumped up and down. Like a teacher's pet, he waved his overly enthusiastic hand. The man stubbed out his cigarette and shook his head. He argued with a woman standing next to him. He pointed to his watch and scolded us for being late. "Why you not stick with your group?" In an English accent so different from what I'd heard on Mother Superior's television, he barked at us for ten minutes. "So we were supposed to follow a group! Mai Ly's commie badge. Cutting through lines. It got us nowhere ... um ... Get it?" Through clenched teeth, Tuan muttered his frustration to me.

The group waiting outside for us was a bunch of half-white kids and their Vietnamese chaperones. Neatly combed hair, starched clothes, newly cut fingernails. They looked ready-made for America. Sitting on their suitcases, many kept busy with their Vietnamese-English dictionaries. Some just yawned looking at swarms of mosquitoes. Others sucked on pens searching for inspiring words to write Grandma. Barely a few hours after emotional goodbyes, they already missed home. Would home miss them? Would home miss any of us? That was a question on all our minds.

Our voices brought the kids out of their brooding. Right away, a chorus of bad words greeted us. "Fuck your mother, Black One! We've been waiting half an hour! It's damn hot out here!" An auburn-haired boy came up to me with a fist ready for punching. He placed it just below my chin, his stone ring scratching my newly shaved face. He dared me to move. I did not. He maintained that position until Tuan came to my rescue. My brother-on-paper didn't barter vulgarly like a mango vendor at Ben Thanh Market. No, it was the calmness of an antique dealer that saved me from a punch. Welcome to the Philippines.

Pogo Anyone?

THE PHILIPPINES. WE were there to learn about America. We were there to be detoxified of our Vietnamese backwardness. We were there—housed and fed—thanks to American generosity.

Our first lesson in American culture vexed Tuan. He felt insulted having to sit through an hour of table etiquette. The use of knives and forks came naturally to him. It reminded him of his former Saigon days dining on *steak frites* at the Cercle Sportif club. Cutting a piece of tough meat was child's play for Tuan. It wasn't for me. A thing called "beefsteak" drove me crazy. I felt like tearing it apart with my bare hand and teeth.

My struggle with a knife and fork bothered Tuan. He slapped my hands for using the wrong utensil. "No! Knife in right hand! Fork in left hand!" I turned around to check on the others. Fortunately, nobody had noticed Tuan's slap. They were all busy chewing and chewing until the toughness gave way to something edible.

A bowl of rice, slices of fried tofu, some cut turnips. They were so much simpler to gulp down with a spoon. Did I miss those orphanage meals sitting by myself? Ducking spit balls while eating. Were they endearing memories? No. I only missed Mother Superior's snake wine. I missed sharing her moments of drunkenness. I remembered finding her on the bathroom floor with a glass of wine. It had shocked me at first. I got used to it eventually. Without a trace of shame, she'd make signs for me to pull her up. I did with much effort. She was heavier than I thought. To thank me, she'd pour some wine straight into my mouth. I'd gulp it down in one shot. "This was your milk in the old days," she'd say, her voice half serious, half mocking.

"Not everything needs knives and forks. Some food can be eaten with your hands," a young man explained. We were in a large whitewashed room, well lit, well aired with two ceiling fans. All 20 of us sat around four wood tables listening earnestly to our American teacher. Our mouths salivated at photos of food. "This is a hamburger, this is a hot dog, this is a sandwich and these are French fries. They can all be eaten with your hands."

Photos of a "pogo stick" put an end to my salivation. It reminded me of my raised eel. Thoughts of eating it repulsed me so much, I gagged. I coughed. Tuan turned around to stare at me. It was a look that said it all. I know exactly what's on your dirty mind, his accusing eyes claimed. That made me cough even more.

"What's wrong, Monkey? You should know all about eating with your hands!" The auburn-haired guy said scornfully. That taunting got some kids laughing. "Shut up and leave my brother alone!" Tuan grumbled. "Fuck your mother! He's black, he can't be your brother!" someone yelled. Vietnamese swear words flew back and forth. Girls giggled hysterically behind their notebooks. Younger boys stamped their feet excitedly. Despite the screaming, our teacher went on with his lecture. He continued showing photos of food as if our discontent mattered little. In the big scheme of things, we were just animals to be trained for his circus. "Remember, no spitting during dinner. And, oh, yes, we cover our mouth when we cough, Nat."

Itchy Feet

OUR LESSONS ENDED after twelve weeks. American culture, geography, history. We crammed our brains with details and succeeded in rehashing them for our exams. To our surprise, we all received the same 80% mark. "Equality and democracy," we whispered amongst ourselves. Like rice water after a first wash, our fathers' Occidental values remained murky in our minds. Yet we were deemed ready for America. "Make your fathers proud. Make America proud. Be good. Do the right thing." Our teacher smiled. He always smiled no matter what. "American optimism," Tuan said and chuckled.

Our last day of class was celebrated with cold Coca-Cola. Loud music played from a tape recorder. Correctly identifying the singer earned us each a dollar. Tuan collected three dollars by guessing "Beach Boys!" three times. Too shy to say "Nat King Cole," I stayed quiet that afternoon. I did end up whistling a Beach Boys song. Something about "California Dreaming" got my fingers snapping.

Thick yellow envelopes awaited us. One by one the teacher called our names. In alphabetical order, he handed us our envelope. He shook our hands and told us once more to Make America Proud. Pointing a camera at us, he ordered us to straighten our backs. "Smile!" he said. We all obeyed.

My fumbling with the envelope infuriated Tuan. He snatched it from me. His long fingernail slid easily through the well-sealed flap. We both blinked at its contents. Fragile and impermanent, our dreams stared back at us: two plane tickets to New York, two entry visas, a fold-out map of America and 50 dollars.

At Manila's airport, my feet tapped impatiently, loudly. They tapped independently of me. Having suffered in silence for so long, they could no longer wait. They wanted to leave the Philippines as soon as possible. To run away from this place that was only a more modern version of Vietnam. They itched to wander fields that had never harboured landmines, to explore country lanes that had never been deceitful with two-faced calmness. In new running shoes courtesy of American churches, tapping to the rhythm of my hiccupping heart, my feet became the voice I never had.

PART 8:
AMERICA

Empty Snow-Covered Fields

JOHN F KENNEDY Airport. USA? Tuan thought he was in another country. The many black and brown faces baffled him. The America of our old TV shows was nothing like this. Yes, Mr. Greg Morris of *Mission: Impossible* was a black man. But the rest? *Rawhide, The Wild Wild West, Bewitched, I Dream of Jeannie, The Flying Nun, Gunsmoke, Green Acres, Bonanza, Lost in Space, Mister Ed.* They were all white. Had America changed? Or was the truth hidden from us?

"Do you feel at home now?" Tuan turned to ask me. "You blend in, I stand out now. Yeah, I might be a 'Chink' to these people, I'm still your big brother. Don't forget that!" The sheer number of dark-skinned people surprised me. This gift of belonging, of finally blending in, brought tears to my eyes. For a few minutes, happiness overshadowed my usual melancholia. Wanting to be clean for America, I asked for a visit to its washroom. There I scalded my hands turning on a wrong knob. Hot water running freely and forever. We were never taught this in our American Culture class.

A large crowd jammed the exit door. People waved and shouted. Some held up cardboard signs with names.

Others just waited patiently, cameras around their necks. Tense, I looked around, wondering if I would ever spot him. Tuan took my hand, trying to calm me. "I've his phone number. I'll call him if he isn't here." Past the exit door, still nothing. No one waved at us. No one called our names. No one took our photos. Tuan's hands shook uncontrollably as he searched for a phone number in his wallet. Mine began to sweat.

Two taps on my shoulder so startled me, I yelled, "No!" A name on a sign got my heart banging. For a moment its beats outraced my internal pendulum. In big block letters I could make out 'Nat Tran,' a name I'd had to learn by heart to recognize as my own. I'd always thought of myself as Black Devil.

I looked at him trying to find traces of myself. He also studied me with curiosity. Next to him, an orange-haired woman dabbed her forehead. The silence of our encounter stretched like a rubber band. It became almost intolerable. Tuan eventually came to my rescue. "Hello, I am Tuan. This is Nat," he said pointing to me. Teary-eyed, Orange-Haired Woman took me in her arms. Michael, my father, just kept staring at us. I supposed he wanted to say things. His lips only twisted soundlessly.

"I'm Amanda and this is Michael! We've been waiting soooo looong foooo this day! Oooo! Did you eat, sleep? Oooo sooorry foooo being late …" In an accent I could not understand, Amanda went on and on. Emotion must've choked her up, eaten her consonants, stretched her O. Maybe it was my ears that didn't hear properly. I was stressed out too.

"Yes, thank you. We sleep well and food very good. Plane trip very nice," Tuan answered in his private-French-school English.

"Yes, thank you. We sleep well and food very good. Plane trip very nice," I repeated, plagiarizing Tuan's speech. Eager to practise expressions I'd learned, I also added my own "Oh yeah, man!"

That "Oh yeah, man!" brought a grin to Michael's face. He reached out to play with my hair. Still without words, he rubbed my shoulders. Finally, he bent down to take my suitcase. Walking ahead, he made signs for us to follow him. We did so in silence. Only Amanda made noises with her sniffling.

Our car ride to New Haven lasted forever. There was so much I wanted to say. My basic English didn't allow it. Simple nouns couldn't capture my flickering ideas. Plain adjectives couldn't describe my foggy mind. I turned to Tuan for help. I shook his shoulders to rouse him. "Please wake up! What do you think of them, these people? I feel strange. Do you feel strange, Big Brother Tuan?" I asked in Vietnamese. "Sshh, your father might understand our language. Be discreet and keep quiet. Let me sleep now!" Tuan closed his eyes. He yawned. He so wanted to return to his dreams of scooter rides in platform shoes.

"You like American music, Nat?" my father asked, each word pronounced clearly and slowly. He obviously had experience speaking English to Vietnamese people. I wondered if this was how he talked to my mother, addressing her as if she were twelve years old.

"Yes, Nat King Cole."

"Wow! Nat King Cole! My mom likes him too! Did you hear that Amanda? Nat King Cole! Haha!" My father looked at me through his rear-view mirror and smiled. I smiled back. Satisfied at our exchange of information, he turned on the radio. Bang-Bang-Bang-Boom-Boom-Boom. I wondered if that was Nat King Cole hitting his drum.

Snow-covered woods. Empty fields. This was America. Out of nowhere, raindrops began to fall. One by one, they dug nests in the grey snow. I so wanted to wake Tuan up. To share with him my first impression of America. Of its vast open space and its mass of dark-skinned people toiling in closed rooms. Without Tuan to help me remember this scene, I'd have to write it all down. A muted monologue accompanied me to New Haven.

"She's Awake!"

MAI OPENED HER eyes. Loud noises echoed in her head. There were footsteps coming and going. A machine beeping. People talking over each other. A familiar voice: "How she doing? How she doing?" The insistent tone bothered Mai. A foreign accent lured her to a time before memory. She wished to slip back to her dreams. Whiffs of rubbing alcohol and disinfectant irritated her nose. Itchy, she attempted to move her left hand. A rigid cast held it back. She blinked a few times before making out wheat-coloured walls.

Or was it the ceiling? Everything was so out of focus. "She's awake!" a nurse shouted.

That outburst frightened Mai. Instinctively, she closed her eyes. Looking up again, she saw three women in white.

"We are glad to see you up. You've been asleep for 42 hours. You are at the Los Angeles County Hospital now. I'm Dr. Juarez, one of your resident doctors. Tell us what happened. Do you remember?"

Mai moved her lips, trying to make sounds. Only unintelligible noises came out of her dry throat.

"Relax. Take your time. Here, sit up, have a sip of water."

Mai coughed, spewing droplets of saliva on her tangled hair. She tried to drink again. On the third sip, a cool liquid descended smoothly down her parched throat. She nodded gratefully.

"Do you remember your name?" Dr. Juarez asked.

"Hmmm ... Mai, I'm Mai."

"Good! Now tell us what happened, Mai."

In a hoarse voice, she whispered, "Monk ... Fire ... Bones ... Baby ... Helicopter."

Exhausted, she stopped.

"And what else, Mai? What happened at your restaurant?"

"Rain ... Credit card ...Gun," Mai said, quivering. Terrified by the recollection, she again closed her eyes. She so missed her dark silent world.

Total Darkness

MAI TRIED AND tried. Only after 20 minutes did she succeed in setting pen and notebook on her left arm. Any wrong movement would double the pain in her fractured rib cage. Her left-arm cast was not an ideal support. Pages kept sliding off. She had no other choice. The table on wheels was beyond her reach. Both knees sprained. Broken ribs. Dislocated shoulders. Fractured left radius and right femur. She felt like an invalid.

Four weeks. It has been four weeks since her fall. Or maybe more. She couldn't remember. Immobilized on a hospital bed, Mai was near her wits' end. Every day, she was promised a 'discharge soon.' Every other day, a new complication would appear to delay her discharge. Wound infection leading to osteomyelitis. Aspiration pneumonia. Acute renal failure secondary to antibiotics. Hallucination due to morphine. She had them all. Mai felt like screaming each time a medical intern tiptoed into her room. Their update on her latest test results left her nauseous. Blocking her ears, she refused to hear more medical terms. Only the notebook and pen kept her sane.

"Problems started long before the kid walked this earth," Mai scribbled with much effort. She grumbled when the notebook slid off her left arm cast. Readjusting her pages, she pondered what these problems were. It had been so long since those Saigon days, cycling to school in a flowing satin *ao dai*. She wondered how its long panels never got caught in her bicycle wheels, how she never fell to damage her white-person nose.

For no reason, Mai decided to fast-forward. "M. is startled by sudden noises. She can make out footsteps coming and going. Regular beeping of a machine bothers her. Disinfectant and rubbing alcohol irritate her nose. She winces hearing a familiar voice in a foreign accent. 'How she doing? How she doing?' it asks ..." Her sixth sentence unfinished, Mai looked up to see a tall orthopaedic resident by her bed. He greeted her with a big grin. Dr. Barnes. Young, dimpled, square-jawed, confident in his manners. Who could resist him? He was so different from those medical students bothering her every morning with their tiresome questions. "Can we listen to your heart? Can we listen to your lungs?" Mai wondered which secrets seeped from her heart? Which forbidden tale accompanied each of her breaths? Did the stethoscopes transform her mournful sighs into songs of longing? Why did the students return every day asking for more?

"We've got good news, Ms. Tran! Today's blood tests came back normal. X-rays show your leg fracture healed. Everything's good. We will cut the casts tomorrow. You'll go home next week and continue physio on an external basis. Would you like that?"

"Yes, I'd like that. Thank you, Doctor."

Her pen and paper beckoned. Mai's mind refused to

cooperate. It was impossible to refocus on her writing after the orthopaedist's visit. Her thoughts wandered back to that stormy night counting money in her restaurant. Memories of a burning monk also resurfaced to play tricks on her. She saw a blade of grass growing out of a crack in the asphalt. She saw her father sucking on a young girl's nipple. She saw a tiny brown baby whimpering on her abdomen. She saw Saigon's boulevards plugged by cars while American helicopters flew overhead. She saw a soaking wet Yves St. Laurent, hands shaking nervously. She saw a bunch of credit cards and credit card receipts crammed into his jacket's left pocket. She saw the butt of a gun sticking out of his other pocket. She felt again a shove, a blow, a fall, pain and darkness. Total darkness in total silence.

Ironed Panties

THE FORGIVING LIGHT of a 20-watt bulb could not mask Amanda's changed face. It revealed all. Her wisp of grey hair, her bald spot, her puffy eyes. Michael studied them with alarm. Even in sleep, the lines crisscrossing her forehead refused to relax. New frowns. They were not there four months ago, Michael told himself. He bent down to kiss her head. "Goodnight, I love you," he said softly.

Michael decided to seek company. He needed to get stuff off his chest. Since Nat's arrival, conversation at home had disintegrated into superficial talk. Hand gestures, short sentences, loud repetitions. It was the language of children. Or was it the language of dog trainers? Michael thought simple phrases would bring him closer to his son. It didn't. It only taxed his patience. Nat's neutral smiles and obedient nods only frustrated him.

Tuan's presence helped ease their awkwardness. He spoke for Nat when the boy couldn't string his words together. He translated Michael's American expressions using his new dictionary. To Amanda, he gave only compliments. From her writing skills to her sports trophies, from her cooking to her looks, Tuan went out of his way to make her blush. Those blushes, he collected them like coins in a piggy bank. Frugal, he'd save them for rainy days. Amanda's blushes would double after his washing of the dishes. They would triple after his scrubbing of the floor and quadruple after his ironing of underwear. This peculiar habit puzzled Amanda. She'd never seen her mother iron underwear back in Pembroke. In fact, she'd never heard of such a waste of effort. "Oh, we do this all the time in Vietnam," Tuan insisted as he handed her a dozen pressed panties and boxer shorts.

Michael wasn't blind. Tuan as Nat's half-brother? Impossible. That story didn't click. Their age difference, their physical features—nothing lined up. Was Tuan a cousin? An uncle? Or even a total stranger? Such deceit didn't surprise Michael. Having been to Vietnam, having seen desperation up close, he'd recognized the many facets of misery. The wheeling and dealing, the lies, the petty theft. They were survival tactics. They were rocks giving rest to those swimming against a current of indifference.

Tuan accidentally revealed his true identity one day. Seeing *Rambo* on television, he unwittingly bragged about having a similar outfit as a kid. "Oh, I used to torture Mai with my plastic gun!" he blurted out. Immediately he clenched his teeth. To atone for his blunder, he went searching for clothes to iron. He ignored Nat's glare on his way out.

A stranger in her house worried Amanda. Despite his hard work and compliments, she wished Tuan to be elsewhere. She found his good nature forced, even suspicious.

"What if he's a communist spy?" she asked.

"Ha! Ha! You should stop reading John le Carré," Michael said.

"Don't brush me off, I'm not crazy!"

"Sorry, Amanda, I didn't say you're crazy! But you do have an imagination. I thought journalists are supposed to stick to facts."

"Oh, Jesus Christ, Michael!"

"It's just a joke, Amanda."

"Not funny."

"Sorry. Come here Baby—"

"Don't you baby me!"

Their argument ended in tears, apologies and a noisy session of make-up sex that night. Still disgruntled, Amanda went digging for her ironed panties next morning. She crumpled them all up. Next, she tackled Michael's neatly folded boxer shorts. Wrecking laundry. She was ashamed of her heinous act. She saw herself drifting away from Michael.

Unlike Amanda, Michael enjoyed Tuan's company. With interest, he listened to tales of re-education camps. Descriptions of a young Mai in flip-flops a size too small warmed his heart. He laughed at stories of cops and communists. His eyes bulged hearing of Mai Ly's transformation. He remembered her as a small, timid girl in Mai's shadow. Dressed in her friend's badly fitting clothes, she'd looked out of place on Catinat. Even rolled up, the miniskirt had dropped below Mai Ly's knees. "An important communist cadre now? Producing fake birth certificates?? Ha! Ha! What a story!" Michael said with a hoot. This stranger in their midst would keep him entertained. For a few hours a day, Tuan's tales would help lighten the sadness of accidental fatherhood.

Kissing Her Photo

THE SPRING NIGHT was windy. A three-day downpour had turned grass into mud. Michael decided to go out anyway. He jogged to his usual bar. At 10:50 p.m. on a Wednesday, it was empty. He almost ordered a beer before changing his mind. His favourite barman wasn't working that shift. No use opening his heart to an indifferent college student. Head bent, he ran back to his apartment.

Silence greeted Michael at home. A line of light emanated from the guest room. He wondered if Nat was still awake. Or was it Tuan reading a book? Michael sometimes heard them talking at night. Behind closed doors and in Vietnamese, Nat could talk for hours. His words flowed for Tuan. For Michael, they hesitated as if held back by tangled knots.

Michael went straight to Nat's room. A light knock on his door got no response. Michael entered anyway. A banal image greeted him. Tuan deep in sleep, Nat hunched over a piece of paper. Yet that scene would obsess Michael for years to come.

"You not sleeping?" Michael asked. His son was like a stray alley cat. He never knew if it would jump on him or run away. "What you looking at? Picture? You want to show me? What is it?"

"Hand. Hand and arm. Strange," Nat said. Despite his intensive remedial English classes, despite his nearly perfect understanding of the language, Nat's verbal expression still lacked. He wanted to say so much but could only blurt out two words, "Agent Orange."

"Oh, I see! Yes, Agent Orange is horrible. What happened in Vietnam was terrible. Hey, cute drawing, Nat. Looks like a giraffe. Hey where's the head? Haha! Picture done by one of your ex-girlfriends at the orphanage, I bet!" Nat's pout stopped Michael from saying more. Agent Orange and a headless giraffe, the link had escaped him.

Michael decided to change subjects. He pulled Nat into his office. He sat his son down on a torn leather armchair. "Close your eyes," he ordered. He searched his drawers for the object that would bind them. He remembered hiding it carefully and cursed himself for being too careful. Hidden amongst old Mastercard bills, he finally found it, this souvenir of another era.

"Ever seen a photo of your mother?"

"No, she beautiful?"

"Of course! Now open your eyes." A crumpled black and white photo of a young woman winked at both of them. Right hand playing with her hair, left one shielding a smile, Mai beckoned them. "Come and get me!" she seemed to say.

"What do you think, Nat?"

"Yes, beautiful, my mother. Where's she?"

"I don't know."

"Oh!" Nat exclaimed.

"Well, I'm not sure. Haven't seen her in ages. Last I heard, she had a restaurant in Los Angeles. I have her address somewhere. Gotta look for it."

"Los Angeles, far?"

"Very far. Other side of the country."

Disappointed, Nat turned to Mai's photo. Hoping to recognize himself in her, he studied all her features. Her limp hair, no, not his. Her slanted eyes, not his either. Her downward sloping lashes, no. Her pale skin, no. Her fine, straight nose, yes. This was their only shared trait transmitted over generations. A nose to smell the sweetness of frangipani and the nausea of latrines. A nose to inhale the addictive savour of sex and the stench of abandoned kids.

"You want to see your mother?" Michael's question pulled Nat from his daydream. He stayed silent. His mother, he had imagined her all his life. Had written about her as soon as he could match verbs to nouns. Of course, he wanted to meet her. Only fear of rejection held him back.

"What my mother like?" Nat asked instead.

"We were young and irresponsible. Sorry, Nat."

"You tell me story?"

"Ever heard of 'make love, not war'?"

"No."

"Well, your mother was that kind of woman. She made love instead of war. Making love in times of war, she thought she could fool fate. You know, laugh and enjoy life instead of hiding in fear. We wanted to have fun before rockets killed us. Sorry. We were stupid."

"Why you leave her?"

"I didn't leave her! I had to go back home and she was in a convent. Impossible to contact her." Michael grimaced as memories of a French nun re-emerged. Two blue, unflinching eyes. Pouting lips mocking his accent. Her condescending tone of voice. Her cold hands snatching his letter to Mai. He regretted not punching her that day.

"Tell me more."

"Tomorrow, I promise. It's late now."

"You give me photo?"

"Sorry, I can't. It's the only photo I have of her." Nat wheezed at these words of stinginess. "OK, OK. I'll make a photocopy for you next week."

"A what?" Nat asked.

"A photocopy. I'll show it to you next week." Too tired to go into further details, Michael turned to his paperwork. He avoided his son's curious eyes.

Nat caressed his mother's image. His index finger traced a line down her hair. He wondered if they smelled of lemon and cinnamon. He wanted to ask Michael this but was afraid to voice such nonsense. He handed his mother's photo to his father. Michael took it back with care. He blew dust from it. He studied it for a long time before putting it away. Michael's gesture reassured Nat. He imagined his father still secretly in love with his mother. He imagined Michael kissing Mai's photo in the solitude of his study. That would explain his reluctance to give her away.

Dismissed by Michael, Nat returned to his room. From the floor, Comrade Number Two's drawing stared at him. Her deformed arm. He'd promised her. He must keep his promise. He must show it to Michael. Must tell him about her two lone fingers. Agent Orange. Must remind him of his brief Vietnamese stint and all its consequences.

Michael sighed as he sorted his Mastercard bills. It was late. He was tired. The work must be done.

"For you. Agent Orange arm," Nat announced. Michael jerked at his son's interruption. It disrupted his train of thoughts.

"Thanks, Nat." Absent-mindedly, Michael folded Nat's gift in half. He placed it inside his desk drawer, turned off the light and got up. "I'll look at it tomorrow. Time to sleep now." A yawn made its way across his face. A yawn that Nat registered and dared not protest.

A Baby Photo

"**M**A, THIS IS my son, Nat."

"Lord, oh Lord, we finally meet the boy! It's been months!" Michael's mother exclaimed. Taking Nat's hand in hers, she pulled him into her kitchen. A feast of roasted ham and beans awaited them on a well-dressed table. Silver plated cutlery, dishes from the same set, fresh carnations. Michael nodded in appreciation.

"Hello, Mrs. Ross, nice to meet you."

"What Mrs. Ross? I'm your Grandma! Call me Grandma! You look just like little Michael!" Cupping Nat's face with her wrinkled hands, she planted two kisses on his cheeks.

"And Ma, he likes Nat King Cole too!"

"Lord, oh Lord! Come here, my dear. Sit down. Stop talking. Eat, eat both of you!"

Roasted ham pleased Nat. Baked beans not so much. He'd have preferred rice. He longed for rice. Nat's uneaten beans didn't insult his grandmother. She was glad to have leftovers. It meant less time by her stove, more time on her rocking chair. Those beans, she'd eat them in front of her television later. In the darkness of a bare living room, she'd scream out answers to *The Price Is Right*. "$129.95! $129.95!"

"Come see your dad's old bedroom. But first, what's 264 to the power of 5?" Taken by surprise, Nat could only stutter. The math wasn't hard, he just needed paper and pen to figure it out. "Oh. Not a math genius like your dad, eh? He's special, your dad! That's OK, Nat. You're probably good at other things."

Michael's old room impressed Nat. Glued against his closet door were a dozen cut-out images of a beautiful black singer. Nat noticed her name: Natalie Cole. He wondered if she were related to his namesake Nat King Cole. Large posters of curvy women filled the other walls. Tall, muscular, dark-haired, blue-eyed, big breasted. They were all flawless. Their wavy hair, angular jaws, slim waists and long legs were almost identical. It was hard to tell one from another. Photocopies. This must be what Michael had meant by a 'photocopy,' concluded Nat.

Ten minutes ogling photocopied women gave Nat a stiff neck. Slowly he let his eyes wander about. A framed photo on a chipped student desk stirred his curiosity. He had no trouble recognizing Michael's dimples. A dimpled black baby hugged by a white man. A white man with red hair and dimples. The photo baffled Nat. He shook his head. He didn't want to know more. With a clumsy hand, he hid the frame under Michael's old baseball hat and scrambled out.

"Umm, nice room, Grandma! Umm, movie now, Michael?" Nat's words jolted his grandmother. She didn't like his 'Michael' bit. She'd rather hear Dad,

Daddy or Father. Dumbfounded, she stared at Nat. He only lowered his eyes. Months of practice had given no result. Dad, Daddy, Pa, Father, he had repeated them using different intonations, different accents. He still could not address his father by such terms of endearment. Out of his mouth, the words sounded as fake as those photocopied women.

Pick and Choose

GOING TO THE cinema for Vietnam War films was Nat's favourite pastime. He laughed at Chinese American actors pretending to be Vietnamese communists. "Too fat to be real communists!" he said, chuckling. He corrected their bad accents out loud and shrugged when told to shut up. Frustrated by Nat's persistent giggling, some viewers would march out to demand a refund on their tickets.

The war movies reminded Nat of old TV newscasts he'd watched in Vietnam. Grainy black and white images of destruction accompanied by melodious tunes. They'd soothed him in those days. Slow-motion scenes of bodies unearthed had calmed his eyes. Soft music had rocked him to sleep in his plastic bag. For years, he'd associated television news with a lullaby. Nat wondered if Michael felt the same. He wondered if Michael's recollection of the war was not somehow pasteurized—transformed into some black and white snapshots of jungle scenes—minus the heat, minus the humidity, minus the sounds of ricocheting bullets. Nat wanted so much to share this thought with his father. Proper sentences, however, refused to form in his mind. Only random words spewed forth. He couldn't line them up in the correct English order. His chaotic tongue, he couldn't straighten it out. Better to keep quiet, he told himself. Silence had worked in the past. It had kept communist scorn at bay. It had been his wall of self-defence in the charged atmosphere of self-criticism.

Watching movies became a weekly activity for father and son. Their outings didn't bring them closer, didn't bridge their distinct worlds. For two hours, the film only spared them the curse of unspoken reproaches. It only dulled the discomfort of their glances accidentally crisscrossing each other. That was enough for Michael. On his dark theatre seat, he'd imagine shadowy scenes he dared not acknowledge in bright daylight. Between shots of exploding bombs, he'd see a silent Amanda with deeper frowns, more numerous wrinkles. He'd imagine picking strands of red hair from their bed and searching them for her fragrance. An empty bed made for two. He knew he couldn't tolerate it a second time. In that unlit theatre, an unbearably morbid thought crossed his mind. If he had to save one of them from a sinking boat, he'd choose a redhead over his own flesh and blood.

Unsolicited Revelations

"**I**T'S JUST A language barrier," Michael said to Amanda. "Extra English lessons will fix it. I mean Nat has no problems with math in school. He's a smart kid." He paid for expensive private lessons and waited. He waited for the day he could get through to his son. Waited for the moment he could share with Nat his own experience of being lost as a child. Michael waited a long time. The schism between them ran deeper than he'd thought.

Half a year of English lessons later, Nat still bowed. He still sported his ghostly smile. Like the slaves in *Gone with the Wind*, he still nodded automatically, even good-naturedly. No authentic words ever escaped his mouth. No real emotions were ever shown. Tired of staring at Nat's empty face, Michael decided to let his guard down. He knew only genuineness begets genuineness.

"Come, Nat. Let me tell you a story," Michael said one day. "It's a story no one else has heard because I haven't been able to tell it to anyone. Not to Amanda. Not to my mom. It's a story I've tried repressing all these years. Because it's very unpleasant. Years ago, when I was your age, I had a very good friend. David. David Kirby his name. He brought me to fancy parties at his friends' house. We had a car accident after one of those parties. David went into a coma and died a year later. A policeman interrogated me on the road. He hit my head, my shoulders. Pushed his baton against my throat. I couldn't breathe. I tried protesting. 'If you can talk, you can breathe,' he shouted back. He removed the baton only to punch me in the chest. I can still picture his furious green eyes as he screamed at me. Those punches in the head made me dizzy, I couldn't think straight. I only remembered feeling guilty. Guilty about David's coma. You know, he was drunk yet I'd asked him to drive. The police beating, perversely, I thought I deserved it. I should've felt indignant, revolted, I only felt shame. Shame for all the injustice people dished out. Shame for being part of that lineage. You know, my father was a white policeman. My mother never talked about it but I knew. I knew the day I found his photos and an old police badge hidden in her drawers. All those years watching police brutality on television has hardened her. She no longer cries. She only shudders now. Don't get me wrong. Most policemen are very decent. Even very good. Still, the shame is there—"

Nat's waving hands interrupted Michael's talk. He didn't want to hear more. The sting in his eyes increased with each unsolicited revelation. His vision blurred. "Enough!" he said. He ran outside before Michael could see tears on his cheeks.

Back to the Womb

AMANDA WRAPPED AN apron around my waist. She watched keenly as I peeled a potato. She raised her thumb when I finished my work. "Good job, Nat! Next, we do carrots." Amanda didn't know it but I was also watching her. Her orange hair, her green eyes, her white skin. They had so disarmed me. She could not be real, I told myself. I scrutinized her every move. Behind closed doors, I listened to her conversations. They were only talk about her next writing assignment. I spied on her in the kitchen and saw nothing suspicious. All her groceries came from a supermarket. *Betty Crocker's Cookbook*, a manual she consulted every night, did not seem malevolent. If anything, magic floated like pollen from its pages. Amanda was no White Devil.

"This is how we make soup," Amanda said as she dumped two chicken breasts into a pot of water. She turned around to catch me gazing at her bare shoulders. She continued chopping as if nothing had passed between us. "Onions, go wash some more onions," she said in her light, singing voice. "It's a bit humid today, isn't it?" I was just a poor, backward kid not deserving of her niceties. She gave them to me anyway.

Her soup finished, Amanda turned on the tap to wash her hands. In contact with hot water, she groaned, "Ohhh!" My rush to help with an ice cube brightened her face. "Thanks, Nat!" she said. For my gesture of concern, she gave me two freshly baked chocolate chip cookies. Chocolate chip cookies, chicken noodle soup, spinach quiches, mushroom pizzas, Caesar Salad. Amanda wanted me to try them all. It was re-education camp for my taste buds, she jokingly said. The more she cooked, the more I fell in love with her food. Chewy grilled cheese sandwiches, crispy chicken wings, juicy hamburgers. They were all new sensations for me. If I could, I would say a Hail Mary for Betty Crocker. Unfortunately, I'd forgotten those words. Far from Sister Tam, I'd turned into an amnesiac Catholic.

Michael and Amanda's place looked nothing like what I'd seen on television. There were no colourful flowers painted on their walls. "Wallpaper, we hate that," she declared when I asked about them. There was no large chest to show off ornate dishes. "China cabinets, we hate those too." There was no candle on their dining table, no fruit bowl on their kitchen counter, no calendar glued to their fridge. There were only piles upon piles of newspapers stacked everywhere. *Yale Daily News, New Haven Register, New York Times, Washington Post.* These were Amanda's decoration. Instead of paintings, news clippings of her works covered each wall. Novels and sport trophies from her youth lined three bookcases. Old war photos hid cracks sprouting from the fireplace mantel. A black and white print of soldiers startled me. I gasped as I recognized my father in that photo. This younger version of Michael could've been an older version of me. I saw through his downcast eyes, tight lips and sloping shoulders. It was an image of the loneliness I knew so well.

"Sit down Nat," Amanda said, pointing to a wicker chair next to her. "Do you want to meet your mother?" she asked, looking straight into my eyes. "I think you should meet your mother." Out of her pant pocket appeared a crumpled piece of paper. I recognized my mother's name. Mai. I pushed that scrap of paper away. It hovered in the air then silently landed on my sandals. Amanda leaned down to pick it up. She showed it to me once more. 2437 Carlyle St. #7, Los Angeles, California flashed before my eyes. My heart began to tighten. The chest pain was so intense, it reminded me of rocks thrown my way at the orphanage. If only I could bleed to show Amanda the state of my despair. That piece of paper confirmed what I'd long suspected: my parents had been in contact all this time. Yet my mother had never asked for me, never written me, never wondered what my voice sounded like.

Amanda coughed. She wanted to bring me back to the matter at hand. "You and Tuan, you both should be with your mother. Not here. Tuan should take you to California to be with her. What do you think?"

"Michael OK with this?"

"Listen, your father got you out of Vietnam. He got you accepted into this country 'cause he's American. He cares about you. He loves you. Me too. Really. Do you remember your first home? No, it's not that orphanage. Your first home was your mother's womb. Deep inside her, you felt her every movement, digested all her sorrows and joy, swam in the plenitude of her belly. You could hear what she heard, taste what she ate, sense what she thought. That is where you belong, Nat. You should look for that home now. And Nat, I want you to know you can always return here if things don't work out in California. Your bed will still be here. I'll always be here. Understand?" Amanda lifted my chin as she repeated her words. "Look at me," she insisted when my eyes wandered away from hers. "You should write your mom this week. I'm sure she'll be happy to hear from you. In the meanwhile, I'll write your story for the newspaper. Next, we'll organize some bake sales to raise money for your plane tickets. All's good!"

"I write stories too," I whispered. Amanda turned to me with surprise. "Oh?" she remarked. "I'll tell you some of your dad's stories later. He has some wild ones!" She left me hanging there, my mouth open, my body shaking. Come back! I want to hear those stories now, I pleaded in my head. Tell me I was wrong in my description of him. Tell me he had a happy childhood. Tell me he didn't suffer like I did. The bullying, the abandonment, tell me he knew nothing of that.

Come to California

ON HIS BED, Tuan turned the photocopied image of a young Mai over and over. The years had blurred his memory. Mai's straight slim nose, a solitary hair sticking from her earlobe, her awning-like lashes. Tuan had forgotten. Now he remembered. He imagined Mai stepping out of that photo, her eyes gazing over everything except him. He imagined Mai crossing the street to avoid him only to stealthily turn around for a view of his back. She had been in love with him all those years. Too self-centred, he'd failed to notice her. Mai's heart, he'd probably broken it many times over. What would he say to her now? Would he beg her for a dishwasher job at her restaurant? Yes, he would.

"So they want us out of their house," Tuan said. "I don't blame them. We've been here long enough. What, four months? Five months? I lost track of time, Nat."

"Eight months and three weeks."

"That long?"

"Yes."

"No wonder they're fed up with us! So did you write your mother?"

"Yes. She wrote back. Very short letter. It says: 'Come to California if you want.'"

"So California Dreaming it will be! Do you remember that song, Nat? We heard it in the Philippines."

"Yes, Beach Boys."

"Do you remember that nice teacher always smiling?"

"No more talking, please!"

Sullen, Nat got up from the floor. He went to his bed. There he burrowed his face in a pillow. He could not suppress a sob. America was full of deceit. Friendly, smiling Amanda, her warm suppers every night, the movies every week. It was just a show. He was still a brown kid nobody wanted.

Television Reruns

I COULD NOT sleep after that living room scene with Amanda. Her bouncing footsteps, her swinging arms said it all. She had already imagined a future without me, without Vietnam weighing down on her conscience.

The apartment was dark except for the television light. It was silent except for Michael's snoring. His prostrated body on a lumpy sofa pained me. Saliva dripping from his opened mouth, clothes wet with beer stains. This was not the image I had of my father. I felt sorry for him. I felt sorry for us. I felt sorry for bringing discord into his love life. Gently, I settled next to him. His hand in mine, I spent the rest of that night watching muted reruns of *Mission: Impossible*.

The TV show brought back memories of a eucalyptus-scented room. Those were simple days and I so missed the security of that plastic bag by a doorknob.

Los Angeles 1989

A STOOPED ORIENTAL woman opened her door a crack, the security chain securely in place. Two men in T-shirts and identical black jeans stood facing her. She blinked seeing a young dark-skinned guy with kinky hair. He scared her. She shook her head. "No, no want encyclopaedias! No insurance! No Jehovah! Go!" To her surprise, one of them addressed her in Vietnamese.

"Good afternoon, Aunty. Do you remember me? I'm Tuan, your neighbour in Saigon." Her eyes narrowed, the old woman tried putting pieces of her past together. There were too many parts missing to solve this jigsaw puzzle. She wondered if this wasn't some kind of a scam. Newspapers were full of stories like this—people getting mugged in their houses by con men pretending to be long-lost family members. She tried reaching for her butcher knife hanging inside a canvass bag by the window. The young man's sudden coughing fit frightened her. She put a hand to her face. She didn't want to catch his germs. Television newscasts were also full of germ stories lately. Rock Hudson. Rock Hudson this. Rock Hudson that. She stepped back and waved him away.

"Don't know any Tuan in Saigon. What do you want?"

Tuan reacted to such caustic words with a smile. He started by describing their neighbourhood. Its mango trees. Its hibiscus flower shrubs. Its barking dogs. Its crowing roosters. Its pastel-coloured houses. Shovelful after shovelful, he dug a tunnel into her brain. He brainstormed with her past. He placed her memory on a treadmill and forced it to run. The exercise succeeded in bringing forth images of long ago—of Mai's lemon and cinnamon hair, of Professor Minh's private math classes, of a burning monk on their street.

"Oh ... OK! I remember now! You look different. Sorry. Who's the kid?"

"He's Mai's son. I think Mai is expecting us."

"What??"

"Yes," Tuan said, surprised by such a forceful "what?" While he admired Mai's ability to keep a secret, he found shameful her lack of candour. He felt bad for Nat. The kid's silence, shuffling feet and downcast eyes worried him. In a sincere gesture of brotherhood, he wrapped his arm around Nat's shoulders. He announced once more, "This is Nat, Mai's son."

"Oh, My God!" Mai's mother shouted. She slammed her door and staggered inside. She banged her head against a plaster wall. Two picture frames fell off their hooks. She didn't care. She continued her self-flagellation. Meeting Mai's illegitimate child after all these years was shock enough. Seeing him a black man was beyond belief. Of all Mai's scandalous acts, this had to be the worst. It was a slap to her face. A shredding of and stamping on her ancestors' lychee white genes.

A pulsating migraine put an end to her head banging.

She wobbled to the bathroom. Half-heartedly, she wiped the smudges tears had left around her eyes. She combed her hair. She sprayed perfume on her neck. She wanted to look decent for Mai's son. Dreadful or not, he was still her grandson. She owed him a cup of tea. Perhaps even some mangoes. Ready to change strategy, she marched out, expecting to see two pairs of distressed eyes. Only a note with a phone number gazed up at her from the dusty floor mat.

"Mai, Mai! What did you do? What did you do?" she yelled till her voice broke.

The Legacy of Professor Minh

I **FINALLY TALKED** to her. A month after that unwelcomed encounter at her door, she left a message at my hostel. An invitation for tea. I asked Tuan to come along. I knew I couldn't do it alone. Her greeting was still without warmth, her eyes still fixed on my wiry hair. However, she did invite us in. The dark, narrow corridor smelled of incense and ripe durians. Three cups of newly prepared jasmine tea released steam into her already stuffy living room. Tuan bowed to her fat plastic Buddha, who welcomed us with a detached smile from his position on the mantel. Copying Tuan, I did likewise. Lines of red liquid seeped out of her mouth as she talked. A betel chewer, I assumed. Her jerky hands motioned us to a gold flowered sofa. We followed in silence.

I looked around, hoping to see my mother. I only saw her photo on an end table. Breathless, I searched for her photocopied portrait in my knapsack. Comparing them, I goosebumped. A young Mai by a beer stand. An older Mai in a restaurant. Yes, it was the same woman. I tried listening for her movement from the other room. Perhaps a cough or a hum. Or even a sigh. I heard instead neighbours' music wafting through an open window.

"Is my mother home?" I finally asked. "No, she left," came the disappointing answer. Left where, for how long, when will she be back, I wanted to continue. Tuan's shut-up-look put a lid on my inquiries. I turned my attention to my hot tea and choked on its bitterness.

"Your, your mother's gone forever. But hmmmm ... Hmmm she left something for you," my grandmother said, stumbling on her words. Rummaging through her shopping bag, she took out a leather-bound notebook. "It's all nonsense English writing. I can't understand this stuff. Maybe you can."

"Gone forever" didn't surprise me. Yes, my mother has always been "gone forever" from my life. Gone from the very first day till now. She who had pushed me away as I lay shivering on her stomach, who had never left me a photo when she took off for America, who had never bothered to send a few words of comfort during all these years—why should I be sad at her absence on this occasion?

"What happened, Aunty?" Tuan asked in a low voice. Quietly he inched closer to her.

"Don't know," she replied, her hands fumbling with a broken remote control. Unable to get her television working, she groaned. She stared at her empty wall.

"When?" Tuan whispered. After punching a few buttons, he managed to fix her remote control. He upped the volume to its maximum.

"Eight month ago."

Tuan's puzzled look chafed my grandmother. She spat into a Kleenex. "Letter to Mai's kid two months ago? That was me. I wrote that note."

"I don't understand."

"You don't know whole story??"

"No, Aunty."

"I thought everybody knew. Vietnamese community is so small. Lots of gossip. Can't hide anything from anyone. Anyway, Mai fell down last year. A robbery at our restaurant. A credit card thief. He pushed her. She lost consciousness for a few days. Brain concussion, doctors said. Also broke her ribs, arm and leg. Shoulders got out of joint. Twisted her knees too. Must have been bad fall. Must have been a violent push, doctors said. At least she wasn't shot, they added. Mai was in the hospital for months. She got better. Was supposed to come home and then ... then, then poof! Doctors said she got blood clots in her lungs. I didn't understand. They said blood clots happen when a patient stays in bed too long. Blood clots can kill, they said. I still don't understand. She was in hospital, why didn't they save her? They should have saved her! She survived the war. Communist rockets didn't kill her. Her own blood clot did. Her own flesh and blood killed her. Ironic, no?" Grandmother sobbed. Her sentences became unintelligible. An index finger in front of his lips, Tuan eyed me. He made signs for her to calm down. At once the sobbing stopped. Her words dried up.

They thought I heard nothing when I heard everything. They thought I understood nothing when I understood all. "Her own flesh and blood killed her." Those words would remain with me forever. Did I kill my mother with my skin colour? Did her shame of me drain her will to live? I had no answer to those questions sitting on my grandmother's couch that afternoon. I still have no answer now.

"For my child," my mother's notebook began with those three simple words. Her "my" got my head twirling so fast I almost fainted. All my life I thought I belonged to no one. Now I realized—much too late—that I was a "my" to somebody. With sweaty hands, I turned the pages. I pored over her writing. I read till my eyes burned. She'd exposed herself so intimately on those pages. Yet her sentences remained unscrutinised, her tragedy unacknowledged.

My mother's life, my life—we were two parallel lines forever separated. Way before my birth, our fates had been decided. Professor Minh's sexual perversity, my mother's rebelliousness, the racism of the times ... and the war, how could I forget the war? The legacy of Professor Minh, the legacy of the war ... that was me.

Pages of Longing

"**P**ROBLEMS STARTED LONG before the kid walked this earth," my mother had written in her notebook. "Trouble started years before my birth," I'd also written in my homework booklet. Hers were in English, mine in Vietnamese. How was it that our phrases matched so well? In which way did she transmit to me her fear, her passion? Without ever meeting, we'd told each other our stories, imagined the other's tales. Through our sentences, we'd dialogued. Through our pages of longing, our destinies had crossed again and again. My book for her—a present eight months too late in coming—lay in my knapsack. "IN THE BEGINNING" I'd written on the first page. Messy handwriting in red ink beckoned further exploration. Sentence after sentence, I re-read my words of loneliness. I realized then they were also her words.

Yes, problems started long before my birth.

New York, 2020

WE MISS THAT thriving era of McDonaldism. It was what gave us our first decent jobs after months of digging for worms. At $1.50/hour and 50 cents a bucket, the digging broke our backs. Our eyes twitched trying to see through the darkness with only a headlamp. If some worms dried out, our wages would be cut in half. As an expert worm digger, Tuan knew how to keep them fresh and slimy. Spit, he would spit on them. "Being paid to dig up worms! Only in America," he exclaimed good-naturedly. His enthusiasm soon wore off as memories of the re-education camp returned. "Watered-down rice and floating worms, I could taste it again," he said. One day without warning, he gave me his can full of wiggly worms and walked out.

McDonald's beckoned and Tuan responded. He performed so well he became a manager within three years. And wherever he went, I went. If only Mother had known I followed in her footsteps—serving food to Americans in this dream city that was L.A. If only she could've seen me—neatly cut hair, clean blue shirt, ironed blue pants, shiny red tie—perhaps she would've smiled.

We laboured night and day and we succeeded,

Tuan and I. Our 60-hour work week left us sleepless, it
didn't dull our survival instinct. From worm-pickers to
McDonald's managers, we slowly climbed our way up.
Along the way, we shared one large French fries order
after another. Tuan laughed, comparing them to the
frites at Saigon's Givral Café.

A three-page letter from my father brought us back
East. He apologized for his yearly Christmas card, our
only mode of communication up till then. In his late middle age, he wanted us to be near, to reconnect. Childless,
Amanda regretted pushing me away decades earlier. She
wondered if I had kids. She so wished to be a step-
grandmother, to hold a baby in her arms, to whisper to
it words I've never heard: "I love you ..."

To lure Tuan and me back East, my father offered to
contribute financially to our dream—a bar on a leafy sidewalk. Months of searching brought us to our ideal spot:
Atlantic Avenue corner of Smith Street, a stretch of
Brooklyn alive with high-heeled ladies and sandalled
workers. Just for him, I gave the place a nostalgic name.
I recreated the spot where it had all begun for him
and me.

Our Catinat Boulevard Bar had clients overflowing
onto the pavement. Ex GIs, Vietnamese expats, curious
Americans brought there by the intriguing name would
wait in line for a seat. On summer afternoons, we would
sell one beer after another on our patio. A grin on his
face, Tuan would greet customers with his V for victory
sign. Twice a month, my father would come with colleagues from Yale University. Tipsy, he would repeat
those same stories about a beer seller named Hung on

Saigon's Catinat Boulevard. A man with a huge tattooed eagle on his arm also dropped in. He'd read Amanda's *New York Times* article on me. He told me he had once loved my mother. My heart throbbed hearing his words. The Mai he knew was so different from the frivolous girl Mai Ly had befriended. She was nothing like the make-believe Viet Cong kid Tuan had played with. She was far from my father's romantic memory of a first love. "All those early years here, she'd been looking for your father to help track you down," the Bird Man said. "It was not easy starting her life from scratch. She had a tough time. Try to forgive her." I did, I replied.

Amanda's piece travelled continents. Mai Ly found me after reading it online. Her English is all good now, she wrote. She even has a Facebook account, she bragged. Sister Tam, who had replaced Mother Superior after her death, had laughed excitedly when shown my photo in the *New York Times*. "Our little novelist is a big shot now," the sister had exclaimed. Her enthusiasm soon waned. After a few minutes, she shook her head and pushed Mai Ly's laptop away. Too many compli-cated English words. She couldn't understand those so-phisticated sentences, couldn't follow their twists and turns. Amanda's gimmicky retelling of facts left her cold. She'd rather read my candid tales of zucchinis and eels. "Why Nat not writing his own story? He should," she simply said. Then she inquired about my mother.

My mother. Years later, I still think of her. How many times did I re-read her notebook? Many times. I am perusing it now. Perhaps for the last time. A mere five dozen pages to chronicle a life. So devoid of details, yet so dense. How I'd like to memorialize her! To prolong her words. To resuscitate her sentences. To pay tribute to her resilience—the resilience of innocence. I've grafted my tale onto hers. I have added action scenes. I have tweaked her descriptions. All for nothing. More showing, less telling, they insisted. Where is the arc? they asked. Make your characters more memorable, your scenes more compelling, they said. No, I cannot. There is no time to change my story. It does not matter anymore. I'll go taking with me all the memories that matter to no one. An orphanage in Cholon. A plastic bag by the doorknob. A eucalyptus-scented nun. A polka dotted girl. A beer stand on Catinat Boulevard. A comrade sharing my mother's name. A pair of Agent Orange arms. A young man in platform shoes. And an image I could never forget: a baton pressed against the throat.

A baton pressed against the throat.

The last line of my manuscript stands desolate on a laptop screen. It cries out for company. No, my tale must end here. My hands ache and my throat burns. I hear chanting outside. There are loudspeaker voices reclaiming the story of a people, my people. There are police sirens muzzling them. Muzzling us. Too exhausted to go downstairs, I look out from my window. Feverish, I put an icepack on my forehead. I cough. My mask falls from my hands.

XXXXXXXXXXXX

WHEN **NAT FAILS** *to answer my message, I worry. It is unlike him. After two days of silence, I call our friend, the sup. We find Nat slumped over his desk, a thermometer in hand, mouth gasping for air. My voice rouses him. Slowly he opens his eyes and just as slowly, closes them. His attempt at a smile ends with a series of coughs.*

I stay on after the ambulance leaves. They tell me to go home. I won't. I pace up and down. There are picture frames displaced when two medics rushed in with their stretcher. I pick them up, these black and white photos of old events. My eyes burn seeing them again. Our last day of "school" in the Philippines. Me drinking Coca Cola and Nat holding a yellow envelope containing our plane tickets to New York. Our first American dinner with Michael and Amanda in a room full of newspaper cut-outs. A photocopied image of young Mai playing coy on Catinat Boulevard. Only three pictures to capture our past ... All that time together yet we never really talked. Never opened up. Never dared tell each other our stories. Four decades later, I still don't know him, this "half-brother" of mine.

I am thirsty. I go looking for a bottle of beer. Nat's kitchen is a mess. There are torn bits of paper scattered everywhere. I could make out words here and there. Sorry, sorry, sorry, they all say the same thing. Your story … not a good fit. Not a good fit, not a good fit. Too many grammatical mistakes, mistakes, mistakes. Try elsewhere, try elsewhere, try elsewhere. Wish you luck, wish you luck, wish you luck.

Near a coffee machine, a neater stack of paper catches my eye. On the first page, the words "Catinat Boulevard." Curious, I go over them. Chapter after chapter, I finally hear stories I've blocked out all these years. I laugh then shudder with sadness. A shy boy hiding in the shadow, shrouding his skin colour to escape his tormentors. A young man burying his grief under pagefuls of precocious words. I recognize him now.

Back home, I send a quick message to Amanda. Please come to NYC. Nat's in the ICU, under ventilation. Can you also take a look at his writing, I text. Of course, coming in an hour, she answers within ten minutes.

Amanda's early phone call wakes me at 5 a.m. She says she's been crying the whole night. Nat's manuscript is all wet with her tears. "What an incredible tale! I'll contact friends at Penguin Press. We'll try to get it published. No, we will get it published. This story must be told," she whispers before hanging up.

A week later, Nat is still at Mt. Sinai Hospital. Doctors say he's doing better. His oxygen level is increasing. His fever is under control. They are weaning him off the ventilator. I jot down everything they tell me, careful not to miss a single word. This is one hospital scene I intend to end well. Unlike David, unlike Thu, unlike Mai, I'll make sure Nat comes home safe and sound. And when he does, I'll tell him I wrote the last chapter of his novel.

Acknowledgements

A heartfelt Thank You to Anita Anand and Julie Roorda for the invaluable editorial advice, David Moratto for the book design and Michael Mirolla for believing in this project. Your patience is greatly appreciated.

Thank you also to all my friends who have read the first draft of this story and encouraged me on: Ian T. Shaw, Susan Doherty, H. Nigel Thomas, Cora Siré, Timothy Niedermann and Sadiad Youssouf.

Lastly, I want to thank the Canada Council for the Arts for their financial support, enabling me to take time off work to write this story.

About the Author

Caroline Vu (full name: Caroline Vu-Nguyen) was born in Vietnam during the height of the Vietnam War. She left her native country at the age of 11, moving first to the US, then to Canada. Her first novel *Palawan Story* won the Canadian Author Association's Fred Kerner Prize in 2015. The same novel was a finalist for the Concordia University First Book Prize. *Palawan*, the French translation of *Palawan Story*, was shortlisted for the 2018 Montreal Metropolis Bleu's Prix de la diversité. Caroline's second novel, *That Summer in Provincetown*, has been optioned for a film. After extended stays in Europe, Latin America and Ontario, the author is now back in Montreal with her two daughters. She works part time as a medical doctor.